NECESSITY

NECESSITY

D.W. BUFFA

Copyright © 2018 by D.W. Buffa
Cover and jacket design by 2Faced Design
Interior designed and formatted by E.M. Tippetts Book Designs

ISBN 978-1-947993-08-2
eISBN 978-1-947993-25-9
Library of Congress Control Number: 2018930270

First hardcover publication April 2018 by Polis Books, LLC

1201 Hudson Street, #211S
Hoboken, NJ 07030

www.PolisBooks.com

POLIS BOOKS

Also by D.W. BUFFA

CHAPTER ONE

Ithough was a strange case, a great case, a case that, once it got to trial, might well change forever the history of the United States. Other presidents had been murdered, but no one who had killed a president had ever been brought to trial. I did not want any part of it.

"You have to take it," insisted Albert Craven. "This is what you do; this is all you have ever done. Why wouldn't you want to do it?"

Despite his age, there was not a line on his smooth, round face, not a wrinkle in his small, manicured hands. He sat there in his expensive tailored suit and his polished shoes, shirt cuffs precisely positioned an exact half-inch below the suit coat sleeves, a kind of permanent presence in his prosperous well-being. The founder of one of the oldest law firms in the city, a lawyer who had never tried a case, he had made a career of listening with endless patience to a client's habitual complaints, and then with sympathetic understanding assuring them that there was nothing to worry about, that most problems were solved with time and forbearance. I started to laugh.

"Why don't you take it, Albert? You've practiced law a lot longer than I have."

As if praying for patience, he closed his eyes and slowly shook his head. He often did that with me, but then, when he opened his eyes, he looked at me in a way I had not seen before.

"This is serious. You're Joseph Antonelli. How many years has it been since you came here, to San Francisco, to try a case, a case you won—"

"A case I damn near lost!"

"A case you won. And then you stayed, and I'm very glad you did. I admire what you do. God knows I could never do it. I'm not asking you to take the case; it has nothing to do with the firm. It has nothing to do with me. But what happened...it isn't a question of someone's guilt or innocence; it isn't a question of whether someone has or hasn't committed murder. It isn't a question," he went on, moving forward until he was sitting on the very edge of the blue wingback chair, "of whether or not you can win an acquittal. The question—the serious question—is what effect the trial will have on the country."

Picking up my fountain pen, a present he had once given me, I began to twist the corrugated black barrel back and forth between my fingers. It was ten o'clock on a Monday morning, the second week of September. Outside the window, the sky was a relentless gray, the last remnant of the lingering overnight fog.

"Do you know why I became a defense lawyer—one of the reasons? Because a trial, a criminal trial, has a beginning and an end. You try the case, the jury brings back a verdict. That's the last I have to deal with it."

"Unless you lose, and then there's an appeal. But I forget, you never lose. But what does this have to do with—"

"We're still litigating the Kennedy assassination. This trial will go on forever, there will never be an end to it."

"There will be a verdict; there will be—"

"Years, decades, of questions about what happened, whether there was a conspiracy, a cover-up; whether the defense attorney was part of it, whether he was in on it—whatever that 'it' might be. I've got other things to do than spend the rest of my life answering questions about what happened, or didn't happen, at a trial. And besides," I added with a shrug, "everyone says Fitzgerald confessed." I put down the pen and reached for the newspaper that lay folded on the side of my desk. "Here, look at—"

"I've read the paper," he replied, becoming for some reason more determined, more intense. He did not raise his voice, he seldom did that, but there was no mistaking what he felt. "It says there are reports that he confessed." He paused long enough to give me a look that told me he knew something. "The reports are true. Fitzgerald has confessed." Craven did not wait for the obvious next question. "There is still going to be a trial. He wants one, and the government insists on it."

I had no idea how Albert Craven had come into possession of this information, but I had long since stopped being surprised at anything he had come to know. He knew everyone, and no one, it seemed, had ever kept anything secret from him. Husbands might lie to their wives, and wives their husbands, but they would confess to him everything they had done.

"He's confessed, but both he and the government want a trial?" I suddenly realized what was going on, or thought I did. "He wants to make the case why he was right, he wants to be a martyr to a cause, while the government wants to show that he is a murderer and nothing more. It's a show trial, that is what it is going to be. And that is another reason why I won't do it," I insisted, waving my hand to stave off any more argument.

"Well, will you at least talk to his wife, listen to what she has to say?" I started to shake my head, but Craven was already on his feet. "She's waiting in my office. It won't take more than a few minutes. Talk to her. If you still don't want to do it, that will be the end of it. I promise."

I did not know Kevin Fitzgerald, but I knew enough about him to know I did not like him. The youngest of California's two U.S. senators, he had been the next great hope of the Democratic party, someone who might very well become president, if not in the next election, the one after that. I did not care about his politics; it did not matter to me whether he was a liberal or a conservative. What did matter was that he did not really seem to believe in anything except whatever anyone else believed. Ambition—the desire to be recognized as someone important, the need to feel not just recognition, but the approval of vast numbers of people, the applause of the crowd, the drive to be thought of as exceptional, better than anyone else, someone others would envy and, if they could, try to imitate—was the reason for everything he had ever done. It was, according to the received wisdom of Albert Craven's circle of privileged, wealthy friends, the reason why he had married Tricia Raintree. Ambition meant nothing without money, and she had more of it than nearly anyone else her age. Good looking, if not quite beautiful; charming in her conversation when she was talking to someone she wanted to impress; quick in her ability to calculate her own advantage; and, as I was about to discover, as determined to get her own way as any woman I had ever known.

She did not bother to knock. She swept into my office as if I had come to see her. Had I gotten up to greet her, she would have taken my chair. I pretended to study a case file that lay open on my desk. She took the wingback chair Albert Craven had used and did not say a word. She did not move, she just waited as if she had all the time in the world, as if she did not care in the least if I ever looked up. When I finally did, there was just the hint of a smile on her lips, the knowledge that whatever else I might think, I could never think she needed anything from me. It was the assumption of men with too much money and women who thought themselves irresistible; it was an assumption that, especially in this situation, had no connection with reality.

"The answer is no, Mrs. Fitzgerald. I won't represent your husband."

Tricia Fitzgerald glanced at her long, painted nails, deciding, as it seemed, whether they had been done properly or exhibited some slight imperfection.

"My husband has been accused of murder. I wanted to talk to you about representing him. They tell me you're the best there is. Albert—Albert Craven—is an old family friend, and..."

She was looking past me, out the window, as if suddenly taken by something she had just remembered. Her mouth twisted at the corners, and then, as if to punish itself for this failure of control, tightened into a spiteful grimace.

"Murder. That seems a strange way to describe it. He didn't murder anyone. You aren't a murderer if you acted in self-defense."

"Self-defense? The president tried to kill him, and he—"

"I went to law school, Mr. Antonelli. I took criminal law. Self-defense isn't just when you act to save yourself."

"He acted to save others?" I asked with a doubtful, measured smile.

Instead of an answer, instead of an explanation of what she meant, she began to look around the room, pausing once or twice to make a more careful appraisal of what she saw.

"You have very good, very expensive, taste, Mr. Antonelli. There isn't anything here—not the chairs, not the sofa, certainly not the Persian rugs—that was bought off the floor. The books, law books almost all of them, though I notice you have some other things as well—first editions?" she asked, certain with all the certainty of money that she must be right.

"No, at least not that I'm aware of. Just some old books I inherited."

She got up and walked across to the bookshelves, pulled out a volume from a middle shelf and opened it.

"Aristotle!" She laughed, masking her disappointment. "No, I imagine it wouldn't be a first edition. And why would you want one if you don't read Latin."

Greek, I wanted to tell her, but there were other, more important errors with which we had to deal.

"You've done very well," she continued, putting the book back where she had found it. "I had heard that about you, that you only take cases that pay extraordinary fees."

I tried, with only partial success, to conceal my irritation.

"The last case I tried, a trial that ended just last week, there was not any fee at all."

She moved with such a light step that she seemed not to move at all, motion nothing but the sudden exchange of one place with another. She had been standing next to the bookshelves on the other side of the room, now she was sitting in the same chair she seemed never to have left.

"And why did you do that, Mr. Antonelli?" she asked in her breathless, lilting voice, her large, dark eyes full of laughter.

She seemed more like a college girl on a date than a woman married to a man about to go on trial for his life. I had the feeling that, for her, the present moment was always everything. There was no past, no past that counted; the future, when she thought about it, was only the extension, the inevitable, expected realization, of what she wanted now. It was not that she felt entitled, that might have required an explanation, a reason why. It never would have occurred to her that she needed a reason for anything. The world belonged to her because the world had always been, and always would be, whatever she wanted it to be.

"Well, why did you do it, take a case for nothing?"

"Because the kid was guilty."

"Because the kid was...? That seems a little strange."

"It isn't strange at all. He was eighteen years old, a black kid, goes to city college, wants to become a lawyer—just like you. His mother screamed at some drug-dealing gangster type in the neighborhood where they live and this lowlife breaks her jaw for her trouble. So the kid, my client, confronts the guy and beats the hell out of him. He gets charged with assault. The law says he should have called the police, that it's a crime to take the law into your own hands, that it's a crime to do physical violence to someone, no matter what the cause. The prosecution offers him a deal, a very good deal, as those things go. He pleads guilty to misdemeanor assault and gets a year probation. I told him the hell with that, we're going to trial. The jury took maybe five minutes, and that was only because before they announced their verdict—their unanimous verdict—they asked the judge if they could ask a question: why was the district attorney's office prosecuting someone who should have been given a medal?"

Tricia Fitzgerald jumped on it. It proved everything, everything important, everything that was needed to show me that I should do what she wanted me to do.

"That's what everyone is saying about Kevin: instead of being prosecuted for murder, he should be given a medal, that he saved the country, that he—"

I stopped her with a look.

"Everyone is saying? I read the papers. Whatever anyone thought about the president, no one is saying your husband did what was right."

"Maybe not the editorial writers for the *New York Times* or the *Washington Post*. What else could they say? But if you ask them what they really think, whether the country is better off without that mindless narcissist in office... Look," she said, leaning forward, a stern, implacable expression on her thin, high-cheek-boned face, "go on the internet, read what people are writing, read some of the blogs, turn on your television set, watch the cable channels. There is a feeling that it was all inevitable, that it was going to happen, that he brought it on himself, that he put the country in a terrible position: a man who wasn't the least bit qualified for the office and no way to get him out of it. Everyone understands that, everyone—"

"Not everyone," I interjected. "And it wouldn't matter if they did."

"Are you sure? Are you sure it wouldn't matter, that it doesn't make a difference? What did you just tell me about this last case of yours—that it didn't matter that what the law said, everyone thought what he did was right!"

She settled herself back in the chair and while the fingers of her left hand drummed a slow, methodical beat on the arm, studied me with a new, a different, curiosity.

"You take some cases for free, and you can do that because of how much you make from your other cases. I know a few things about you, Mr. Antonelli. It's odd we've never met. When Kevin was mayor, and even now, when he is in the Senate, there is scarcely any social event of any real significance we haven't attended. And I'm not sure I remember going to any when Albert wasn't there. But I don't remember ever seeing you, even once. I asked Albert. He said you're always too busy, that you work all the time. I don't believe that, Mr. Antonelli, I don't believe that at all. I don't believe for a moment that you're this perfect recluse who spends all his time at home or in court."

Leaning back, I stared straight at her. It was the habit of a lifetime, learned early in court: never look away from a witness, never let them think you aren't giving them all your attention, waiting for the first inconsistency, the first even minor mistake, by which to discredit their testimony and destroy their credibility.

"I'm not reclusive at all. I spend a lot of time going different places in the city. I talk to a lot of people, some of them, I confess, people I've never seen before and will never see again. It's the magic of the city, the reason I stayed in San Francisco: all the familiar strangers and the mystery of their lives. And if I don't go to the kind of social events you spend your time going to, there are two reasons for that. If you go to a hundred of them, it only means that you have had the same conversation a hundred times with the same people. The second reason is that the only time I am reasonably certain the person I am talking to might actually tell me the truth is when I have them as a witness in a courtroom and they are under oath. Not always, you understand, but some of the time. Now, if you're so certain that everyone thinks your husband deserves a medal for what he did, what is the real reason you want me to take this case?"

"Why did you take that case you told me about, the one the jury took five minutes to decide? There is only one reason: you didn't think anyone else could do it, prove him innocent when there was no question that, according to the law, he was guilty. The difference between that case and this is that what you did for free, you can do for more money than you or any other lawyer has ever earned! It isn't my money, Mr. Antonelli, it isn't my family's money—though we would be glad to pay whatever you wanted, if we had to. It's money that's been coming in from all over the country, all over the world; so much of it we've had to hire people to keep track of all of it—thousands, hundreds of thousands, of small donations to a legal fund we had not even thought to set up before it started coming in."

Quite on purpose, I glanced around the opulent furnishings of my office, almost none of which I had paid for because, with his usual generosity, Albert Craven thought I should have a place to work almost as expensive as his own.

"I don't need the money, and I have never taken a case because of what I thought I could make."

"Then take it because we both know that if you don't do this, if some other lawyer tries to defend him, my husband doesn't have a chance. He confessed to what he did. That doesn't make him guilty. I remember from law school—surely you haven't forgotten—almost the first thing they teach you in criminal law—"

"Self-defense, the defense of others?"

"The law of necessity, that there are times when it is not only your right, but almost your duty to kill."

CHAPTER
TWO

I t was not true that I never attended any social events that involved some of the most important, or whatever they might think of their own importance, and best-known people in the city. I was the frequent, if sometimes reluctant, guest at the dinner parties Albert Craven liked to give for a small gathering of ten or twelve from among his endless list of wealthy and socially prominent friends. I had told him that afternoon, after my meeting with Tricia Fitzgerald, that I was not going to take the case. He did not try to talk me out of it; he did not really say anything except to remind me that I was expected for dinner that evening and, at least until then, to keep an open mind. I had no idea what he was talking about, but I had known him long enough to know that, for all his surface amiability, despite the careless manner with which he sometimes dismissed something out of hand, there was always something left unsaid, some deeper meaning that would come out later.

Craven lived in one of the pastel-colored houses that without any room between them lined the street across from the marina and the yacht club on the other side. The fog, which had vanished late that morning, giving way to a bright blue picture-perfect sky, had started back, a thick gray veil towering up from the sea, out beyond the Golden Gate. Children with their parents, women with their dogs, walked and ran and talked and shouted on the tan sliver of a beach where the small grass park abruptly ended. In the distance, the other side of the bay, out where the bridge stopped and the headlands of Marin rose up from the water, the lights of Sausalito began to glitter in the darkening light of dusk. I rang the bell, hoping I would remember the name of Albert Craven's latest wife.

"Isabel," she said the moment Mrs. Albert Craven opened the door, and without the slightest sign of embarrassment or hesitation, ran her long fingers through my unkempt hair and kissed me affectionately on my cheek. "And I'm the fourth...or, let me see, I think that's wrong," she added quickly, striking a pose of gleeful confusion. "I think the fifth. Come in, Joseph Antonelli."

She kept chattering away as she led me toward the dining room, regaling me with one absurdity after another.

"Between Albert and myself, I think we must have going on a full dozen—marriages, I mean. He was always marrying the wrong woman, and I was always marrying the wrong man. He was always losing money in divorces; I was always getting rich. A dozen marriages, and God knows how many years. Albert, as you know, is older than sin, and I—believe it or not—am no longer a young virgin. Hell, I'm not sure I ever was—either of those things, I mean: young or a virgin," she remarked to her own vast, full-throated amusement.

The dining room had changed. Perhaps after this many marriages it had become a habit to start each one by giving everything a new appearance. I had been too preoccupied trying to decide exactly what it was about Tricia Fitzgerald that I did not trust to pay much attention to the fact that the house, which had for years been pale yellow, had recently been painted pale blue. The change to the dining room was too dramatic not to notice. The mirrors that had covered two facing walls to give the room a feeling of infinite space in which a dozen guests seemed the central part of an endless banquet hall had been taken down. The glass chandelier that had cast a glittering light on the eager faces below had been replaced with indirect lighting from canisters inside the ceiling. The room had become warmer and more intimate, softer and more sedate, a place for quiet conversation. I remembered, like a missing friend, the lost sense of boisterous excitement, the sound of younger voices all clamoring for attention.

I was the last to arrive, though I had actually been a few minutes early. Everyone was already seated, and a maid was moving from one guest to the next pouring wine. The room went silent. Albert rose from his place at the far end of the table, motioning for me to take the empty chair halfway down, directly across from one of the most strikingly beautiful women I had ever seen.

"The famous Joseph Antonelli, the man we have all been waiting to meet," she said in a voice that made you think of those cool summer nights and long summer days when you knew, with all the certainty you would ever feel, that those days and nights would never end and that you would spend every one of them with the girl you were with, the only girl you ever wanted to know.

I looked at Albert Craven, standing there in his dark blue blazer and understated tie, waiting for him to explain. I knew that he always acted with my best interest at heart, but whatever he was doing now had been done behind my back. "I'm not going to do it, Albert," I insisted before he could begin his well-rehearsed remarks. I raised my empty glass and nodded toward the maid, who immediately brought the bottle.

Albert threw up his arms, a gesture of polite despair, an apology for his evident failure, and sank back down in his chair. With his hands clasped in front of his chin, he leaned forward. A thin, cunning grin ran unmolested across the gentle contours of his mouth.

"I think you are; you really have no choice."

I sipped on the pinot grigio, my eyes moving from Albert to the gorgeous woman sitting opposite me.

"No choice at all," she said, as if the decision had already been made. "Everyone here agrees. You're the only one who can do this, the only one who can make it right."

Make it right? What did she mean? I shot a glance at Craven.

"Just listen," he urged before retreating into an enigmatic silence.

"Yes, just listen," said a tall man in his early sixties with hooded gray eyes and a tangle of unruly gray hair. He had the cultured look of a classical musician and a voice thick as velvet, but J. Michael Thomas had never played an instrument in his life and his only connection to the arts was the large financial contributions he regularly made to a half-dozen different museums. If he gave a lot, he had a lot to give; more, it was rumored, than anyone else in the city and as much as anyone in the country. "We asked Albert for this meeting. We all wanted to meet you, to talk to you, to make sure you understood what is at stake here. This isn't about someone's guilt or innocence; it isn't whether Kevin Fitzgerald should be punished for what he did."

"Punished?" A woman, somewhere in her forties, with frantic hands and nervous eyes, could not wait to break in with an opinion of her own. "He did everyone a favor. Saved the country, far as I'm concerned. It isn't a crime when you kill a tyrant, someone who doesn't give a damn about the law, someone willing to commit treason, someone who—"

"For God's sake, Naomi," yelled her partner, Angela Baker, sitting three places down. "I didn't like him any better than you did. No, don't interrupt," she continued. "That isn't the question. The question is whether no matter how bad he was, you can allow someone to commit murder. He didn't have to do it, you know. Fitzgerald—we all know him, how much he always wanted to be, had to be, the center of attention. But to kill—murder—the president! They could have impeached him."

"Impeached him? That would have taken forever."

Even in a coat and tie Evan Winslow looked rumpled and only half dressed. His shirt was not quite tucked in, the tie not quite pulled up. He seemed disconcerted, constantly fidgeting with his stubby fingers, constantly shifting his line of vision. There were those who thought him a financial genius; there were others, more envious, who thought him an idiot, dumb luck the only possible explanation for his success. Either way, he had been a shrewd investor when it came to politics. No one had contributed more to winning candidates. The only one he had not backed had been Kevin Fitzgerald.

"Impeached him?" he repeated. "That would have taken a little more serious effort, a little more strength of character, than our good friend Kevin Fitzgerald has ever exhibited."

Dinner was served, but no one paid much attention to what they ate. There was only one thing on their minds, and only one thing on mine.

"I've listened, I've heard what you have had to say. Some of you hated the president; some of you apparently did not think all that much better of the senator. Some of you think killing the president is something that, if it isn't worthy of praise, should not be punished. Some of you think that, like any other crime, it should. But I haven't heard anyone tell me why you think I should take on Fitzgerald's defense as opposed to some other lawyer."

"Perhaps they don't know the reason," said someone who had not spoken before, a man who spoke English with the formal precision of a second language. "Perhaps it is simply something they feel."

"Jean-Francois Reynaud," said Craven, introducing the guest who sat on his right, "the French Consul."

He looked the part, with the calm, easy manner of someone trained in all the arts of misdirection, the studied expression of friendly indifference, the languid charm of the detached observer willing to offer an occasional remark but always without commitment, willing, if called upon, to hazard a guess about the direction of affairs, but never without the stated assurance that, more often than not, he had been proven wrong about such things. Years earlier, or in older movies, there would invariably have been a cigarette dangling from his fingers.

"If I may speak for everyone here," he said, without any obvious doubt that, for some reason, he could, "the feeling, not just in this room, is that after what has happened, a trial, to have anything like the desired effect, has to be comprehensive. What I mean is that nothing can be left out. The truth, whatever the truth is, has to be told. Anything less than that, anything less than the whole story—what happened, why it happened, who was involved, who was not involved—and nothing will ever get back on the right track again. Everything and everyone, all of it has to be brought out into the clear light of day. And that won't happen if some other attorney takes this on. Forgive me for putting it this way, but Americans, and especially American lawyers, are too much in love with technique, with the way things are done, with how they happen. You haven't the same interest in what those things are. You lack any real understanding of history. The great nineteenth century historian Jacob Burckhardt once said—and please forgive me for this—that 'barbarians and American men of business lack all knowledge of history.' This, however, seems not to be a deficiency you share. You seem actually to have a serious interest in such things. That is the reason why you are the only one who can do this, take on a case that is in every sense truly historical."

It was not clear to me why he was here, or why he would have an interest. And while I understood that Albert Craven knew everyone in the city, including the various foreign diplomats stationed here, I did not understand why he had decided to include Reynaud instead of one of a dozen others. After all the other guests had left, he tried to explain.

"I'm sorry about this, Joseph. I should have said something to you. I know that now. But they were all so insistent. They wanted to talk to you, try to convince you, but they wanted to get together first, to make sure they knew best how to proceed. As you could see, it didn't work out very well. They're still in shock. Everyone is. They don't care—they're frankly rather relieved—that the president is gone. What they're worried about is what is going to happen now, not just the immediate reaction, but the long-term consequences. And they don't really care, most of them, what happens to Kevin Fitzgerald."

I shook my head, remembering Evan Winslow.

"Some of them seem like they wouldn't mind if he was drawn and quartered." I was curious. "What is the reason Winslow doesn't like him? It seemed almost personal."

Albert emitted a low, knowing laugh.

"Personal? Yes, I suppose you could say that." He tucked his chin and gave me a look that seemed to taunt me with my ignorance. "You met her. She was sitting right across from you. The one you couldn't take your eyes off. I'm sorry. Things got started so suddenly, when you first arrived, I forgot all about introducing people. Tangerine Winslow."

"His wife?" I exclaimed, unable to hide my astonishment, and, perhaps, my disappointment. "She's married to him?"

"Doesn't make any sense, does it?" He slid the wine bottle we had been sharing across the table to me. We were sitting in the kitchen, new white tile everywhere. "She's the reason why he hates Fitzgerald. They were friends. He thought they were friends. He had money, a lot of it, but, as you no doubt noticed yourself, not much else. Fitzgerald was outgoing, good looking, full of charm, and full of praise and compliments for those like Winslow who were helpful to him. The first time Fitzgerald ran for mayor, Winslow headed his finance committee and did a wonderful job of it, got people to contribute who had never contributed to a candidate before. He also contributed a lot of his own money. And then, just days before the election, he finds out that his great good friend, Kevin Fitzgerald, has been sleeping with his wife."

Albert Craven sighed with sorrow, less at the predictable improprieties of vain and ambitious men, than at the absence of all reasonable honor and pride in the minds and souls of men who have had the misfortune to fall in love with beautiful women.

"What really almost killed him, the real reason he hates him, isn't that

Fitzgerald slept with his wife. The real reason is that his wife was going to leave him to marry Fitzgerald instead. She would have, too, according to what I've been told, but Fitzgerald, who was still single at the time, was too worried about what the scandal might do to his career."

"And so she stayed married to Winslow instead."

"As I say, it would have killed him if she had ever decided to leave."

"But he still wants Fitzgerald to have a fair trial?"

"No," said Craven, shaking his head emphatically. "None of them care anything about that. They want more than that. We all do. Jean-Francois said it best. It would be one thing if this had happened somewhere else— back East somewhere, or in the Midwest, or even the South. If it had to happen anywhere, it should have happened there. If it had been some demented loner, some white racist who thought the president was not going far enough, some half-educated fool who thought it would make him famous, everyone would have said all the usual things: what a tragedy it was, how violent we as a country have become, and then felt a private sense of relief at having finally reached the end of all the mindless, all the dangerous, nonsense to which we had been subjected. But it happened here, on Air Force One while it was parked at SFO; it happened here, in San Francisco, the place every conservative, and not just every conservative, thinks of as the gay and lesbian, the transgender, capital of the world, the place where we would rather give a home to a Muslim terrorist than a white straight couple who take their kids to church. That is bad enough, but then the killer—the assassin—is a sitting U.S. senator who just happens to be the former mayor of San Francisco. Do you know who those people were this evening? The civic and cultural establishment of the city, or to be more precise, the most important dozen members of that establishment. And they're all scared to death. They might be glad the president is dead, they might wish they had done it themselves, but they know—they think they know—what will happen if they don't scream louder than anyone else that Kevin Fitzgerald should be punished to the full extent of the law."

Craven poured himself what was left in the bottle, looked at the room still remaining in the glass, got up and went over to a cabinet and pulled out another bottle.

"A friend of mine," he remarked as he twisted the corkscrew with a practiced hand, "wanted to 'get back to the land.' He bought a vineyard and a winery up in Napa. Given what he paid, better pretend you like it. The cost of producing it was astronomical." He took a long, slow drink, swishing it around his mouth before he finally swallowed. "Not bad," he judged, wrinkling his nose. "Actually, I don't really know if it is or not. Would you like a scotch and soda instead?"

It was late, and I had had enough, and there were still things I wanted to know.

"Why the Frenchman? What is his role in this? There was a reason you invited him. I understand what you were telling me about what the others are afraid of, why they want…what is it they really want? Some kind of trial of reconciliation, something that gives them immunity, removal of responsibility, exoneration for anything they might have said or done that might have contributed to the climate in which something like this could happen? Because if that is what they're after, they're not likely to get it from me. I don't try cases to make people feel better about themselves; I try cases to win. Never mind that now. The Frenchman, Jean-Francois Reynaud. What does he have to do with this? He wasn't here to remind me about the deficiencies of American education."

Albert looked down at his hands. He seemed to grow older, more fragile as he sat there, contemplating what he was going to say. Something was haunting him, perhaps a secret that he could not tell, a secret to a mystery no one else suspected.

"People tell me things they shouldn't. It is why I have so many friends, some of them quite disreputable," he remarked with a gentle, forgiving laugh. "Maybe it's the face I have, maybe it's my manner, maybe because, unlike you, no one would ever look at me and think me any kind of threat. I never slept with other people's wives; I quite frequently never slept with one of my own. It's why Isabel married me; it's why, at my age, I married her. She likes you, by the way. She told me so. That's unusual with her. She doesn't like many people, and even those she likes she doesn't like to any great degree. But she likes to talk, and she can talk to me. The day after the assassination, Jean-Francois came to see me. He told me things, things I had no right to know. He was here tonight because he believes what he said about the potential consequences of a trial. He was here because, as he told me, before he fully commits himself, he wanted to meet you in person."

"Fully commits himself? To what?"

"I don't know, or rather, I'm not sure. I have my suspicions. In any case, he now wants to see you alone. He asked me if you could meet him tomorrow at the consulate for lunch. I hope you will. No, I'm asking you to do it. See him, see Jean-Francois, and listen to what he has to say, and then, before you make a final decision, go and see Fitzgerald. Hear his side of it."

I left Albert Craven's house and started walking up the street to my car. The fog had settled in again and I could barely see a block ahead. I did not notice the car that was following me until I heard a door swing open and a now familiar voice asking me to get in.

"I thought you might need a ride home," said Tangerine Winslow, sitting bright and shiny in her cream-colored Bentley.

"It must be an hour since you left."

"I had nothing else to do."

"Except wait for me?"

"Except wait for you."

"Because you thought I might need a ride?

"Because I thought you might need a ride."

"To my car, parked half a block from here?"

"To wherever you decide you might like to go."

"I was thinking I might go to the airport and catch the next flight to London or New York."

The words, my words, came with all the ease of words written in advance, words half forgotten and suddenly remembered, words spoken by a stranger while I listened, wondering what he might say next.

"And were you thinking that you might not want to go alone?"

It was a dare, nothing more and nothing less, a way to test the limits, her limits as much, or more, than mine.

"Either way, it doesn't matter; but if I go, I might not be coming back."

"You'd stay, in London or New York? You wouldn't come back, not ever?"

"Not if I were running away with a woman married to someone else."

"You might get tired of her, married woman or not, and then run away again."

"I've been known to do that," I admitted, "but never without regret."

She smiled softly in the night, and I knew that though she would not do it, run off with me, someone she had only just met, she thought it was something lacking in herself, the failure to yield to unqualified romance, to risk everything on a single, unknown chance.

"I've been known to want to," was all she said. "And, who knows, maybe one day…but there are first a few other things I need to do. One of them," she said as she started the engine again and began to drive, "is to tell you that I don't believe for a minute that Kevin did it."

I looked at her, wondering if she meant it.

"Kevin would not have had the courage. He's always been a coward. It's the reason he married who he did, the reason—I'm sure you've heard—he wouldn't marry me. He wanted money, lots of it, and marriage was the only way he was ever going to get it. I can't complain. It's what I did myself, married for money and nothing else."

"The papers all say he confessed," I reminded her.

"Kevin Fitzgerald has never told the truth about anything in his life. Now, last chance," she whispered with a glance that suggested endless possibilities, "London or New York?"

CHAPTER
THREE

I t was neither London nor New York nor any other, closer place. She dropped me at my car and I drove the short distance home, the apartment I had purchased on Nob Hill before prices became outrageous and the city started to become a place for only the richest of the rich. If I ever decided to sell, I would have a small fortune and nowhere to live. That wasn't true. I could live, and live well, in other places, but San Francisco was home; more than home, it was the hidden secret of existence, the secret you could never solve, or even fully understand, but somehow still gave you the sense that somewhere, just beyond your fingertips, was the meaning of what you did. San Francisco was a mistress, always changing, and never changing at all. There was nowhere else I wanted to be.

The doorman greeted me the way he always did, calling me Mr. Antonelli, though I had often asked him not to, and then hurried to the elevator to push the button and in that way reduce by all of two or three seconds the time I had to wait. It was a useless gesture, but one in which he took a certain pride, a way not so much to be helpful as to show that he was more than willing, eager, to give whatever assistance he could. He had done the same thing a thousand times before, but now, suddenly, it taught me the necessity of the choice I had to make; it taught me that I did not have any real choice at all. The doorman did his job; no one asked him if he would rather do something else. And if he had his job, I had mine. I tried cases; it was all I knew. And if I had reached the point in my career where I could pick and choose the cases I wanted, I had still the obligation not to do so on the basis of my own convenience, much less the fear that I might lose.

By the time I met Jean-Francois Reynaud the next day for lunch, the decision had been made. I told him as we sat down in a back booth at a fashionable bar and grill a few blocks down the street from the French Consulate what I was going to do. Reynaud nodded politely, as if he had expected nothing else, caught the attention of a passing waiter, who, like everyone who worked here, must have been in his seventies, and ordered a drink. He looked as if he needed it. With his elbow on the table, he glanced up at the framed black-and-white photograph on the wall.

"Joe DiMaggio. I like coming here. You get the feeling that nothing has changed since the 1950s. You get the feeling," he added, watching the waiter walk away, "that he, and the others, all started here and never thought to leave." With his finger he traced a thin line across the hard, polished table. "There is so much going on, so many things I have to do," he said quietly and without explanation. The waiter brought his drink. Reynaud picked it up, barely took a sip and set it down again. He searched my eyes.

"I asked to meet you. I had heard about you, of course; you could even say I followed your career from a distance, though that would not tell the whole story and would, in a sense, be misleading. Part of my job is to know what goes on in the city, and not just the city; to know the principal actors, the men and women who, in their different ways, contribute to what goes on. I would have come to know something about you in the normal course of events, a well-known criminal defense attorney, but most of what I know about you is through my old friend, Albert Craven."

"You must have an easy job. Albert knows everyone, and if you know Albert, you wouldn't need any other source of information."

"Yes, except that our mutual friend is a master of discretion. Tell him something in confidence and—I needn't tell you this, I'm sure—it goes with him to the grave. And despite that engaging manner of his, he is not a gossip. He won't tell you anything he doesn't think you need to know, though perhaps he tells me things he wouldn't tell too many others. We've been friends for more than twenty years."

This was a surprise. Until last night, I had never heard him mention his name. Reynaud's eyes brightened.

"Last night was the first time you had ever heard my name. That is what I mean. He's careful that way, you can trust him that way. We met when he was on his honeymoon—I'm not sure which one it was. Poor Albert, he has a Frenchman's weakness without a Frenchman's talent for self-deception. He thinks infidelity inexcusable; we think it a condition of existence. He and his new bride stayed at our castle." He threw up his hands, dismissing the exaggerated impression this would almost certainly create. "A castle, as distinguished from a chateau; an ancient place built in the thirteenth century, but a place in which to live, not, like Carcassonne, a fortress built for war. We—my wife and I—restored it, and for a while ran it as a place for travelers to stop. It's just outside Agen, which is about a hundred miles south and slightly east of Bordeaux, and a three-hour drive from Spain.

Albert and his new wife, whose name I'm afraid I don't remember, spent a week with us. Then, after that, for a while they came every year."

This, while interesting, told me nothing about why Jean-Francois Reynaud, a French diplomat, would have an interest, much less try to involve himself, in whether I would become a lawyer for Kevin Fitzgerald.

"It's very simple," he remarked in response to the question I had not asked. "Albert told me he trusted you more than anyone he knew."

"That was nice of him to say. But what difference could that make to you? No one from your country is involved. It did not happen on French soil."

He raised his left eyebrow.

"Are you sure it didn't? Happen on French soil? Or, to be more precise, are you sure it matters where it happened? Everything is connected. What happened here might as well have happened in France, for all the difference in the effect it will have. Yes, I know, Bridges was your president, Fitzgerald your senator; the crime—the assassination—changes, could change, the whole political dynamic in this country. But consider," he said, leaning forward with a sudden sense of urgency, "consider the effect Bridges had on what we in Europe are faced with. Consider the situation where, for the first time since the Germans were defeated in the Second World War, we find ourselves without any reliable American guarantee. Consider what will happen if this assassination should lead a majority of your people to see Bridges as the victim of some left-wing conspiracy. Consider what will happen if they start to believe that Bridges had been right after all, that all the investigations, all the talk of some conspiracy with the Russians, was nothing more than made up lies, that he was murdered to make sure he could never be exonerated; that he wasn't murdered to stop him doing any more damage to the county, but to stop him changing the country in the way it needed to be changed. You've read Shakespeare?"

The question came so quickly, without so much as a pause to signal a new subject, a different inquiry, that it took a moment to catch up.

"Shakespeare? Yes, some. Why?"

"You've read Julius Caesar?"

"It's been a while."

"Someone—I've forgotten who—wrote that there was a chance, when Caesar was murdered, if someone had seized the moment, to restore the republic; that everyone was in such a state of shock, of disbelief, that they would have followed anyone who had the will to lead. But instead—civil war, thousands murdered and the beginning of the Augustan Age in which power become more absolute, more concentrated in a single man, an emperor, than it had ever been before."

"Do you think that is what is going to happen here? We have had the normal succession. The vice-president has been—"

"I don't know what is going to happen here. I only know what almost happened here. I only know that everything that came out about Bridges and the Russians only scratched the surface, that if he had lived, the world would have changed in ways no one would have thought possible."

"Then why the reference to Julius Caesar? What analogy are you trying to draw?"

"Caesar was murdered because he was a threat to the continued power of the Senate; in other words, a threat to what was left of the old, established institutions of the Roman republic. Bridges, with nothing like the genius of Julius Caesar, was surrounded by people who, in the name of a new nationalism, were moving him in the same direction—government by executive order, demands that the Senate change its rules so that everything could be done by simple majority, direct appeal to the public in short, sometimes mindless, statements giving his own, authoritative opinion—opinion, not argument—about every matter of public, and even, on occasion, private concern. He is murdered, like Caesar, by a member of the Senate, murdered because of the threat he has become. Who decided whether Caesar's murder was justified, whether it was murder or tyrannicide? It wasn't debated in the Senate, it wasn't brought for judgement to some court. The people of Rome were asked to decide, and they did—by backing one claimant to power or another in civil war.

"What I said to you last night—there is more at issue here than the guilt or innocence of one lone defendant in a murder trial, more at issue than whether you or any other attorney can win an acquittal for your client. What is at issue is nothing less than the question of which way history takes us, what kind of history we make ourselves. That means, Mr. Antonelli, what kind of history we think we have already, whether what we think has happened is, or is not, true."

Jean-Francois Reynaud was talking with more animation and more intensity with every word. Leaning on his elbows, his face between his arms, his hands seemed to be moving in several different directions at once. He looked a little like a prisoner speaking from behind the bars of his cell. Then, just as he was about to start another sentence, another long excursion through the obscurities of time, he stopped.

"But we should eat," he remarked, and with that he beckoned to the stoic, white-haired waiter and we ordered lunch.

"I should tell you," he started up between bites of his salad, "that if this had happened in France—I mean if everyone involved had been French—

all you would have had to do is make sure a woman was involved. We have a long history of forgiving crimes of passion. There was a trial once, early in the twentieth century, if I remember right, for a woman—I forget if it was the mistress or the wife—who showed up at the other one's front door and shot her five times. She was acquitted of the murder. It was ruled an accidental death. Five times!" he repeated, marveling at what he seemed to think an exquisite example of fairness and good judgment.

"But as to your question," he said, shoving aside what was left of the salad and ignoring altogether the main course he had ordered. "The importance of what happened—not the murder, but what happened before, what made that murder almost inevitable."

He paused, lifted his glass and for only the second time took a drink, this one with the slow reluctance of a thought come unbidden to the surface of his mind.

"The French Revolution. Everyone murdered everyone else, everyone who got power by killing whoever had it, then, the new possessor, murdered for the same reason. And all of it done in the name of democracy and equality, the twin standards, the two driving forces, of the last two hundred years. There is no aristocracy of any kind anymore; no hierarchy, no set of established beliefs that differentiate among the various levels of accomplishment; nothing to mark the difference between better and worse; no accepted form of argument by which to test the reasonableness, or even the necessity, of what we do, the only basis of judgment is what a majority— any majority—happens to feel at any given moment, every opinion, every belief, as good or evil, as any other. This is the world in which we live, the world that made someone like Walter Bridges possible, the world that allowed someone of such astonishing ignorance and incapacity claim to know better than anyone else how to solve problems no one had solved before, the world that made it possible to claim to be a patriot while acting the traitor. It was all true, Mr. Antonelli, every rumor, every whispered allegation. We have it all, everything, all of it on tape. It is the only chance Kevin Fitzgerald has, isn't it, to show that he acted to save the country from something worse than murder?"

"But what makes you think that I, or anyone, can—"

Reynaud called the waiter over, paid the bill and got up to leave. He pointed to the tan briefcase placed next to where he had been sitting.

"Don't forget your briefcase, Mr. Antonelli. I know you wouldn't want to lose what you have inside."

And then, before I could say a word, before I could ask a question, he was gone. Whatever was in the briefcase, it was now my possession, free, so far as I now knew, to do with as I wanted. I was tempted to open it right there and thumb through the contents to see if I had really been given what he had appeared to promise: proof that the president was everything his adversaries had said he was. Or had Reynaud given me even more than that, something no one had dared think possible? But temptation yielded to a strange, unaccountable fear. I looked around, the victim of what I tried to dismiss as paranoia, the feeling that I was being watched, that among the dozens of people sitting at dozens of tables, someone had me under surveillance. I left the restaurant and, clutching the briefcase, walked half a block, stopped and looked back. The streets were crowded, but so far as I could tell no one was following me. I laughed, or tried to laugh away my fears, but I could not quite shake the feeling that something was not right.

The building that for more than forty years had housed the law firm that Albert Craven had begun, the law firm in which he was the only listed partner still alive, was just a few short blocks away. Built just a few years after the earthquake that had leveled the city in 1906, it showed scarcely any signs of age on its front facade and none at all in the plush, modern surroundings of the two floors on which the firm did its own, quiet, business representing companies it had taken care of since the beginning of their respective existence. "We were all just kids," Craven liked to say, "usually broke and always in debt. Now we're all old and rich and there isn't one of us who wouldn't give it all away if we could only go back and start all over." It was a well-intentioned lie, but also, for that dwindling group of aging clients, a way to forget, and, as it were, make time to atone for what some of them they had cheated and stolen to acquire.

The receptionist, a smartly dressed women of an indeterminate middle age who wore rings on her fingers and bracelets on her arms, always quick and alert, raised her hand as I passed.

"You have a visitor waiting in your office. Kevin Fitzgerald's wife," she whispered as I moved closer.

"She didn't call? She just walked in?"

"That's right. She said she knew you would want to see her."

"Does Albert know she's here?"

"He's still out," she replied, smiling with her eyes. Craven frequently had lunches that lasted until dinner. There was always someone dying to tell him a story.

Tricia Fitzgerald was waiting for me, all right, and she was not particularly pleased about it.

"You didn't see Kevin yesterday. I told him you'd be there, that you would go over to the jail and talk to him. I told him—"

"Good afternoon, Mrs. Fitzgerald," I said as I settled into the dark blue leather chair behind my desk. I was careful to place Reynaud's briefcase next to me on the floor as if it were my own and I put it there all the time. "What can I do for you?"

"You know damn well what you can do for me!"

"Represent your husband. Yes, I know. But you were here only yesterday. Did you think that I—"

"Kevin has been in custody for more than a week!"

She said this as if that were the limit of her patience, the limit of how long she could wait for anything. Her husband was all she cared about, but if he were convicted, I had very little doubt he would rather quickly become part of her unremembered past.

"If I take your husband's case, there would be conditions," I informed her.

Anyone else would have agreed at once. She demanded to know what those conditions might be.

"How old are you?"

The question surprised, and irritated, her.

"What difference does it make how old I am, what—"

"That's the first condition. You—and your husband—answer any question I ask. I decide what is relevant and what isn't."

Her chin came up a defiant half inch, anger flashed across her eyes.

"I don't think—"

"There are a lot of lawyers, Mrs. Fitzgerald; good ones, all of them eager to take this case. You won't have any trouble finding one."

"I'm thirty-two," she announced, mastering for the moment all her latent hostility.

"Understand, right at the beginning, I'm going to need to know everything about you, everything there is."

"But I'm not on trial, I'm not accused of anything. I'm not the defendant."

"Don't be too sure. Things come out in a murder trial, things that suddenly become important, things that make a jury believe, or refuse to believe, that the defendant is someone who isn't the kind of person who would have committed the crime. What was his state of mind? Was he angry, upset, because his young and beautiful wife was having an affair, that she was about to leave him for another man?"

She did not protest the way some women might have done, fearing what I might think their silence to mean. She had too much an instinct for her own advantage, too much the sense of her own interest, to allow herself an emotional reaction. If she had an affair, she would never feel guilt.

"Or if it were to come out at trial that the defendant had been cheating on his wife," I went on, describing with analytical clarity the way that what might have seemed exclusively private matters could prejudice a jury. "You won't find it in any of the jury instructions, it isn't what the judge says concerning what they may and may not consider, but once a jury thinks a defendant someone they would never trust, the verdict is all but certain. So, no, Mrs. Fitzgerald, there isn't anything that isn't relevant, nothing that you can hold back because you don't think it important or that it isn't anyone's business."

"Kevin has never cheated on me, and I have never cheated on him," she said, cool and self-assured. "And if you're thinking that wives don't always know what their husbands have done, we aren't like other married couples. We both understood the political damage something like that could cause."

It was a curious way of putting it. She understood, as well as he had, the danger involved. It was not just his behavior, but hers as well, that might cause scandal. The possibility of indiscretion had, as it were, never been just on one side. I had the feeling that this had been discussed and decided, fidelity part of a check list of what his, or rather their, political ambition required.

"What about before you were married, when your husband was still single?"

She started to laugh, wondering if I was really that out of touch with the way other, younger people lived their lives.

"Kevin was young and good looking, wonderful to be with. He had his share of girlfriends. He had…I'm not quite sure what you're asking."

"Did he ever have an affair with a married woman? Did he have an affair with Tangerine Winslow, Evan Winslow's wife, while he was running for mayor?"

"That never happened," she insisted, shaking her head. "It was a rumor, nothing more. Kevin told me that it never happened."

I now knew what I had not known before: Kevin Fitzgerald did not always tell the truth. Or was she the one who was lying? Was this just another way she protected her husband? We talked for another thirty minutes. I was not so much interested in the answers she gave to the questions I asked, questions that had mainly to do with the basic elements of their respective biographies, as in the way she continued to assume that if everyone did not already think her husband had done a very great thing, they would after everything came out in the trial.

"Kevin was on the Senate Intelligence Committee. He knows things other people don't; he knew what was going on, he knew what was going to happen if someone did not stop it."

"He told you that?" I asked, intensely curious. "He told you he knew what was going to happen?"

"Not what it was. He couldn't do that, he couldn't tell anyone, not even me, about the classified material he had seen. But, yes, he told me that however bad the things that had been done before, what was going to happen, what these people—what the president and the people around him—were going to do was worse, much worse. 'Catastrophic' was how he put it. He was worried, Mr. Antonelli, more worried than I had ever seen him. You have to help, Mr. Antonelli; the story has to get told. He saved the country."

I promised to see her husband, but I did not promise that I would take the case. I might still change my mind after I had seen him. I told her only that I would make a decision after I talked to him. She did not have any doubt, once I met him in person and listened to what he had to say, what my decision would be.

"There is something you should know," she remarked as she rose from the chair and in that effortless way she had started to turn toward the door. "All those millions of people who think what Kevin did was right, all those millions who keep sending money, who keep expressing their support, want more than an acquittal. They want him to lead the country."

She said this with all the shining certainty of a triumph long foretold, like the dream of the fanatic who thinks her every fantasy destined to come true. I remembered what Jean-Francois Reynaud had told me at lunch, the eager willingness, both in ancient and modern times. to find in murder a political excuse.

A few minutes after she left, there was a soft knock on the door and Albert Craven walked in.

"Jean-Francois Reynaud—"

"I was just thinking of him."

"He called a few minutes ago. He asked me to tell you that he wondered if you could return sometime tomorrow what he gave you at lunch today. He said it's quite important that he have it back, and that you would understand."

I picked up the briefcase and placed it on my desk. Whatever was inside, it was something no one outside the French government was supposed to have.

"Do you know what documents are in here?"

"Only in the most general terms. Jean-Francois would not tell me more than that they were highly confidential, that only a few people in the highest positions in the French government knew of their existence, that no one in American intelligence had been told about them and never would be."

"But he gives them to me?" I asked skeptically.

"I think he must have explained that to you already. They have an interest, all of Europe has an interest, in making sure that the truth, all of it, gets out. You'll need this, you'll need to know what they know, for the defense. It isn't what happens to Kevin Fitzgerald that concerns them; it isn't their concern whether a jury finds him guilty or not. It is the reason Bridges was murdered—what he did that led to this—they want out. For obvious reasons, they can't be seen involved. It is an American murder and an American trial. Everything is now in your hands."

CHAPTER

FOUR

I forgot all about dinner, I forgot about everything except what I was reading, each page more compelling, and more damning, than the one before, all of them together a complete indictment of Walter Bridges. Everything I had read before, what from almost the beginning of his administration had been reported with growing alarm and disbelief in the papers, had been true, and yet none of it close to the real truth, the organizing principle of what had been attempted. I sat at my desk, reading some things three and four times to make sure I really understood the darker nature of what, by any definition, was clearly subversion. I was afraid to leave the office, afraid to take home with me this astonishing dossier compiled by agents of French intelligence, afraid that if I let it out of my sight for even a few moments it might disappear; afraid that what I had thought my ungrounded fear from earlier in the day that I was being watched, being followed, might not have been groundless after all. I read until I could read no more. A few minutes past two in the morning, I locked the briefcase and its incredible contents in my desk and went home. The first rose-colored light of morning began to paint its way down the steel towers of the Golden Gate when, my head still full of what I had read, I finally fell asleep. A few hours later, showered, shaved and dressed, I was on my way to the county jail and my first meeting with Kevin Fitzgerald.

He seemed oddly disengaged, as if what had happened had nothing to do with him. He spoke like someone describing not what he had done, but what he had seen, a witness, not a participant in something the significance of which he had not yet fully grasped. Or was it the other way round? Was it that he understood better than anyone the nature of his achievement? He was in jail, but he was not being held in a normal cell, one of those narrow, dismal places of confinement. It was a light, airy room that must have been used as an administrative office. There were bars on the two windows high up on the wall opposite the door, but the door itself was a normal wooden door, not one made of iron. The bed was a regular twin bed with a box spring mattress. There was a wooden table, and on the table a laptop computer. The bathroom, which had a shower, had a separate entrance of its own. Four large, overstuffed canvas mailbags were stacked close together against the wall on the far side of the table.

"Fan mail," explained Fitzgerald.

Gesturing toward a faded, slightly tattered green easy chair the near side of the table, he sat in a straight back chair in front of the computer. If he had not been wearing the tan shirt and pants of an inmate, I would have thought I was in the private rented room of a writer working all alone on his novel.

"Trish told me you would be coming," he said with a friendly, easy grin that could not quite conceal the coldness of his eyes.

He was smaller, thinner, than he looked on television or in the photographs I had seen in the papers. His hair was straight, black, parted sharply on the side, his eyes set evenly apart, his nose an almost perfect line and his mouth pulled back at the corners as if on spring set hinges. It left you, that look of his, with little doubt that time could not measure the interval between the instant he once he grasped the reaction you were hoping for and the reaction he would give. I decided to shake him out of his self-complacency

"You lied to your wife, why would I think you wouldn't do the same thing to me?"

I said this so matter-of-factly, with such an obvious unconcern what he answered, or even if he answered at all, that he had begun to smile, the way he ingratiated himself with any well-meaning constituent who asked a question of no particular significance. The smile died on his lips. A question of his own shot through his cautious eyes.

"Lied to my wife? I don't know what you mean."

"Lied to her when you told her you had never had an affair with Evan Winslow's wife."

He looked at me, incredulous.

"You talked to Trish about...? I didn't lie. It never happened. I never had an affair with Tangerine. Winslow lied about it; he started that rumor. I knew her, I knew them both. We were all good friends once. But it was in my first campaign, when I ran for mayor. Evan was doing all the fundraising, contributing a lot of his own money. He thought it meant he would have a place, an important place, in the new administration when I won. He also seemed to think he could tell me what I had to do as a candidate, what I had to say, what positions I should take. When he found out that none of that was going to happen, that he could not control what I did, there was a big blow up. He thought I had used him, used him for his money; he swore he would get even. His wife, Tangerine—have you ever seen her?—there's only one reason she would have married a guy like him. She was probably sleeping with all sorts of people. It was easy to start a rumor that she was sleeping with me, that it was the reason he quit. He wasn't going to tell the truth, that he quit because he couldn't buy himself a place in city hall."

If I had not seen her, if I had not heard from her that she would have left her husband and married him, if he had not had the kind of ambition that required money, I might have believed him. He was that good. Only seasoned politicians and courtroom lawyers can convince themselves the lies they tell are only the truth.

"I didn't lie to my wife," he insisted, indifferent, as it seemed, whether I continued to doubt his honest word. "And I won't lie to you, if that is what you came to find out—whether you can trust me to tell you what you want to know."

Reaching inside my briefcase, my own, not the one that belonged to Jean-Francois Reynaud, I pulled out a yellow legal pad and, with the fountain pen I always carried, began to scribble a few brief notes, the shorthand summary of what I would need to remember.

"Let's begin at the beginning. The place it happened. Why here, why San Francisco, why on board Air Force One?"

He nodded slowly, and looked off to the side of where I sat waiting to hear what he was willing to tell me about what had happened just ten days before.

"I did not plan it in advance," he said suddenly.

"Why were you there, then, if you didn't go with that purpose in mind?"

"I didn't say I didn't go there with that purpose."

"You didn't...?"

"I didn't know if I would get the chance. I didn't know if I would even see him; close up, I mean, close up and alone. There were other times, other places—Washington, the White House, where I had been invited to meet with him, but always with other members of the House or Senate. I thought, when I learned he was making the trip to San Francisco, that there might be a chance to see him alone. I was part of the greeting party, the elected officials who stand on the tarmac to welcome the president when he visits the state."

"But you got on the plane."

"That was just chance. The plane was a few minutes early. One of his staff people comes down the staircase and tells me that Bridges wants a word. I was taken to his cabin. That's where I found him, all alone. As soon as I was inside, the door shut behind me."

I knew what had happened, everyone in the country knew what had happened then. What I did not know was why Fitzgerald had been so eager to confess.

"You think I should have denied it, said someone else must have killed him?" he asked with a jaundiced, thin-lipped smile. "I understood immediately the situation I was in."

Had he? I wondered.

"But you didn't confess right away. They had you in custody, held incommunicado, for three full days."

"Want me to tell you that they beat it out of me, like in some old movie? That confession is my best defense."

"The law of necessity?"

Fitzgerald pointed toward the bursting bags of mail, tens of thousands of letters which, he informed me, were running ten to one in favor of what he had done.

"They call me an American hero, another Nathan Hale, a patriot willing to die for my country. And those are just the one who write letters. For every one of them there are a thousand others registering their approval, and if not always their approval, their sympathy, for what I was forced to do. There isn't a jury anywhere that is going to convict me of murder."

This led to a question, cruel in its implications and impossible to answer, because, if it were true, every thought of heroism was destroyed.

"Is that what you believed when you killed him? That you could never be convicted, that you could do it and everyone would applaud?"

"I wasn't thinking about the consequences; I thought about what I had to do."

"There has never been a trial for the assassination of an American president," I reminded him. I wanted him to understand that in something this unprecedented, there was no basis on which to assume that murder might be forgiven. "There are a lot of people on death row who thought they killed someone who deserved to die."

"There isn't anyone on death row—at least no one who deserves to be there—who killed someone who was a threat, an imminent threat, to the lives and the well-being of every citizen in this country. Call it a presidential assassination if you want to, but it isn't as if I killed Kennedy or Lincoln!"

I now knew enough, thanks to Jean-Francois Reynaud, to know that Fitzgerald was more right than he knew. But he was already too certain of himself, too certain that everything was going to go his way, to tell him this.

"You have the reputation of a serious man, Mr. Antonelli. It is even said that you read serious things. Have you read any Russian history?"

"Some," I replied, wondering at his interest. "When I was in college I took a course on the Russian Revolution, and I've read some things over the years. But most of what I read about Russia was Russian literature: Tolstoy, Dostoevsky—"

"Pushkin," he added, picking up the thread. "*The Queen of Spades* is a great story," he added with a reader's eager nostalgia.

It surprised me that he had read Pushkin; it would have surprised me had he mentioned any Russian author's name. I had thought him one of that breed of politician who lived his life as a cliché.

"Pushkin, Chekov, Lermontiv, I read them all, including, of course, *War and Peace* and *The Brothers Karamazov*. You can read all the so-called experts in the field, all the dull, painstaking studies, the economic projections, the political analysis, but it is only what great writers write that tell you what is essential about a people, another country's way of life. Someone once wrote—I've forgotten who it was—that by showing how corrupt, how ineffective the Russian aristocracy had become, *War and Peace* made the Russian Revolution not just possible, but inevitable. A Marxist would never believe that, but then no Marxist thought the revolution, the revolution that would destroy capitalism, could possibly start in Russia where capitalism barely existed."

Fitzgerald tapped two fingers on the table as he thought about what he wanted to say. He was bending forward, leaning toward me, an arm's length away. For a moment he did not say a word. His eyes drew close together and his lips pressed tightly as he worked through whatever problem he was trying to solve.

"I'm not the empty-headed fool you think I am," he said suddenly.

"I didn't…" I started to object, but quickly changed my mind. It was not a time for false politeness. I did not deny he was right. "Why do you think I would think that?"

His eyes flashed with recognition, an acknowledgement of candor.

"Why wouldn't you, someone who reads Tolstoy and Dostoevsky and then reads in the papers the kind of things I say. Don't think for a minute that I don't wish I had been able to talk at a higher level, or that I haven't thought myself a coward for staying within the predictable limits of everyday speech. But that's just it, you see: I can't connect what I would like to talk about and whatever everyone wants—or thinks they want—to hear. But you, you've read things, then remembered, thought about, what you've read. The Russian Revolution: you could draw a line, all the way through, starting with what Tolstoy wrote about, the war with France, Napoleon's invasion, draw the line through the rest of that century right up to the Russian Revolution and beyond: Lenin and the Bolsheviks, Trotsky and the so-called Permanent Revolution, the belief that what had started in Russia would soon spread, would have to spread, through Europe; Stalin and his insistence on Socialism in One Country, the necessity for Russia to look within, to build itself up against the world outside that was intent on destroying what Communist Russia had to do. And then, once Stalin was in power, the countless murders, the millions of peasants killed in order to collectivize agriculture, the attempt to monopolize every aspect of Russian life, and then, finally, the Show Trials, the state-run accusations that those high-ranking Communists who had opposed what Stalin had done had not only been mistaken, but were traitors to the cause, agents of the capitalist powers, proof, the only proof needed, their own confessions in open court."

"The show trials of the thirties, Bukharin and the others. Koestler wrote the book."

"*Darkness at Noon*," said Fitzgerald, surprising me again by the breadth of his knowledge. "I read it more than once. Someone charged with crimes he did not commit agrees to confess to those crimes in open court, crimes of high treason against the Communist party, crimes that will cost him his life. And why does he agree? Because—"

"Because the Communist party is the chosen instrument of history, and he cannot deny his guilt without denying his own belief in history; he cannot deny his guilt without denying the only thing that gives meaning to his life."

Fitzgerald sat back, studying me with a new interest.

"Koestler's book is based on what happened to Bukharin, who, as you know, was not the only one prosecuted for something he did not do, but his was the most important trial because he was the highest ranking member of the party accused. It is the same position I'm now in."

How could he possible think that? The difference was too obvious.

"Bukharin confessed to something he did not do. Are you saying that your confession isn't true, that—"

"I'm saying that the government wants to use my confession in the same way the Russian—the Soviet—government used Bukharin's and the others: to show the world that not just those in power, but a whole way of life, is under threat and that something has to be done to stop it. That meant execution for the Russians under Stalin; it means the same thing here. That's why, don't you see, it's so important that the trial becomes more about the so-called victim than the question of who killed him. The only question is why Walter Bridges had to die. It has to be a show trial, but one in which the government—the president—is put on trial!"

"Have you ever been involved in a trial?"

"I didn't go to law school, I'm not a lawyer, if that's what you're asking."

"What I'm asking is have you even watched a trial, a criminal trial, watched it start to finish, watched jury selection, listened to opening statements, followed the testimony of the witnesses, observed the different ways in which the prosecutor and the defense attorney conduct a cross-examination? Because if you haven't done that, you have no idea what can happen. You can't just decide you're going to make the trial about the president. The prosecution can call as many witnesses as it likes, introduce all the evidence it thinks it needs, and everything the prosecution does will be to show that there was no excuse for what you did, that Walter Bridges could have been not just the worst president, but the worst man who ever lived, but that you had no right—no one has the right—to decide on your own that it's okay to kill someone else.

"No, don't bother," I said as he began to interrupt me with an argument of his own. "I know what you're going to say. I don't disagree. It's probably the only hope you have. But you're making a huge mistake to think you can persuade a jury—any jury—by simply telling your story. You aren't going to be on the floor of the Senate speaking to a respectful, silent audience of your fellow senators; you're going to be on the witness stand, answering questions, every answer subject to immediate attack by a prosecutor who wants nothing more than to cut everything you say to ribbons."

Fitzgerald was not convinced. He might have to answer questions, but he would decide how long those answers would be. He had spent half his life taking questions from an audience, questions that had not always been friendly. He knew how to handle people.

"I'm told that one of the rules in politics, something you learn almost at the beginning, is that if someone asks you a question you can't answer, answer one you can. You won't be able to do that here, not when you're a witness in a trial. Do anything but answer directly, you, and the jury, will immediately be reminded that you haven't answered what you were asked, reminded in a way that will leave no doubt in the minds of those jurors that there is something you are trying to hide."

I had spent my life trying cases, and he had never seen one, but he knew better what was going to happen. He was sure of it. This was different, this would be no normal trial. Hadn't I already said so myself; hadn't I told him what he undoubtedly had known, that there had never been a trial of someone accused of assassinating the president of the United States?

"Tell me something," I said as I prepared to leave. "I first started reading about the Russian Revolution when I was in college. What about you? When did you first get interested, when did you first read those Russian writers we were talking about: Pushkin, Turgenev and the others?"

"I read a few things early, when I was still a student, but most of what I've read—all the really important things—just a few years ago."

"When you were already in the Senate?" I asked, just to be sure.

"That's right."

"When you were on the Intelligence Committee?"

"Yes."

"When you first became aware of what the Russians were doing, how they were establishing relationships with Americans, Americans who were private citizens, Americans who had certain kinds of financial interests that involved Russian companies, Russian investors and banks, people who were connected, one way or the other, with the Russian government?"

"Yes, but how did you—"

"I'm not the empty-headed fool you thought I was," I remarked with a quick sideways smile as I got to my feet. "I have a few sources of my own."

After nearly two hours with Fitzgerald I still was not sure why he had done what he had. He had made it sound almost accidental, something he had decided he had to do, but, despite that apparent decision, had never really planned. If he had not suddenly been given the opportunity, suddenly found himself alone with the president, it might not have happened at all. But why—and this was a question the prosecution would never ask—if it was obvious, necessary, that something this drastic had to be done, if it was the only way to save the country, had he not planned every step in great and meticulous detail? And why, if it was all so damn obvious that there was no other choice, had he acted alone? Why had he not engaged a group of like-minded men, formed a conspiracy that by the sheer weight and numbers of those involved, other senators like himself, turned murder into what could then be claimed was an act of public need and retribution, given it at least the color of shared sacrifice to a sacred ideal. Had this involved only private individuals, if the victim had not been the president, there might not have even been a charge of murder. In the absence of sufficient premeditation, it might have been pleaded down to manslaughter.

"It isn't a criminal case," replied Albert Craven when I mentioned this to him in his office later that same day. "It's a political case, a political trial. I scarcely need to explain that to you."

He sat behind the black Victorian desk, ugly beyond description, that had been the unwelcome gift of one of his first wives. He had hated it, as anyone would, but he was too soft-hearted to think of getting rid of it, even after the divorce. He thought it rather nice of her to think it would help to cushion the blow of her decision to leave if she left it with him. It had become a kind of ritual, a way to keep intact the line of shared memories, that each time I came in to see him, I would manage, now without any conscious awareness, to shudder at the sight of those large, thick, circular legs spiraling up to four carved Herculean figures on whose respective bent backs rested the weight of that enormous monstrosity, ready, at any moment as it seemed, to crash through the floor below.

"Isabel wants me to get rid of it." With Buddha-like serenity he tapped his fingers together. "A new, modern desk, all glass and steel. It gives her something to do, change everything out of all recognition, make everything new. She mentioned, just this morning, that I need to change my wardrobe. You've never been married. There are certain advantages in that. Funny, I never seem to remember that. You would think I would, having had so many chances to learn that particular lesson. One advantage," he said with a burst of energy as he jumped forward and slammed the palms of his hands on top of what remained a soundless pile of wood, "is that when you're single and a married woman wants to see you, there is at least the chance that what she has in mind is illicit, especially if she is remarkably good looking and married to a man she quite properly despises."

"Then it isn't my new client's wife?"

"Then you've decided for sure to take the case," he remarked, the gleeful good humor vanishing from his eyes. "Good. Very good. Whatever happens, at least we can now be sure that the truth—whatever the truth is—will come out."

"You said a woman, a married woman, wants to see me."

"I did, didn't I," he replied, the eager anticipation, if a little less mischievous, coming back in his eyes. "Tangerine Winslow. You must have made an impression the other night at dinner. She didn't want to call you directly. She asked if I could arrange it. She said that if you were going to take the case, there was something you should know."

Resting on his elbows, he folded his hands together and held them close to his mouth. He looked at me with a slightly puzzled expression, wondering, as it seemed, how far he should go, how much he should tell me, whether he had the right to interfere.

"She is one of the most beautiful women I have ever seen, and easily the most dangerous."

"Dangerous? What do you mean?"

"I'm really not sure. But every time I see her, I remember an old story about a woman who lived in ancient Greece or Rome. She would sleep with anyone for a price, but the price was unusual—your life. One night, and the next day you died, died by your own hand, suicide the price of carnal knowledge. A price, apparently, a great many were willing to pay."

"You think that is what Tangerine Winslow might charge?" I asked with a quick, dismissive grin.

"No, but there are other things, other costs you might not think that much different. I told her I would do what she asked, let you know she wanted to see you. I didn't tell her that I would tell you that you should. And the truth is that I think it might be the biggest mistake you could ever make."

"Well," I said, as I stood up, "I can at least promise I won't be running off with her to London or New York. I have a trial to get ready for." Then I remembered. "But she said there was something about the case I should know?"

Something about the case, that was what I told myself as I walked into the Mark Hopkins Hotel and took the elevator to the restaurant at the top where I had agreed to meet her at the bar. I was right on time, nine o'clock, and she was not there. I ordered a scotch and soda and stared at the lights of the city, and the lights of the bridge, and the lights dancing in the distance the other side of the bay in the Berkeley Hills. The place was full of well-heeled tourists, the out of town guests staying at what, along with the Fairmont across the street, were the best-known hotels on Nob Hill, places you could brag about when you finally had to leave and go back to wherever you had come from, full of all the excitement that came with telling everyone that San Francisco was everything you thought it would be and even more. They were not all newcomers, of course; some were old enough to have started coming here half a century before, when travel took longer and people stayed longer in the same place, and when instead of a quick drink on the way to somewhere else, afraid that otherwise something might be missed, most of those who came to drink, drank until last call, drank and talked and drank some more when, if you were lucky, you might see that great scoundrel of a lawyer Melvin Belli on a three-day drunk with some of his famous hard drinking Hollywood friends, when Herb Caen, chronicling all the city's glorious indiscretions, might be seen scribbling a note to himself, perhaps thinking already of the line he would later use when, dying of cancer, he would tell ten thousand of his closest raucous friends at a downtown rally in his honor that he had dreamed he had died and gone to heaven and that after he had a chance to look around, St. Peter asked him what he thought of heaven: "It's very nice," he said he told St. Peter, "but it isn't San Francisco!"

There were people at every table, scarcely any room left at the bar. The noise was not deafening, but loud enough that the bartender had to lean forward to hear my order. And then, suddenly, the noise stopped, the only sound a kind of puzzled hum. Turning around, I immediately knew the cause. Tangerine Winslow, looking just like Elizabeth Taylor, looking just like Natalie Wood, looking just like every movie star you had ever seen, was walking across the room as if the place belonged to her. Everyone was watching, certain they must know her, certain she had to be someone famous, wondering why they could not remember her name. She came straight toward me, and I felt that long forgotten rush of boyhood pride and pleasure in the knowledge that she had come to be with me. She took the empty stool next to me and without a word, or a look of greeting, asked the bartender for a glass of wine. She stared straight ahead, an enigmatic smile of Egyptian secrecy moving catlike across her firm, full mouth.

"I'm late," she said, as if I was not there and she were speaking to herself. "I don't know why I can so seldom be on time. Do you think," she asked, turning suddenly to me, "it's because I spend too much time getting ready? Too much time worrying whether you will be as interested in me as I would like you to be?"

Wearing a black, low-cut dress, with diamond earrings and a gorgeous diamond necklace, she had thrown her fur coat over the back of the high-backed leather stool with the careless gesture of a woman who took for granted that whatever clothing or jewelry she wore owed all their luster to her.

"I heard a story," I began, nursing the scotch and soda, "not that long ago, about a woman who lived a long time ago, a woman so beautiful that she would only sleep with a man if he agreed to kill himself the morning after they spent the night."

"And did she sleep with many?" asked Tangerine, sipping on her wine.

"Endless numbers."

"Then she was a fool."

"A fool?" I laughed. "Why?"

"Because at least once in a while she should have found one worth sleeping with twice." Her eyes still on me, she took another slow drink. "And would you like to know if I ever have—found someone I wanted to sleep with twice?"

I caught myself, stopped while I still knew what I was doing.

"You already answered that."

"Yes, of course. Kevin, that's who you mean. And you're right, I did— and I would have for who knows how much longer. Yes, I admit it: I was in love with him, in ways I had never been before."

I felt a slight sense of disappointment, a tinge of regret, a feeling, not jealousy exactly, but something more like envy, not of Kevin Fitzgerald, not of him directly, but the wish that it could somehow have been me; the sense of something lost, not something I had ever had, but, if I had had that chance, would have wanted.

"You remind me of him a little," said Tangerine, as if she could read, not my mind, but something deeper, the thought that has not yet come, but would. "It isn't that you're about the same age. You don't look anything alike. His looks are all surface; you're are more ingrained, more a true reflection— if I'm any judge—of who you really are. Yes, that's the difference, I think. You don't care what other people think about how you look. You never think about yourself that way. That's what makes you so attractive: it never occurs to you to wonder if you are. What you have in common, why you remind me of him, is the way you both are so single-minded, so obsessed with getting what you want. It's the reason, unless I miss my guess, why you never lose a trial. You won't allow it to happen. You'll spend all your time, concentrate all your energy, on only that one thing: winning, finding a way to convince a jury that the only choice they have is to find the defendant not guilty. Am I wrong?"

"You've left something out: most of the people I've represented should have been found not guilty."

"Most, not all?"

I let that question pass in silence. The difference between the guilty and the innocent was not always as clear as everyone would like to think.

"And Kevin Fitzgerald, what is he so single-minded about? In what way is he obsessed?"

"Haven't you figured that out yet? He wanted to be mayor so everyone in the city would know who he was. He wanted to be a senator so everyone in the state and a lot of people in the country would know who he was. He wanted to be president so everyone everywhere would know who he was."

"Wanted to be president?"

"Yes, wanted, because now I think he wants more than that. It's the only thing I can think of that might explain what he is doing."

"You still don't think he really did it?" I asked, wondering why she would not accept the obvious fact.

She smiled, took another drink from her glass and fixed me with a glittering smile.

"You live just down the street, on California, just before you get to Grace Cathedral. Am I right? That means it is only a five-minute walk away.

And that means," she added, her glance now subtle and profound, "in ten minutes we can be in bed."

CHAPTER
FIVE

There was a question I always asked, a question which from the first case I ever tried changed the way a jury viewed its responsibilities, a question that taught them it did not matter if at the end of the trial they thought the defendant must be guilty. I always led up to it the same way, starting with the first juror I questioned on voir dire, a simple inquiry that invariably elicited the same, surprised, reply.

"Tell me, do you believe everyone should obey the law?"

"Yes, of course," was always the response, given with a rush of sincerity lest anyone suspect that they might ever do anything wrong.

And then, quicker and in a more serious tone of voice, the unexpected challenge: "Even you?" Followed with the question that settled everything: "At the end of the trial, the judge is going to instruct you that you must find the defendant not guilty unless the prosecution has proven the defendant guilty beyond a reasonable doubt. My question, then, is this: If, at the end of the trial, after you have listened to all the witnesses, after you have heard all the evidence, after you have discussed the evidence with the other jurors, if you think to yourself that the defendant probably did it, but that the prosecution has not proven it beyond a reasonable doubt, will you obey the law and return a verdict of not guilty?"

No one had ever said no, no one had even hesitated to say yes. Of all the trials I had won, most of them had been won because of that one question, won before the first witness had even been called, won because the jury now understood that they were not there to decide what really happened, but whether the prosecution had proven that their version of events was, beyond any serious doubt, the only true one. That one question was the best weapon a defense attorney had, and it was a question that in the trial of Kevin Fitzgerald I could not ask.

Everyone knew what had happened, everyone who sat in the jury box, the twelve men and women who would decide the case, knew the defendant had committed murder. Fitzgerald had told them, he had told the world; there was not anyone anywhere who had not heard about his confession. Kevin Fitzgerald, the junior senator from California, had murdered Walter Bridges, the president of the United States, and there was not any doubt, reasonable or otherwise, about it. The only question was whether it was really a crime.

I greeted the first juror, a middle-aged woman who worked as a nurse in a local hospital, like a long-lost friend

"You work in the emergency room at UCSF—the University of California San Francisco," I added for the court reporter, hunched over her stenographer's machine, "up on Parnassus Street. You have to make life and death decisions in that job, don't you?"

She had kind, gentle eyes, but quick, alert, attentive.

"We do whatever we have to do, and yes, sometimes it is life and death, but," she added with a modest, self-effacing smile, "those decisions are usually made by the treating physician."

"Sometimes to save a patient, it's necessary to remove a limb, isn't that true?" And then, as she nodded her agreement, "Because you know that if you don't, the patient will die, and because your responsibility is, if I can put it like this, to the whole patient, not just to a part?"

"Yes."

"Tell me, Mrs. Huddleston, did you vote for Walter Bridges in the last election?"

I had known for weeks that I was going to ask this question, and I had known exactly what the reaction would be. Raymond St. John, the prosecutor, was on his feet, thundering his objection. The courtroom, crowded to capacity, hundreds of people who had lined up hours before the trial started, was suddenly tense, electric, everyone looking to the bench. The judge fixed me with a lethal stare.

"You are not to ask that question of this juror, or any other juror! How someone voted has no relevance to this case."

"It has every relevance, your Honor," I replied, rising from my chair at the counsel table. I spoke in a calm, measured voice, showing, as best I could pretend, my respect for her judgment and the law.

I had tried other cases in the courtroom of the Honorable Evelyn Patterson. She liked a little too much the prerogatives of her position. When she came into court, she always came a few minutes late, and while she talked to jurors as if they were all now best friends, she too often treated the lawyers in her courtroom like errant schoolboys not smart enough to learn the lessons she was so well-prepared to teach. She was also a perfect addict for publicity. If this was the trial of the century, she was going to make sure she played the main part. When St. John, who had ambitions of his own, agreed with the media that the trial should be televised, she told me in open court that my objection struck her as outdated and even quaint. When I replied that, "I hadn't realized that time, and not the law, was the proper basis for a legal judgment," and then had the temerity to ask whether she had decided to schedule the trial with commercial breaks, "thirty second spots during cross-examination," she became, for some reason, quite livid. And now, the first day of trial, the very beginning of jury selection, I had set her off again. I could not have been happier.

"It's obvious, your Honor. We are not here to decide if the defendant, Kevin Fitzgerald, caused the death of Walter Bridges. We are here to decide if Kevin Fitzgerald had not only the right, but the duty, to do so. The answer to that question depends, in turn, on whether Walter Bridges was himself guilty of a criminal conspiracy. I am entitled to find out whether this potential jury member, and every other prospective juror, is, because of their political beliefs, prejudiced against the defendant."

"It may be obvious to you, Mr. Antonelli, but it isn't obvious to me. Now ask your next question, if you can think of one that might be allowable."

Still standing, I turned back to the jury box.

"Did you at any time believe the president was a clear and present danger to the country?"

"Mr. Antonelli!" cried Patterson, halfway out of her chair. "You ask another question like that and you'll be watching the trial on television from your cell in the country jail! Don't doubt me, Mr. Antonelli. I won't hesitate to hold you in contempt."

Slowly, I turned and faced her with a look that dared her to do it.

"I'm here defending a man on a charge of murder. The defendant is accused of the assassination of the president of the United States. I can think of no more serious charge. If I seem to push the boundaries of what is considered normal practice, if I ask questions that are not often asked in a court of law, it is because there is no precedent—no accepted, established rules—for a case, a trial like this. But I will try, your Honor, to stay on point, and to not incur the court's displeasure."

"Tread lightly, Mr. Antonelli. Ask your next question."

I sat back down, leaned back and began a quiet conversation with the juror.

"You didn't go to law school, did you, Mrs. Huddleston?"

"No, I didn't."

"If you had, you would have taken in your first year the course on criminal law. Almost the first thing they teach you is something called the law of necessity. One of the examples they always talk about involves mountain climbing. Imagine there are six climbers, all roped together, climbing high up on a mountain, a sheer drop of a few thousand feet below them. The climber last on the rope falls and is dangling in midair. You're the climber just above him. You can't hold him. There is too much weight. You have two choices, and only two choices: hang on as long as you can, knowing it is only a matter of time before not just you but everyone else will be sent flying to your deaths, or you can cut the rope and save yourself and the others by letting that one climber die. What would you do, Mrs. Huddleston, if you had to make that choice?"

She shut her eyes and shook her head at the agony of the choice, the necessary choice, that would have to be made.

"Cut the rope, sacrifice one to save the others."

"That happens in an emergency room, doesn't it? If there has been a mass shooting, or a terrible accident involving more victims that can be taken care of at the same time, choices have to be made. If there is someone who seems certain to die no matter what you do, you take the next victim, the one you think you can save. No, never mind, Mrs. Huddleston, you don't have to answer that."

Raymond St. John was as good at prosecuting cases as there was. There was nothing of the aggressive self-righteousness, the insistent display of their own rectitude, that too many other prosecutors wore like a badge of honor. He did not need to separate himself from the follies and vices of the criminals he brought to trial. Friendly, easy going, the first to shake your hand on those rare occasions when you won a case against him, he gave the impression that, but for the luck of birth and education, he might have made some unfortunate mistakes of his own. It may have been connected with the fact that, just below the surface, there was a sadness, a sign of something lost, I had seen in the faces of other men, men who had, for all sorts of reasons, become alcoholics and, for different reasons, then recovered. He still moved with an athlete's efficient speed, the way he must have done on the football field in college when he was an all-American running back. Even standing still, he seemed to be in motion.

He did not ask many questions in voir dire, and those he did ask were for the most part variations on the same theme. He did not care, it did not matter, how you had voted; it did not matter if you had admired or hated Walter Bridges. He only cared that you could put aside your political beliefs, whatever those beliefs might be, and act the part of good citizen, dedicated to the rule of law. The question, the only question, was whether you would base your verdict on the evidence and the evidence alone.

It was standard, textbook procedure, conducted, however, with unusual skill. The questions reminded everyone what their duty was; the manner in which he asked the questions told them he was someone they could trust, as fair-minded as anyone they could find. There would not have been a problem in any other trial. There would not have been a problem in this one if I had not, by those first few questions by which I had incurred the angry rebuke of the judge, encouraged one of the last jurors to ask St. John when he was finished if he could ask him a question of his own.

"You're prosecuting the case for the government. Does that mean you voted for that criminal son of a bitch?"

I bit my lip not to laugh. Patterson banged her gavel so hard it was a wonder splinters did not start to fly, banged it over and over again before she could quell the bedlam of the crowd. She turned a sharp, unforgiving eye on the juror, who sat smirking, triumphant and unrepentant in the back corner of the jury box.

"You're excused, Mr. Sherman. Your services will not be required."

"No, in answer to your question," said St. John as Sherman left the jury box, "I did not vote for Walter Bridges when he ran for president."

I started to object, to raise all the hell I could, but I knew it would have no effect.

"So you agree," I shouted to no one in particular, "that Walter Bridges was never qualified to hold the office, that he was a danger to everything we—"

"That's enough, Mr. Antonelli!" yelled the judge over the noise of her own gavel beating back the noise that hit with hammer-like force from the audience behind me.

Another prospective juror was called by the clerk to take the place of the one just dismissed. St. John acted as if nothing had happened, and that Marcia Vernon, a black woman in her early twenties, was a close, personal friend. He smiled at her, she smiled back. He was sitting at the counsel table farthest from the jury box on my right. He bent forward, as if to get closer.

"You were in the courtroom when we started voir dire, and you heard Mr. Antonelli, the very capable attorney for the defense, describe that dreadful scene—and he's right, we all heard about it our first year of law school— with the mountain climbers, that to save everyone else the rope has to be cut, sending one of them to a certain death. But, and this is my question, would your answer be the same if it was clear that the others were strong enough, and that there was time enough to pull that climber to safety? That, as I think you will see, as the evidence will show, is precisely the situation here. Murdering the president, even if you believe the president should be removed from office, was not the only available choice. The law of necessity does not apply."

Finally, we were done, we had finished voir dire, a jury had been empaneled, seven women and five men, the oldest sixty-eight, the youngest, the last juror chosen, only twenty-three. Most of them, I was willing to guess, had not voted for Walter Bridges, and all of them, I was all but certain, willing to follow the law to whatever verdict the law required. It was, I thought, a good jury, as fair-minded and impartial as anyone could have hoped; a jury, in other words, with which Kevin Fitzgerald had very little chance to win.

He did not care about his chances. He knew more about the shifting allegiances of the public mind than any courtroom lawyer ever could.

"You heard what that juror said, what he asked St. John."

"The juror who isn't a juror anymore, the juror who, if he had kept his mouth shut, might still be on the jury, a potential vote for you and acquittal?"

"The point is that he said what everyone else is thinking."

"The point is that you don't know, any more than I do, what anyone else is thinking."

"What's wrong with you? Can't you see what's right in front of your eyes? You saw the way they were looking at me. I'm sitting where you had me sit, in the chair closest to the jury box. Did you see anyone pull away, act like they didn't want to be too close to someone accused of murder?"

We were alone in the courtroom, everyone gone except the two guards waiting to take Fitzgerald back to jail had left. The late-day sun shone through the windows high on the wall above the empty jury box. I loosened my tie and, sitting back in the chair, crossed my arms, stretched out my legs and stared down at my shoes. He was not wrong in what he said. There had been no sign, not the slightest, of any kind of aversion, the only reaction to their close proximity an almost casual curiosity about what he was like. They had looked at him the way they might have studied some celebrity, wondering whether he was just like what they thought he was when they had seen him in a movie or on television. I felt like saying that just because they liked you didn't mean they wouldn't hang you. I told him instead that they were always going to be looking at him, even if sometimes out of the corners of their eyes, measuring his reaction to everything that went on, especially when a witness for the prosecution said something especially damaging.

"Listen to me. This isn't like some committee hearing in Congress; it isn't like some political rally. You don't get to ask questions, you don't get to give speeches. You listen, you observe, and no matter what you hear, no matter how wrong or stupid it is, you follow every word, and you never look surprised. No matter what. Because you know things no one else knows. That is what you have to make them feel: that whatever they hear, whatever a witness says against you, they're only saying it because, if they aren't lying, they don't know the whole story, that the testimony of the prosecution witnesses are only fragments, parts of a puzzle only you can solve. Our case, your defense, rests entirely on the proposition that you knew things few if any others did, and it was that reason—what you knew—that caused you to do what you did. Do you understand me? Do you understand what I am trying to tell you?" I asked, raising my eyes to meet his waiting, anxious, utterly impatient gaze.

"We've been through this a dozen times. Damn near every day."

"And we'll keep going through it—every day the trial lasts, if I have to—until it's second nature, the only way you know how to think!"

"I'm not—"

"I know, an empty-headed fool. It might be easier if you were. You might not spend so much time questioning my judgment."

"I've never questioned—"

"Only every day."

"I've just asked questions about what you plan to do. That's all."

"And you never seem to believe me when I tell you that I never know what I'm going to do, that something always happens at a trial that no one expected and no one could have guessed, something that usually changes everything. And if you don't see it when it happens, if you are so locked in to what you think is going to happen next, you'll miss the chance that may never come again, the chance, sometimes the only chance, to get the verdict you want."

"So we just sit there and wait to see what happens?"

"No, you just sit there. I'll have other things to do."

"What about what I asked you about before? I want to hold a press conference, go on some of the morning shows. Everyone wants to hear my story."

He was impossible. He could not stand confinement, not because, like other people, he hated imprisonment; he could not tolerate the absence of an audience, the presence of reporters asking questions for all the millions out there who, he was certain, could never get enough of him.

"Why not wait," I suggested with weary, half-closed eyes, "until you're convicted. Then you can give any speech you want for everyone who watches your execution on television."

He thought it quite funny. Placing his hand on my wrist, he gave me what some might have thought a politician's meaningless assurance, but seemed to me something he thought settled in advance.

"It will never happen. It's what you said before: I know things that no one else does. And besides, you're not a bad lawyer. Look at it this way: you've never lost a case and I've never lost an election. The odds are in our favor."

There was something so astonishingly, brilliantly arrogant about him that it somehow did not seem arrogant at all. It almost seemed understated, like the bragging of a modest boy, laughing at his own exaggeration. I watched him leave, marveling at the way he made the two guards think he was doing them a favor by letting them come along. When he reached the door, he turned his head just enough to wink at me. Kevin Fitzgerald could convince anyone of anything. He was sure of it, so sure he was willing to bet his life on it.

CHAPTER

SIX

"Is the prosecution ready to call its first witness?" asked Judge Patterson. She was bending forward with a somewhat exaggerated look of anticipation, as if, like an actor on the stage, she wanted to make sure she played her part with enough emphasis for those in the back rows of the theater.

Raymond St. John was already on his feet.

"Yes, your Honor. The prosecution calls Jonathan Reece."

With a chin that seemed to slope away into his throat, a nose too long for his face, and dark, deep-set eyes with which he viewed his enemies with hostility and his friends with suspicion, Reece raised his hand and, with what to some of those who had followed his White House career seemed like reluctance, swore to tell the truth.

"Would you state your full name for the record?"

"Jonathan Edward Reece," he replied, shifting around on the witness chair, trying to get comfortable.

"How are you employed?"

"Assistant to the president—or, rather, I was assistant to the president."

"Walter Bridges?"

"Yes."

"You were with President Bridges on Air Force One on the flight from Washington to San Francisco?"

"Yes."

"Would you tell us, in your own words, what happened when the plane landed?"

"You mean when I found—"

"No, start from the beginning, if you would."

Reece looked puzzled. He still was not sure where to start.

"I'm sorry," apologized St. John with a friendly shrug. He glanced across to the jury box. "I should have been more specific," he explained, and then turned again to the witness. "When the plane landed, did the president ask you to do anything?"

"Yes. He said that Fitzgerald—Senator Fitzgerald—had been asking to see him; that he was waiting on the tarmac and that I should bring him on board. He said he would see him for ten minutes in his cabin."

"Did he tell you why Senator Fitzgerald wanted to see him? And why he wanted to see him at the airport, instead of back in Washington?"

Reece had a whiny, strident voice, every word a complaint.

"He didn't have to; we all knew the reason—"

St. John quickly raised his hand to stop him. His manner, though friendly, was still formal. St. John, as good a prosecutor as there was, always kept a distance.

"When you say, 'we all knew the reason,' whom do you mean?"

"Everyone who was close to the president. Fitzgerald—Senator Fitzgerald," he corrected himself for the second time, "had been making a lot of accusations—false accusations—about things the president had supposedly done. He was always on television, claiming that while there was not any evidence yet, it was only a matter of time; that with all the investigations going on, it was only a matter of time before evidence would be found."

Satisfied that this answered the question, Reece sat back and waited for the next question. St. John asked again: "What was the reason—what did the president tell you was the reason—Senator Fitzgerald wanted to see him?"

"To tell him about something he said he had found, something he wanted to give the president a chance to explain. But," he added before anyone could draw the wrong conclusion, "the president knew it was a bluff, that Fitzgerald didn't have anything—there was nothing to have—and that what he really wanted was a private meeting he could talk about."

St. John pretended to be confused. Without a question, just a look, he invited him to explain.

"He was always going on television, talking about how important the investigation was, and how, as a member of the Intelligence Committee, he could not talk about what he knew, which gave the impression that what he knew and could not talk about would be more damaging to the president than anyone could imagine. That's what the president thought, what we all thought was the reason he wanted a private meeting: so he could tell everyone that he had met in private with the president and discussed things he could not yet reveal. I mean, what could sound more damaging than that?"

With a serious, thoughtful expression, St. John nodded as if this explained a great many things that might otherwise pass unnoticed.

"That was the reason, then, that the president agreed to meet with him on Air Force One, just after it landed in San Francisco, to keep the meeting short?"

"One of the reasons; there was another one. The senator would be standing there with the greeting party, just one of the public officials who are always there to welcome the president wherever the president travels. If Fitzgerald is invited up to see the president, no one is able to suggest that he confronted the president with some new, explosive evidence. It's all too casual."

"Let me make sure we all understand this. It's your testimony that Senator Fitzgerald had been asking for a private meeting with the president in Washington, a private meeting in the White House?"

"Yes, but as I explained, that wasn't going to happen."

"If it had," said St. John with a look of practiced outrage, "we might have had a murder in the Oval Office!"

I was on my feet before he had finished the sentence, shouting my objection. Judge Patterson waved me back to my chair and with withering contempt threatened St. John with perdition.

"Not here, counselor, not in this courtroom! You want to testify, I'll let Mr. Antonelli call you to the witness stand and put you through whatever cross-examination he thinks proper."

For the first time, I began almost to like her.

It was not widely known, but Raymond St. John had years earlier been a drunk, and then, to his great credit, had stopped drinking altogether. The story, which was too sad not to be true, was that he had come home one night at three in the morning, and his teenage daughter, confined for life to a wheelchair with muscular dystrophy, had been waiting for him in the living room and with one short sentence brought him to his senses. "You are a disgrace," she told him, and the next night, instead of a bar, he went to his first meeting of Alcoholics Anonymous.

Like a lot of recovering alcoholics I have known, Raymond St. John had lost the capacity for extremes. There was no burst of anger, no outraged indignation; nor, on the other hand, even the smallest sign of chastened hope or sullen despair. Without emotion of any kind, he waited until Patterson finished, and when she had, turned back to the witness as if there had never been an interruption. It was easy to imagine that he started every day with a list of all the things he had to do, and easier still to imagine there had not been a day since he stopped drinking that he had failed to do even one of them.

"Tell us what happened, after you brought Senator Fitzgerald onto Air Force One."

Resting his elbows on the wooden arms of the witness chair, Jonathan Reece hunched forward, gazing into the middle distance, trying, as it seemed, to remember every detail.

"I came down the stairs, went across to where he was standing and told him the president had asked me to come get him, that the president could spare a few minutes. He followed me up to the plane and to the president's cabin."

"When you got there, to the president's cabin, what happened then?"

"Nothing. I mean, I left him there and went back to where the rest of the staff were waiting in the mid-section of the plane."

He had left something out. St. John reminded him what it was.

"You didn't just leave Senator Fitzgerald at the door to the president's cabin. Someone else was there, weren't they?"

"Oh, yeah. Besides one of the Secret Service agents, Ellison was waiting."

"Ellison?"

"Richard Ellison, the president's chief of staff. He had been meeting with the president when I was sent to get Fitzgerald. He was there, at the door, when I brought him."

"Senator Fitzgerald, the defendant, you mean?"

"Yes. Ellison was standing there, waiting to take him inside."

"And did he take him into the president's cabin?"

"Yes…I mean, he must have. I didn't actually see him do it, open the door and take him inside. As soon as I had Fitzgerald there, I left, as I said before. I had to get my briefcase and a few other things. We were about to get off the plane and get in the cars waiting to take us into the city."

"To the Mosconi Center where the president was scheduled to speak at the technology conference?"

"Correct."

"And that is the last time you saw the senator?"

"No, I saw him a few minutes later, when the Secret Service had him in custody, when they were taking him off the plane. I didn't know what had happened. And then everyone knew, and everyone was running all over the place. We didn't know," he explained, turning now for the first time to the jury. "We didn't know if this was just the beginning, if a terrorist attack was underway, if Fitzgerald had orchestrated the whole thing: killed the president while some other friends of his, other people who hated the president and what he was trying to do—save the country from attack— were going to start killing everyone else on the plane!" he exclaimed, raking Fitzgerald, sitting next to me, with a harsh, combative stare.

"You didn't know if this was the start of an attack—a terrorist attack, is the way I think you put it—on everyone on the plane?" I said in a calm, even voice as I rose slowly from the counsel table to begin my cross-examination. "Is that what you said?"

"Yes, I did."

"You were afraid that Senator Fitzgerald might have 'orchestrated'—I think that is the word you used—an attack with other people. Is that what you said?"

"That's what I said, and I meant it."

"You brought Senator Fitzgerald onto the plane, correct?"

"Yes, that's what I said. Yes."

"And you did that because the president asked you to do that, correct?"

"Yes," he replied, tight-lipped and cautious.

"Because Senator Fitzgerald, according to your testimony, had been asking for a meeting." He started to answer, to give another one-word reply, but I talked right past him. "And because, as I believe you put it, everyone knew why he wanted a meeting with the president, the decision was made to invite him onto the plane for a brief meeting of just a few minutes. Isn't that what you just said?"

"Yes, that's right; that was the reason."

"Senator Fitzgerald was there, on the tarmac, part of the group of public officials there to greet the president on his arrival. I think that's what you said."

I paused, as if I wanted him to be sure. He looked at me as if he could not understand why I would think it necessary.

"Yes, he was there as part of the greeting party."

"He didn't know he was going to be invited on the plane, did he? I mean, he had asked for meetings in Washington. He had not asked for this meeting on the plane?"

"No—I mean, yes, that's right."

I threw up my hands as if nothing he had said made sense. Smiling in a show of sympathy, I shook my head.

"He's there as part of the greeting party. He doesn't know he's going to be invited onto the plane. And yet your first thought when you see him being led off the plane is that he had orchestrated a conspiracy—a terrorist attack!—and everyone is in danger. But then you're used to that, aren't you, Mr. Reece—finding a terrorist attack everywhere you look, seeing danger everywhere, except, of course, among your Russian friends! Withdraw the question!" I fairly shouted before the judge's gavel struck. "Yes, I know, it isn't a question I'm allowed to ask," I added before she could open her mouth. "Tell me, Mr. Reece," my attention suddenly, abruptly, back on him, "when you went to get Senator Fitzgerald, did you search him for a weapon?"

He looked surprised.

"No. I didn't see any reason—"

"Did you ask anyone with the Secret Service to make sure he wasn't armed?"

"No, as I say, I didn't—"

"See any reason; yes, precisely. You didn't see any reason because it never occurred to you that Kevin Fitzgerald might be an assassin. Why was that, Mr. Reece? Because he doesn't look like one, because he is a United States senator? Why, exactly, did you not imagine the possibility that he might be a threat?"

Jonathan Reece was faced with the apparently obvious fact that the man he had let on the plane was an assassin. How had he not known to take the simple precaution of a search? He seized not on an explanation, but an excuse.

"He didn't have a weapon, he did not have a gun; that isn't how he killed the president."

"But you obviously did not know that when you let him on the plane. That couldn't possibly be the reason you didn't have him searched—because you knew he would kill the president a different way—was it?"

"No, of course not."

"The reason you didn't have him searched, the reason you never thought him a threat, is because he had never made a threat against the president, or anyone else; never made so much as a threat to commit violence against another human being in his life, isn't that so? And why, Mr. Reece, what reason can you give the jury that explains why someone like Kevin Fitzgerald, a respected member of the United States Senate, a man many expected would one day be a candidate for the presidency himself, a man who has never been accused, much less convicted, of a crime, a crime of violence or any other crime, suddenly, from out of nowhere, take it upon himself to kill Walter Bridges, unless it was the only way to stop Bridges from doing something that could not be allowed? Can you answer that, Mr. Reece? Can you tell this jury how this could possibly have ever happened?"

There was not a sound in the courtroom, not a whisper, when I finished. They sat there, the hundreds who had come to observe, the hundreds who had come to report, stunned into silence by the violence of my question.

"Why it happened?" said Reece, slowly, burning with resentment. His knuckles went white as he squeezed the arms of the witness chair to stop himself hurtling across at me. "Why it happened? Because he could not stand the fact that he and his liberal friends were losing. Because it made them all crazy that someone like Walter Bridges who had never been in politics, never run for office, never been in government, never been an insider trading favors, doing everything to stay in power, had won the presidency and doing everything he had promised the American people he was going to do! That's why he killed him—hatred, pure and simple."

I smiled, and moving from the side of the counsel table where I had been standing, moved closer.

"These promises you say he made. You were there when he made them, weren't you? One of the more prominent members of his campaign."

"I was in the campaign…yes."

"You were with him almost every day, you were with him on election night. Tell us, if you would, what was his reaction to the outcome?"

"What was his…? He won, what do you think his reaction was?"

"I ask the questions here, Mr. Reece, not you. Now, what was his reaction?"

He hesitated, not sure why I would suddenly ask a question that seemed to have no possible connection to anything he was there to testify about. He tried to shrug it off, a question of no importance.

"He was, of course, pleased, honored at the result."

"That he had just lost the popular vote by a margin in the millions?"

"He won the presidency!" he fired back. "Who wouldn't be pleased, honored, at that?"

"But he knew, didn't he, that a majority in the country would always see him as a loser, isn't that right, Mr. Reece? And didn't that start to gnaw away at him, make him a little bit crazy every time someone brought it up?"

"He won the election, and by a large majority, in the electoral college."

"Yes, we've heard that argument before," I said in a scornful, dismissive voice that, as I had hoped it would, made him bristle. "He won the election because he won the electoral vote and, what had happened only once or twice before, lost the popular vote. So, he comes into the presidency, the choice of only a minority, and his support in the country, instead of going up, keeps going down. It keeps—"

"I fail to see the relevance of this, your Honor," objected St. John. "What difference does the president's standing in the polls make? The question isn't whether Walter Bridges was popular; the question, the only question, is whether the defendant committed murder."

Evelyn Patterson turned to me.

"It's relevant, your Honor. It goes to the inconsistency in the witness's testimony."

"For that purpose, I'll allow it. But get to the point, Mr. Antonelli."

I took another step forward. I was halfway down the jury box, just a few feet from the witness stand. With my hand on the jury box railing, I looked straight at Reece.

"You said it's your belief that the reason Walter Bridges was killed was because he was 'doing everything he had told the American people he was going to do.' But isn't it true, Mr. Reece, that the president had not done even one of the things he had promised?"

"No, that's not true, that's—"

"He promised to change the entire American healthcare system, promised that everyone would have coverage, promised that everyone could afford it. He hadn't done that, had he, Mr. Reece?"

"He couldn't get Congress to act; he couldn't—"

"He hadn't done what he promised. He promised to change the whole system of taxation, to make it more fair and equitable. But there isn't any real tax reform, is there, Mr. Reece?"

"But that wasn't his fault. That was the fault of—"

"He promised to keep Medicare and Medicaid and not to touch Social Security, and he did just the opposite, cutting, one way or the other, all three. Or, rather, tried to, because, as you were just trying to tell us, everything he tried to do was stopped by Congress or the courts. Stopped, Mr. Reece, because of the sheer force of numbers, the great and growing majorities that came to view Walter Bridges unfavorably. Isn't it the case, Mr. Reece, that in the last polls taken before his death, Walter Bridges's favorability rating had reached a new record low, not just for him, but for any president in our history? Is that true or not?"

"He would have turned it around when the truth came out, when all the lies that were told about him were proven false, when—"

"The point, Mr. Reece, is that no one had to stop Walter Bridges from doing what he had promised the American people he would try to do. He had no support in the country, and therefore no possibility of support in the congress. Senator Fitzgerald did not have to kill the president to stop him from carrying out his promises; Walter Bridges had already stopped himself!"

As he left the witness stand, the sense of relief that nearly every witness felt when their testimony was over, when they could finally start to relax and let down their guard, suddenly vanished. His jaw clenched and a slight but perceptible shudder passed through his body when halfway to the railing he heard me inform the court, "The defense reserves the right to recall Jonathan Reece as a witness." Let him, let the other witnesses for the prosecution, worry about how much I might know.

The second witness for the prosecution nodded to the first one as they passed each other in the middle of the courtroom's central aisle. After a few quick questions, the necessary preliminaries to the substance of his examination, Raymond St. John got down to business.

"The previous witness, Jonathan Reece, testified that on the day of the president's death, he brought the defendant, Kevin Fitzgerald, onto Air Force One and left him with you just outside the president's cabin. Is that true?"

Richard Ellison had wavy black hair that swept straight back from high on his forehead and a slightly puzzled expression in his eyes as if he were never quite sure that you really meant what you said. It was like watching your tax accountant wonder whether you had made an honest mistake or were trying to make him an accomplice in your attempt at evasion. The dark suit he wore seemed, from the way the jacket button held, just a size too large.

"Yes, that's true. He brought him onto Air Force One and left him there with me."

St. John was standing in front of his counsel table, the one farthest from the jury box, which meant that Ellison looked at him at an angle away from the jury. He moved across to a position directly in front of the witness stand, just to the side of where Fitzgerald sat. The jury could now not just hear the witness, but see clearly his expression. More importantly, the witness could now look at them each time he answered one of the prosecutor's questions. It may not seem like much, but it is easier to trust someone who looks at you when they are talking than someone who seems to be looking off in a different direction. St. John was far too experienced to allow it.

"This was because the president said he would see the senator for a few minutes, a brief meeting, on Air Force One?" he asked, his arms folded over his chest, glancing down at the polished hardwood floor.

"Yes, that's correct. It was—"

St. John held up his hand.

"You needn't tell us the reason. That has already been established. Senator Fitzgerald had been asking to see the president. This was a way to get it done without taking up too much time. What I want to ask you is what happened after Mr. Reece left you with the senator?"

Twisting his head slightly to the side, Ellison looked at him with his puzzled eyes. He did not answer. St. John rephrased the question, made it more precise.

"Was anything said, was there any conversation?"

"Nothing, really; just a few words," he replied with a shrug.

"Can you recall what those few words were, as exactly as you can?" asked St. John with the patience and indulgence of a helpful friend.

Ellison looked out at the sea of faces in the courtroom, at the television cameras in the back, at the crouching photographers who had, over my objection, been allowed inside. He seemed ill at ease with what he saw. He was used to crowds, used to the scrutiny of television, but he was not used to court. He had answered, thousands of times, the frantic, shouted questions of reporters, answered, dozens of times, the more methodical inquiries of political analysts on the news shows; he had never testified in a criminal case, never had to face a cross-examination about anything he might have said. He answered each question St. John asked him, but almost every time he did, he looked at me, a quick, furtive glance, as if he were trying to guess what I might try to do with what he had just said. St. John sensed his uncertainty.

"There is nothing to worry about," he assured him. "It is perfectly understandable if you can't remember exactly what was said. Given the traumatic nature of what happened, what you witnessed, it is a wonder you can remember anything at all."

"He said he was glad to see me. I remember that. And I remember I said that it was nice to see him as well, that I was looking forward to the chance to see a little of the city. He said that next time, I should come out on my own, a few days vacation, and that—I remember this—that if I did, I might have to quit my job because I wouldn't want to leave. I remember thinking that he was a lot nicer in person than the way he seemed when I watched him on television tearing into the president."

He was looking at the jury, talking to them like they were old friends. He had been taught at least that much about testifying as a prosecution witness in court.

"Is there anything else?" prodded St. John. "Anything that made you think that something was not quite right?"

"I didn't think anything of it at the time. Like I said, he seemed nicer in person than what I had thought before—but his eyes, they kept moving all around, first one direction then another. He never looked straight at me. As I say, I didn't think anything of it, but now, looking back, he must have been nervous, worried about what was going to happen if he went through with what—"

"Objection!" I cried, flying out of my chair. "The witness can't testify about what he thinks the defendant was thinking!"

"Sustained!" ruled Judge Patterson with a cautionary glance at the witness. "You can testify to what you actually observed, not to what you think may have been passing through another person's mind."

"Tell the jury what happened next," said St. John. His expression was serious, troubled at what he wanted everyone to see he knew was coming. But the reply was anti-climactic.

"I opened the door and told him he could go in."

I could not understand why St. John seemed so surprised. What different testimony had he expected?

"You opened the door and let him in. And then what happened?"

Ellison looked at St. John, then looked at the jury, and then looked at St. John again.

"Nothing."

"Nothing? I'm sorry, I don't think you're following me."

"And here I thought a prosecutor was not supposed to lead his own witness!" I remarked from my chair.

"Enough, Mr. Antonelli. Don't interrupt," warned Judge Patterson.

I got to my feet, and with a cursory bow of my head, prayed forgiveness.

"I will, like his witness, try to follow whatever Mr. St. John finally decides he wants to say, your Honor."

For one brief moment, Evelyn Patterson seemed to relent, to take it as a short reprieve from the serious, and sometimes intense, business of the court. But only for a moment.

"Enough. No more. Sit down. Mr. St. John, get on with it."

"You open the door and Senator Fitzgerald goes into the president's cabin. Did you go with him?" asked St. John in a sharp, no-nonsense voice.

"No, it was a private meeting: only the president and the senator."

"When was the next time you saw the senator?"

With his eyes open wide, Ellison scratched the top of his eyebrow with the back of his thumb, still astonished by what he had seen.

"I saw him bending over the body of the president, the knife still in his hands, the president's blood all over him."

"The president had been stabbed?" asked St. John quickly as he stepped forward.

"Yes, I don't know how many times, but at least half a dozen; stabbed in the throat, stabbed in the stomach, in the chest. That's what I saw, that is what I'll never forget."

St. John was finished. It was my turn to ask questions. Ellison sank back in the witness chair and tightened his eyes. His mouth twitched nervously at the corners. Embarrassed, he switched positions, sat straight up and raised his chin.

"It's all right, Mr. Ellison," I remarked in an affable, reassuring tone. "I have just a few questions."

He scratched his chin, tossed his head to the side and then look up at me with mild suspicion.

"When you opened the door, did you check with the president to see if it was all right to let the senator come in?"

He thought about it, and he kept thinking about it.

"It's a simple question, Mr. Ellison. Did you ask the president—"

"No," he said with sudden emphasis. "The president had said to bring him in a soon as he got there. He wanted to get it over with as quickly as possible."

"So you opened the door, let Senator Fitzgerald in and, I assume, shut the door behind him, correct?"

"Yes, correct."

"And the next time you saw Senator Fitzgerald was when you found him with a knife in his hands, bending over the dead body of the president—is that your testimony?"

I asked this in a way that made him think I had not believed anything he had said. His answer was brief, and belligerent.

"Yes, that's what I said. That's what happened."

"You didn't testify—the prosecution did not ask—how long the interval was between those two events. How much time, Mr. Ellison, between the moment you let the defendant into the president's cabin and when you found him bending over the body?"

"Ten minutes, exactly ten minutes."

He said this as if it was something to be proud of, an example of proven efficiency.

"Exactly ten minutes. That is an interesting way to put it. Exactly ten minutes. What happened to make you enter the cabin exactly ten minutes later? Did you hear something: screams, the sounds of a struggle?"

"No, it wasn't anything like that. It's when the president told me to come in."

I threw up my hands.

"I'm sorry. You hadn't heard anything, and when you went in the president was dead, so how—"

"Ten minutes. Exactly ten minutes. That is how long the president told me to wait before I came in and reminded him it was time to leave. Ten minutes, exactly ten minutes, that is how long he wanted to let Fitzgerald have. Ten minutes," he repeated, the last words the president had ever spoken to him. "Exactly ten minutes, not one minute longer. That's what he said."

"I see. That explains it. One last question. During that time, those ten minutes, where were you, and what were you doing?"

"I stayed close, not far from the door, going through some of the things

I had to get ready for later, when the president got to where he was going to be speaking."

"And you didn't hear anything from inside?"

"You can't hear anything. It's completely soundproof in there."

I was finished, for the moment. I waited until he had taken a few steps from the witness stand before, once again, informing the court that I reserved the right to recall the witness, this time as a witness for the defense. Ellison stopped in his tracks, looked back for just a moment with his puzzled eyes and then quickly left the courtroom.

CHAPTER
SEVEN

"You were the first agent on the scene, the one who first responded to Richard Ellison's—the president's chief of staff—cry for help?" asked Raymond St. John as we began the second day of trial.

"That's correct," replied Milo Todorovich, who had been the head of the president's Secret Service detail. "I was maybe twenty feet away from the door to the president's cabin when I heard Ellison start shouting."

"And what did you see when you got there?" asked St. John in a voice that seemed to underscore by its quiet calmness the violence of the scene the witness was being asked to describe.

"The president was laying on the floor. The senator, the defendant," he added, nodding toward Fitzgerald sitting next to me at the counsel table a dozen short steps away, "was standing over him, holding a knife."

"What did you do, Agent Todorovich? What was the first thing you did when you saw the president lying there and Senator Fitzgerald standing over him?"

"I pulled out my gun, told the senator to drop the knife and to back away."

"Did he drop the knife and back away?"

"Yes. He didn't give me any trouble."

Milo Todorovich had the habit of his profession. Every movement seemed controlled, nothing sudden, nothing ever hurried; his eyes, on the other hand, seldom still, sliding constantly from side to side, everything within his range of vision under constant surveillance. You could imagine him a cowboy, a gunfighter, in an old western, leaning against a hitching post at the end of town, whittling on a stick, taking in everything that was happening with a single, lethal glance.

"He didn't give you any trouble?"

"He did what I told him. He dropped the knife…" He caught himself and with a swift, sideways motion of his head berated himself for his mistake. "He didn't drop it, he kneeled down and placed it carefully on the floor. Then he stood up and stepped away, just as I told him."

"And that is when you went over to the president to see if he was still alive?"

"He was dead. No question. I checked for a pulse, just to be sure. Then I summoned everyone else, the other agents on the plane, and we sealed the room."

"Did the defendant say anything, did you ask him anything?"

"No. He didn't say anything and I didn't ask. We got him off the plane. He was interrogated later."

There were other questions, and other answers, but none of them deviated from the central theme the prosecution was determined to pursue.

The defendant had been found, with the murder weapon in his hand, kneeling over the victim's dead body. Within those narrow confines, St. John went into painstaking detail, asking the witness to describe, as exactly as he could, the blood on the body and on the floor, the position of the victim's body, the way the defendant had looked when he first saw him; everything, no matter how seemingly inconsequential, he had seen. It was repetitive, tedious, and all done for the single purpose of adding color to the dull abstractions of what everyone had heard so often in the public accounts of the assassination that they had become desensitized to the grim realities of the violence with which Walter Bridges had been killed. It was only after Todorovich had gone through what was essentially the same set of facts a half-dozen times that the prosecution introduced the photographs taken at the murder scene.

After they were marked into evidence, I watched twelve faces give expression to the horror, the disbelief, the decent revulsion they all felt as these graphic pictures of murder were passed through the jury box. It was one thing to read a story in the newspapers, one thing to listen to a well-dressed, even-voiced newscaster reporting a crime; it was something else to see the twisted features, the blank-eyed stare, the bloody throat and clothing of a man lying motionless on a blood-soaked floor. Some of the jurors glanced at the photographs and immediately looked away; some studied them more closely, trying perhaps to see if there was something, some detail, they had not expected to find. All of them, when they were finished and handed them to the next juror, became more serious, because suddenly more convinced of the gravity of their obligation.

I approached the witness with all the solemnity of someone come to pay their last respects at a funeral.

"It must have been quite a shock, finding the president like that. No matter how well-trained you are, still, it must have taken a moment to realize what had happened."

"It took a moment, that's for sure. Even when I saw him, knew he was dead, it didn't seem quite real. Shock? Yes, I suppose you could say so."

I started to ask another question, but there was more he wanted to say. He looked at the jury.

"We're trained to protect the president, to take a bullet if we have to. When this happened, when I heard Ellison yelling for help, I knew something must have happened, but I never thought…I thought he might have fallen down, an accident, or had a heart attack, a stroke. Because of his age, how overweight he was, we knew there was always a chance of that. But…to find him like that, murdered by someone with a knife, on the plane! It was impossible, it could never happen!"

I moved to the far corner of the second counsel table, the one where Raymond St. John was sitting wondering what I was going to do. The witness now had to turn away from the jury to look at me. The jury could look directly at me, but if they looked at the witness at all, they could see only the side of his face. I started pacing slowly back and forth, a pensive expression on my face, doing what I could to make the witness, and the jury, believe the question I was about to ask had a high order of significance. In a jury trial, everything you did, every movement, every gesture, was important. It was how a jury learned to trust you. What had started, years before, as conscious duplicity had now become second nature. There were times I even thought it real.

"Agent Todorovich, you've been in the Secret Service for more than twenty years, but this was your first involvement in a murder investigation, is that correct?

"That's right."

"You're trained to protect the president, not investigate a crime?"

"Yes, but—"

"You picked up the knife, the knife you say had been in the hand of the defendant, didn't you?"

"Yes; no one else was there. I wanted to make sure Senator—I mean, the defendant—didn't try to get it, didn't try—"

"He had put it down, the moment you told him to. Your gun was drawn. You—"

"You're right; maybe I shouldn't have done that. But—"

"You didn't put on any gloves, the sort police detectives wear to avoid contaminating evidence, did you?" I asked, still pacing back and forth, but faster with each step I took. "You didn't think to preserve the evidence—the knife, the murder weapon—in a way that would not distort, would not destroy, whatever fingerprints there might have been?"

He did not like the question. He would have taken a bullet for the president—any president.

"I'm not questioning your courage, Agent Todorovich. No one doubts that. What I'm questioning is the reliability of the evidence."

He had an answer to that, an answer that was as obvious to me as it was to him.

"The knife was in his hand; he had blood, the president's blood, all over him. And he confessed. So what difference does it make if—"

"The difference between evidence that is properly collected and evidence that is not should be obvious to anyone, Agent Todorovich, and not just to a trained detective. The meaning of that difference in this case remains to be seen."

I stopped pacing, and with my right hand sliding across the front edge of the prosecution's table, moved slowly toward the jury box. I stood right next to it, tapping my fingers on the railing, and looked directly at him.

"You were part of the president's detail from the beginning, weren't you, beginning when he first got the nomination?"

"That's right. Almost two years."

"You were in a position to observe his behavior, his conduct; you were in the room sometimes when he was talking to people, am I right?"

"Yes, I was."

"Did you consider him stable, in complete control of his faculties?"

"Objection!" cried St. John. "The witness isn't a trained psychologist, he isn't a physician."

"We make judgements about this sort of thing all the time, your Honor," I insisted. "Your Honor isn't a trained psychologist, you aren't a physician, but you have, on more than one occasion told me, told everyone, that I didn't know what I was doing."

"That's true, Mr. Antonelli," remarked Patterson, leaning forward with a shrewd grin. "But I have never questioned whether you were 'stable,' or in 'control of your faculties.' Though, now that I think of it, perhaps I should have. Perhaps later in the trial. As to the prosecution's objection, I'll overrule it, so long as it is understood that this is not expert testimony."

It took a moment for Todorovich to consider how he wanted to respond.

"He was always polite and straightforward with me, and with the other agents. He knew we had a job to do. He never questioned anything we did, or anything we asked him to do."

I took a moment to let him consider my disappointment in his response.

"I'll ask you again. As you watched him over the course of two full years, did you think he was always stable, or were there times when he seemed erratic, impulsive, not in control of himself? Let me be more specific. Did you ever see him go off into a towering rage, screaming at people?"

"That could happen," he said, watching me with careful eyes.

"That did happen, you mean?"

"Yes."

"More than once?"

"Yes, more than once."

"How often?"

"I really couldn't say; I couldn't—"

"All the time, wasn't it, almost every day? Isn't that the truth, Agent Todorovich? Isn't that what happened? Wasn't he almost always in a rage against somebody—someone on his staff who hadn't done what he thought they should have done, or someone he saw on television? Isn't it true, isn't it a fact, that on at least three separate occasions he broke a television set, threw something at it, because he was so angry at what someone was saying about him?"

"That happened," he allowed. "He could get upset."

I looked at him, incredulous at the way he was trying to dismiss the significance of what Bridges had done.

"Upset? Is that what you call it? Upset, when he shatters a television set; upset, when he reduces one of his press secretaries to tears because he didn't like the way she had done her hair, didn't like the dress she wore, when she briefed reporters after he sent out another one of his famous incoherent attacks on what he had read that morning in the *New York Times*! Upset—"

"Objection! Perhaps, your Honor, Mr. Antonelli might try not to become quite so upset himself," remarked St. John with a slight, mocking smile.

"I agree," I replied before Patterson could think to make a ruling. "I shouldn't be upset." Pausing, I looked from the bench to the jury. "I apologize. There is never any excuse to lose your temper, never any excuse to throw things, never an excuse to berate, to ridicule, someone who is just trying to help you. And I promise," I said, turning back to the witness before St. John could object again, "not to get upset, so long as you simply tell the truth. You testified that when you entered the president's cabin, he was lying on the floor, and that Senator Fitzgerald was standing next to him, correct?"

The speed with which I had moved from the issue of the president's stability to what Todorovich had seen threw him off. His eyes widened with surprise before he was able to focus his attention on the question I had just asked. He was not sure he had heard it right.

"The president," I repeated, "he was on the floor?"

"Yes, that's right."

"He wasn't in his chair, behind his desk?"

"No, he was on the floor."

"Walter Bridges was a large man, was he not? Over six feet tall, well over, what? Two hundred thirty, two hundred forty pounds?"

"That's about right, maybe even a little over two forty."

"And there was blood on the body, and on the floor next to him. There was also blood—the jury has been shown the pictures—on the chair and on the desk, is that correct?"

"Yes, that's correct."

"That's what you saw, what you observed, when you came into the cabin?"

"Yes."

"Did you then assume that the president had been stabbed to death while he was sitting in his chair and that he had then fallen forward, and that was the reason he was on the floor?"

"That's right. It had to have happened that way."

"Just a few questions more," I assured him in a friendly voice. "You were with the president for two years, which means you were also in fairly close proximity to the people who were close to him, people on the staff who spent time with him every day, who traveled with him when he made a trip, like the one to San Francisco, on Air Force One." He started to answer, but I raised my hand and continued with my question. "What was the opinion of the defendant, Kevin Fitzgerald? Did the president or those around him think Fitzgerald was someone they could work with, someone who had an open mind, willing to listen to what they had to say?"

"Just the opposite. They thought—they all thought, from the president on down—that the senator would oppose anything and everything. They thought he was likely to be the candidate they would have to face in the next election, that everything he did was because he wanted to be president himself."

The first rule of cross-examination, as every halfway decent lawyer knows, is never ask a question if you don't know the answer the witness is going to give. But this was not a case that could be played by the rules. The question I had was too tempting to worry whether I might be wrong in what I could only guess would be the answer.

"Tell us, Agent Todorovich, isn't it true that one of the times Walter Bridges broke the screen on a television set he was watching the defendant, Kevin Fitzgerald, say something he did not like?"

Todorovich scratched the side of his prominent, smooth shaven chin.

"I don't know; it might have been."

I turned and started back to my place at the counsel table, and then, as if I had just remembered something I had wanted to ask, a minor matter of no great importance, I stopped and looked again at the witness.

"In which hand was the defendant holding the knife?"

He had thought he was finished and had started to relax.

"The right hand or the left?" I insisted.

"Right hand."

"You're sure?"

He wondered why it was important. He looked a little worried.

"Yes, I'm sure. He had it in his right hand."

"And was he holding it with the blade pointed up or pointed down?'

I was not asking questions just for the sake of asking them, but neither did I have a clear purpose in mind. Fitzgerald had killed the president; how he had been holding the weapon was in that sense irrelevant, but I had to find out everything I could, perhaps stumble on something that would add some force to the argument that he had been compelled to do what he did, that there were convincing reasons why, instead of murder, this was death by necessity, that Fitzgerald had acted to save the country, that it was, to use the phrase that had never been used in an American court of law, not homicide, but tyrannicide. There was almost no chance this was going to be successful, which left no alternative but to search for even the slightest flaw in the prosecution's case, something on which to raise a doubt, something that, in closing arguments, I could use to give the jury a reason to think that a guilty verdict was not as obvious as it seemed. Had Fitzgerald been holding the knife pointed up or pointed down? I made it sound like it was the most important issue in the case, the issue on which everything else in the trial would ultimately depend. The jurors leaned forward, waiting to hear what the witness would say.

"I'm not sure," he admitted.

"You're not sure?" I asked, as if that one admission would cost the prosecution any chance they had at a conviction. "Not sure. But you saw him over the body, the knife in his hand, and you don't...? Never mind. We can come back to that later on. You testified," I said, moving back to where I had stood before, in front of the jury box, "that you then got the defendant off the plane."

"Not alone; I had help."

"Help? Did you need help? Did Senator Fitzgerald try to resist, try to escape?"

"No, he didn't."

"He did what you told him to do. That's what you said before. He put down the knife—whichever way he had been holding it—and waited while you finished what you had to do. And then you, with the help of some others, took him off the plane. Where did you take him?"

"To a hangar, the other side of the airport. We cordoned off the area, made sure there was no one in the vicinity who was not authorized to be there. We held him there."

"That's where he was interrogated?"

"No, we held him there until the decision had been made where to take him."

"And that was where—to jail in the city?"

"To an undisclosed location."

"You can disclose it now."

"No, I can't. I don't know where he was taken. I was not part of that."

I looked at the jury.

"An undisclosed location, and you don't know where it was. You don't know who conducted the interrogation, who interviewed the defendant? You don't know anything about this confession the prosecution made so much about in its opening statement?"

"Only what I've heard."

"What you heard?" I asked with a glance full of skepticism.

"That he confessed to what he did, what I saw him do."

"Bending over a body with that knife you don't remember how he held? Yes, we all remember what you said about that. Just one last question. Did you ever hear the president, or any one around him, express any fear that Senator Fitzgerald might be a threat, someone who might commit an act of violence?"

"No, never."

I walked back to my chair, and for the second time changed my mind. Todorovich had one hand on the arm of the witness chair, starting to get to his feet.

"You came running to the cabin because you heard the president's chief of staff, Richard Ellison, shouting for help. He was there, in the cabin, at the same time as the defendant, Senator Fitzgerald. He was there before you. How much before: a few seconds, longer?"

"As soon as he opened the door, he started yelling and I was only a few short steps away. I dashed past him. He was still at the door."

"I see. And you came through the same doorway, the one that opens out into the corridor, not the one on the other side, the one that connects with the president's bedroom. Is that right?"

"Yes, that's right, the same door."

"And when you called for help?"

"Everywhere at once."

The moment I was finally finished, Raymond St. John was on his feet, calling his next witness. There was something clocklike in the precision with which he organized everything in the order of time. The first witness, Jonathan Reece, had told the beginning of the story, the opening chapter, how the villain of the piece, Kevin Fitzgerald, had made his first appearance on stage. The second witness, Richard Ellison, had read aloud the second chapter of the tale, what Fitzgerald had done. The next witness, Milo Todorovich, had in the third chapter given all the details of the outline given in the chapter just before. It was a simple, straightforward chronology, a story anyone could follow. The killer had come on board, and the killer had killed, and though there had not yet been a witness to say so, everyone watching, from the twelve members of the jury to the millions watching on television, knew that the killer had admitted what he had done. The president was dead. Kevin Fitzgerald had murdered him. That would have been sufficient in other times and in other places to order the defendant's immediate execution, but this was an American trial and even the obvious had to be proven.

Dr. Hubert Rudner was wearing a new suit. The trial was on television and he wanted to look his best. His practice may have been limited to dead bodies in the morgue, but he had friends and relatives who were sure to tune in. As the county coroner, he had testified in dozens, perhaps hundreds, of trials before, but he seemed stiff and self-conscious, every word prefaced by a hesitation. He did not want to make a mistake, say something that might be misconstrued. Slightly bald, with a large, off-center nose, and a crooked, off-center mouth, he had begun to perspire from almost the moment St.

John asked his first question.

"Did you examine the body of President Bridges?"

"Yes," replied Dr. Rudner, his gaze wandering past St. John to the crowd behind him. "I did."

"Were you able to determine the cause of death?"

"Yes. The president—I mean, the decedent—was killed by a stab wound to the throat. It severed the carotid artery. Two stab wounds, two to the throat."

"Two in the same place?" asked St. John patiently. "The same side of the throat?"

"No, not exactly," he replied.

His eyes kept moving between St. John and the courtroom crowd. Casually, with his hands on his hips, staring down at the floor as if he were thinking how best to ask the next question, St. John took two steps to his left. He was directly in front of the witness, better able to hold his attention.

"One stab wound to the artery, the other...?"

"The larynx."

"Were there other stab wounds on the body?"

"Several others, in the stomach, in the chest."

"Were you able to determine from the nature of the wounds the kind of weapon used to inflict them?"

"A knife, a knife with a serrated blade."

St. John walked to the clerk's table, below and just off to the side of the bench. The clerk, an Hispanic woman with a friendly face and soulful eyes, handed him a cellophane bag already marked as an exhibit. He handed it to the coroner.

"Is this knife consistent with your description?"

After a brief examination, the coroner agreed it was. Other witnesses would be called to establish that it was the knife found at the crime scene and that the blood found on it matched the blood of the president. And that was all. The coroner had given the prosecution what it needed, proof that Walter Bridges had actually died, proof that he had died of wounds inflicted by a knife. I was not interested in anything he had just proven.

"As part of your autopsy, you weighed the body?"

"Yes."

"How much did Walter Bridges weigh?"

Hubert Rudner glanced down at a notebook he had brought with him. He was nothing if not meticulous.

"Two hundred forty-seven pounds."

"He was how tall?"

Another quick glance before he answered.

"Six feet, two and a half inches tall."

"He was, under the current medical definition, obese, correct?" I asked, as if this was only to establish the necessary biological background.

"Yes, somewhat, I would say."

"A heavy man, not easy to push around; someone, for example, that a normal-size person could not simply lift out of his chair and throw across his desk."

I could sense a slight unease, the glimmer of a doubt, of suspicion, as St. John began to wonder what I could possibly be after. The line of inquiry did not, on the surface, make any sense. What St. John did not know was that I agreed: I did not know what I was after, only that I had to keep searching, asking questions that would bring out every fact I could, and hope that at some point something would happen that might give meaning to what would otherwise have no significance at all.

"So what we know for sure is that, whatever happened inside the president's cabin, the defendant—look at him, he isn't big enough, is he?— didn't attack the president and throw him on the ground. That seems a safe assumption, doesn't it, Dr. Rudner?"

I looked at the jury and let them wonder what it might mean. I had no more questions and Dr. Rudner was excused. Reminding the jury that they were not to discuss the case with anyone, Judge Patterson adjourned the trial until tomorrow.

Something had been bothering me since the testimony of the day before: those ten minutes that Bridges had insisted were the absolute limit on the time he would spend meeting with Fitzgerald alone. Had they talked for a while, had that talk become an argument, had the argument turned violent? Where had Fitzgerald gotten the knife, and why had he brought it with him if he had no reason to think he might be invited on board to meet the president alone? Fitzgerald dismissed it all with considerable impatience.

"Why are you so damn concerned with things like that? This isn't a murder trial where you try to prove I didn't do it. This is the trial—I keep telling you this—where you let me show everyone that I did what I had to do, that stopping Bridges was no more murder than killing someone on the battlefield."

The analogy disturbed me, not because of the comparison it drew, but because he had not seen the fatal flaw.

"You don't kill someone on the battlefield after you have taken him prisoner."

He laughed at my strange innocence. The guards who stood talking to each other the other side of the empty courtroom looked over for a moment, decided everything was all right and went back to their own conversation.

"Prisoner? It was the other way round. I know what some people are saying: that if he was as guilty as I said he was, if he had committed crimes against the nation, I didn't need to kill him. There was impeachment, there was the twenty-fifth amendment." He laughed again, but quietly and with a bitter edge. "The last person in the world who would have invoked the twenty-fifth was the vice-president, and he's the one who has to start it. Impeachment was impossible. Even if there had been enough support in the House and Senate, there wasn't time. That's what no one seems to understand—yet. Because I'm going to tell them, I'm going to make them understand what they were planning, what was going to happen next. There wasn't time." And then he said something so ominous I shuddered. "It may already be too late."

CHAPTER

EIGHT

I met Jean-Francois Reynaud in the same dark bar and grille where, weeks earlier, we had lunch. This time we met for dinner. It was not a very popular place at night. The daytime clientele, the businessmen and women with offices in the newer high-rise buildings, who crowded the bar for an hour or so after work, had long since left. The place was all but deserted.

"I've been there, in court, almost every day," remarked Reynaud, blowing gently on a bowl of soup. "It's an interesting thing, an American trial. Are you winning?"

I broke off a piece of French bread and took a bite. I had not noticed him in court, but then, I had not noticed anyone. The crowd was background, nothing more. I could have looked at my best friend, if I had one, and not known who he was.

"Winning? At this point, I'm not sure I could even tell what that means. But if you've been there, you can probably answer that question better than

I could."

Nodding, Reynaud raised another spoonful to his mouth. There was a sly look in his eyes, as if he were enjoying a secret of his own.

"You're better, much better, than anything I expected. I know your reputation, I know what Albert told me, but until I saw myself what you do, the way you ask questions...it isn't what you ask, but how you do it. I watched the witnesses. It was fascinating. Three questions into it and you have them thinking that the answers they gave are exactly—and I mean this—word for word what you knew already they would say. I could almost imagine that they start to wonder whether, somehow, you had written the answers yourself and they were, without knowing how it happened, simply reading what you wrote. You should have gone into politics."

I was not sure that I had anything like that kind of effect, much less that kind of control, with the witnesses I cross-examined. In any event, it did not matter. There was only one way to win, and the odds against it seemed immense. Reynaud knew what I was thinking, what I wanted and had to have.

"I'm not sure I can do what you ask," he said, setting down the spoon.

He wiped his mouth with a white linen napkin, crumpled it up and then, thinking better of what he had done, folded it neatly and placed it on the table next to his plate. He studied it a moment, decided it was not quite right and pushed it first one way, then the other, watching with a slight, world-weary smile the inching movement toward a perfect alignment. Pressing his lips together, he nodded his head in a measured beat, keeping time to the two-sided argument going on inside. He stopped and looked across the table.

"It's the only chance I have," I reminded him. "What you gave me, what

I read, it's devastating, proof beyond anything anyone here has ever thought about what Bridges, what his people, were doing with the Russians. But without the documents themselves, and without someone to testify that they are authentic, there isn't much I can do."

Reynaud's nostrils flared open as if he were sniffing the air to discover the source of some strange scent. He darted a glance, first in one direction, then another, searching, as it seemed, for the best way to explain his dilemma.

"I asked for approval before I gave you that briefcase full of documents assembled by French intelligence, and I was given that approval, but with the understanding that that approval had never been given. Not only that, never requested."

"I'm not sure I understand." Then I thought I did. "It was all right to do what you did, but only so long as no one ever discovered what you had done."

"Yes, precisely; which was the reason I was in such a hurry to have them back. If you need to go through them again, I could arrange that. It might have to be at my office in the consulate. But as to whether you can have any of them for use in court, whether anyone would testify how they were obtained…that would have to be decided at the highest level."

"Why? If you think it important—if the French government thinks it is important—that the whole truth of what happened come out, if you believe what you said that first time we met, that night at Albert's house, that everything had to be brought out into 'the clear light of day,' and what you told me later, when we were here before, sitting in this same restaurant, that the importance of what happened was not the murder, but what happened before, what made the death of the president all but inevitable. No one will ever know that unless I can bring it all out in court."

"I agree. Perhaps there is a chance. But you must understand the difficult position the government is in."

He glanced around the nearly empty restaurant, the habitual reaction of someone trained to the belief that he is never safe from surveillance and has to watch every word.

"You read the transcripts of what was said, meetings between several different members of Bridges's inner circle and certain well-placed people connected with Russian bankers and other men of business. What you don't know—and I can give you this—are where those conversations took place."

Reynaud sat back against the corner of the booth and folded his arms across his chest. A smile of grudging admiration cut sideways across his face.

"If you walk the streets of London, there are cameras everywhere; if you sleep in a Moscow hotel, everything you say or do in bed is recorded. If you use a computer anywhere in the world, the Americans are aware of what you are doing. We are not so indiscriminate in France. We have at least that much respect left for the private rights of individuals. But if you happen to be a Russian oligarch meeting an American public figure in a Paris restaurant, or a Paris hotel, we think it only prudent to learn what we can about any potential threat to what we in the West think important to preserve. So, to be more precise, when the president's son-in-law decides to have dinner with Oleg Kryshenko, the head of one of the biggest Russian banks and one of Vladimir Putin's closest friends, we, so to speak, invited ourselves along. And are very glad we did. Nor was that the only dinner between someone close to Bridges and a Russian we surreptitiously attended. Fitzgerald was right, more right, I think, than he knew. But no one knows—not the Russians, not the Americans—what we have. They don't know, and we don't want them to know, that they are always under surveillance when they visit France. If you use this, I must rely on your discretion not to reveal your source."

"If I don't have the documents, the transcripts of those meetings, I may not be able to make any use of them at all."

Reynaud gave me a knowing look.

"I have a feeling you will be able to find a way."

"But if I can't, if it's the only way to bring out the truth, the whole truth, about what was going on, what made it... What did you mean, a moment ago, when you said that Fitzgerald was more right than he knew?" I asked, suddenly grasping the potential importance of that seemingly chance remark.

Reynaud tapped two fingers on the table as his gaze drew inward. The look on his face was as serious as I had seen.

"I can't tell you that. Not yet, anyway." He reached across and for a moment held my wrist, and with a penetrating gaze tried to assure me that it was not because he did not trust me. "I may know in a few days. It is a question of current debate." He let go of my wrist. "There is another conversation, one that involves someone else in Bridges's inner circle. All I can tell you for the present is that it took place just a week before the assassination and that it involves what you might call double treason."

"Double treason? If it happened just a week before the murder, is that what you meant when you said Fitzgerald was more right than he knew, because he did not know about what was said in that conversation?"

Twisting his head to the side, Reynaud studied me as if I had not understood a thing.

"Fitzgerald did not know anything about what we know. You're the only one outside French intelligence who has seen any of this. Fitzgerald had his own sources in American intelligence. We stopped sharing with the Americans almost two years ago, when we learned what they were doing, or beginning to do: the destruction of the Western alliance, this new notion of theirs that diplomacy, like business, is a series of deals, each one independent of the others, with no other consequence except the terms of each arrangement. These people have no understanding of history, their own or anyone else's. They cling to this belief of theirs that flies in the face of all the evidence, that there are no permanent interests, no permanent values, that the only serious obligation is to take advantage of the next opportunity, whenever that might arise; this belief that there are no limitations, that history starts with them, that history is whatever they want it to be; this childlike delusion that you can have whatever you want simply because you want it."

Reynaud gave me a long, searching look. He sat back and shook his head.

"Kennedy read Gibbon, read Churchill, read a lot of great things, and he wrote some interesting things of his own about former courageous members of the Senate who had risked and even lost their careers over a principle. If Walter Bridges ever read a serious, much less a great book, in his life, he never mentioned it. And what he wrote, or had others write in his name, isn't worth the paper it took to print it. He knew nothing about the past, and like too many other people now lived only in the present moment. What was the nature of his appeal? It wasn't because, like Kennedy, he could give a speech. It was his insistence that every problem would disappear because everyone else in politics was stupid and he was smart. He was going to make sure everyone had a job, everyone had healthcare they could afford, the country would have the best roads and bridges and the best transportation system the world had ever seen. The country would be safe from terrorism, there would be peace in the Middle East, peace all around the world, and all if paid of by reducing taxes and getting rid of regulation. And if it didn't all work out the way he promised, it only proved that he was smart and everyone in Congress and in the courts were stupid, just as he had always said. Remarkable, that anyone could have thought him competent to hold any public office, much less the presidency of the Untied States. If Kennedy were alive, if he was still a young man in his forties, he might be tempted to write a sequel to Gibbon and call it *The Decline and Fall of the American Empire.*

"That really is the point I am trying to make, what I think you need to understand. Remember our last conversation, what we talked about, what happened after Caesar's death, what could have happened but did not. Instead of a return to a republic, the Romans concentrated even more power in the hands of a single man, an emperor who, whatever lip service he paid the Senate, controlled everything, even people's private lives if they were prominent enough. Don't misunderstand: there is no comparison between Julius Caesar and Walter Bridges. Caesar was a military and political genius who understood that Rome had changed and that the Senate had become a feeble-minded debating society without the will to concentrate on any more great endeavors, interested, most of them, only in keeping and enlarging what they owned. Bridges thought the only great thing in the world was himself. The only thing they have in common is the manner of their deaths. Although," he said, growing hesitant, "even that isn't quite so clear." He shot me a quizzical glance. "It was not done in a public place in front of witnesses, and Fitzgerald, so far as we know, acted alone.

"But, listen, listen," he said, holding up his finger and waving it back and forth, impatient with himself. "I was wrong. There is another comparison. Or there might be. After Caesar's death, the speech by Marc Antony: 'I come not to praise Caesar, but to bury him.' The speech in which he so deftly pours scorn on what Brutus, who had explained what he, with others, had done, by saying that it was not that he 'loved Caesar less, than did other men,' but that he 'loved Rome more.' The vice-president, now president, the speech he gave at the funeral, insisting that those who hated Bridges hated him because he loved America more, that it now fell to those still living to carry on the great unfinished work. This is what you need to understand. This trial, what happens here, is the hinge on which everything will turn, the door that either opens or stays closed, whether your country thinks Walter Bridges a victim, a martyr to a cause, a cause which will now be given far more power than it had before, or a traitor, a would-be tyrant that Kevin Fitzgerald stopped, the only one who knew how to stop the country from becoming a place where the old, established institutions that kept your democracy alive becomes nothing more than hollow shells, government become a private business."

We talked all the way through dinner, or rather Reynaud talked and I listened. It was a seminar in modern and ancient history, a series of brilliant analyses that exposed the fault lines of our existence, the unexamined but questionable assumptions on which we led our thoughtless, careless lives. It was only after the dishes had been cleared away and we were sitting over coffee that Reynaud asked a question that made me, for a moment, stare at him in speechless wonder.

"So, tell me," he asked with a rare sparkle in his eyes, "how are you enjoying your affair with the ravishing Mrs. Evan Winslow?"

With anyone else, even Albert Craven, I might have lied. But I could not lie to Jean-Francois Reynaud; he was much too French to have believed it. I took refuge in understatement.

"It's a pleasant way to spend a few innocent hours."

Reynaud's thick eyebrows shot straight up. His head flew backward.

"Innocent! I should think her rather more inspiring than that!"

"What made you suspect I was having an affair with her?"

He shrugged off even the possibility of a doubt.

"I saw the look on her face that night at dinner when you walked into the room."

I had been too taken, too overwhelmed by her stunning good looks to notice any reaction, much less any response to my own.

"If you were French, you would have known immediately. Americans always think an affair is something to be hidden, disguised, kept private from the world. We think an affair the only reasonable result of an attraction between a man and a woman, and what difference if they are married to other people. After all," he said as he generously paid the bill, "if it gets too involved, if some jealousy occurs, the one who is jealous can always shoot their rival and, in a French court at least, have the chance of an acquittal. But don't worry, your secret is safe with me. If you have a jealous husband on your hands, it won't be because of anything I have said to anyone. But really," he asked with mild astonishment, "how could anyone doubt that a woman who looks like she does could ever stay faithful for long? It is against all the laws of nature."

Tangerine pretended to be hurt when, later that night, I told her what Reynaud had said. I had driven over to Sausalito and her house on the steep hillside that looked out across the water to the city. They had houses everywhere, but this one, she had made it clear to her husband, was her own private retreat, the place she could come to be alone. I parked at the top of the narrow drive and walked down the wooden steps to the door of the chocolate shingle-sided home, watching the lights of San Francisco dance in the starry night darkness above the steep shingled roof. She answered the door while I was still three steps from the bell.

"He said that?" she asked with her mouth turned down at the corners and her eyes alive with all the excitement of things still bright and new. "But you told him, didn't you, that I would always be faithful to you."

"Always. Or at least until tomorrow."

We were sitting on the sofa, looking out through sliding glass doors. The moonlight made a shadow drawing of the Golden Gate on the bay below. She hit me gently on the shoulder with her hand.

"You might have trusted me at least a week."

I wondered if anyone really had, and then realized that it had probably never been a question. She was so good looking, so damned irresistible, that the only thing you could think about was being with her. There was nothing after that.

"You had dinner with him. Did he have anything interesting to say?"

"Everything he says is interesting; but no, nothing in particular," I replied, keeping the confidence I had been given.

"And what did you think of what happened at trial today?" she asked, picking up from the coffee table in front of us the drink she had made.

"Did you watch it on television? What did you think?"

She became serious. Holding the glass in both hands, she stared down into it.

"I think...I don't know what to think, except you are a great lawyer and

Kevin doesn't look anything like a man on trial for murder." She thought a moment. "You know what he looks like, sitting there? The way he looked when he was sitting at the front table at one of those fund-raising dinners, hundreds of people in the room, waiting to give his speech."

I had not thought of it, but she was right. It was exactly what he looked like: eager and alert, everything in place, suit pressed, tie straight, shoes shined, hair combed, teeth brushed, just waiting for the moment to jump to his feet and flash that winning smile, the perfect candidate, ready to tell you everything you wanted to hear. And yet…

"There is a little more to him than that, I think. He knows he's on trial for murder. He understands the seriousness of the situation."

"I don't mean that he doesn't. He always has—understood his situation, I mean. Understood, and been ready to do what he has to do to meet it."

I sat against the corner pillow and watched the way she held herself with such perfect ease, the way she gave even the slightest movement of her hands, the slightest movement of her eyes or mouth, a meaning, and as many interpretations as you could invent.

"Faithful for at least a week," I repeated her teasing rejoinder. "How faithful do you think you would have been if Fitzgerald had been willing to give up his ambition and married you?"

An instant's anger flashed in her eyes, replaced a moment later with a glance of bittersweet nostalgia.

"The honest answer is I don't know. Maybe until someone like you came along. But I would have tried; really, I would have tried. Enough of that now. You probably didn't see the coverage today, what they're saying about you and the trial and what is likely to happen, all those self-proclaimed experts on television, or what they're writing in the papers."

I did not care what anyone was saying on television; I did not care what anyone was writing in the newspapers. I just wanted to watch her talk.

"It all depends on the channel you watch. Whatever they're saying on one of them, they're saying something completely different on another," she explained, her dark eyes glittering with the antic memory of what she was now so eager to describe. "There is one guy—he really hates you—who says it's just disgraceful, that it should not be allowed, to raise as a defense that Bridges had to die, that it is 'okay to kill someone if you don't happen to agree with what they think.' I think those are the words he used. Then—and when you think about it, it is really quite funny—he quotes that line from some play Shakespeare wrote: 'The first thing we do, let's kill all the lawyers.' He said it with one of those grim smiles that makes you think he wants you to think he is only kidding, but that he really means it, or at least wouldn't mind if someone did it. Then there are the ones on the other side. They won't come out and say that Kevin did what he had to, they won't go that far. No one wants to be the first to come right out and say that Kevin saved the country and should be acquitted, but you can hear it in their tone, see it in the way they talk among themselves, the sympathy they feel. They call it a tragedy; they never call it murder. Tragedy, because Kevin Fitzgerald thought he did not have a choice, not because Walter Bridges was killed."

She sat on the edge of the sofa, her knees close together, holding her drink in her hand, smiling into it as if she were looking into a mirror, seeing not her own reflection but a portrait of her own remembered past.

"Do you know how I got my name, why my parents called me Tangerine?"

I did not know, I could only guess, but I guessed with unknown knowledge, a sense that there could be only one reason.

"The song."

She looked from her glass to me. She was not surprised, only curious.

"The lyrics started bouncing through my head the moment we were first introduced."

"My father loved that song; my mother did not like it. What mother would? A song about a woman who men adore, a woman all the talk of the Argentine. My father was always more the romantic. But he married my mother and spent his life with broken dreams. He had to make a living. He sold insurance. He worked in an office. During one spring break while I was in high school, I met him one day for lunch, and when we were walking back to the building where he worked, he told me—and I never forgot the look in his eyes when he said it—that work, work like his, was just another name for slavery. He died of a heart attack when he was forty-seven, a sad, desperate man who never got tired of telling me that I should live life like an adventure and never settle for anything else. My mother hated him."

"Hated him?"

"He was a dreamer, which, for her, meant he was useless. It's the reason she thinks I have a perfect marriage—Winslow money—the same reason my father would be so disappointed. So, tell me, Antonelli," she said as she turned to me with sad, wistful eyes, "what do you think? Was my father right, should life be lived like an adventure, or my mother, who thinks I can marry for money and not be a whore?"

It is not true that you can learn to know someone over time; you knew them, if you ever know them, the first time you meet them and their eyes tell you that you had not just met them after all. I had not known what I was going to say until I heard myself say something I never thought I would, and knew immediately that I meant everything I said.

"Then leave your husband and marry me."

She tossed her head and laughed, a soft, sweet laugh that taught me perfect happiness and changed my life forever.

CHAPTER
NINE

Jenny Ann Carruthers had served three terms in Congress from a district just outside Charleston, South Carolina before deciding to join the then new administration of Walter Bridges. She had the Southern manner of easy, slow familiarity, and the polished smile of an insincerity so congenial that instead of rampant duplicity, seemed to practice the closer intimacy of the acknowledged thief. She could lie to your face and with those long, batting eyelashes of hers fan away your resentment. You knew she would never tell the truth, and you found yourself admiring the consistency with which she lied. She was the best press secretary Walter Bridges could have found. I had no idea why Raymond St. John was calling her to the stand. It did not take long to find out.

"Would you tell the jury what your job was when you worked for President Bridges?" asked St. John after he had her state her name for the record, a name that was slightly different than the one she had used since her first campaign for public office. Jennifer Anastasia Carruthers was a little too aristocratic, a little too formal, for a constituency raised on television. Everyone felt comfortable with Jenny Ann. All the political consultants had said so.

She turned slowly, her flat, rather narrow chin staying steady in the arc, and faced the jury. It was part of her training to look at the cameras, to look at those you wanted to convince instead of one of those baying reporters who were always jumping up and down with their arrogant insistence that you answer only them.

"I served as White House director of communications during the presidency—the all too short presidency—of Walter Bridges," she replied in an accent that screamed its Southern origins.

Fitzgerald tugged my sleeve.

"She was born and raised in Pennsylvania, went to Yale, married a med school student. First time she ever saw South Carolina was when he took his first job at a hospital and they moved there," he whispered.

St. John stood at the far corner of his table. There was nothing but empty space between him and the witness, or between him and the jury. Instead of moving closer the way he usually did, to take up a more conversational tone and make the jury feel more involved in what was said, he stayed where he was. He did not want to block the view of the television cameras; he wanted this witness in particular to have the chance to talk directly to all those millions watching. He wanted everyone to see and hear the prosecution's preemptive strike.

"You were his press secretary, and in that capacity, were you in fairly regular contact with the president?"

"Every day. Several times. I went over with him every press release issued in his name. Discussed with him each morning the questions that were likely to be asked in that day's briefing. Asked if there were any announcements he wanted me to make. Asked if there were any matters, especially related to national security, he did not want me to discuss. So, yes, I was with the president, every day, from early morning until sometimes quite late at night."

"In addition to your discussions with the president about what you, and other people in the White House, were going to tell the press, were there conversations in which you discussed with the president news stories written about him?"

Jenny Ann Carruthers looked not at the jury as she had before, but at the courtroom crowd and the cameras in back.

"President Bridges was very concerned with the kind of coverage we were being given. He did not understand—really, none of us could—why the press was spending so much time reporting about things that had never happened, stories in which they almost never bothered to provide the names of any of their so-called sources."

"Stories about Russian involvement in the last election? Russian money, Russian banks…stories like that?"

"Yes, that's exactly right. There was nothing to any of it, nothing at all, but that didn't make it stop. They kept repeating it, every day in the press, every day on television," she said, outraged at how she and the president had been treated. "There was nothing to it," she repeated. "Nothing but made up lies. The people who hated us—the people who hated him—would take a perfectly ordinary meeting—someone talking with the Russian ambassador; someone not even in the government, an old friend of the president, having a business meeting with a foreign investor—and turn it into a conspiracy, subversion, an attempt to destroy American democracy. It was disgraceful, that's what it was!"

I was on my feet, ready with an objection, when, changing my mind, I just stood there, too confused to speak.

"Mr. Antonelli?" asked Evelyn Patterson, peering down from the bench. "Do you wish to make an objection?" she asked in a way that left little doubt she would sustain it.

"I was going to, your Honor," I admitted. I scratched the back of my head. "And I probably should. Instead of answering the prosecution's question, the witness is giving a speech. But, to tell you the truth, like everyone, I like a good story, especially one filled with myth and fantasy. So, no, your Honor, I think I'll just sit back and listen."

A whisper of laughter rippled through the crowd, silenced by a glance of disapproval from the bench. Jenny Ann Carruthers looked at me as if I were the one who should be on trial for murder. Raymond St. John ignored the interruption and continued as if I had not said a thing.

"It's your testimony here today that, so far as you have any direct knowledge, no one connected with the president was involved with the Russians, or with anyone else, in an improper way?"

"That's correct, Mr. St. John. There was no truth to any of it."

"I want to move on to something else. The trip out here to San Francisco. You weren't with the president. Was there a reason?"

"There wasn't really any reason for me to come. The speech had been written, all the arrangements made. There were other people who could handle the press covering the trip. There were a thousand things to do in Washington: the president's legislative agenda, the need to work out our communications strategy, the—"

"Yes, I understand," interjected St. John, determined to keep her on point. "You weren't on the trip, but did you help plan it?"

"Yes. It was partly my idea. We had lost California in the election, and we probably were not going to win it next time either. But it was important to communicate the message that the president was president of all the people, not just those who voted for him. That one reason, there were others. We thought the Bay Area—because of Silicon Valley—would be the perfect place to give a speech on the way technology could be used to jumpstart the economy, to get it moving again the way it should, the way President Bridges was determined to do."

"You said there were other reasons. That was one of them."

She glanced briefly, but only briefly, at Kevin Fitzgerald sitting next to me. For a second time he tugged my sleeve.

"When she was in the House, they used to say she was the one member of Congress you could always trust to keep her word, if only she could remember what it was. It's why she has always been such a good liar: she can't remember far enough back to know that what is coming out of her mouth isn't what she has always believed."

I started to turn my attention back to the witness. He tugged again.

"Be careful dealing with her. When it comes to what she wants, she's lethal."

"The other reason," prodded St. John when Carruthers seemed to hesitate.

"The defendant, Senator Fitzgerald."

"Would you explain to the jury what you mean?"

Jenny Ann Carruthers took a breath, not a deep one, but the kind you take at the last second, when it's time to deliver a speech, a dramatic part, something you have made an effort to learn by heart.

"Senator Fitzgerald had, from the beginning, opposed everything President Bridges said or did. It was clear to the president, it was clear to all of us, that he had decided that open and aggressive opposition was the best, and probably the only, opportunity he had to get his own party's nomination and run against the president in the next election. The president was never one to run away from a challenge. We decided to take the fight to the senator's home ground. He had not left us any choice."

"He hadn't left you any choice? I'm not sure I understand," said St. John in a way that suggested he really had not understood what she was driving at.

"The senator had made threats," she replied in a voice harsh, brittle and combative. "He had threatened the president's life!"

The courtroom erupted. There were shouts of protest, shouts, though fewer of them, of support. Reporters, too astonished to shout anything, looked at each other as if for confirmation that they had heard the same charge. Judge Patterson pounded the gavel as hard as she could, twice, three times, and then, as the noise subsided, promised expulsion to anyone who raised their voice again. St. John was more surprised than anyone. It was all he could do to conceal his displeasure at a witness giving testimony he had not heard from her own mouth before. In all the commotion I was the only one to notice the anger in his eyes, his only thought that Jenny Ann Carruthers had damn well better be able to prove what she had just alleged. He was cautious.

"You're testifying, here today, that the defendant, Kevin Fitzgerald, threatened to kill the president?"

She did not hesitate.

"Yes, and he did it in public, on the floor of the United States Senate. He said—and this is a direct quote—that the country could not survive another two years of a Bridges administration, and that the only way to save the country was to get rid of Walter Bridges! And after what he's done, we know exactly what he meant, don't we?"

Human intelligence, often traced on a curve from stupidity to genius, should perhaps be thought of in terms of a circle on which you always ended with the two of them so close together they overlapped. For a moment no one knew what to make of what they had just heard. The courtroom was silent. Raymond St. John was speechless.

"Mr. St. John, do you have any more questions of the witness?" asked Judge Patterson, staring in wide-eyed wonder at Jenny Ann Carruthers.

"Yes, your Honor. Ms. Carruthers, would you like to clarify what you just said? You testified that there were several reasons why it had been decided to have President Bridges give a speech in San Francisco. The last one you mentioned is because the defendant had threatened him. Did you mean to say that Senator Fitzgerald threatened to murder the president? Or did you mean to say," he went on, encouraging the suggestion that she must have meant something else, "that Senator Fitzgerald, in a speech he gave on the Senate floor, threatened some kind of political action as a way to end the president's hold on power?"

Jenny Ann Carruthers looked at Raymond St. John with the contempt of the bully for the weakling too scared to fight.

"My meaning is plain enough. Fitzgerald threatened the president. Then he killed him." She turned to throw a challenge at the jury. "How much more evidence do you need than that?"

Without another word, without even the usual, and traditional, thanks to the witness for her testimony, without even bothering to acknowledge formally the end of his direct examination, Raymond St. John, lost in some unsettled thoughts of his own, walked to the other side of the counsel table and silently took his seat.

"Mr. Antonelli?" asked Judge Patterson, quiet and subdued. "Do you wish to cross-examine the witness?"

I did not move. I just sat there as if I could not decide. I let Jenny Ann Carruthers wonder whether I might be reluctant, even afraid, to try to match wits with her. Slowly, and with an effort that suggested I was still not sure, I pushed myself up, shook my head as if at an unavoidable ordeal, and leaned my hip against the table and stared up at the ceiling.

"The speech, the speech given on the floor of the Senate. Would you quote me that line again?" I asked, my gaze descending until my eyes squarely met hers.

"He said the country could not survive another two years of the Bridges administration, that the only way to save the country was to get rid of Walter Bridges."

"Yes, very good. And I can tell the jury and everyone else who is listening that that is exactly what Kevin Fitzgerald said in that speech he gave in the Senate."

A small, vindictive smile marched triumphantly across her mouth.

"And, if you would not mind, now that you have quoted that line, quote the line right after that. You remember!" I remarked when her only response was a blank stare. "The line that says, 'Impeachment is the only way we have to rid ourselves of what is almost certain to turn out to be a criminal enterprise the likes of which we have never seen in our public life.' Surely you can't have forgotten that, Ms. Carruthers. I remember distinctly seeing you on television, in the White House briefing room. It was all the reporters wanted to know about: what the president thought of Senator Fitzgerald's call for his impeachment!"

She was halfway out of the witness chair, protesting what she called my deliberate attempt to mischaracterize what she had said.

"Quoting someone, you think distortion?" I asked with a smile, walking in a half circle in front of the two counsel tables. "Because the meaning of what the senator said isn't what you said it was?"

"He said they had to get rid of him. That's what he did."

"Yes, perhaps, but that raises the question, doesn't it, of why? You testified that Senator Fitzgerald was considered the most serious, and determined, political opponent Walter Bridges had. You testified that you and others in the White House, including especially the president himself, thought the senator the most likely opponent the president would face in the next election. Isn't that what you said in direct response to the question Mr. St. John asked?"

"Yes, but—"

"And if you thought Senator Fitzgerald was that formidable an opponent, would it not be safe to say that you had your reasons?"

"Reasons? What do you mean?"

I looked at her, incredulous.

"What do I mean? You've been a member of Congress, you were involved in the president's election. You're considered a very good political operative, someone who knows her way around politics, who knows what it takes to put together an effective campaign. There were reasons why you thought Kevin Fitzgerald a threat, a political threat. What were they? Had you done private polling on the likely result if the two of them ran against each other?"

"Yes," she replied with some reluctance.

"And who won in a matchup like that?"

"The senator."

"By what margin, in the last poll that was taken?"

"Fitzgerald was ahead fifty-six percent to thirty-two percent."

"The rest undecided?"

"That's right." She looked at the jury, anxious to explain something she thought it important everyone know. "It seems like a large margin, but the election was two years away, and once we put an end to all the groundless rumors, all the false reporting, once we got Congress to concentrate on the president's agenda, those numbers would turn in a hurry."

"But they had not turned yet. And so you sent the president to California to give a big speech, a speech that was never given, correct?"

"The president was murdered!"

"The speech was never given. Who wrote that speech?" I asked with an urgency that for a moment caught her off guard.

"There were several writers involved, several people who—"

"It was written by Michael Donahue, wasn't it? Michael Donahue, who was the principal foreign policy advisor to the president. Michael Donahue, who is now the new chief of staff."

"The speech was about technology and the world, so, yes, Michael would have been involved."

"Involved? No, he wrote it. That speech was supposed to set a new direction for the country, that speech was going to describe how with the new technology the country could chart a new course in which our first, our only, duty was to ourselves. Isn't that correct? Isn't that what Walter Bridges was going to say in that speech, nearly every word of which was written by Michael Donahue?"

"The speech was never given! Kevin Fitzgerald made sure of that. Maybe that was his idea of how to save the country, stop anyone from saying anything he might disagree with!"

"Your Honor!" I shouted as she gaveled the courtroom to order. "Would you please instruct the witness what it means to be one?"

Evelyn Patterson and Jenny Ann Carruthers were about the same age, but years apart when it came to their understanding of what was tolerated in a public forum. Carruthers might ignore a reporter; she could not ignore this judge.

"You give answers to questions, truthful answers, the shorter the better. Do anything else, Ms. Carruthers, and I assure you the White House will be getting along without you while you have an extended vacation right here in San Francisco, though not in one of our better hotels. In brief, Ms. Carruthers," she added with a steely-eyed stare, "don't…with me, understood?" She paused just long enough to make sure the question answered itself. "Your witness, Mr. Antonelli."

"You agree that Senator Fitzgerald was the biggest political threat you faced, correct?" I asked, boring in as I moved closer. "You knew that in a head to head matchup he won by more than twenty points, isn't that correct? You knew, in other words, that Kevin Fitzgerald had nothing to worry about, that he was almost certain to be elected president in the next election, not two years away. There was no reason for him to do anything but wait, isn't that right?"

She could not wait to answer, to show everyone what a fool I really was.

"But he didn't wait! He murdered him!"

I was less than an arm's length away. I took a single step back.

"Which can only mean that something had happened, that he had learned something that told him he could not wait, that something, something drastic, had to be done to save the country. What do you think that was, Ms. Carruthers? What was going on, what was the president, what were you and your friends in the White House, doing that would make someone think they had to kill the president the United States, whatever might happen to them?"

"There was nothing going on!" she cried, her face red with rage. "Nothing!"

"You were director of communications under President Bridges. And you still have the same position. Were you asked to stay on during the transition, until the vice-president—I should say, the president—has assembled a staff of his own?"

This seemed to quiet her. She was back on solid ground. She was proud of her position, proud that she deserved to have it.

"The president has asked me to continue the work I had been doing. There aren't going to be any changes. The vice-president—all of us—are determined to finish what we started."

"There aren't going to be any changes? That isn't quite true, is it? Some changes have already been made. Richard Ellison, who was chief of staff, isn't chief of staff now, is he?"

She dismissed this as a minor matter, the normal, routine shuffling that follows every change of administration, even a transition as tragic but as seamless as this. Ellison, she insisted, had not been replaced, he had been given the main responsibility for the domestic policy agenda. I repeated the question.

"He isn't chief of staff anymore, is he?"

"No, as I just said, he's been—"

"The new chief of staff, the person through whom everything, including the domestic policy agenda, will go is Michael Donahue, isn't that correct? Michael Donahue, who—"

"I'm sure this is all quite fascinating," said Raymond St. John, rising from his chair to state an objection. "But it isn't clear what connection the defense thinks there is between the question of White House staffing and what is at issue in this trial."

"Mr. Antonelli?" asked the judge. "Is there a connection? Because otherwise it is difficult to see the relevance of this line of questioning."

There was a connection, a serious connection, but I had learned it through Jean-Francois Reynaud, and I could not yet reveal it.

"I'm finished with the witness, your Honor."

Jenny Ann Carruthers was excused. She left the courtroom without looking at Kevin Fitzgerald or anyone else. She had looked at him only once, and then only briefly. She had never looked at him when she was accusing him of murder.

Fitzgerald had not noticed.

"I was too busy watching the way the jury was watching her," he explained that evening when I visited him in his unusually comfortable cell. "They didn't like her. Hardly anyone ever did."

He sat on the edge of the bed. His dinner tray, which he had barely touched, lay on the floor next to him. The room seemed smaller. There were more bags of mail, double the number there had been just a few days before. The letters he had opened, the samplings he made that, as he informed me, showed that a majority had been written to show support, were stacked on the table he used as a desk. The numbers who had sent messages on their electronic devices exceeded anything that had been seen before.

"We're winning," he assured me with the same bright, artificial smile he must have flashed to a thousand different audiences.

"You might be winning in the country, but you're not winning in court."

"The trial has just started."

"The trial is damn near over. All that's left for the prosecution is to introduce your confession."

For a single, fleeting moment, he seemed to lose confidence, but then, remembering who he was, he was as brash and as defiant as ever, convinced that everything was under control.

"Which is when the trial really begins, when the prosecution rests and it's our turn. Cheer up, Antonelli, there's nothing to worry about." He got up from the twin bed and walked over to the stack of open mail. "Everyone knows what I did, and nearly everyone understands it was necessary, that there wasn't any choice, that it was either Bridges or the country."

Did he really believe that, I wondered. Whatever he may have read in the letters he had been sent, however much the sentiment expressed in them was running in his favor, he read the papers, pouring over every line of the coverage of his trial. He had to have known that on the question, not whether Walter Bridges had been fit to be president, but whether there could have been any justification to kill him, less than a third of the American people were willing to go as far as that.

"I know what you're thinking," he said with that unerring instinct he had for what was going through other people's minds. It was the politician's clairvoyance, to know in advance the weak point of their own argument. "But you're forgetting that most people aren't going to admit they approve. That's a secret they'll share only with themselves, and maybe," he added with the shrewdness of a thought just discovered, "not even with themselves. They'll act on it, though, when they have the chance, when they're voting in the jury room, or at the polling place. You'll see. I'm not wrong about this."

His confidence seemed absolute, and yet he kept glancing at all those mail bags stacked on top of each other, appealing, as it were, to that vast anonymous public opinion that was the only jury he seemed to take seriously.

"We have some work to do," I reminded him.

For the next two hours we went over what I thought the remaining prosecution witnesses were likely to say. But I was mainly interested in getting him to go into detail about his confession. It struck me as remarkably vague, a bare outline of the crime. What was the reason he had not been asked about his motivations, why he had decided to kill the president? His response did little to fill in the gaps.

"I told them what happened. I was not going to tell them any more than that."

"Most people who confess to a crime want to talk about why they did it; they want to get it all off their chest, make a complete confession."

"I'm not most people, and this wasn't a crime. It was an act of defense!"

"You did not think it would be better to tell the whole truth, not just what you did, but why?"

"A confession like Bukharin made in those Russian show trials under Stalin we talked about?" He shook his head. "Bukharin's confession was made in open court, which, you might remember, is where I'm going to make mine."

"But not to announce you're guilty, like Bukharin, but to insist on your innocence, like…" I could not remember a comparison I could draw. The case against Fitzgerald had no obvious precedent.

"When you kill the king, they call it tyrannicide and throw flowers at your feet, but only if, after killing him, you wear the crown. But you're on trial for your life, and Steven Spencer, who was vice-president, now sits in the Oval Office."

"A borrowed crown, to use your analogy; one that won't be permanent."

"Is that your plan: walk out of court a free man and run against him in the next election?"

Fitzgerald gave me an odd look.

"Not after what I have to say in court."

"Then you wouldn't—"

"Yes, I would—I will. But Spencer won't—he can't."

It was like listening to what Lenin must have talked like in the sealed train in which the Germans brought him back to Czarist Russia. The Germans hoped he would cause dissension in the Russian army and help them avoid defeat in the First World War; he planned on causing more than disaffection, a revolution that would bring him, and those who followed him, to power. Sitting in his cell, Fitzgerald was already thinking how his trial for murder would be his springboard to the presidency. It was more than stunning, it was madness.

"They were all involved—all of them. The Russian thing was real. There are no coincidences. Listen, it isn't that difficult to understand. Bridges was going to lose. It was not going to be close. Now, imagine you're someone close to him, someone who does business in Russia. You know a lot of people, you have Russian friends, people you do business with. It doesn't have to be anything criminal—money-laundering, that kind of thing— legitimate business, all of it above board. Whatever else was going on, whatever else may have happened, just assume that everything up to that point had been perfectly legal. You're having dinner with some Russian investor, some partner in some international enterprise. The conversation turns to the campaign. The Russian mentions that he had heard there is a lot of information, really damaging information, on the other candidate. He wonders if you think Bridges might be interested, whether Bridges might be able to use it. He may be able to get it for you—he knows some people—but only if it is kept completely secret. The people he knows can't afford to be involved. Bridges hasn't got a chance, but now you have a chance to help. Your friend tells you that everything can be arranged. All you have to do is get someone in the Bridges campaign to open a line of communication so they can decide the most advantageous times to release what they have. You don't ask how any of it was obtained. It's out there, why not use it? Collusion doesn't mean that everyone agreed to something in advance; it doesn't require a conspiracy. All that is needed is that you do something that helps someone do what they had planned all along. That is one of the things that happened. There were others."

"Other things? Such as?"

"Michael Donahue. It almost doesn't matter what involvement he had with the Russians in the election. He's a bigger threat than that. He discovered history too late to understand it."

CHAPTER
TEN

Albert Craven dropped into the chair in front of the desk where I was working, unbuttoned his suit coat, placed both hands on his stomach and rolled his small, round head from one side to the other as if to make sure that nothing in my office had changed.

"You're here because it's Saturday and you don't have to be in court, and because, usually, you have nowhere else to go. I'm here because it's Saturday and I'm meeting someone for lunch." A faint whisper of a grin slid without effort across his pear-shaped mouth. "I come in almost every day, though I don't really know why. All it does is interfere with lunch. The only reason I make an appearance is so the junior partners downstairs know I'm still alive. That way they have an incentive to keep working until all hours so I might decide one day to move them to an office here, upstairs. What do you think about doing something different, after you're finished with this godforsaken trial of yours? We'll leave the firm, leave all my aging, ungrateful clients, and we'll start all over, just the two of us, an office somewhere—"

"South of Market, so you can get away from all your monied friends?" I taunted gently.

"Nothing that drastic," replied Craven, wrinkling his nose in genuine distaste. "You can go on representing all these murderers, rapists and thieves. I'll keep going to lunch so I can keep telling you what everyone in San Francisco is talking about. The difference is that I won't have to feel guilty about what I'm doing. Someone else can look after the bright new futures of a few dozen over educated men and women who think billable hours the only true measure of a lawyer's life. Really, Antonelli—I mean it."

I could not count the Saturdays I had heard this same lament. This time, instead of a vague promise to consider his vague offer, I accepted on the spot.

"It's a great idea. I'm ready for a change. You have a deal. Give me a week or two after the trial to get everything in order. It will give me something to look forward to."

Albert took a deep breath and sprang forward.

"Would you really? I had no idea… Well, let me think about it. It could be complicated. A lot of old business to unravel. But what the hell, why not?"

I wondered if he really would, whether he could separate himself from what for more than half his long existence had defined who and what he was. There was an immediate appeal, of course, the unexpected chance to start over, to go back to a young man's dream, build from scratch a second, better practice, one in which he would not have to be ready at a moment's notice to sooth the ego of some old client who had, as so many of them now seemed to have, a thousand complaints and a thousand excuses.

"You came in here for a reason," I reminded him as he gazed past me, imagining what a change like that might mean.

"Yes," he replied, a little embarrassed that he had let his attention wander. "The trial. Everyone is talking about it; it's about all they talk about. But that isn't what I wanted to tell you. Well, yes, it is. But something quite specific: what you did on cross-examination, what you did with Jenny Ann Carruthers when she quoted that line from Fitzgerald's Senate speech, that there was no choice but to get rid of Bridges. What everyone is marveling over is how you could that very instant quote back to her the very next line, the one that destroyed her interpretation of what he had said. I know you never stop working, that there is no end to your preparation, but how in the world did you ever do that, remember a line from a speech no one now remembers?"

"It was easy," I said, passing it off with a shrug. "I just made it up."

He jolted forward, slammed his hand on my desk and laughed so hard I thought he might cry.

"You did what?" he sputtered. "Made it up?"

"Sure, why not? I didn't lie. I didn't know what he said, but when I heard the line she was quoting, I knew he had to have said something like what I quoted back. It only made sense. What was he going to say after a sentence that, taken by itself, could seem so sinister? That the president needs to die, that someone needs to kill him? He had to give it a reasonable definition. And if he didn't do it in the very next sentence, he would have had to have provided some clarification sometime soon after that. And what was I going to do? Ask that smug, self-satisfied and, unless I miss my guess, utterly remorseless Jenny Ann Carruthers to tell the jury what else Fitzgerald might have said? There is a rule which, unlike most rules of what you should and should not do in court, actually sometimes makes sense: when in doubt, be decisive. I was not taking much of a chance. She isn't someone who spends any time looking at anything except what seems to her immediate advantage—none of them are, the people who worked for Bridges that I've seen so far. She had one line in a speech. She probably got it from someone else. She never would have thought to read the speech, the whole speech, herself. They live in their own talking points world. One thing I'm sure of: there isn't one of them that will bother to check to see whether I quoted Fitzgerald accurately."

"You've put me in another impossible situation, Antonelli." The laughter had faded away, moved from his voice to his eyes. He had the excited look of a secret he would have given anything to share. "I'll have to keep listening to everyone talking about your meticulous, painstaking preparation, how you committed to memory everything Kevin Fitzgerald ever said, how you were just waiting to destroy the prosecution's witness with a single line that no one else remembered. By the time they quit talking about it, everyone will think you know everything everyone has ever said. And all I can do is smile and never tell them all you did was guess!"

"I have a better idea," I said, speaking out loud the thought that had just flown through my head. "Tell them the truth. They won't believe it, and they'll be more convinced than they were before that I know a hell of a lot more than I really do. The truth," I went on, with a bitterness I did not try to conceal, "is that I wish I had followed my own first judgment and never gone near this case."

"Why? You've done extremely well, better than any other lawyer could have done."

We had known each other too long for false modesty, or false confidence.

There was no one else, no one at all, with whom I could have a conversation in which nothing was held back. There was nothing I could tell him that would make him change his mind about me, nothing that would lead him to seriously question anything I had done, nothing that would make him question anything, except how, if I were in some difficulty, he might help. Albert Craven was the only real friend I had.

"The question isn't whether I can win this case, whether I can persuade this jury that what Fitzgerald did does not amount to murder. If you could tell me right now that Fitzgerald was going to be acquitted, walk out of that courtroom a free man, able to resume his own political career, I couldn't tell you that would necessarily be a good thing. It isn't clear to me that we wouldn't be better off—that the country wouldn't be better off—if Fitzgerald were found guilty and sentenced to die. That would put an end to it, wouldn't it?" I asked, wondering how much I believed of what I was saying.

"By better off, I assume you mean, because it would stop people thinking it was ever okay to kill a president, whatever he might have done?"

Sitting sideways to my desk, I stared out the window at the cloudless autumn day, and in the distance, down through the narrow street, the gray water of the bay.

"If Fitzgerald were to be acquitted, it will only be because he has convinced everyone that what he did saved the country. And maybe most people will believe him, but there will be a lot of them who won't. Fitzgerald will run for president. He's already planning his campaign. Forget what that election will look like, forget what Jenny Ann Carruthers and everyone else backing Spencer will be saying—that the choice is between a murderer and the man who kept the country together after the assassination—imagine what it will be like if Fitzgerald wins, if he becomes president. Everyone who compares the death of Bridges to the death of Julius Caesar—how long before they start comparing the administration of Kevin Fitzgerald to Richard III?"

"And if he isn't acquitted?"

"Maybe something even worse." For a moment, I thought hard, trying to put a shape on what I had not yet been able to draw into focus. "Fitzgerald did them a favor. They admitted it. What was the situation, what did Carruthers say under oath? That Fitzgerald was their biggest problem. They thought he was almost certain to be the opponent they would face in the next election. He was winning by huge margins in the polls. Yes, it was early; yes, a lot could still happen. But, though I did not press the point with her, the only things likely to happen were things that would hurt their chances: more investigations than anyone could count, a legislative program that was never going to get off the ground. Bridges was not going to win re-election, but now Bridges is dead, and the candidate they feared the most is on trial for murder and is almost certain to lose, which means that everything Fitzgerald thought he had to stop goes forward, and anyone who so much as dares to challenge what they are doing will be accused of approving murder."

Craven listened intently. He did not disagree with anything I said, but, as he explained, it really did not matter that the consequences of the verdict, whatever that verdict was, might be tragic.

"In a way, it makes everything easier. All you have to do is make sure the truth comes out. It is the only way something like this never happens again: if we understand what it was that made Kevin Fitzgerald think he had to do what he did."

I swung around and rested my elbows on the desk. Picking up a pencil,

I held it at each end, twisting it slowly in one direction and then back again, watching the changing light on the smooth yellow surface, the way the six sides moved in and out of the shadows, like a trial in which you could never see everything all at once.

"It all comes down to that, what Fitzgerald thought," I remarked as the pencil kept turning in my hands. "What Fitzgerald thought he knew."

Dropping the pencil on the desk, I watched it roll away. With a rueful look, I let Craven know that Kevin Fitzgerald was like no client I had ever had.

"I told his wife that first time you sent her in to see me that there could not be any secrets, that I had to know everything about both of them. I told her, and later I told him, that I would decide what was relevant and what was not, that there was nothing private anymore, nothing they could conceal."

"And?"

"Let's just say that he doesn't always tell the truth. But the real problem is that he doesn't lie. He's evasive. I have to put him on the stand. It's the only defense he has: what he knew, what he had learned, the reason why he had to do what he did. It is all about this Russian business, but it's more than that. He has told me that much, but nothing more. Vague hints that Bridges was about to do something that would have changed everything, something that, once it was done, if he got away with it, could never be set right. That's as far as he would go. It will all come out at trial, when he testifies under oath."

"But why won't he tell you? You're his lawyer. What is he worried about?"

"I think he's worried about what might happen to me. He told me it was better if I didn't know; that way I wouldn't have to lie if someone asked me.

He's too smart to think I would tell someone just because they asked. He thinks I might be in danger, that there are people out there who are worried about what he might know, what he might be getting ready to tell the world."

"There have been some threats," he reminded me. "There have been letters."

I dismissed them for what they were: hollow threats from hollow people, not worth the trouble to report. Craven, because he had never practiced criminal law, thought they were too serious not to report and had turned them over to the police.

"I'm in an unusual situation, Albert. Fitzgerald isn't going to tell me what he is going to say before I call him to the witness stand. And I won't—I can't—tell him that I may know more than he does about what Bridges and his people were planning."

"Jean-Francois," said Craven, not a bit surprised.

"Without whom I would know almost nothing, and with whom," I added with a wistful grin, "I cannot prove anything I know."

"I wouldn't worry too much. One thing I can tell you about my old friend Reynaud is that he is one of the most resourceful men I have known. If there is a way to get something done, Jean-Francois will find it."

Craven's eyes grew bright. There was a glint of recognition, the sudden grasp of a new idea, a connection he had not drawn before.

"It's interesting, isn't it, how little relation there is between someone's intelligence and what happens to them in life? You don't notice this so much at the beginning, or even through most of your career, but now, looking back, it is really quite astonishing. Jean-Francois—he should have been the French ambassador, even the French president, but he spends all these years in a consulate. True, it's in San Francisco, and far from complaining about it, he has always acted as if there was no place, other than Paris, he would rather be. But I've met the French ambassador, here, at a reception a few years ago, and in terms of sheer intelligence and both breadth and depth of learning, there was no comparison, and perhaps that is the reason: his superiors understood that the comparison would never favor them. Then, at the other end of things, the sheer ignorance of Walter Bridges. You never met him, did you? I did, some years ago, here, in San Francisco. He was trying to negotiate with one of my clients the construction of a high-rise apartment building.

"It was probably twenty years ago, but watching him later on television, he didn't seem to have changed as he got older. He was polite, well-mannered, did not argue over anything. But you knew right away that he already knew exactly how things would turn out, that he would agree to so much and no more, and that if he could not get what he wanted, that was fine with him. There were always other buildings, other places. He wanted you to feel he was doing you a favor even to consider doing business with you. Part of it, of course, was the whole New York attitude: San Francisco is a nice little place to visit, but it isn't where the action is.

"Everyone got into the habit of talking about him, when he was in the White House, as a narcissist, as if that could not be said about half the people in America, and good deal more than half of everyone with money. He was simply narrow minded, like a lot of people who think that anything beyond their own range of interest not only isn't important, but—and this is the point—that no one else really thinks anything else is either. This world, your world, my world, is the only world there is, and because, for the last forty years or so, we talk about the rich almost as much as they talk about themselves, if you have made money, a lot of money, that can only mean that you have more intelligence, and more talent, than anyone else around. What difference does it make whether you head a company or the country? You're in charge: everyone has to do what you want.

"What no one wants to believe is that people like Bridges—and God knows I've represented a lot of them—really think that making money proves how smart they are. They have sold the country on that idea. Everyone wants to get rich. And they believed Walter Bridges when he told them all they had to do was listen to him. He did not give political speeches before he became a candidate; he didn't, like Ronald Reagan, go around the country talking about the country's problems and what should be done about them. He made a fortune as a motivational speaker. He would teach you, for a price, how to be great. And then he tells you, after you have paid, that deep down you were great already. And after hearing what you have always wanted to hear, you feel good about yourself, and only later notice that, great or not, you are now in debt."

Craven got up from the chair and walked over to the window behind my desk. It was Saturday morning. He had a luncheon appointment, but even if he had not he would have been dressed in a suit and tie. He could not help himself. He still remembered when all the men wore coats and ties and women wore hats and gloves, when San Francisco demanded, and deserved, at least that much respect.

"The city has gone to hell, Antonelli; nothing is as good as it used to be. Everything has changed, and yet, damn it, if anything, I love it even more. It's like falling in love with a woman, a woman who falls in love with you, and then, without your ever quite knowing why, she isn't in love with you anymore. It breaks your heart, but it has the curious effect of making you remember what you were in danger of forgetting, why you had fallen in love with her in the first place. You can't make her fall in love with you again, but you don't want to lose her."

He had been looking out at the skyline of the city, remembering when the clocktower on the Ferry Building could be seen from every hill in town. I thought that was what he must be thinking, but he was not thinking that at all. With his hands shoved down in his pants pockets, he turned his head just far enough that I could see the look in his eyes, the look that managed to mix a kind of grudging admiration with a warning.

"It's a feeling a little like what Evan Winslow must be feeling now, a feeling he has no doubt felt before when his wife was going to leave him for Kevin Fitzgerald, but perhaps not with quite the same intensity as now, when she is in process of filing for divorce."

I met his gaze, and waited.

"There is no point telling you," he continued, peering down at the floor as he kicked at the carpet, "that I'm worried about you." A smile full of mischief flickered on his lips. "I'd be lying, and it wouldn't change anything you're going to do. Tangerine Winslow…I wonder where she got that name. It fits, though. But that other rumor going around, that's a rumor I'd never believe: that she's getting a divorce so she can marry Joseph Antonelli, the famous lawyer. The day you get married, Antonelli, is the day I remain divorced!"

I started to say something, though I wasn't sure what, but he cut me off. He was having too much fun to stop. Clasping his hands behind his back, he wandered around the room.

"It's part of your charm, the reason women are always so intrigued:

someone who isn't married and isn't even gay. They're intrigued, the way you seem so detached, giving everyone the impression that you must be living the kind of life they wish they had."

Finished with his brief tour of my office, he took his chair. There was a more serious expression on his face.

"I told you she was probably the most beautiful woman I had ever laid eyes on, and I also told you she might be the most dangerous. I was right, wasn't I? Look what she has done to you, made you join the race of mortals. And I remember the story I told you, about that woman in ancient times…"

"I haven't promised to kill myself, Albert, but…"

He caught my meaning, and let it go.

"I still can't believe it, but good for you! I have a hunch you'll do better at marriage than I ever have. Just be careful. I have a hard time believing that Evan Winslow will just let her go. He's never cared what she did, as long as she did not leave him. I'm serious, be careful. I'm not sure there is anything he wouldn't do when he realizes that she means it, that the divorce is real."

"How did you hear that she was filing for divorce? Who told you?"

"Her lawyer, the one she went to. He's an old friend."

Everyone was his old friend.

"And he's the one who told you it was because she was going to marry me?"

"Yes, and if you're worried about anyone else finding out, he's the only one who knows. I certainly won't tell anyone. I'll keep your secret as long as you want."

He was right. It was a secret. Tangerine had told her lawyer, but she had not told me.

Sometimes the easiest way to hide is not to hide at all. Tangerine met me when I got off the ferry from the city and we walked along the streets of Sausalito like just any other pair of out of town visitors. My name might have been reasonably well known, and my picture had been in the papers a few times, and anyone who had been following the trial on television would have seen me often enough, but dressed as I was in an oxford shirt with a sweater thrown around my shoulders, a baseball cap, and dark glasses, no one gave me more than a passing glance. Tangerine was a different story. Even with her hair pulled back in a schoolgirl ponytail, wearing sandals and a simple summer dress, every one stopped to notice. The attention did not bother her. I suppose she was used to it, something that was always there wherever she happened to go. Distant, unapproachable, beautiful beyond description, a woman no man would be fool enough to make a pass at, and no woman would even think to envy or resent. All anyone wanted to do was look. It made them feel better, knowing that someone could really look like her. I suggested it might be more appropriate if I walked three steps back. She slapped me gently on the shoulder and said two would be enough.

We walked along a path that led across a small grass park. A few young children scampered along under their parent's watchful gaze. A couple of wizened veterans of the place, with gray stubbled faces and stiff curly hair, with strange tattered hats and mongrel dogs with tired legs and tired eyes, lay stretched out under the late day sun, resting up for another night of endless drinking. We were holding hands and I could not remember when we had started. The path now ran close to the rocks which, just a few feet below, were beaten by the tide. A few minutes later we were inside the Spinnaker, a restaurant on wooden pilings with glass-sided walls looking out over the water. We had reserved a table at the far end, on the side that faced the city. It was a place I had always liked. San Francisco floated like an island in the distance. If you stayed here long enough, you could watch the city melt away in the golden darkness of the night.

"Do you ever think of me during the trial? Probably not, you have too many other things on your mind."

"Yes, I have too many other things on my mind. No, I don't think of you at all during the trial, not even once."

She did not quite believe me.

"Not even once?"

"Nope. Not once. Not ever."

I could have drowned in her eyes. I wanted to laugh, and she knew it, but to my own astonishment, I discovered that I was serious. I had told her the truth, but the truth had a meaning that I now found fascinating, and perhaps a little…not terrifying, that would be too strong a word, but hazardous, a chance venture into the unknown.

"I don't think about myself while I'm working. I don't wonder how I'm feeling, or what I might do later, while I'm in court. That's why I don't think of you. It's strange, I can't explain it, but you've somehow managed to become more a part of me than I am myself. If that makes any sense."

It made perfect sense to her, and so she laughed and told me I was mad and that she would love me forever. Her voice was now an echo in my mind, words were lost, a silent look all that mattered.

We finished dinner and were drinking coffee when I remembered what had been, until the moment I saw her waiting at the ferry landing, the first thing I was going to ask her.

"I understand you're starting divorce proceedings. Rumor has it you want to marry some lawyer."

It did not surprise her that I knew. Nothing ever did. Whatever happened, she always seemed to be expecting it.

"My lawyer is one of Albert's many good friends. I knew he would tell him, and I knew Albert would tell you. I didn't need to say that I wanted a divorce so I could marry someone else. I didn't need to say it was you. But this way you would have a chance to deny the rumor and steal away into the night. Great headline, don't you think: 'Trial Stopped. Lawyer Can't Be Found. Chased Away by Woman He Only Just Met.'"

"Is that true?" I asked. "Did we only just meet? I can't remember when we didn't know each other."

"That's because," she said, finishing the thought in that breathless voice of hers, "you and I both came to life in the same moment. We met and life began. It's as simple, as wonderful, as that."

And I knew, as well as I had ever known anything, that she was right.

We left the restaurant, and because our only destination was each other, found an empty bench in the park we had walked through earlier, and for a long time sat in silence, watching the sun set the sky on fire as it slid slowly down to the sea. We stayed there until darkness came and the lights on the seven hills across the bay began to glisten like a dancing girl putting on her bright bangled sequin shoes.

CHAPTER
ELEVEN

Evelyn Patterson smiled at the jury. She seldom smiled at anyone else, and almost never at a lawyer in her courtroom, unless it flashed with caustic contempt at what she thought a failure of the deference owed her. It was, now that my head was full of the history of revolutions, like the way so many kings and queens had tried to put their aristocracies, all those privileged noble powers, in subjection: encourage all the forces of democracy with promises of fair treatment and in that way win their gratitude and loyalty. The courtroom was her kingdom, a place where, she insisted with her friendly, watchful eyes, she, and not some paid for lawyer, would tell them what to do and how to think. She, and she alone, would decide what was evidence and what was not. The queen would determine what was good for them to hear.

It was a measure of how habit replaces thought, that you could search for years in all the textbooks ever written and nowhere find a statement of what was obvious to anyone who had spent time in an American courtroom:

the jury was the only purely democratic element in the American system of government. No one was elected to the position, no one ran for the office, no one was appointed. No one was given the job because they had contributed to someone's campaign for governor or mayor. Jurors were chosen the way office holders had been chosen in ancient Athens: the random chance of names drawn from among the citizens. That was the only qualification - citizenship. There were no others. College educated, people who had never read a book, everyone, every citizen, was qualified equally in the eyes of the law to decide the life or death of anyone accused of a crime.

But they were never allowed to exercise this power by themselves. There was always a judge to give them guidance, which, during the course of their service, was absolute. Her decision was final. She ruled the courtroom like a master ruled her slaves. She might be gentle, she might be forgiving, or she might be vengeful and vindictive, but, either way, she never had to explain. Praise you, thank you, or damn you all to hell, if you were a lawyer in her courtroom, you could only stand and listen, and then, when she was finished and you were permitted to speak, say, "Thank you, your Honor," and like a chastened schoolboy sit back down. Kevin Fitzgerald, the man I was defending, had confessed to killing the president because the president's actions had been, or were about to become, tyrannical. Watching Evelyn Patterson, I thought I knew what Fitzgerald must have felt.

The smile for the jury turned to a baleful glance when she turned to Raymond St. John.

"Is the prosecution ready to call its next witness?"

"The prosecution calls Carson Youngblood."

Fitzgerald touched my arm. He knew the witness.

"He's the one—"

"I know," I whispered back. "You told me. I believe you."

He had told me about Youngblood, what Youngblood had done, and I had never doubted that what he said was true. But he had never quite believed me. Some things are too incredible to be believed all at once, if they are ever believed at all. It did not make any difference how many times I said it, he could not quite shake the feeling that I had the same kind of doubt he would have had if someone had told him the same story.

The witness was sworn in. St. John stood at the far end of the jury box, two steps from where Fitzgerald was sitting.

"Would you state your full name for the record?"

"Carson Allen Youngblood."

"How are you employed?"

"I'm with the Secret Service," replied the witness in an understated manner.

St. John, ready with the next question, hesitated.

"You're the head of the Secret Service."

"Yes," said Youngblood with what seemed almost a show of indifference.

The job, not the position, was what mattered. You could see it in the way he held himself, the absence of almost any movement, like a bent coil, ready on the instant to spring forward. He never looked at the jury, the way prosecution witnesses are taught to do. His eyes stayed on St. John, the better, as it seemed, to react to whatever the prosecutor might decide to ask.

"Were you with the president when he flew out here to San Francisco?"

"No, I was in Washington. I was not part of the president's detail."

"When did you find out that the president had been killed?"

"Within minutes of when it happened. Probably less than a minute after agent Todorovich entered the president's cabin and found him lying dead on the floor."

"What did you do when you learned what had happened?"

"I flew right out."

"To take charge of the investigation?"

"Yes, that's correct."

"Isn't that a little unusual? Wouldn't the FBI, not the Secret Service, conduct an investigation into the death of the president?" asked St. John cautiously, as if there were something that neither he nor the witness wanted to reveal.

"That's right; normally, they would have. Our job is to protect the life of the president. The president had just been killed. I had to find out how that could have happened. There wasn't any mystery about who had done it. That wasn't the kind of investigation that had to be made. We weren't looking for the killer. He was already in custody. He had already confessed. We needed to make sure that everything was put on record; we needed to make sure there were no unanswered questions."

St. John moved immediately to the central question, the only one that seemed to count, the one that would leave the jury no alternative but to convict.

"Did you conduct the interview with the defendant, Kevin Fitzgerald?"

"Yes, I did."

"And did he make a full and voluntary confession? Did he confess to the murder of the president, Walter Bridges?"

"Yes, he did."

St. John walked across the front of the courtroom to the court clerk's desk. She handed him a document which he then handed to the witness.

"Is this the confession, the written confession, that, in your presence,

Kevin Fitzgerald signed?"

Holding it in both hands, Youngblood read it over and assured St. John that it was.

"Would you please read it aloud for the jury?"

Lethal in its consequences, it was as simple and uninspiring as a grocery list. There was a date and time, Youngblood's name as witness to Fitzgerald's signature and three short sentences, the bare recital of the facts of murder. Fitzgerald had stabbed Walter Bridges in the throat and in the chest and stomach. He had meant to kill him. He was not sorry that he had. It was "the only way he had left."

"The only way he had left?" I asked as I got up from my chair at the counsel table and began my cross-examination. "The only way he had left to accomplish exactly what?"

Even on cross, Youngblood did not look at the jury. He looked at me, not as he had with St. John, to be quick with his response, but to take my measure, to determine how best to evade telling me anything he did not want me to know.

"This is his written confession, what he put down," he said, nodding toward the document he still held in his hand. "You would have to ask him what he meant."

"There is scarcely any need for that, is there, Mr. Youngblood? There isn't anyone in this country who doesn't know what he meant. It's been in every paper, on every news show. He told every reporter who would listen, he said it when he was first arraigned on the charge. He killed the president because—surely you heard this—it was the only way the country could be saved. But he didn't tell you that, not once, in the whole time he was in your custody. Is that what you want this jury to believe?"

Now, finally, he looked at them.

"It's his confession. What he said at the time."

"At the time. And just how long was that time, Mr. Youngblood?"

He did not like being called mister. He preferred agent or director, which was the reason I would not call him either one.

"How long, Mr. Youngblood; how long did this interview last?"

His gaze was just coming back to mine. The answer was out of his mouth before he had time to think about it.

"Interview? Which one?"

"More than one, then. That would make sense," I remarked, running my hand along the railing of the jury box. "You held him for three days before he was brought into court and from there to the jail where he has been held ever since. How many interviews did you have with him during those three days, Mr. Youngblood? Two, three…more than that?"

When I asked a question, I looked at him, and the moment I finished, I looked at the jury as if I were ready to laugh out loud at the answer Youngblood was sure to give. I knew things, and Youngblood knew I knew them, and we both knew that he would never, even under oath, admit what had happened.

"I really don't know. Several times."

"Several times. Interviewed in the same place?"

His only reply was a blank stare.

"The same place, Mr. Youngblood? The 'undisclosed location' that your agent, Milo Todorovich, has already told us about?"

"What about it?"

I shot him a withering glance, daring him to continue to try the court's patience.

"Where was it, this 'undisclosed location' where you kept the defendant locked away for half a week?"

"I can't tell you that."

"You won't tell me that!" I shot back. I looked up at the bench. "Your Honor?"

The queen was livid. Drumming her long, sharp nails on the hard surface of the bench, she looked down at the witness and let him know that he had no more importance in her courtroom than the bailiff, and probably a good deal less than that.

"We will be glad to let you decide at your leisure, in a place not far from where others who ignore the law spend their days and nights, whether to ignore an order of this court to answer truthfully any question one of the attorneys thinks to ask and that I have not ruled inadmissible. There is nothing inadmissible about the question you were just asked. Trust me when I tell you that you had better answer."

"It's classified!" he protested, angrily.

She did smile at the witness, but only to underscore how ridiculous that protest was.

"Not in my courtroom. Now answer the question."

I saved him the trouble, and did what I could to cause him more.

"You had him taken to an Air Force base fifty miles from here, isn't that correct, Mr. Youngblood?"

"We needed a secure location, somewhere the senator could be kept safe, somewhere—"

"Safe?" I asked, raising an eyebrow. "You were concerned for the safety of the defendant?"

"Yes, of course. After what happened, after he killed the president, you had to know there would be a lot of people who would start thinking about killing him."

"You mean people who thought Walter Bridges a great man, someone who should be president?"

"Yes, and we were right. In those first few days after the assassination, the death threats—people who wanted vengeance, who wanted to get even with Fitzgerald, Senator Fitzgerald, for what he had done—the numbers went through the roof!"

"So your first thought was for the safety of your prisoner?" I asked, staring at him from beneath my lowered brow, trying hard, as I wanted the jury to believe, not to laugh.

"It was one consideration."

"Because of all those death threats you talked about; even though, it is safe to say, not one of them had yet been sent? He was held in an airport hangar, no one was allowed anywhere near him, no one knew yet what had happened, no one knew that Senator Fitzgerald was being held, no one except the Secret Service agents who were, per your instruction, waiting for you to arrive. You should be congratulated, worried about threats that had not been made!"

He started to speak; I waved him off and moved two steps closer. I was now halfway down the length of the jury box.

"When your plane touched down at the airport, it went directly to the hangar where the senator was being held. He was put on that plane, and you then took off and flew to the military base where you held him until four days later he was handed over to the local authorities, here in San Francisco, and finally brought into court. Isn't that what happened?"

"That's right."

"Three days and three nights before you released him to the jurisdiction where he should have been taken the moment he was found in the president's cabin with the murder weapon in his hand?"

"Look, it wasn't like this was any normal kind of crime!" he fairly shouted. "He had just murdered the president of the United States! It was a political assassination! Do you have any idea how many questions that raises? How many questions have to be asked? So, yes, we took Senator Fitzgerald into custody, and we kept him there until—"

"Until you got out of him everything you thought you needed, answers to all those questions you thought you had to ask. How did you ask them?"

Youngblood blinked.

"What do you mean?"

"I mean, how did you ask them? Did you sit across a table and ask questions the way you would if, for example, you and I were having a conversation? Did you ask them, Mr. Youngblood, the way I'm now asking questions of you? Ask a question, listen to the answer, then ask another one?"

He tried to shrug it off, to dismiss by the admission of a minor difference the importance of what I asked.

"He was in a secure facility; he was not in open court."

"He was not free to leave; though, come to think of it, neither are you. But I think we all understand what you mean. He had just killed the president. He was your prisoner."

"He was a prisoner."

I looked straight at him, then lowered my eyes to a spot on the floor and nodded as if this had settled the issue and it was time to move to another line of inquiry.

"And as a prisoner, he had the right to be treated the way we treat anyone arrested for a crime—whatever that crime might be. Is that correct, Mr. Youngblood? Isn't that the law?"

Youngblood became solemn, subdued, searching my eyes to see how far I was willing to go, to see whether I thought he would really tell the truth.

"There was nothing wrong with the way he was treated."

My eyes shot wide with wonder and then, shaking my head, I walked to the counsel table and stood behind Fitzgerald, sitting in his chair closest to the jury box.

"These questions you thought so important, so vital, to get answered— what were they about?"

Youngblood knew where I was going, but I was almost certain St. John did not. Youngblood was on his own, with no time to think. He acted on instinct, the way he had been trained.

"The president had just been murdered. A United States senator had killed him. The first question, the only question, was who else was involved? If there was one who wanted him dead, there might have been others. And if they had murdered the president, who were they planning to murder next? We had no idea what we were dealing with. If there was a conspiracy, if Fitzgerald had not acted alone, were they going to stop with the president? What about the vice-president? Would they murder the president just to let the vice-president take over? The first thing I did, after I was told about the murder, before I ever reached the plane, was to direct that the vice-president, the Speaker, everyone in the line of succession, be taken to the secure places that had been set up for use in the case of a terrorist attack on the White House or the Capitol."

"You thought it might be an attack, not just on the president, but the whole leadership of the government?"

"Yes, exactly; that's why—"

"Why you did what you did: asked Senator Fitzgerald to tell you what he knew. We understand. And what did he tell you? Did he tell you he was part of a conspiracy?"

"No, he didn't."

"Did he tell you that there had been anyone else involved, that someone else might have helped him in some way?"

"No."

"Did he tell you that he had discussed what he was going to do with anyone else, come to them for counsel or advice?"

"No, he said he had never even mentioned the possibility to another person."

Smiling, I looked over at the jury, and then turned for just a moment to the courtroom crowd.

"Not even when he told the Senate of the United States that the presidency of Walter Bridges was a threat to the country, a remark which, for some reason, Jenny Ann Carruthers insisted was a threat on the president's life? Never mind," I said, turning back to the witness. "You don't have to answer that."

I had caught a glimpse of a now familiar face sitting in the very last row, and with that glimpse proved myself a liar as I tried without complete success to banish from my conscious mind the thought of her.

"Did he tell you anything that suggested, in any way, the involvement of other people?" I asked with the vanishing remnant of a smile that only made sense to me.

"No, nothing."

"He told you, in other words, that he had acted alone, didn't he?"

"That's what he said."

"But that wouldn't have been the end of it, would it? There were other things you wanted to know. You knew he had killed Walter Bridges. He told you no one else was involved. You must have asked him why he did it, what reason could have led him to such a drastic act. He's a United States senator, his career—his life—all in front of him. What did he tell you when you asked him why he had given all that up to murder Walter Bridges?"

Genuinely puzzled, Youngblood furrowed his brow and slowly shook his head.

"He never really answered that question. He said he did not have a choice. He kept repeating that. He did not have a choice, because he had to stop Bridges from doing what he was about to do, that there was not time to stop him any other way."

"Did he strike you as in any way demented, delusional, irrational, out of control, someone who did not know what he doing or what he was saying?"

"No, not at all. He was as calm, as collected, as anyone. It surprised me a little."

"Surprised you?"

"I would have expected more emotion—anger, rage, contrition, sorrow—something by way of reaction to what he had done. The impression I got instead was of someone intensely interested—that's the only way I can describe it—intensely interested in everything that was going on, as if he wanted to make sure he would remember it all later, every detail, every word. It was as if he was making mental notes, the way someone does when they are planning, first chance they have, to make a written record of everything they had observed."

I did not doubt he was right. Fitzgerald was playing for the highest stakes imaginable, perhaps the highest stakes any American had ever played for. He had killed a president to become a national savior, killed the president to become the president and maybe even something more than that: the new founder of a new republic. Why would he not be thinking of how to chronicle the importance of his own, historic achievement. Kill the king and wear the crown, or be drawn and quartered for your trouble.

"He answered all the questions you asked, all the questions you asked during those three days in close confinement?"

"He answered what he was asked."

"He confessed to his crime?"

"He did."

"That written confession you read into evidence?"

"Yes."

"And he didn't say anything, nothing that was written in that confession, about the reasons why he did it? Even though, as you just testified, he kept telling you that he had to do it, that it was the only way to save the country?"

"He didn't include it in his written statement."

"Or you didn't include it when you had that statement typed up."

"Are you saying that—"

"The reasons weren't that important, were they?" I asked, my voice harsh, demanding, insistent. "What was important was finding out, as quickly as possible, whether anyone else was involved, if there was a conspiracy, if other people were at risk. Isn't that what you told us just a few moments ago, that you had to take him into custody, had to take him to a place where no one could interrupt what you were doing? Isn't that what you said?"

"Yes, there wasn't any choice. We had to—"

"Had to find out, whatever you had to do. You asked him questions, he answered them, correct?"

"Yes, he answered them."

"And you believed him, believed he was telling the truth when he said he had acted alone, that no one else was involved."

"Yes, I believed him, believed he had acted alone."

I cocked my head, and with a broad, knowing smile told him he was a liar.

"No, you didn't; you didn't believe him at all—not at first. It was only after you had tortured him, over and over again, and he kept telling you the same thing, that what he did, he did alone, that you finally decided he was telling the truth. Isn't that right, Mr. Youngblood? You tortured him, because it was the only way you could be sure that someone else the Secret Service was sworn to protect did not get murdered as well!"

"That isn't true!" he cried, sitting bolt upright. "That's a damn lie!"

"Is it?" I asked as I quickly moved across to the clerk's table and picked up an exhibit of my own. "This photograph was taken by someone from quite a distance away, but perhaps you can identify the man being led by two other men to a plane, the plane in which you had just landed."

I handed him the photograph. He glanced at it and handed it right back.

"The defendant, Kevin Fitzgerald."

"Are you sure? Do you want to look again? You can't really see his face in this picture. He's wearing a black bag over his head."

"He had just murdered the president! Did you think we were just going to walk him to the plane?"

"No, but I would have thought, as willing as he was to talk about what he had done, and the reasons why he had done it, that you might not have subjected him to sleep deprivation in a windowless cement cell in which there was no furniture of any kind, and with lights so bright that even with your eyes shut tight it was never dark."

Youngblood denied it.

"That isn't where he was kept. He had a bed, he was allowed to sleep."

"And after he told you what he knew, gave you answers to your questions, told you no one else was involved, you had his head covered again, didn't you?"

He just looked at me. It was his word against the word of a confessed assassin.

"You had to know if he was telling the truth, so you used that technique that serves a double purpose: it gives you the information you want, and it doesn't leave behind any evidence of what you did. Kevin Fitzgerald was waterboarded, wasn't he—over and over again, and always the same question: was anyone else involved, was he part of a conspiracy. And each time, over and over again, the same answer, screamed so often that, finally, you believed him. Isn't that right, Mr. Youngblood; isn't that exactly what you did: tortured Kevin Fitzgerald until he almost died? What would you have done then, dropped him in the ocean from your plane and called it accidental death by drowning? That's all, Mr. Youngblood, your time as a witness is over. Your time as a fit subject for investigation is, I hope, only beginning!"

CHAPTER TWELVE

Every day, from the moment the doors to the courtroom opened until Evelyn Patterson ended the proceedings with a caution to the jury not to discuss the case with anyone, Tricia Fitzgerald sat in the first row, directly behind her husband. It was a lawyer's trick, by now become a habit, to put there the wife, the husband, the mother, the child, anyone who proved by their presence that the defendant was not entirely without redeemable qualities. She played her part as well as anyone ever had. She never wore the same thing twice, but always came dressed in conventional, conservative clothing. Her hair, her makeup, everything was done to give an impression of middle-class normality. She was, she seemed to say with every careful breath she took, just like everyone else. Or rather, what everyone else placed in her unenviable position would like to be: a woman loyal to a fault, who, whatever her husband might have done, would never think of anything but how she could make easier whatever road he might now have to travel. She was a charming, accomplished fraud.

"That photograph. We want it."

She was sitting on the other side of my desk. There was a brittle edge to her voice.

"What photograph? What are you talking about?"

It was nearly six o'clock. I had been in trial all day, and had barely had time to loosen my tie when she walked in.

"The one you introduced into evidence, the one where Kevin is being led away by those two thugs, the one with his head covered in that black hood. That photograph!"

She said this as if it were somehow my fault that her husband had been treated like someone who had just assassinated the president.

"It's in evidence. It doesn't belong to you."

"You must have copies."

"It's in evidence. It will stay in the court file."

"We're going to need it!" she persisted. "After the trial is over, after Kevin is acquitted. We need it to show how far these people were willing to go, what Kevin was fighting against."

I was too tired to put up with this, too tired of her constant intrusion into what I was trying to do, the endless questioning, the endless complaints.

"What he was fighting against? You think what Youngblood did was bad? You think your husband was mistreated? If I had been in Youngblood's shoes, I would have done exactly the same thing he did."

She did not believe me. It was obvious that, for whatever reason, I was lying. She was certain of it.

"You spent all day destroying him, you took him apart. There isn't anyone who believes he was telling the truth after what you did to him on cross-examination. Everyone knows what he did, how he had Kevin tortured!"

Leaning back, I searched for wisdom in the ceiling.

"Do you know how easy it is to change the meaning of things? Everything would have been different if he had not lied, if he had just admitted what he had done, that faced with the possibility that others might be targets, he had to do whatever was necessary to find out. And if that meant waterboarding, it's a small enough price to pay. I would have done exactly what Youngblood did, and so would your husband."

I kept watching her, wondering when there would be some change in that impassive face she wore like a shield to her emotions; I wondered if she had any real feeling at all. It was all too analytical, the way she listened, waiting to respond. Her eyes never moved.

"You're wrong; Kevin would never have done anything like what they did to him."

It was almost predictable—maddening, but predictable—how she could ignore whatever might contradict her interpretation of events. Her husband would never countenance torture for the same reason Youngblood had lied about it. Among civilized people that sort of thing was never done. I was not in a mood to indulge her sensibilities.

"Youngblood, though he won't admit it, did what he thought was necessary to save the government, the duly elected government, of the country. But you think it wrong?"

"Torture," she replied, with complete moral certainty, "is never right."

"If necessity is never an excuse for torture, it's a good thing you're not on your husband's jury."

"Why? I don't—"

"Necessity is no excuse for torture, but it is for murder? You see no inconsistency, no hypocrisy, in that?"

She thought she better teach me law.

"The law of necessity: kill someone because it is the only way to save others. The mountain climbers on a rope, remember? There aren't any cases where torture is allowed."

"There aren't any cases where murder is allowed when necessity isn't imminent."

"But it was imminent, the threat to the country Kevin stopped."

"Maybe, if Bridges had his finger on the nuclear trigger and Kevin had to stop him. Haven't you wondered why he doesn't really talk about what it was that was so awful, so terrible in its consequences, that he had to do what he did?" I searched her eyes for the answer to the question I had not been able to get Fitzgerald to address. "Every time I ask him, he says it will all come out when he testifies."

"He's probably just protecting both of us. It's obvious, isn't it? Kevin knows things. Bridges is dead, but his people—some of them testified in court—were involved, whatever he was doing. Kevin can't tell anyone, not until he's on the witness stand. Then the whole world will know."

My eyes started for the ceiling again, but I was now too angry to search for reason.

"That's what he says. But how exactly does that protect you or me? If they grab you off the streets, how are they supposed to know he never told you? After you've been tortured? He isn't protecting you, and he isn't protecting me. He's protecting himself."

She did not protest; she did not even disagree. She seemed puzzled, not by anything that had been said, but by her own failure to have grasped this simple fact. Her loyalty had betrayed her, made her accept at face value what, as it turned out, was false coin. Her husband was holding something back from her. She was not as much interested in what it was than in why he might have done it. The look on her face asked the question for her. I was not much help.

"I told him at the beginning, I told you both, that I had to know everything, that I expected answers to any question I asked. But he won't tell me anything about the reason why he did it, why he thought he had to do it, nothing beyond vague assurances that there was not any choice. Sometimes, I have to tell you, I almost think he isn't sure himself, that he's still trying to come up with an excuse, an explanation that he can use to argue that what he did was the selfless act of a hero, a patriot. It makes my job almost impossible. He gets on the stand, tells his story, and then, hearing that story for the first time, I have to somehow come up with the kind of corroborating evidence that will convince the jury that he is telling the truth, and that it isn't something he made up."

"He isn't making anything up. Whatever happened, whatever he found out, it's the truth," she insisted, a little too forcefully.

She was struggling to maintain the confidence of her belief that her husband would never lie to her. She felt even more compelled to prove that what he had done was on a level higher than what his enemies were capable of attaining.

"The law of necessity. Even if you were right and torture was in some circumstances the only choice, it was not the case here. They knew, or should have known, that Kevin acted alone. Remember what the first witness for the prosecution said: they only decided when they landed in San Francisco to invite Kevin aboard the plane. There could not be a conspiracy, because no one else could have known when Kevin would have any contact with Walter Bridges."

Unless the conspirators had agreed in advance to act whenever they heard that the president had been killed. But there was no point in mentioning this to her. It was useless speculation about things that had not happened. Better to leave her what was left of the certainty of her belief that her husband had done nothing not the part of ancient heroes, the men who had conquered kingdoms and brought new prosperity and glory to the lands they now ruled. Not every fairy tale is false.

She left my office an hour after she had come, and I knew she would be there the next morning, sitting in the same place in court, ready with an eager smile of encouragement when, in full view of the jury, Kevin Fitzgerald, just before he took his seat next to me, would with unmistakable affection turn and smile at her. It was one of the only things in this bizarre trial I could honestly predict.

There was an inch-high stack of phone messages on my desk, half of them from reporters hoping to get me to say something about what the defendant was planning to do, some from prospective clients with the mistaken belief that a lawyer in a trial on national television must know what he was doing, and, I suspected, the hope that their case might end up part of the pictured memory that had almost completely replaced written history in the public mind. All of these could wait. There were two that could not. The one from Jean-Francois Reynaud was brief but urgent. I called the private number he had left and got a recording. Thirty seconds after I left the message that I was returning his call, he called back. Could I meet him at eight o'clock in the place we had met before.

The other message was from Tangerine, telling me she would call later. I felt like a kid in high school, wondering if the girl he kept calling would ever come to the phone. I started to call her, then thought better of it. If she had wanted that, she would have asked. I had an hour before my meeting with Reynaud and at least four hours of work to get through. It was the necessary preparation for another day in trial: witness statements, biographies, background information, every imaginable detail about the lives of anyone the prosecution was likely to call, including especially the witnesses who had already testified and I was in all probability going to recall as witnesses for the defense. Most of it was dry, routine, the dull, dreary catalogue of what, for most of them, had been the anonymous steps up the public ladder: elections won, elections lost, positions taken, positions changed, loyalties given, loyalties denied, the slow transition from the bright-eyed eagerness of the young reformer, certain that they could never be corrupted, to the squinting self-confidence of the political operative learned in all the virtues of deception. Criminals of the kind I usually represented were more honest. They did not lie about what they were. Politicians, those I was reading about, cared only about the image they created, the image they thought other people, those vast majorities they wanted, needed, to have, wanted, needed, to have of them. It was a mistake to call them hollow; they were solid glass, reflecting back whatever you came looking for. But not all of them. There were a few who were exactly what others thought they were. Their error was the failure to understand that the sincerity of their belief did not make their convictions true. The ones made of solid glass led wherever others wanted to go; these people would take everyone in one direction, whether anyone else wanted to go there or not. The best example was the witness the prosecution was going to call next, the new president's chief of staff.

I did as much as I could until it was time to leave. There was more work to do, but I could get to it later tonight or early in the morning. Jean-

Francois would not have called if there was not something more important than a last review of material I now knew almost by heart. I left the building and started looking for a cab. It was not yet dark and the streets were full of noise, cars jammed close together, drivers honking, shouting, their impatience. People waited in a bunched-up crowd for a red light to change. Smart-looking couples hustled down the sidewalk, eager to get to dinner. An old, gray-haired lady pulled a tattered canvas two-wheeled cart in her heavy, thick-soled shoes. The blind man at the corner newsstand carefully counted out change by the measured touch of his aging fingers.

"Let me give you a ride."

The backseat door of a long black Lincoln had opened just in front of me. The voice seemed familiar; the face, when he leaned across the backseat and repeated the invitation, was the last one I expected to see. Without hesitation, oblivious to everything except an extreme curiosity to know what Carson Youngblood thought he was doing, I got in.

The driver, wearing dark glasses though it was now twilight, immediately started up the street.

"I wanted to apologize," said Youngblood, more relaxed and far friendlier than he had been in court. "I don't have to tell you that I lied. My only excuse is that I didn't have any choice."

I did not know what he was after, why he was doing this, but I did not like it. Did he expect that I would give him my approval, tell him that I understood, that there were no hard feelings?

"You lied under oath. That's called perjury. But I don't think I have to tell you that, do I?"

Youngblood looked at me for a moment, then looked out the window on his side of the car. He did not say anything, nothing, not a word. We sat in silence as the car moved steadily through traffic, until we were on the street that ran the length of Golden Gate Park.

"Where are we going? I have somewhere I have to be. You offered me a ride, not an invitation to a kidnapping."

Youngblood laughed. He turned away from the view out his window.

"I can't be seen with you. I can't afford to have anyone know I've even talked to you. There are some things you should know, things that might help you understand the situation you're in."

He seemed friendly enough, but his words seemed like a warning, perhaps even a threat.

"There was not any other way to talk to you. I couldn't call your office and make an appointment."

He seemed to think this quite funny. The reason escaped me entirely.

"So you decided to pick me up outside my office. How did you know I'd be there? How did you know what time?"

Youngblood rolled his eyes, and bobbed his head from side to side.

"You go back to your office every day after trial, and sometime later you leave. Why? Did you think you were under some kind of sophisticated surveillance? I'm afraid not, Mr. Antonelli. We just waited up the street. It's old fashioned, I know, but it works."

We had reached 19th Street and turned right through the west end of the park. The road led directly to the bridge.

"This happened to me once before," I remarked as we approached the toll plaza. "A few years ago. There was a case involving another U.S. senator, Jeremy Fullerton. He wasn't, like Fitzgerald, accused of anything. Fullerton was murdered, and I was defending a young black college student charged with killing him. He had not done it, and eventually he was cleared. He finished college, graduated from medical school and is now a physician. Fullerton, on the other hand, had not lived such an honorable life. He had been involved with the Russians—yes, it happened before— had taken a lot of money from them, funded his campaign, financed the way he lived. Everything had been arranged by an old Russian spy, a man named Bogdonovitch, who had stayed in San Francisco when the Soviet Union collapsed and he was, as he used to put it, suddenly out of a job. Bogdonovitch killed Fullerton, but that's another story. In the middle of the trial, someone with the government—our government—did what you're doing now, took me for a ride over the Golden Gate and gave me all the reasons why I shouldn't dig too deeply into Fullerton's past, that it would be better if this one kid got convicted than what Fullerton had been doing ever came out. He was very clear, this member of the government. He was sitting in the backseat, just like you are, and he had a driver, just like you have, and they stopped in the middle of the bridge and told me to get out and to think about how many people jumped off the bridge, their deaths declared suicide, as I walked to the other side."

"And did you, think about what he told you while you walked to the other side?"

"Not a lot. I was thinking mainly of how goddamn cold it was and how much I hated heights. Now, if you're going to threaten me, go ahead and do it, but if you think it is going to make any difference…"

He ignored me. We continued on in silence, across the great bridge with the long, twisted cables that look like harp strings in the somber light of dusk. When we reached the other side, he tapped the driver on the shoulder and told him to pull off at the vista point on the right. The car came to a stop and we got out and walked to the guardrail at the edge of the sheer cliff and, hundreds of feet below, the swirling waters of the bay.

"What my agent, Milo Todorovich, told you when you were cross-examining him in court is true. Bridges was everything he said he was: violent temper, unable to concentrate on anything for more than a few seconds, watching television all the time, the only thing he seemed to care about was what people were saying about him."

Far away and yet close enough to touch, the city started flickering into life. I shoved my hands in my pockets and listened carefully to what Youngblood was saying, wondering why he had gone to so much trouble to bring me out to this deserted place on the far side of the bridge.

"I've been thirty years with the service, and I've seen and heard some things that make you wonder what would happen if people really knew the kind of men they have sometimes elected to be leaders of the free world. But whatever their failings, there wasn't one of them who did not have some idea of their responsibility to the office. Bridges did not feel any responsibility for anything, except to himself. Listen," he went on, staring across at the dancing lights of the city, "even that isn't quite true. Every president we have had felt a responsibility to himself—it's the nature of ambition. They wanted to leave their mark, to be remembered for doing things for their country, important things. They did not always succeed, probably most of them failed, but that was what they wanted. Do you know how often, usually late at night, some of them decided they wanted to go out to the Lincoln Memorial, go out there when no one else was around. They would stand there, looking up, and you knew that they were wondering if they would ever have the chance to be tested like Lincoln was, and, if they were, whether they would reach that kind of greatness. You could see it on their faces, the hope, the doubt, and the regret; regret that they had not lived in earlier times when they thought things were not as complicated, as difficult, as they had become. But Bridges? It's the last thing he would have done; it's the last thing he would have thought about. You want to know the secret that explains what Bridges was? It's easy. Nothing existed except what he wanted now, this minute. Everything was impulse. He was nothing but a child, an overgrown child who would crush anything, or anyone, he did not like. He did not like Fitzgerald, he did not like him at all. He didn't invite him on the plane."

I did not understand at first what Youngblood was saying. It had come too fast, without a pause. Then, when it hit me, when I realized what he had said, I still was not sure what it meant.

"Bridges did not want to see Fitzgerald. There was a big fight about it," explained Youngblood.

"A fight? Between Bridges and…?"

"Michael Donahue. Ellison was chief of staff, but Ellison did not carry any real weight. He was there to make sure everything was scheduled properly, that everyone knew what they were supposed to do. If he had an opinion about anything, he kept it to himself. Donahue was the only one with real influence; the only one Bridges never screamed at—until that day on the plane. Todorovich was standing just outside the door. The door was open. He heard everything. 'I'm not going to see that son of a bitch!' Bridges shouted. 'Why bother? He wants to run against me. What am I going to tell him, that it isn't going to happen, that he'll never get the chance? That would be smart as hell, wouldn't it?'"

"He said that?" I asked sharply. "He said, 'he'll never get the chance'? What did he mean? Do you know?"

Youngblood narrowed his eyes, concentrating on what he remembered.

"Todorovich told me what he heard. He remembered it almost word for word, and I wrote it down so I would not forget. That's what Bridges said. I'm not sure what he meant. But whatever he meant, it did not stop Donahue from insisting that he meet with Fitzgerald when they landed. He said that the reason Bridges did not want to was the reason why he should. 'We have to do everything we can to keep him in the dark.'"

"In the dark about what? What were they planning? Fitzgerald was not going to be able to run against Bridges, and they wanted to keep him from finding out how they were going to stop him? That has to be it. They must have had something on him, something they could use to keep him from trying to run against Bridges for the presidency. But for some reason they didn't want Fitzgerald to find out."

Youngblood was not listening. He was too absorbed in what he had been told, the story he was now trying to tell me with as much accuracy as he could.

"Bridges didn't care. Fitzgerald and 'all the others like him, could go to hell.' He wasn't going to see him and there wasn't any point trying to get him to change his mind. Donahue told him he did not have any choice. Fitzgerald had already been invited. It was too late to tell him the meeting had been cancelled. That's when Bridges went ballistic. He started screaming obscenities, accusing Donahue of always doing things behind his back, always telling him one thing and doing another, always—"

"He said—Donahue said that Fitzgerald had already been invited? When was this, after they had landed?"

"No, not after they had landed—during the flight."

"Jonathan Reece, the president's assistant, testified that he was sent down from the plane to invite Fitzgerald on board."

"I know; I heard. I have no reason to think he was not telling the truth."

"And Ellison testified that Bridges told him to do it. He never mentioned Donahue. What made Bridges change his mind? Why did he decide, after screaming at Donahue that he would not even talk to Fitzgerald, to invite him on Air Force One?"

The prospect of a brief face to face meeting with Fitzgerald had made Bridges apoplectic. It struck me as a case of nerves, tension reaching a breaking point when something is about to happen that, one way or the other, will change everything. What could they have been planning, what could they have had on Fitzgerald, that would have put Bridges so much on edge?

"Something they made up, something that isn't true, something that, if anyone found out, would blow up in their faces?" I ventured.

Youngblood kicked at a rock on the pavement, put his hands on the small of his back and after one last glance across the bay, gave me a strange, ironic look.

"A false story, with just enough circumstantial evidence, that he was planning to murder the president? It's not impossible. They said the purpose of the trip was so that Bridges could speak at the tech convention. That was what the public was told. But he was here to do a few other things as well. He was scheduled to meet privately with a couple of executives from companies that specialize in cyber warfare, how you screw up someone's electronic system, how you protect your own system from someone's interference. This is the interesting part. The two companies involved work with the government on some really highly classified things—you never heard this from me—the kind of cyber warfare that makes the attack look like it comes from someone else. They can invent anything, create a whole chain of evidence, email messages, phone records, anything they need to make you believe that something has happened that never happened at all."

With a grim expression, Youngblood searched my eyes, as if I knew the answer to a question he was almost afraid to ask.

"Do you think Fitzgerald did the right thing? I'm sworn to protect the life of the president, but before Bridges, I never had to ask myself if my oath included someone who might be planning treason. That's what Fitzgerald thought, isn't it, that killing him was the only choice he had? Ever since it happened, I keep wondering if he was right. I brought you out here to clear my conscience. I don't know how important it is, but I thought you should know why Bridges was coming out here and what happened on the plane, when he and Donahue got into it."

He would lose more than his career, he would be facing the possibility of prison time for what he had told me. I trusted him; I hoped he trusted me.

"I won't use any of this in a way that can be traced back."

We started back to the car. The lights from the Golden Gate cast everything in shadow.

"You had Fitzgerald for three days. Anything you can tell me, anything that struck you as peculiar?"

It was an unusual question for a lawyer to ask about his own client, but, as Youngblood instinctively understood, there was nothing normal about the series of events in which we had both found ourselves involved. His first reaction was to emit a short, almost noiseless laugh, a grunting acknowledgment of the obvious, that everything about it had been peculiar. Then he changed his mind.

"The most peculiar thing was that it was not really peculiar at all. It was fascinating—though let me add right away that I only thought about it later—that he did not seem the least bit angry or upset. He never shouted, never demanded an attorney, insisted on his rights, never showed the least bit of defiance, and he never, not even once, showed any sign of feeling guilty about what he had done. He treated us with—and I know this must sound strange—complete respect. And it wasn't just because he thought we were only doing our jobs. He seemed interested in how we did them. It was like a training exercise in which he was playing the part of a captured terrorist, going through an interrogation, being waterboarded, as if it were all pretend, knowing that he wouldn't be treated nearly as harshly as he would if it were real; knowing that, at the end of it, he would not only walk away but join in the discussion about the ways in which we might improve the technique. I can't quite put my finger on it. Maybe it was because he believed what he did was right; maybe that is the power of being willing to become, if necessary, a martyr to a cause. But I think it was something more than that. I don't think he thinks he is guilty of anything; he thinks he is innocent."

Jean-Francois Reynaud was still waiting, an hour after I was supposed to meet him. He had told me it was a matter of some urgency, but that meant in the French translation, as he explained to me with Gallic calm, that it was also urgent that he not leave before he saw me.

"I was taken for a ride," I remarked as I slid into my side of the booth.

"Not for the first time, I imagine,' he replied with a droll smile. Sitting against the corner of the booth, a drink in his hand, he shoved a plain manila envelope across the table. "You may find these of some interest," he said as I pulled out a handful of documents and, what surprised me more, half a dozen photographs.

"These are...?"

"Photographs taken of various meetings between several different Americans and several different Russians. The Americans—you will find three of them—are all people you know. One of the Russians is a banker who is close friends with Putin, one is the Russian ambassador to France, while the other is a general in the Russian army, the head of their cyber warfare division. Now, there are certain rules..." Pausing to take a drink, his expression could not have been more serious. "You can keep the photographs, and you can use them any way you see fit. The only condition is that you do not reveal to anyone at any time where you got them or who took them. They can't be traced back to us any other way. The documents, the transcripts of what was being said when the photographs were taken, are the transcripts I gave to you before. My government won't allow them to leave my possession, but there is no objection if you want to study them and taken any notes you please. But, again," he continued, "you do so on the condition that you never reveal how you have this information. Are we agreed?"

"And where am I supposed to work my way through all this," I asked, thumbing through a pile at least six inches thick, "if they have to remain in your possession?"

Reynaud shrugged his shoulders as if the answer was plain to anyone with the limited intelligence needed to see it.

"Why, right here, of course!" He lifted his hand to signal the waiter. "I have a very good relationship with the owner. I may be his best customer.

Would you like something to eat? I've had dinner."

I ordered a sandwich and coffee; he ordered a bottle of sparkling wine.

"It's champagne, rather good champagne, but because it comes from California and not from France, they can't call it that. Some think it unfair, but we own the name, and we are, if nothing else, meticulous when it comes to language. Champagne is, always will be, French. So, while you work through all these astonishing papers, I will sit here and consume each glass of this American imitation and pretend I know the difference."

Reynaud had emptied the bottle sometime after midnight, before I finally finished.

CHAPTER
THIRTEEN

Michael Donahue was the prosecution's last witness, and even as he was being sworn in, I was not certain why Raymond St. John had decided to call him. He had proven his case: Walter Bridges had been murdered, stabbed to death with a knife; the defendant, found next to the body, the knife still in his hand, had confessed to the crime. All the elements of the crime had been proven beyond any, much less a reasonable, doubt. My confusion ended with the prosecution's first question. I had forgotten that this was as much a political as it was a criminal trial.

"When did President Bridges first come to believe that Senator Fitzgerald might be willing to do anything, including violence, to keep him from accomplishing what he had promised the American people he would do?"

"Objection!" I cried before I was halfway out of my chair. "One, it's hearsay; second, it's completely irrelevant to the case!"

St. John had prosecuted too many cases not to come equipped with a practiced smile that advertised indulgence for the ignorance with which an objection has been made.

"The witness is testifying to what he was told directly by the president; not what he thinks the president may have thought. And with regard to what is relevant and what is not, I would remind my learned friend that it is the defense, not the prosecution, that wants to argue the law of necessity. The prosecution is certainly entitled to show that the defendant had threatened violence before this so-called necessity could ever possibly have arisen."

Evelyn Patterson tapped the eraser end of a pencil three times in quick succession on the bench. Then she tapped it once against her chin.

"Yes, all right, I'll allow it." She bent her head toward the witness stand on her left. "You may answer, Mr. Donahue."

Donahue was tall, overweight, with sloping shoulders and a double chin. His hands were small, soft and puffy. His heavy-lidded eyes were as strange as any I had seen. Grayish-blue, they moved with a kind of relentless irritation, as if everything that came under their stern, implacable scrutiny invariably failed to come up to some standard of his own devising.

He had listened to the question, he had listened to the judge rule on my objection, and he had not moved. He just sat there, slouched in the witness chair, wishing he did not have to be here at all.

"When did the president first decide Senator Fitzgerald was a threat?" repeated St. John.

"Within twenty-four hours of the election. As soon as it was known that Walter Bridges was going to be our next president. No, I'm wrong," he said as he lurched forward and pointed a short, accusing finger at Kevin Fitzgerald, sitting next to me. "You started making threats before all the returns were in, before the votes were counted. You don't remember? On television, you said that if Bridges won, it would be the worst thing that had ever happened to the country. And then you said, remember, that there wouldn't be any way Bridges would be able to serve a full term. You'd make sure it never happened!"

"Your Honor," I complained, "would you please instruct the witness to address himself to the court and not attack the defendant!"

"Sorry, your Honor," apologized Donahue before she could reply. "But after what he did, I just couldn't…"

St. John caught his eye, stopping him before he could say another word.

"A lot of things are said in the heat of a campaign," he reminded him. "Isn't it possible that Senator Fitzgerald meant those remarks in a purely political sense, that he would oppose him in the Senate, try to block whatever the president might try to do, even, in the most extreme case, try to remove him from office through impeachment?"

The impatient eyes of Michael Donahue opened wide with contempt.

"There isn't any doubt what he meant: the president had to die."

There was a hush in the courtroom, everyone waiting to see what was going to happen next. Donahue turned and faced the jury.

"He told me a week after the election, during the transition. I visited him in his Senate office. We hoped that, despite everything that had been said during the campaign, we could develop a working relationship with the other side. No one had been more vocal in their criticisms of Walter Bridges, but we knew Senator Fitzgerald was an intelligent man, and though we disagreed with his politics, we thought we might find at least some common ground. But he didn't want to talk about anything except the election, how Bridges should never have won, that there were too many questions about how it had happened, that the whole thing was a sham. The only real question was how much Bridges knew about what the Russians had done. I tried to point out to him that whatever the Russians may have tried to do, they had not changed any votes. All the votes had been counted and Walter Bridges had won the election. I kept insisting that the only real issue was whether we could now work together for the good of the country, or whether he and the other members of his party were more interested in trying to destroy a presidency just because they lost. That is when he told me that a Bridges presidency would not last, that someone was sure to kill him. And then he added—I'll never forget it—that if no one else did it, he might have to do it himself!"

Fitzgerald had me by my sleeve, insisting it had never happened. I looked at him and, knowing the jury was watching, nodded my agreement. I scribbled a note to myself on how to use this on cross, and then watched while St. John led his witness step by step through what was meant to be the final, crushing blow to our only hope of a defense.

"The defendant's anger, his willingness to threaten violence against the president, was based on his belief that the election of Walter Bridges was in some sense illegitimate, the result of foreign interference?"

"They were all angry about that, Fitzgerald more than most. It wasn't just that they had lost, it was that Bridges was going to change things in ways they had not been changed before. We weren't going to be bound by what Washington thinks, by what, no matter which party is in power, are the agreed upon limitations of what can be done, or even thought about. They were right when they accused us of being revolutionaries. That is exactly what we were, though not in the way they meant it. They thought—Fitzgerald thought—we were there to declare war on government, that we were going to dismantle the Washington bureaucracy. They never understood—they still don't understand—that we—I mean, President Bridges—was determined to change not just the way government works, but the way government thinks, what its purpose is."

The more Donahue spoke, the more, it seemed, he wanted to say, and the less St. John wanted him to go on. He tried to keep him on point.

"The defendant was angry about the election and a week or so later told you that if someone else did not do it, he would kill the president," said St. John, as calm as if he were relating a well-known story. "Were there any other occasions when, to your knowledge, the defendant did or said something threatening?"

"Almost every speech he gave on the Senate floor, almost—"

"Objection!" I said without raising my voice or rising from my chair.

"Sustained. Mr. Donahue, you were asked a specific question. Give a specific answer, if you can. Were there other, specific threats of the kind you just described?"

Donahue was not interested in what Evelyn Patterson thought was the way he should answer. Grim-faced and determined, he stared straight ahead until she finished.

"Every speech he gave, and almost every day the Senate Intelligence Committee met."

"Mr. Donahue, I—"

But her complaint died in a sea of noise, everyone talking at once, wondering what secret information Donahue had decided to reveal. The proceedings of the Senate Intelligence Committee were always kept confidential. But that apparently was not going to stop Donahue from using what he knew to attack the credibility of the defense. St. John did not know what to make of it.

"Every time the Senate Intelligence Committee met, Senator Fitzgerald would insist that the president had to go, that—"

"Objection!" I shouted, springing out of my chair so quickly that it almost tripped over. "This is the same thing another one of the prosecution's witnesses tried to do, twist the meaning of words out of all recognition."

"Mr. Donahue!" shouted Judge Patterson in her turn. "Damn it, look at me when I'm talking to you. You're not in Washington now, you're in a court of law. Either answer the question you're asked or face the consequences."

St. John started to ask another question, but Patterson did it for him. With a glance that promised a long stay in hell if he did not do exactly what she told him, she asked him point blank if he had himself ever heard the senator threaten the president during a session of the Senate Intelligence Committee. When he answered, with a show of reluctance, that he had not, her glance became deadly.

"You're not on the committee, you're not a member of the Senate. The only time you could have heard Senator Fitzgerald make such a threat, or make any statement at all, is if you were there as a witness, under subpoena, isn't that correct, Mr. Donahue?"

"That's right, and...?"

It was a challenge he should not have made.

"And, Mr. Donahue? And? Well, how about this, were you there, a witness under subpoena?"

He looked away, waiting for the prosecutor to get back to business.

"Answer the question, Mr. Donahue!" She was furious, and not just with the witness. "Mr. St. John, you will instruct your witness to answer or he will not be the only one held in contempt!"

"Yes! I appeared before the Senate Intelligence Committee. And, no, I was not under subpoena. I agreed to testify."

"In connection with the Russian investigation?"

"I'm not at liberty to say."

"I'll take that as a yes. And during your appearance as a witness, did Senator Fitzgerald make any threat against the life of the president?"

"No."

"There," she said with a flash of condescension in her eyes, "see how easy that was. Now, Mr. St. John, you may continue with your witness, now that he has learned how to behave like one."

I had seldom seen anything like it. For a moment, St. John was too stunned to speak. Then, before Donahue could say something else to antagonize the court, he changed the subject in a way that made it seem he had not changed the subject at all. He was simply moving to the logical next step.

"The Senate Intelligence Committee was investigating Russian interference in our election. Was that the reason the president had come out here to California, because he was concerned with what the Russians had tried to do?"

Donahue sat forward, intensely interested, not so much in the question but, it seemed, in anticipation of his own response. It was the look you sometimes saw in an actor's face that quick split second before he said his lines in a stage performance. His lips had begun to move, a mute rehearsal, before St. John had finished asking the question.

"He was here to speak at the technology conference, but he was also here to meet with some people from Silicon Valley, the leading experts on the kind of cyber technology that the Russians were using, experts who were best equipped to create the technology needed to make sure our elections would always be secure from interference, whether it was the Russians or anyone else. All the things people like Kevin Fitzgerald said they wanted done, Walter Bridges was doing them. And if Fitzgerald had not murdered him, Walter Bridges would have made certain that this country, and everyone in it, was safe and secure."

Leaning back in my chair, my elbows on the arms, I spread my fingers wide apart and slowly pressed them together just beneath my chin while I studied Michael Donahue's ever shifting gaze. I was in no hurry. This was going to be a very long cross-examination.

"You graduated from Princeton with a degree in history, and then law school at Columbia, is that correct?"

"Yes."

My left hand fell to my chest and I scratched briefly at my chin with my right. I was, quite on purpose, lackadaisical.

"Walter Bridges, on the other hand, went to business school, is that right?"

"Yes, he got an MBA."

"In business school, when you get an MBA, you study accounting, finance, things like that, things that have mainly to do with money, am I correct?"

"Yes," he replied, not at all certain where this was going.

"You don't study history, or political science, you don't learn about the great revolutions of the past, you don't learn about the American Revolution or the American Civil War, you don't learn about the history of this country, you don't learn what led to our entry into the First World War, or the Second, you don't learn anything at all about the history of our relations with other nations—you learn about money, how to make it, how to run a company, how to measure profit and loss on a balance sheet. Is that a fair description of the differences in your respective educations?"

He shrugged his indifference and said that he supposed it was.

"That put you in an interesting position, didn't it? You're a well-educated man, while Walter Bridges, according to the standard implicit in your education, was not."

"I'm not sure I know what you mean."

Slowly rising from my chair, I looked at him, and then at the jury. I began to move toward him.

"Of course you do. You knew all about history and politics and the law. Walter Bridges only knew how to make money. I take it you never thought to give him advice about how to do that, did you?"

"No, I never did. I'm not sure I would have known how."

"But it didn't work the same way, the other way round, did it? Bridges did not know anything—he had never studied, the way you had, history and politics and law—but that did not mean, did it, that he always took your advice?"

Donahue thought me naive.

"He was the president. I was just one of his assistants."

"You were more than that, Mr. Donahue. You were—what was it you were called?—the White House intellectual, the mind behind the power, the architect of the new world Walter Bridges was going to build. But that did not mean that he always agreed with what you said, or that he even always listened, did it?"

"I think I just answered that."

"Perhaps. You testified that shortly after the election you met with

Senator Fitzgerald in his Senate office. Is that still your testimony?"

"Of course it is. Did you think I—"

"Just the two of you? There was no one else in the room?"

"No, just the two of us."

"And it was in that meeting that the senator said...I want to make sure I have this right," I remarked as I went back to the counsel table and glanced at the notes I had made. "According to you, the senator said if no one else killed him, he might have to do it himself. Is that still your testimony?"

"That's exactly what he said."

"You were with Walter Bridges when he was giving speeches during the campaign. You were there, were you not, when he told people at his rallies that they should 'beat the hell' out of protesters? Did he mean it, is that what he really wanted them to do?"

"No, it was just a way of expressing his contempt for people who were trying to stop him, interrupt what he was saying, but—"

"When he said he could shoot someone on a public street in front of a crowd of witnesses and people would vote for him anyway, did he, so far as you know, really intend to see if he could do it?"

"No, he would never have—"

"And when he said, after the Supreme Court ruled against him on an issue he had staked his reputation on, that the best thing that could happen is if half the justice were carried out on stretchers, did he mean he thought half the member of the court should be shot dead?"

"Absolutely not. He meant that half the court were too old, that they ought to be replaced with justices young enough to do the job."

"In other words, the only threats that were real were the ones made against the president, threats that no one but you seem ever to have heard!"

He grabbed both arms of the witness chair and started to shout back. I did not give him the chance.

"Why were you on Air Force One? Why did you make the trip out here? Why didn't you stay at your office in the White House? Why did you come to San Francisco?"

The questions came in such rapid fire succession that Donahue had to wait a moment to make sure I was through.

"It's what I said earlier: we were here to meet with the best people in technology there are."

"'We were here.' You keep saying that. There seems to be no difference, at least in your mind, between you and the president. And that hasn't changed, has it? You're still in the White House, only now, instead of a senior policy advisor, you're chief of staff; which means, I imagine, that you can speak of 'we' with even greater confidence than you could before."

I shook my head at the arrogance of it, the exaggerated sense of his own importance. He believed everything that had been written about him. He was smarter, far better read, than the president he worked for; better, more able, than anyone else on the White House staff. He had a reason for his belief. No one could match his intellect, no one, that is to say, who was in any position to rival him for power. Fitzgerald thought him overrated, the books he had read in college, the assigned reading in courses he had to take, the books from which he had learned only what he needed to pass exams, the only things he had ever read. The degrees he held were impressive, but mainly to those, like Walter Bridges, who did not have them.

"And that was because, as I believe you just testified, the president was concerned with what had happened in the last election and wanted to do everything possible to make certain it never happened again, is that correct?"

"Yes, the president was very insistent. You see," he went on, turning to the jury, "no one had been affected more by what happened, by the Russian attempt to interfere. They weren't successful, but that did not stop the president's opponents—people like Senator Fitzgerald—from making all sorts of allegations, suggesting that the president not only won because of what the Russians had done, but that people in the campaign, even the president himself, had been working with the Russians, that there had been coordination, collusion, and that nothing the president wanted done should be allowed to pass until everything had been investigated. So, yes, the president was concerned. His presidency was being held hostage to these vicious, unproven because unprovable, allegations of criminal wrongdoing."

"Criminal wrongdoing—is that what you call treason?"

"I object to that remark, I—"

"The president did not want to meet with Senator Fitzgerald, did he?"

"I...not particularly. Fitzgerald had several times asked for a meeting with the president, but we—I mean, the president—did not see any reason, not after what Fitzgerald had been saying."

"But he met with him on Air Force One when it landed here, in San Francisco?"

"The senator was part of the greeting party. Wherever the president goes, he is met by the most important local public officials. Obviously, Senator Fitzgerald was included in that group."

"He met with him on the plane, not the tarmac."

"We had landed early. It was decided that this would be a good time to let Senator Fitzgerald have a few minutes. It was a way to end his complaint that the president would not see him."

"So it was decided at the last minute, so to speak, after the plane landed, when you realized there was time?"

"Yes."

"A last-minute decision. Are you sure of that?"

Curious, he tried not to show it.

"Yes, a last-minute decision."

"You're under oath," I reminded him in such a quiet voice it got everyone's attention.

"Under...? I'm aware of that."

"Then stop lying. It was not a last-minute decision. It was a decision you had argued about almost from the moment you took off from Washington, an argument that became heated, an argument in which the president told you—and this is a direct quote—'I'm not going to see the son of a bitch.' It was an argument in which he told you that Fitzgerald wanted to run against him, but that—and this is another direct quote—'it isn't going to happen, that he'll never get the chance.' Are you starting to remember now? The argument in which you told the president that he had to meet with Fitzgerald because, 'We have to do everything we can to keep him in the dark.' In the dark about what, Mr. Donahue? That you were going to be meeting with people who could help make sure no one ever interfered with our elections again?"

Donahue was adamant. It had never happened. He had never argued with the president. It was possible someone might have overheard part of the conversation he had with Bridges on the plane; there had, as he remembered it, been some discussion of Fitzgerald, the way he was always playing to the cameras, hinting at things that the Intelligence Committee might be looking at. There was no doubt that they had spoken, if only briefly, about what to do with Fitzgerald at the airport. There were going to be cameras and reporters everywhere, and you could never be sure, with someone as eager for attention as Fitzgerald, what he might pull. It was, as best he could now recall, only when they landed early that they decided to give Fitzgerald a few minutes on the plane. It would solve two problems at once: stop Fitzgerald from complaining that the president would not meet with him, and keep him out of view so he could not try to upstage the president on his arrival.

"And I'm sure we all believe you," I remarked dryly when he finished. "Just as I'm sure we'll all believe all the rest of your testimony."

"Your Honor?" objected St. John.

"You know better, Mr. Antonelli." Patterson would have gone much further, giving me no end of a scolding, but she had taken such an intense dislike for the witness that she made it seem she thought me guilty of only a minor indiscretion.

"The president wanted to meet with people who could help protect our elections from electronic attack?"

"Yes, that's right."

"What we're really talking about is cyber warfare, isn't it? The kind of thing the military knows how to do. Correct?"

"Yes, that's right."

"The people you were meeting with, though not in the military themselves, were, I take it, experts in the technology used for that purpose— cyber warfare. Would that be correct?"

"That's right."

"You've met with people like that before, haven't you? Cyber warfare specialists?"

"In Washington, part of the intelligence community. Yes."

"Not just in Washington, Mr. Donahue, but other places, other countries, as well. As a matter of fact, Mr. Donahue, you've met with some of who I think it fair to say are some of the world's leading experts in this field. And you did this even before Walter Bridges was elected president. Because it is true, isn't it, that you met with the very man in charge of the Russian attempt to interfere with the election, Sergei Rostov, a general in the Russian army!"

Donahue's face turned red. He pounded his hands on the arms of the witness chair.

"That's a damn lie! Nothing like that ever happened!"

"You never met Rostov, you never talked to Rostov?"

"No, never!"

Three quick steps and I was back at the counsel table, drawing from out of my briefcase three photographs. As I started back to him, his eyes went cold and his face went rigid. His fingers squeezed hard the wooden arms of the chair.

"Here, tell us, who is sitting across the table from you in this photograph—the large, balding man in the dark, three-piece suit? You don't remember having dinner with General Rostov in a Paris restaurant in June, five months before the election? If you have any questions about the date and time, you will find them recorded on the top left corner."

I waited in the awkward, endless silence for a response.

"Don't remember? Here, this second photograph, perhaps it might help. It shows you entering the restaurant, walking next to Rostov. Or this last one, which shows you standing on the sidewalk, shaking hands with him when he left. It's odd you can't remember," I taunted him as I returned to the counsel table, where I opened a file folder. "Odd, given the conversation you had, the plan, the detailed plan, by which the Russians agreed to release information damaging to the other side, and to do it whenever you told them the time was right. Do you remember this now? Is your memory starting to come back? Let me help you. General Rostov said, 'We have people at Wikileaks. They use what we give them the way we tell them to.' And you said, 'Just so long as none of this can ever be traced back to me.' And Rostov asked, 'Does Bridges know what you are doing, because if he doesn't, as you'll understand, we lose some of our incentive?' And you reply, 'He knows what you want. He doesn't see any problem with it.' Really, Mr. Donahue? He did not see any problem with what the Russians were asking for?"

"I had dinner in Paris. I was there early that summer. I stayed for four days. It was my chance to get away for a while, before the convention, before the campaign really got started. I was invited to dinner by a Russian businessman, someone the president had known for years. At the last minute, he had to cancel and he sent this Rostov instead. I did not know he had any connection with the Russian government, much less the Russian military. He told me he was a partner of the president's friend. He told me—you're right about this—that he had friends—that was how he put it—who had some damaging information that might be helpful to the Bridges campaign. They wanted to help him. They had a way to take it public, but they would rather know from us the best time to do it. I knew this was treacherous ground. So instead of making some kind of definite commitment, I put him off with a promise to let him know. And as for the question about whether Bridges knew what I was doing, I was not doing anything except the vague promise to get back to them."

"And what Bridges was willing to do in exchange for Russian help? That didn't mean anything, either?" I asked, wondering if there was any lie he would not tell.

"I had no idea what the Russians might have wanted. As I say, I kept everything vague. Let me be completely honest with you," he went on, turning again to the jury. "If the Russians, if anyone, knew something damaging to the other side, or damaging, for that matter, to Walter Bridges, the one thing certain is that they were going to use it. When I heard what Rostov—that was not the name he used with me—had to say, I thought the best thing was to string him along, play for time, until we found out what was really going on."

It was outrageous, without precedent, Donahue's utter disregard for the truth. The worst part was that I had the sense he did not think he was lying at all. The truth for him was however you decided to interpret what you saw happening all around you. He did not doubt for a moment that he had played the Russians, taken what they could give, without even a promise, a real promise, that they would get something in return. It was the great discovery of the century that there was no order in the universe, only chaos on which you could, if you had sufficient wit and daring, create an order of your own invention. Alternative facts was not some misspoken phrase, it was the working hypothesis of the new reality."

"You didn't know what the Russians wanted, so you decided to remain noncommittal, play for time. Is that what you want us to believe?"

He did not answer, he just looked at me with a blank expression, as if, having answered the question once, he did not have to answer it again.

"You did not, in other words, reject out of hand this offer of Russian help from a Russian general you claim you did not know was a general, much less what he did for the Russian government?"

"As I just finished testifying, I didn't know what—"

"Yes, we remember," I said, cutting him off with a dismissive wave of my hand.

Unbuttoning my jacket, and with my hands on my hips, I peered down at the floor. The silence in the courtroom was so complete I could hear my own breath. Everyone—the jury, the crowd, the swarm of reporters—was waiting for the next question. They had followed every word the way a concert audience listened to every note in a well-played symphony, caught up in the music, not a thought for the complications of the orchestration. It was only when it ended that anyone would start to remark on the flaws in the performance; only when the witness left the stand, only when that day's proceedings came to a close, that anyone would begin to ask how much the witness had said was the truth and how much were the fabrications of a liar and a cheat. That judgment was always informed, at least to some extent, by their reputation, what we knew, or thought we knew about them outside their time as a witness in a courtroom. If someone like Mother Theresa were to testify that the world was flat, you might think her mistaken, but you would never think she was telling you something she did not honestly believe. What I had to do was make the jury believe that if Michael Donahue testified the world was round, it would be enough to make them doubt the evidence of their own senses.

"You hated Kevin Fitzgerald, didn't you?" I asked, my eyes still on the floor.

"No, I wouldn't say that I hated him."

"He was leading the opposition, standing in the way of what you wanted to do."

"That doesn't mean I hated him."

"You testified that, in that meeting you had with him in his office, he threatened to kill the president."

"What is your question? Whether I hated him?"

"No," I said, lifting my head and staring hard at him. "My question is, who did you report it to?"

"Report...?"

"Someone has threatened the life of the president. That is a crime. Who did you report it to—the Secret Service, the Capitol police?"

"I didn't report it. I didn't think it was necessary."

"Not necessary to report a crime? Is that because it never happened, Senator Fitzgerald never threatened the president, or because you had more important questions to deal with?"

He glared at me, and then, remembering where he was, sat straight up and with a show of formality raised his chin.

"I didn't report what the senator said because I hoped he would come to his senses. And as to your reference to 'more important questions,' you'll have to be more specific."

"Yes, let's be more specific. You studied history in college, and history, as you understand it, follows a certain path, correct? It isn't just a series of disconnected events. History has a purpose. Isn't that what you have said, what you have written?"

"Do I believe that history has a purpose, that it is moving in a direction, that it is possible to anticipate what will happen in the future? Yes, in a general sort of way. It isn't like trying to predict who is going to win the next election, or what might happen in the Middle East, but in terms of the broad movements in the world, the fundamental changes that may take place over long periods of time, then, yes, in that sense I believe that history can be understood."

"The history of the future determined by the history of the past?" I asked, as if I were just trying to be sure I fully grasped his meaning.

"That is a fair statement."

"You have a theory about this, don't you?"

"A theory? I—"

"A theory that starts from the premise that conflicts keep getting bigger. The American Revolution, for all its importance, was a smaller conflict than the Civil War, and the Civil War was smaller, in terms of numbers, than the First World War, and the Second World War was larger still, the biggest conflict the world had ever seen. This leads to the question that seems to have been at the center of all your thought: if conflicts keep getting bigger, what great conflict is coming next? And you had an answer to your question, didn't you?"

I asked this with an even temper and a steady gaze, the way it would have been asked by someone in an audience to which he just lectured on history and what it means. The difference was that this was a courtroom jammed to capacity with people who had come to watch a murder trial, and millions more watching on television. He was supposed to be a brilliant strategist, with a clear vision of how America's place in the world had to change. He now had to prove it. He leaned forward.

"The biggest conflict, the one that is taking place world-wide, the one we have to win, is the conflict between Islam and the West. There are terrorist attacks everywhere—Europe, Africa, Asia—all from the same cause, the same belief that Islam is the one true religion, the Koran the word of God and that anyone who doesn't believe is an infidel and deserves to die. It is the biggest threat we have ever faced and most of the people in government refuse to acknowledge it. They think that all we have to do is practice tolerance, treat everyone the same, and worry more about offending someone's religion than how many might die the next time we get attacked at home."

"And that is the reason—the failure of government to appreciate the danger we face—that you, and Walter Bridges, spoke so often of what you and others call the 'Deep State,' the permanent government, the officials who stay in power regardless who is elected to Congress or the presidency, correct?"

"The people who think that nothing has to change."

"And when you talked about 'deconstructing the administrative state,' that is what you were talking about, wasn't it, changing in fundamental ways the American government?"

"Yes, precisely. We need to change the way we do things to meet the changing threat."

"Because the threat isn't what it was during the Cold War, it isn't what some other country might do—it is the threat of terrorism that can come from anyone at any time, not just from an organized, established military power. Correct?"

"That's right," he replied emphatically

"Which means, does it not, that all the institutions, all the alliances which were established at the end of the Second World War to protect us against the kind of military threat posed by the Soviet Union are now obsolete. They serve no purpose in a world in which the issue is whether Islam or the West will triumph. Is that correct?"

"Yes," he replied, but now tentatively, and with guarded suspicion.

"In a world like this, in a conflict like this—the biggest conflict, I think you put it—we have to be ready to join forces with anyone who views terrorism as much a threat as we do; willing, if necessary, to let them have their way with other, lesser nations if that is the price we have to pay to get them to work with us?"

He did not want to answer.

"Any nation, any group—the Russians, if they can give us what we need. Isn't that correct? The Russians, if they'll help, and help not just against the terrorists, but against our own government if it is the only way to get rid of that Deep State which, as you just testified, refuses to take seriously the threat we face? The Russians, whose help you told General Rostov you, and Walter Bridges, would be—and this is a direct quote—'more than grateful to receive'?"

CHAPTER
FOURTEEN

I was furious, and I let Fitzgerald know it.

"The prosecution is finished. Donahue was his last witness. Now it's our turn, and I have no idea what I'm going to do! No idea at all!"

"You destroyed Donahue, you destroyed them all, every witness the prosecution called. St. John is the one who should be worried."

"Are you out of your mind?"

I sat down on the easy chair in the cluttered room that served as his temporary cell. The mail bags were now stacked to the ceiling. The table was filled with pages and pages of handwritten notes, some of them, I assumed, the fragmentary starting points for the speech he was going to give in court, while others, the plans he was making for when the trial was over and he was free to go about his business. It was the one thing he had not kept secret from me. He was going to run for president, or rather, not run for the office, but receive it by acclamation.

"Bridges is dead, but they were all involved—Donahue, Reese, Ellison, that idiot Jenny Ann Carruthers, the vice-president. The country won't stand for it; they'll all have to go."

Had he forgotten that the line of succession still held, and that he was not on it?

"You think too much like a lawyer. Consider the politics of it, what the country wants, what the country feels. Remember what happened, after Bridges died? The funeral, what they tried to do—make it into a spectacle, a day of national mourning, the casket on a horse drawn carriage, like what was done when Kennedy died, the color guard, the slow procession down Pennsylvania Avenue. And what happened? Hardly anyone came out to watch; a few stragglers stopped to stare, anyone else on the sidewalk hurried to go somewhere else. It was an embarrassment. Spencer, the vice-president, tried to say something in his speech but… Now he's the president, but only until everything comes out. Then he's gone. The line of succession, that won't matter. Before he leaves office, Spencer will have to choose me—the country will demand it—to be vice-president, which means—"

"That when Spencer resigns, you become…"

It would in anyone else have been megalomania of the most ludicrous kind, an ambition so far out of keeping with any reasonable chance of achievement as to constitute cause for involuntary commitment. But whatever Fitzgerald might be, he was not insane. Calculating, shrewd, and, given what he had done, either ruthless or courageous, willing to assassinate a president either to save the country, as he insisted, or, with the same excuse, to create a place in history that would make him live forever in the memory of men. He and Michael Donahue were, in this respect, not that much different. Only one of them, however, was on trial for his life.

"That's the advantage I have," he explained. He sat at the table, a few feet away, his eyes glowing with an inner light, the vast certainty with which he now could see the future. "I stopped it, stopped what they were about to do. When the country hears what it was, there will be no doubt that I had to act. Who else do you think they will want to lead them then?"

"Listen to me. We go back to court tomorrow morning. The judge is going to ask if the defense is ready, and if we are, to call our first witness. How do you think I should answer that, what do you think I should tell Patterson, that the defense doesn't know if it is ready or not, and in any event could not even guess who it might call first?"

Fitzgerald did not care.

"It's up to you who you call, isn't it?"

I could have murdered him then and there. He was the strangest combination of shrewd intelligence and simple stupidity I had encountered. He could think three moves ahead of anyone in politics, could analyze the strengths and weaknesses of a friend or an adversary quicker than anyone since Lyndon Johnson, but it was all instinctive, something he could do without any real understanding of how he did it. But because he could do it, because he had always been able to know what others would do before they knew it themselves, he assumed, and never questioned the assumption, that things would always work out the way he wanted and expected. And they always had. Everything, even murder, could be used to his advantage.

"A lot of things are up to me," I replied in a low voice full of a warning he did yet understand. "I don't have to call any witnesses at all. Tomorrow morning, when the judge asks if I am ready to proceed, I can just announce that the defense rests. Then it's up to the jury to decide."

He thought I was kidding.

"But you're not going to do that," he said, beginning to show the first signs of doubt.

"I may not have any choice."

He looked at me, astonished. He began to be nervous. All his well-laid plans now perhaps in jeopardy; his chance to tell the jury, to tell the country, what he had done and the great, good reason he had done it, about to be taken away.

"You never call a witness when you have no idea what they are going to say. You have refused, time and time again, every time I asked you, to tell me what was so damn urgent, what threat, what danger so immediate that you had to kill Walter Bridges, what was so incredibly important that you could not stop it by any other, lawful, means."

His friendly, publicized eyes went cold.

"You can't stop me from testifying. A defendant has the right, the absolute right, to testify in his own defense."

"Is that what your wife told you, what they teach in law schools?"

I did nothing to hide my derision. Both of them had from the beginning promised to tell me whatever I wanted to know. Neither had kept their word.

"What they don't teach in law school, what you are about to learn, is that lawyers, like politicians, can throw out the rules when no one else is following them. You don't want to tell me what you're going to say in court, you'll say it in court with someone else to represent you. I'm done."

I grabbed my briefcase and started for the door.

"Wait! Don't go. I'll tell you what you want to know."

For the next two hours I listened in growing amazement to a story I would never have thought possible, a story that made every rumored allegation of what had been done by Walter Bridges and those around him seem nothing more than the mindless antics of schoolyard boys. It was an indictment more damning, more devastating, than any criminal charge I had ever read.

"I didn't know if you would believe me if I told you everything at the beginning, if you hadn't first heard the testimony—what you drew out of the prosecution's witnesses on cross—about what Bridges and the others had done and were planning to do." With a quick, troubled expression, he added, "I wouldn't have believed it if someone had told a story like this to me."

Now that I knew what Fitzgerald was going to say, I knew the kind of questions St. John was likely to ask on cross. Fitzgerald had anticipated most, though not all of them.

"The ten minutes, the time you were alone with Bridges on the plane. I'll ask you about that. All the prosecution can do then is try to follow up. The fact that you did not know you would be invited on the plane. Why, in that case, did you have a knife? St. John is good. He'll do everything he can to cast doubt, anything that shows, or seems to show, an inconsistency, he'll be all over it. Why did you have the knife?"

Fitzgerald smiled, then looked away. He began to rummage through the notes scattered over the table. He seemed to be thinking of something, making up his mind.

"I was going to do it when he came off the plane," he said finally. "While everyone was standing around."

Like the assassination of Julius Caesar, I thought, done in full view so no one could doubt who did it or why it was done. I wondered if Fitzgerald had thought about what he might say at the moment he struck the fatal blow. He was too much in love with what he thought the world would think of him to have let the deed go unaccompanied by a few well-rehearsed words.

I remembered an English teacher I had in college who once remarked that the most heroic thing a hero could do was to do something heroic and never tell a soul. If I had had more courage, or more wisdom, I would have told Fitzgerald that.

"In front of all the cameras, in front of all the world," I said out loud before I knew I was saying it. "All right, I don't think there is anything else."

"I'm testifying tomorrow?"

"You're the first witness for the defense."

He had been looking forward to this moment, the chance finally to tell his story for so long, he could not hide, not his excitement exactly, his sense of relief.

"This is the truth?" I asked, searching his eyes as I stood up to leave. "Everything you told me this evening?"

"Every word of it," he swore.

My hand was on the door when I remembered the question I had wanted to ask from the first time I met him, before I had agreed to represent him.

"You lied to me when you told me that you hadn't had an affair with Evan Winslow's wife. Why did you do that?"

He treated the question, the accusation, as without significance. He could not understand why I would even ask.

"I hardly knew you. We had only just met. Why would I tell you something like that?"

Tangerine was not surprised. But there were other things she wanted to talk about.

"This is mine now," she explained, glancing around at what was both the living and dining room of her Sausalito home. "It's all been arranged. I don't need anything else. He can have everything else, the house in the city, the house in Palm Springs, the house—oh hell, we had houses everywhere!" she cried, laughing at the inconsequence of what she had once thought important. "This was always mine. I picked it out, I had it practically gutted and rebuilt, I decorated it, I furnished it, and when you finally came into my life, I got laid in it. Can you think of a better title than that? It's mine, Antonelli, which means it's yours as well." She gave me a glance full of mischief and seduction. "You got laid here, too. Your title is as good as mine."

She was wearing a green skirt and a white blouse, and, as I found out later, nothing else. Walking barefoot on the carpet, she opened the sliding glass door and looked back.

"Come join me for dinner."

We sat at a small round glass table out on the deck. The sky was turning midnight blue and the first stars had begun to shine.

"Drunken chicken," she said, her eyes sparkling at the crazy way it sounded. "A little chicken, a lot of wine. Some other things, too, but I can't remember what they were supposed to be. I guess a lot when I cook," she announced, shaking her head at her own pretended incompetence. Then she laughed again, a soft, gentle laugh that floated birdlike in the air. "Now, eat; it really isn't too bad."

Time stopped. The past had not happened and the future would never come. Words lost their meaning and speech had not been discovered. It did not matter what we had for dinner, nothing had ever tasted as good. A hillside in Sausalito became Babylon, the blink of an eye marked the passage of a thousand years.

"I was there, in court, today, when—"

"I know, I saw…"

"And you thought of me then, didn't you, because—"

"That stupid smile on my face, and I couldn't remember what—"

"But you did, that next question you asked, no one would have thought that—"

"I didn't know what I was asking; I didn't know what I was doing for—"

"For the few seconds it took to put me out of mind." She laughed. "I probably shouldn't have gone, but I wanted to know what it was like, the feeling in the courtroom, the tension, the sense of anticipation. It isn't at all like what you think it is when you watch on television. You're even better in person," she remarked with an innocent smile full of promised evil.

The sky had disappeared, lights were shining everywhere, on the hillside, on the long, curving outline of the Golden Gate, all over the city and then back over the Bay Bridge to the other side of the bay, all of it, every light from everywhere, danced reflected in her eyes. She bent toward me, looking across the top of the wine glass dangling from her smooth tapered fingers.

"It's completely different. Everything is so alive. The cameras show you one thing or another, usually the witness and the attorney asking questions, but when you're there, you see everything, the way the jury is watching, the different expressions on their faces, the different ways they sit. The way the judge stares daggers at whoever she decides isn't doing what they're supposed to do! Tell me about her. What is she really like? She can't be like that at home. Who could live with that?"

"You don't think she keeps a gavel on the table to keep order at dinner?"

"Really, what's she like?"

"I don't really know what she's like. She's married; I think she is. She had a photograph in her office, a family picture: she and her husband and two teenage girls. But when it was taken, whether she's still married… All I really know is that she is as tough as they come in court. She was a prosecutor; supposedly never lost a case. She's well trained. Graduated from Stanford, went to law school at Michigan, came back here to work for the district attorney. She had a chance to go on the appellate court a few years ago but she turned it down. She likes the action, the excitement of a trial. There is nothing like it, especially now."

Sipping slowly on her glass, Tangerine tilted her head to the side, the silent expression of the question she wanted me to answer.

"Everyone, almost everyone, does everything electronically. We don't live in the world anymore, we live in what they call cyber space. People like Michael Donahue seem to think it's the only thing that's real anymore. But in court, in a trial, nothing has changed. It's the same as it was a hundred, two hundred years ago. Some of the evidence is different, but—you saw it yourself today—a man, a woman, is sworn in as a witness, sits there with twelve people observing everything they say, everything they do—every change of expression, every change of emotion—and answers, under penalty of perjury, questions put to them first by one side, then the other. And you never know how anyone is going to do, you can never be entirely certain when you put them on the stand how they'll hold up."

I laughed at what I had just remembered, laughed with the kind of nostalgia you felt for your vanished innocence, the feeling you had when you were just starting out.

"The first time—the very first time—I walked into a courtroom to try a case, something strange happened. I had not been able to sleep more than a few hours at a time, for days I could not stop thinking about what was going to happen, the questions I was going to ask, the thousand different answers I might be given. It was making me crazy, and then, the moment—and I mean the very moment—I walked into that courtroom and sat down at the counsel table, it all stopped. It was like I had come home."

"I can understand that; you were doing what you had always wanted to do. And you knew that after all the years waiting, all the years in school, you were ready."

I had not quite thought of it like that, but I knew she was right. It was what I had always wanted to do—the only thing I had wanted to do.

"But it made me forget something, and even now, after all these years, and God knows how many trials, I look around the courtroom and everyone looks so calm, so self-assured. The judge, the prosecutor go about their business like they have never had a doubt about anything in their lives. Every eye is on them when they speak, but they don't seem aware of it. The witness, who may never have seen the inside of a courtroom before they find themselves swearing to tell the truth, sit there, answering questions as if they did this every day. The jury, called up one by one, walk all alone from the first few rows of the visitor's gallery to the jury box, like being called up to the front of the class in grade school or high school. And then, in front of everyone, including hundreds of strangers and however many millions are watching on television, a lawyer, someone you probably think a trained assassin, asks you questions about your life—where you live, where you went to school, what you do for a living, whether you're married, if you have any children. And they answer, as best they can, and they never, not even once, suddenly forget what they want to say. And so you sit there, watching it all play out in front of you, and you have to remind yourself that what you are really dealing with are people, especially among the jurors, who are so nervous, so self-conscious, so worried they might do something wrong it is a wonder they can stand."

"But you're not nervous, self-conscious?" she asked, just to be sure. "Never?"

"Never. One time only. Today, when I looked at you."

"Liar!"

"I wish I was lying. My knees went weak. I was helpless, astonished I could still speak," I went on, enjoying in all its gleeful extravagance what, at the heart of it, was the simple truth of it. "I thought I was going to pass out; my head felt dizzy. My heartbeat was so loud, I thought that Evelyn Patterson, hearing it, would stare daggers at me for the disruption. I was—"

"You were telling me about her, how she likes being a trial court judge."

"There is a line I heard, years ago, about another judge. 'No one likes her; everyone respects her.' That's not a bad description, and, when you think about it, rather high praise for a trial court judge. You were there. She didn't like what Donahue was doing. She didn't wait for St. John, she asked the questions she had decided the witness should answer. No one does that, almost no one does that. She's more like a British judge than an American one. She never lets things get off track, and if she seems to give one side a little more latitude than the other, it's because the other side has broken one of her rules and she is trying to right the balance."

The candle on the table flickered in the cool night air. Shadows threw a mask over Tangerine's lovely face, but her eyes, left uncovered, held me close in their eager and excited curiosity. She wanted to know everything.

"Everyone respects her, but no one likes her?"

"It's just a line, easy to remember, convenient to use. I'm sure she has friends. But she isn't someone who allows the two things to mix. You see it more in women than you do in men. Women are better this way. She doesn't go play golf on weekends with other judges, or with lawyers. She keeps her two lives separate. When she's a judge, that's all she does, that is all she knows. But when she is with her family, or her friends, she probably never talks about what she does, and never about any trial over which she is presiding. If I ran into her in the supermarket or at a restaurant, she would be polite but distant, ask me how I was, tell me it was nice to see me, and with a smile and a nod be on her way. There is nothing imprecise about her."

"Imprecise? How do you mean?"

"Everything is structured, organized, everything made to fit." I raised my eyebrow at a sudden thought. "But who knows, really; maybe she is so strictly tied to her own self-imposed demands, her expectations of how she has to live, that she'll have a breakdown and end up in an asylum. But I doubt it. Her mind is too good; she has too much depth. Before the trial started, I filed a few motions. It's something you almost always do in a criminal case: move to suppress evidence, more to limit testimony—and you almost always lose. You know that, but you do it anyway because that way, if the verdict goes against you at trial, you have some issues of law on which to base an appeal. Most trial court judges just deny the motion. Evelyn Patterson denied the motion, but she wrote an opinion listing seventeen different points of law to support the denial. She's that thorough; she's that good."

Tangerine got up from the table, went inside and came back with a light gray cashmere sweater thrown over her shoulders. She filled our glasses for the second time.

"And what about the prosecutor, Raymond St. John? What can you tell me about him? He seems very polished, distinguished, never, it seems, thrown off, never out of control. What you were saying about people always looking like they're so calm, so much in command of themselves, when they're really nervous wrecks—he doesn't give the impression that he has ever been nervous about anything."

I searched her eyes, waiting for the spark of recognition that I knew would be there in a moment.

"He was an alcoholic? Like my father? But he stopped drinking, he's a recovering alcoholic? Good for him. It's hard not to like someone who has managed to do that." Staring out into the night, a wistful smile moved slowly across her mouth as she remembered. "It's the way he does everything; the slow, measured way he goes from one thing to the next, concentrating on each thing in its turn. And in that way," she added with a sad, knowing, lost look in her eyes, "ignore the need." She shook her head, banishing for a moment the memory of her father. "I can see that now. How long has it been? Quite a long time, I would imagine."

"Albert has told me stories about St. John, back in the day when he was still drinking. He always managed to get to court; always, somehow, managed to do his job. But weekends! Unbelievable, some of the things he and some of his friends would do. They loved to scare hell out of tourists, and anyone else who happened to be around. One time, St. John himself, according to what became the local legend, went down to Fisherman's Wharf and waited until the ferry was just pulling out. It was a Saturday afternoon, there were crowds everywhere. From out of nowhere, here comes St. John, running as fast he could, clutching a straw hat on his head, shouting for the ferry to wait, that he has to get on board. The ferry doesn't stop, it keeps moving. It's probably twenty, thirty feet away, and St. John, running at top speed, makes a jump for it. Of course, he misses, misses by a mile, and while the ferry chugs away and hundreds of people stare, horrified at what they just witnessed, St. John disappears under the water. Everyone is leaning over the railing, shouting for someone to do something, to save him, but St. John doesn't come up, only that straw hat he was wearing floats to the surface, the sure sign St. John has drowned. The police come, everyone comes, divers search the water, but they can't find anything. His body must have washed out to sea. No one knows it was St. John, no one knows who it was, just some screaming fool who thought he could catch the ferry by setting a world record in the long jump. No one had noticed that St. John had swum underwater to the other side of the pier where his drunk buddies had whisked him away in a car."

I was laughing by the time I got to the end of Raymond St. John's legend making antic. We both were, laughing at the craziness with which so many people we had known had tried to forget their broken dreams, the tragedy of their existence, in the drunken inspiration of joyful mischief.

"The good times ended at three o'clock one morning when he came home and his daughter, confined all her life to a wheelchair, told him what he had become."

I told her the whole, sad story, and then I told her that faced with the same situation I was not sure I would not have done much worse.

"Raymond St. John was a great athlete, a football player, a running back recruited by dozens of colleges. He went to UCLA, led the nation in rushing yards his junior year, and would have played in the pros and made a lot of money, but he hurt his knee his senior year. That's when he decided to go to law school. He wasn't just some jock, a guy who took the kind of classes where, if you're an athlete, you don't have to do anything. He was a serious student. He went to law school at Cal—Boalt Hall—and finished near the top of his class. He could have joined one of the better firms in the city, but he did not want to shuffle papers, draft contracts, negotiate complicated business transactions. He was an athlete, he wanted to play in front of a crowd, or at least an audience, make decisions on the instant, when they had to be made, the kind were there were no second chances, when everything you did had consequences, where, like the games you excelled at, someone always won and someone always lost. He became a prosecutor, and when he was sober, and ever since he stopped drinking altogether, one of the best ones around.

"That's all I can tell you about Raymond St. John, and all I can tell you about Evelyn Patterson. There isn't anything I can tell you about the defendant—anything I'm allowed to tell—you don't already know better than I do."

She stood up and came around to my side of the table and laid her soft hand on my shoulder.

"I never knew anyone named Kevin Fitzgerald; I've never known anyone until I met you. And I'll never know anyone else."

"For at least a week, if I remember what you said."

"Yes, that's what I said, Joseph Antonelli. But each week is renewable, if you want it to be," she said over her shoulder as she walked away.

I cleared the dishes from the table. Tangerine insisted that I turn on the television in the living room while she cleaned up the kitchen. I refused.

"I never do that. I never watch what they're saying on television about a trial I'm in."

"Don't be so vain," she said with a laugh. "They might actually be talking about something else—sports, or the weather. But I'm lying. It's the only reason I would turn it on: to see what they're saying about how brilliant you were today in court."

"Not a chance," I replied. "It's better if you don't find out you're the only one who thinks so."

We were still arguing the point when my cell phone rang. It was Albert Craven.

"Albert, you're up late. It's almost midnight. Is something—"

I felt my throat go dry, and for a moment my eyes went dark.

"What is it?" asked Tangerine, alarmed and a little frightened at my reaction.

"Evelyn Patterson. She's been murdered."

CHAPTER
FIFTEEN

"You won't be testifying tomorrow. The trial has been delayed."

Kevin Fitzgerald looked like he had not slept. His eyes were raw, reddish. He had not shaved.

"They woke me up last night to tell me. The judge…Evelyn Patterson," he said, pronouncing her name in the deliberate way of someone who wants to keep the memory alive. "Murdered! Unbelievable! It's what I was afraid of, what I knew would happen; what's been happening ever since Bridges got elected. Before that, really—all this hatred, all the violence, out there."

He sat at the plain wooden table. The endless scribbled notes, the half-finished attempts at an outline of everything he planned to say when he was called as a witness, had been stacked neatly on the far corner. He had done everything he could to prepare himself.

"Do you know what happened?" His mouth pulled back at the corners, tightening in the grim certitude of a tragedy that should have been foreseen.

"It must have been what she did yesterday, when she put Donahue in his place. That would have been enough." He glanced at the windows, high up on the wall. "That's why they put me in here instead of a regular jail cell. There isn't anyone else near enough to get to me, and no direct line of sight. But I can hear it, when they bring me back from court—there must be thousands of them out in the streets, the ones who think I'm a hero, and all the others who think the trial is a waste of time, that I should just be taken out and shot. There are fights all the time. I've seen some of it from the police van taking me back and forth."

For the only time since I first met him, he seemed to lose all that bright, shining confidence of his, that belief he had that when the trial was over, when the truth had finally come out, there would be no end to what he could do. In ways I had not been able to understand, he had treated the death—the murder, the assassination—of Walter Bridges almost as an abstraction, the way others might think of the violent death of someone they had read about in a history book or a novel. It had never seemed quite real, perhaps because, for Fitzgerald, it had become merely the necessary piece in a puzzle he had made it his business to unravel, perhaps for other, less obvious reasons, but in any event, nothing more than a part of a larger story. There was a reason for what had happened. The death of Evelyn Patterson, on the other hand, was senseless, the mindless act of some deluded vigilante who no doubt thought himself a patriot for acting against the impartiality of a court in a case that, like so many of those who had thought Walter Bridges right to attack the government he had been elected to lead, no right thinking person could doubt the outcome.

"It's what I meant when I told you that it might already be too late. There is a civil war going on," he remarked with profound assurance, "between those who think the country has to change and those who think the country is being stolen from them; between those, mainly in my party, who think everyone has the right to be whatever they want to be, and those who insist we are sacrificing all the old standards to inexcusable self-indulgence. Everyone talks about the great and growing disparity between the rich and everyone else; you would not have that disparity if we still had the kind of agreement we used to have on what the country is supposed to be."

There was a depth to him I had not seen before, a willingness to stare straight into the face of things I had not suspected.

"What is going to happen now? How long will the trial be delayed?"

"I'm on my way to court now. A new judge has to be assigned. That shouldn't take long. The trial is too important to delay it more than a day or two. Even if it was not, when something like this happens, the murder of a judge, no one is going to let anyone think that this court, that any court, can be intimidated. There will be more security than before, a show of force."

I told him I would come back later in the day after I knew more about what was going to happen, and then went directly to the courthouse where everything was bedlam. The police had established a line in front, officers standing shoulder to shoulder in full riot gear, feet spread shoulder width apart. I gave my name, showed my identification, and waited while the officer in charge checked me off the list that had been prepared of those allowed to enter. He told me they were waiting for me in the chambers of the chief judge, Leonard Silverman.

"She was one of the good ones," said the officer, a heavy set black man in his early fifties. "Don't you think so, Mr. Antonelli?"

The courthouse hallway was full of people huddled together outside their offices, some of them in tears, commiserating with each other, trying, and failing, to find a reason why something like this could happen. Three different times someone stopped me to insist that I not change anything in what I was doing, that we all had to do that because it was what Judge Patterson would have wanted.

"No one ever dared disrupt a trial of hers," someone remembered, and the others who heard it all agreed.

When I reached Judge Silverman's office, his clerk, holding a handkerchief to her mouth, shook her head to apologize for her sudden inability to speak. She opened the door to the judge's chambers and with her eyes alone told me to go in.

Raymond St. John was already there, sitting in one of two simple wooden chairs in front of Silverman's desk. The judge was standing up, his back to the room, his hands clasped behind him, staring out the window. He heard me enter and, without looking around, told me to take the chair next to St. John. For what seemed a long time, but probably was not more than a minute or so, he continued to peer out the window and not say anything. The window faced north and you could see in the distance sail boats on the bay under a cloudless autumn sky. The world went on. Nothing, not even a judge's murder in the most important trial anyone could remember, stopped people from going on with their lives. The tourists still filled the streets, the stores and hotels and restaurants were still crowded, the sailboats still bent sideways to the wind on the bay far below.

"Evelyn Patterson was as fine a person, and as good a judge, as I ever knew," announced Silverman in a steady, understated voice. "Her death will change a great many things—she can never be replaced. But one thing it will not change is this," he insisted as he turned to face us. "This trial, these proceedings."

He looked at each of us in turn, making certain that we both understood, and then with a brisk, quick movement sat down in his black leather chair.

Leonard Silverman was five feet seven or five feet eight, slight of build, with a small, ascetic mouth and eyes you would swear could look right through you when he was sufficiently interested in what you were saying not to ignore you entirely. He had that kind of intelligence. He was always interested in learning something worth learning, which was to say something serious and directly connected with the subject under discussion. He had no time for fools, and no patience for the endless digressions with which too many people generally, and too many lawyers in particular, tried to fill out the vacuity of their thought. He would think you garrulous for using four words if you needed only three.

"I've decided to take the case. Starting tomorrow morning, ten o'clock, I'll preside. I've asked the court reporter to type up the transcript of what has happened up to now. I should be able to get through it before tomorrow. The first question is whether either one of you, the prosecution or the defense, have any objection to my stepping in."

If Evelyn Patterson had been all business, ruling her courtroom with an iron hand, Silverman had the lighter touch that came with a mind that moved so quickly that, sometimes, almost before you had realized you were about to make an objection, he was ready with a ruling. You might get no more than the first syllable out of your mouth when you heard, in that sharp and clear, but always gentle, voice, his one-word decision. In his courtroom, everything ran on clean, straight lines. He had never been known to become angry, no matter the provocation. A lawyer who must have been from out of town once became so incensed when Silverman ruled against him on a motion that he threw the law book from which he had quoted some lines from what he thought a parallel case so hard on the table you could hear the echo in the hallway outside. Silverman looked at him with his small, efficient smile and said, "I knew you could be brief if you put your mind to it."

Neither St. John nor I objected. He turned to St. John.

"Before I let you go, what can you tell me, and Mr. Antonelli, about what happened? All I know is that she was shot to death last night when she was leaving the building."

With his elbows on the arms of the chair, St. John held his fingers to his mouth. His eyes, full of anguish, were close to tears.

"The trial ended a few minutes after five; pretty much the same time it ended every day. She had promised the jury, promised us," he added, exchanging a glance with me, "that she would try to keep to that schedule. But she did not go home. In addition to the trial, there were other cases—motions, judgments—the usual business of the court. And you know how she was. She would work all night before she would allow herself to fall behind."

St. John threw his hand away from his face and turned up the palms of his hands in a gesture of helpless despair.

"We should have seen it coming. The crowds around the courthouse, the picket signs—'Death to Fitzgerald,' 'The Case is Fixed,' 'Judges are the Real Criminals.' And then, on the other side, 'Fitzgerald Saved Us All,' 'Bridges was a Traitor,' 'Bridges Deserved to Die.' Since the trial started, there have been nearly a hundred arrests—disorderly conduct, assault, three for attempted arson when some self-proclaimed militia types decided to throw a molotov cocktail at a police cruiser. People are pouring in by the busload, coming from all over. Every bar in town has the television on, everyone watching and drinking at the same time; people parading in the streets, motorcycle gangs, gays and lesbians, anyone who thinks themselves the member of some group seems to think they have to show the world which side they're on."

Silverman had listened, patient and sympathetic.

"And then, last night…" he reminded St. John.

"And then, last night," said St. John, picking up the thread. "Evelyn was leaving. There was still a crowd. Not as large as it had been earlier in the day, but now, because they had been together so long, feelings were more intense, emotions less under control. The moment she came out of the building, the moment they realized who she was, someone shouted out her name, that she was the judge, the one who had given Michael Donahue, who was the closest man to Bridges, such a hard time. Then, suddenly, without any warning, there were gunshots; three, maybe four, and the man who shot her was standing over her, ready to put another bullet in her head, when he was shot and killed. The police, who had been worried about the mood of the crowd, those who had stayed that late, almost all of whom were there to protest against bothering with a trial for someone who should be taken out and lynched, had not noticed Evelyn when she first started down the steps. They heard the shots before they knew who they were shooting at. When they heard the shot, when they saw the gun, they started shooting. It was over in a matter of seconds. Two people dead on the courthouse steps. We should have seen it coming. But despite all the threats, all the shouting, you never think it is going to happen to a trial judge."

Slowly and methodically, holding his left arm across his chest, Silverman stroked the side of his face with the fingers of his right hand. His attention had been intense and complete. He had one, unanswerable, question.

"Do you think this would have happened if the trial were not being televised?"

"Everyone wanted..." Then he remembered, and he looked at me, an apology in his eyes. "You didn't."

"It wasn't because I thought anyone would get hurt. I certainly didn't think anything like this would happen," I explained as Silverman's curious gaze moved from St. John to me.

"I'm rescinding the order. The trial will not be televised. No cameras of any kind will be allowed in the courtroom or anywhere in the courthouse." He looked at St. John. "The district attorney's office can announce that I've made this decision to protect the integrity of the proceedings, that I..." He was thumbing through the court file and saw something that made him stop. "We'll have to have a hearing on this. Evelyn's decision was in response to a motion."

He picked up the telephone and informed his clerk what had to be done. Then he checked his watch.

"Two o'clock this afternoon. The lawyers representing the media will have the chance to tell me why I should not do what I am going to do."

I had four hours. I went first to the jail to tell Fitzgerald that the trial would be delayed only until tomorrow and that Leonard Silverman would be presiding. He was much more interested in what Silverman was going to do about television.

"He can't do that, can he?"

"He can, and he will. Evelyn Patterson was murdered because there was a mob waiting outside the courthouse, because some maniac had been watching on television and decided she should die because of how she handled Donahue when he was on the stand. There aren't going to be any cameras anywhere near the courthouse, not while the trial is going on. The only audience is whoever happens to get there early enough to get a seat inside."

Leaning against the white painted concrete wall, Fitzgerald shoved his hands in his pants pockets and stared down at the floor. He was disappointed, discouraged, but he had the decency to try not to show it. A woman had been murdered. That was more than an inconvenience, but everything depended on the appeal he could make to the country, the story that would explain that he had acted to save the country from a threat it had not known it faced, and now, because of what seemed certain to be one judge's ruling, he would lose the chance to talk to the country directly. He forced himself to agree that the judge was right.

"I suppose he doesn't really have any choice. There will still be reporters there to cover the trial." His eyes brightened. He started to look from one side of the cell to the other. "It might be better that way. What gets written lasts longer; what people read, they remember."

I left him feeling slightly better, and more determined to give the performance of his life when he took the stand in his own defense. It was there, right behind his eyes, the politician's certainty that he could talk his way out of, or into, anything.

There were still all the hours of remaining work that had been left unfinished after I had learned of Patterson's murder. I went straight to my office, or tried to, because when I got there the street was full of television trucks and the sidewalk full of cameras and reporters. They wanted to see what the lawyer for Kevin Fitzgerald might have to say. I was trapped; I could not turn and run away.

"One at a time," I insisted amid a storm of shouted questions.

"What's your reaction to the murder of Judge Patterson?"

I could not tell who among the throng of eager, desperate faces had asked what a high school freshman of no discernible intelligence would have been too embarrassed to ask. I ignored it.

"Is the trial going to be delayed, and, if it is, can you tell us when it might start again?"

"Mr. St. John and I met with Judge Silverman this morning. The trial will resume tomorrow at ten a.m."

The question, and the answer, changed the tone, put a definition on what was acceptable and what was not.

"It's true, then, that Judge Silverman, Leonard Silverman, will take over for Judge Patterson, that he'll preside over the Fitzgerald trial?"

"Yes. We have all suffered a great loss. Judge Patterson was as fair-minded, as able, a trial court judge as there is."

Someone started to shout another question, but I was not finished.

"If this were any other activity, any other line of endeavor, we would all observe a period of mourning. But Evelyn Patterson was a judge presiding over a public trial. She was gunned down by some coward who, though completely ignorant of the law himself, apparently did not like the way she dealt with a witness for the side he wanted to win. We go back to trial tomorrow because it is the best way possible to honor the memory of a woman who devoted her life to our system of justice. We don't decide guilt or innocence in this country by violence. We let juries make that decision."

With a gift for the superficial, a talent for finding the inconsistency that did not exist, a reporter for one of the cable news networks asked what he was certain everyone would want to know and he was the first to discover.

"You can say that representing someone who murdered a president because he did not like what that president was doing?"

"Killed the president, caused his death, because it was the only way to keep that president from doing something that would have been catastrophic for the nation. That is what Senator Fitzgerald will testify tomorrow. It is called, in the law, the defense of others, in this case, defense of the country. The law of necessity, the need, the imperative need, to act, to sacrifice one life when it is the only way to save more than one." Then I added, "You might want to learn something about those distinctions before you accuse someone who might quite possibly know them already of the kind of hypocrisy with which you have just charged me."

I should have added, "you stupid son of a bitch," but there were standards that even a lawyer should try to uphold.

"There is a rumor—more than rumor, a story—going around that Judge Silverman has scheduled a hearing this afternoon. He is considering whether to ban television coverage of the trial. Do you know if this is true, and, if it is, does the defense oppose or support having televised proceedings?"

The reporter who asked this question, short, balding, and aggressive, was being pushed by a dozen others from behind. He shoved a microphone so close to my face, I shoved it back. I was near the door. The pressure from the crowd kept growing until, finally, I managed to get inside and, with the help of the security guards posted in the lobby, got to an elevator and safely to my office. Albert Craven was waiting for me.

"Terrible, just terrible," he kept repeating. "What's happened to us? How can something like this happen? The whole city—the whole country—has gone crazy. Somebody has to get control of this."

He was pacing back and forth. I sat down at my desk and started going through the thick file folder I had abandoned halfway through the night before. Craven was too absorbed in his own distress to notice that I was not paying attention. There was too much to do, and too little time to do it.

"The trial is still on? You go back when? Tomorrow?"

I nodded without looking up.

"Good. Don't let those bastards think they can get away with something like this. Don't let them!"

"Albert, settle down!" I shoved the folder off to the side. "It's all right. Everything is under control."

"Evelyn Patterson is—"

"Dead. Murdered on the courthouse steps. The guy who killed her is dead as well. There is nothing anyone can do about it now. The only thing we can do is to take this case, and everything connected with it, as seriously as everyone should have done at the beginning. This isn't some goddamn television spectacular! A trial—a murder trial—isn't entertainment! This is serious business. Everyone seems to forget that. They seem to think that if it doesn't happen on television, it isn't real, that it isn't important. If this trial doesn't do anything else, maybe it will remind us of what a trial is supposed to be!"

I was lecturing, the last thing I wanted to do, the last thing Albert Craven deserved to hear. I was the one who needed to settle down.

"Sorry, Albert. I shouldn't have gone off like that."

"Why be sorry? I agree with everything you said. Now," he said as he sat down in the wingback chair the other side of my desk, "we need to work out the logistics."

"Logistics?"

"What happened just now outside, that crush of cameras and reporters. It's only going to get worse after Leonard Silverman stops the television coverage of the trial."

"How did you know that? Never mind. You know. What were you going to say?"

"If they can't have cameras in the courtroom, they'll have them everywhere else. You didn't go back to your place last night, did you? Reporters were camped out, waiting to be the first to get your response, have you say something they could use as part of the story they were trying to tell about the murder. They are going to be everywhere you go, wherever they think they can find you. But don't worry. I've got it all arranged."

There was something slightly ludicrous in the idea that Albert Craven, the most socially involved person I had ever known, someone who knew almost as many people as thought they knew him, would take charge of some clandestine plan to move me undetected and unobserved through the streets of San Francisco filled with half the reporters in the world.

"It's all arranged," he said quite seriously, eager to dispel any doubt I might have. "I've worked it all out with Tangerine."

Folding my arms across my chest, I watched with undisguised amusement as he disclosed the secret of his own small conspiracy. I was in the middle of a trial, an assassination that, in the judgement of some, threatened the downfall of the nation, and we were, both of us, feeling the effects of the horrific murder of a judge, a woman, we both knew. But for a few brief moments we managed to forget everything except a grown-up game of cat and mouse.

"You stay at her place in Sausalito; there are only a few people who know about the two of you. Take what you need from the office there with you. You'll be able to work better there than here. Then, in the morning, when you go to court, she'll drive you. Not to the courthouse—someone could see the two of you together and figure the rest out for themselves. She's going to take you to the hospital, UCSF, up on Parnassus. It's not that far from the bridge. She'll drive you into the underground parking structure. No one will notice. You take the elevator to the street and take a cab from there."

"And at the end of the day, when the trial is over?"

"Same thing, only backwards. She'll pick you up in the garage. It's always full of cars, patients and visitors who are only thinking about the reason they're there. No one is going to notice you. And even if someone does, so what? Maybe you're there to see your doctor. It doesn't matter. There won't be any reporters. There won't be any cameras."

"You worked all this out with Tangerine this morning?"

"Yes," he said rather proudly. "Are you jealous? You should be. That story I told you—that woman in ancient times?"

"Suicide the price of one night with her. I remember."

"Well, in the case of Tangerine," he remarked with the kind of cheerful self-effacement I had not seen in a while, "it might have been a price worth paying. And remember, if you think that some kind of flagrant exaggeration," he said as he got up to leave, "you're apparently willing to pay a price even higher— marriage!"

As soon as he left, I picked up the phone and called her.

"Are you sure you wouldn't mind? Albert just told me—"

"This is the first rule of cross-examination, isn't it? I remember what you taught me: never ask a question unless you know how the witness is going to answer."

I could hear the noise of traffic in the background.

"Where are you?"

"On the bridge. I'm coming to get you. You aren't in court today."

I explained that I was, or that I would be in an hour.

"Shall I come meet you at the…no, I suppose I shouldn't, should I? All right, I have to run a few errands. Call me when you're finished. Then, like Albert said, take a cab to UCSF, and I'll pick you up there. And don't worry, I promise to leave you alone when you're working."

It was a promise I hoped she would break. I did not tell her that. I did not have to. She knew.

"I probably won't keep that promise, but I'll try."

I pulled together the various things I would need—the case file, the sheaf of notes I had made from the surveillance transcripts Reynaud had let me read through, two thick legal pads and my fountain pen and ink—stuffed them into my briefcase and went down to Craven's office. His desk, the ugliest piece of furniture I had ever seen, was gone, replaced by a chrome and glass table of some minimalist's arid imagination. For a moment, I thought I had come to the wrong office. Craven seemed to agree.

"Isabel," he explained with a mournful glance. "There is nothing sacred anymore. I always wanted to get rid of the damn thing, and now that it's gone I wish I had it back." His eyes brightened briefly at a fugitive thought. "At least it's in storage, so one day, maybe…" He noticed the briefcase in my hand. "You've got everything? Good. If you need anything, anything you want me to bring you…and if you need to be here, it should be safe late at night, especially after everyone realizes you're never here."

I left the building by a side entrance and walked down the alley to the street behind the building where I had no difficulty catching a cab. I was back at the courthouse a few minutes before two.

The crowd had grown larger. Television trucks filled the streets. Reporters hung about, waiting to see what would happen next. The mood, though still tense, was more subdued than what it had been before. There were still signs and placards, but the more provocative messages had disappeared. No one jeered at me, nor did anyone shout words of encouragement as I made my way to the checkpoint at the courthouse entrance.

The trial, and all the proceedings connected with it, was now under the supervision of Leonard Silverman. Perhaps to honor her memory, he did not change courtrooms to his own. We would continue in the same place we had started, the courtroom that had for years been Evelyn Patterson's undisputed kingdom.

At precisely two o'clock, the door from chambers opened and Silverman walked quickly to the bench which now belonged to him. Because this was a hearing on a motion, or, rather, a hearing in which the judge was effectively asking the proponents of the original motion to show cause as to why it should not be rescinded, I sat alone at the counsel table. The defendant, Kevin Fitzgerald, was not part of the proceedings. Raymond St. John sat alone at the other table. A half-dozen well-dressed lawyers sat in the first row of the otherwise empty courtroom, the legal team there to represent the joint interests of the networks.

I always liked watching lawyers who never tried criminal cases work in court, the bland efficiency with which they went about compiling every conceivable relevant detail that could even remotely contribute to the completely thorough discussion of whatever issue might be raised. It was the reason there were always so many of them. You knew what you were dealing with the moment they walked into court, pulling behind them wheeled cases of essential documents, too heavy, too cumbersome, too organized, to be carried in a briefcase in their hand. They pulled them like the suitcases with which they had rolled through whatever airport they had just landed, as uniform as the dark, neatly pressed, business suits they wore. They were corporate lawyers on whose tombstones would be recorded not the dates of their birth and death, but the total number of their lifelong billable hours.

Quentin Mitford was the epitome of the type. He spoke for all of them.

"It is a basic principle of American law—a basic premise of both the first and sixth amendments to the United States Constitution—that a criminal trial is a public trial. The public's right to know, especially in a trial of this magnitude, is absolute."

Had Quentin Mitford ever tried a case, had he ever stood in respectful silence while a trial court judge told him what an embarrassment to the profession he really was, had he been forced to listen, politely, to some black-robed fool who had not read a law book, or anything else, since the day he passed the bar, tell him that his brief—the one he had worked on for days—wasn't worth his time to read, he might have learned that it is probably not the smartest thing to instruct a judge on the law with a smile as condescending as anything you might have seen on the mouth of an American billionaire when asked by a car salesman which model he thought he could afford. But he was lucky nothing, not even his smug arrogance, could disturb the equanimity of the remarkable Leonard Silverman.

"I'm sorry," said Silverman, leaning forward. "Could you speak louder; I didn't hear you."

Mitford, certain he had enunciated quite clearly every word, seemed puzzled. The smile began to fade. He started again. He got to the third word.

"Oh, that argument! Yes, I'm familiar with that. It isn't any good. You should know that. The public's right to know. That isn't a constitutional principle; it is a bromide, a simple-minded one at that. There is no necessity for television coverage, no necessity for cameras, no necessity, if you get right down to it, for members of the press of any kind to meet the requirement of a public trial. The public, as many of them as can be seated in the courtroom, are free to attend. The court reporter takes down every word that is spoken. In other words, Mr. Mitford, there is a record, a public record, of the trial.

"The issue is not whether television is necessary for a public trial; the issue is whether we can have a trial at all with the kind of coverage that by inflaming the emotions of the crowd has led to the death—the violent death—of a distinguished jurist who was presiding over this trial. The question, Mr. Mitford, is quite simple: can you guarantee this court that continuing to allow your network, and the others, to cover the trial of Kevin Fitzgerald for the murder of Walter Bridges won't continue to create an environment in which something like what happened last night won't happen again?"

Mitford was appalled. Everyone knew what a question like that would mean for a free press.

"You can't mean to suggest that the only way news coverage would be allowed is when the possibility of violence doesn't exist? We couldn't cover—"

"The press can cover whatever it likes. Reporters are free to cover this, and every other trial. Not all media are the same, they have a different effect. When you read something, you think about what you're reading, your mind is engaged. When you see something on television, when you see someone saying something you don't like, you react, and sometimes, Mr. Mitford," he said, his mouth drawn taut, "that reaction can be violent."

Pausing, he nodded twice in quick succession. Discussion was over.

"The court has two obligations: to make sure the defendant receives a fair trial, and to do whatever is in its power to protect the safety of everyone involved in the trial and everyone who works in this courthouse. There will be no further television coverage of these proceedings. There will be no cameras allowed inside the courthouse. I understand the great public interest in this trial and its outcome. For that reason, a third of the seating in the courtroom will be reserved for reporters accredited to legitimate news outlets. That is the order of the court. The trial will recommence tomorrow morning, ten o'clock."

And with that, Leonard Silverman left the courtroom, and the six dark-suited lawyers rolled their cases back to their offices where they would devote even more billable hours to discovering how they might now appeal the issue on which they had just lost. I caught a cab and called Tangerine.

CHAPTER

SIXTEEN

With a black binder in his hand, Judge Leonard Silverman walked briskly to the bench, his slight shoulders straight, his eyes never moving. He placed the binder on the bench as he took his seat. Looking directly at the jury, seated on his left, he raised his right hand, palm down, and then lowered it to signal that everyone in the courtroom should resume their seats.

"Ladies and gentlemen of the jury, my name is Leonard Silverman. I have the unfortunate duty to take the place of my colleague and friend, Judge Evelyn Patterson, who, as you know, was killed night before last in a senseless act of violence on the courthouse steps. Judge Patterson believed, with every fiber of her being, in the sanctity of the law. It is for that reason, the importance she attached—the importance we all attach—to the law, that this trial will not only continue, but continue as if there had never been an interruption. Let me now remind you of where we are.

"At the beginning of this trial, after you were sworn in but before the first witness was called, you were instructed that you had several duties. The first, and the most important, is to listen to all the evidence before you begin to reach any conclusions about whether the defendant, Kevin Fitzgerald, is guilty or not guilty. You are to keep an open mind. More than that, when all the witnesses have testified, when you have heard all the evidence, then, when you begin your deliberations, you are not only to express your own honest opinion of what the evidence means, but you are to listen, and to give credit, to what any other juror, especially one with whose opinion you initially disagree, says and thinks. You are to engage with each other in what is called reasoned argument. If, and only if, you all eventually come to the same conclusion, you may then reach a verdict in the case."

I was watching their faces, the way all twelve jurors carefully followed each word. They had respected Patterson; they would never think to question anything Silverman told them to do.

"This trial, like any trial, as Judge Patterson explained to you, is divided into two parts. Because in any criminal trial the burden is always on the state, by which I mean the prosecution, to prove the guilt of a defendant beyond that famous reasonable doubt, the prosecution always goes first. It calls the witnesses, introduces the evidence it believes necessary and sufficient to prove all the elements of the crime of which the defendant stands accused. In a case in which the defendant is charged with homicide, the state has to prove first that someone—the victim—is dead, then the cause of death—that he or she did not die of natural causes—and, finally, that the defendant is the one responsible, that he or she killed that other person and did it with what is called malice aforethought. This means that they intended to kill the victim and that they did it with an evil intent. Killing someone who is about to kill you, or about to kill someone else, killing someone in self-defense, is not homicide.

"This is the first part of the trial. In the case now before you, the prosecutor, Mr. St. John, has called witnesses and introduced evidence, including, very importantly, the defendant's own confession, sufficient to make out what is called a prima facie case. That means, in plain English, that the evidence introduced so far, if not contradicted by evidence introduced by the defense, would be sufficient to let you, the jury, decide whether the defendant is guilty or not of the crime of homicide.

"Two days ago, the last day of trial, Mr. St. John called his last witness, and, on the conclusion of that testimony, announced that the prosecution rested. That means that while the prosecution may call other witnesses later, if something said by a defense witness requires and allows it, you will hear no more from the prosecution until Mr. St. John gives his closing argument at the end of the trial. We have now reached the second part of the trial. It is the turn of the defense to call any witnesses it chooses and to introduce any evidence it thinks relevant to the case."

Silverman looked out at the courtroom. He wanted everyone to understand what he was going to say next to the jury.

"Ordinarily, it would not be necessary to tell a jury what I have just told you. I do it now for two reasons. This, as you all know, is a trial like no other we have had. There is not anyone anywhere who does not have some interest in what happens here. Not only," he said, turning again to the jury, "what you decide, but how well we all conduct ourselves. We need to remember what a trial is supposed to be. We are not here to settle accounts; we are not here to demonstrate why our politics are better than the other person's. We are here to do our duty in the way I just described: the two-part trial in which the evidence, and only the evidence, decides the only question with which are entitled and obligated to concern ourselves—whether the defendant, Kevin Fitzgerald, is or is not guilty of the crime of which he stands accused.

"That is one reason, there is another. In addition to the obvious reason, this trial is different from most others in that the defendant, having admitted what he did, has raised a defense that, when you get to the heart of it, is a variation on self-defense. When a defendant asserts a defense such as this, the burden of proof shifts to him. It is now his obligation to prove not that he did not do what he is accused of doing, but that there was a compelling, lawful reason why he did it."

Silverman waited to make sure they understood, and understood clearly, what he meant. Then he thanked them for their attention and for the first time turned to me.

"Mr. Antonelli, is the defense ready to begin?"

"We are, your Honor," I replied, standing as straight as I knew how.

"You may call your first witness."

"The defense calls the defendant, Kevin Fitzgerald," I announced with perhaps more confidence than I should have felt.

I knew what he was going to say, at least most of it, but I could only guess, and at that not a very educated guess, at how it would be received. Nor did I know any better, beyond his own sworn testimony, how much of it could be proved. Fitzgerald, for his part, had been waiting for so long for this moment that he was on his feet, heading for the witness stand, before I had finished calling his name.

The moment Fitzgerald took the stand, every member of the jury, all twelve of them, leaned forward, interested, alert, afraid of missing even one word. I started at the end.

"You confessed to killing Walter Bridges, the president of the United States. Why did you do that?"

For an instant, he froze. Or seemed to, because a moment later he was answering the question as if he had not delayed at all. But there had been that brief hesitation, and I was not sure why. Something about the way I had put the question, the form of the words, had made him, for just that quick half second, think.

"I did what I did because I thought—no, I knew—it was the only way to save the country from what Bridges, and those around him, were planning."

"Was your confession in any way the result of coercion? Were you forced to make it?"

"It would not be true to say that force wasn't used, but I told them—the Secret Service—what happened before any force was used."

"The waterboarding that the director of the Secret Service, Carson Youngblood, insisted had not been used?"

"Yes, that's correct," he replied, turning to the jury. "I was waterboarded. It isn't a very pleasant experience. But I understood why they were doing it. I knew what had happened; I knew I was not part of a conspiracy; I knew that no one else was at risk. I knew that the death of Walter Bridges was not a signal for some kind of attack on other members of the government. But they didn't know, and given what they did know, or thought they knew, I understood they could not just take my word for it. They had to be certain."

I stood at the counsel table, next to Fitzgerald's empty chair, close enough to the jury box to touch the railing with my hand, directly in front of the witness stand, a dozen feet away. The eyes of the jury moved back and forth between us.

"You were waterboarded—tortured—repeatedly, and yet you don't seem to harbor any ill will," I remarked with an air of astonishment that was not entirely fictitious.

"They did what they thought they had to do to save the country. I did what I did for the same reason," he replied with a steady, unflinching gaze.

The next question came out of my mouth before I had had time to think about it. Fitzgerald's reply seemed to invite it. There was no second guessing when you had a witness on the stand. Somewhere down below the conscious mind, the questions started to come with such speed that the witness could hear them before you were quite certain what you have just asked.

"You were tortured, and you approve of that? Torture, in this instance, was, in your judgment, justified?"

I was the only person in the courtroom who was not absolutely certain that I knew what I was doing. Fitzgerald, to all appearances, thought it the most reasonable question I could have asked, one directly related to the reason why he was there, on trial for his life.

"Torture, as a general rule, should never be allowed. There are, it seems to me, exceptions. That's where we go wrong," he remarked, talking now to the jury as if they were participants in a private but important conversation. "We think we should always do one thing or the other. We argue that torture, the use of coercion to extract information, is never right, but then someone starts talking of the extreme situation: there is a nuclear device ready to explode, you have in custody the one person who can tell you where it is. Do you hesitate to use whatever means available to force that person to talk? Who in their right mind would suggest that, in those circumstances, you should worry about whether it is right or wrong to violate someone's civil rights? But the fact that there are exceptions, that there are extreme situations, should only go to prove that the rule itself is solid, not that because torture might be necessary in the extreme case, it should therefore, in the interest of some false idea of consistency, be used whenever someone thinks it convenient."

Fitzgerald, as good at talking to a jury as any witness I had seen, looked at each of them in turn, almost as if were reviewing soldiers on parade. And then he added the remark, stunning in its implications, "No one should ever be allowed to kill the president of the United States. But there are exceptions, even to this rule."

I had started at the end. Now I took him back to the beginning. The jury, and everyone else, knew about the crime. It was important they knew something about him.

"You started out, in politics, here, in this city, when you became mayor. Why did you decide to do that, run for mayor?"

"I loved San Francisco. There is no place like it, no place in the world," he remarked, a wistful look in his eyes. "No one really knows how to describe it, no one really knows it. That sounds strange, but that is the secret, the attraction of the place. Maybe it's the bay, maybe it's the fog, maybe it's the Golden Gate, but you're always drawn to her."

It had been a long time since Fitzgerald had been with other people, limited as he had been in his confinement to one visitor at a time. The sudden proximity of an audience made him eager to share his thoughts. He could not wait to tell them everything he could.

"Maybe the best description I ever read about San Francisco is something F. Scott Fitzgerald wrote about New York, just after the Empire State Building was finished. He said it destroyed the sense that the city was the only world that counted because now, when you looked out from the top, you could see where the city ended. When you're here, in San Francisco, or when you drive in from the airport and see it for the very first time, you still get that sense, the feeling that this place is the only world there is, the only place you want to be."

The jury, all San Franciscans, loved it, and for the few moments while he talked, loved him as well. I had to, unfortunately, bring him back to the present.

"You were mayor, but then you ran for the Senate, and six years later you were elected to a second six-year term?"

"Yes, four years ago. I've been in the Senate ten years."

"And you're a member—the ranking member—of the Senate Intelligence Committee?"

"I've been on the committee since my first year in the Senate. And, yes, I'm the ranking member."

"That means you're not the chairman, but you would be if your party was to become the majority, do I understand that correctly?"

"That's exactly right."

"Other than the fact that you could one day become chairman of the committee, are there any other differences between your position as the ranking member and other members of the committee?"

"The ranking member, along with the chairman, is given unfettered access to intelligence. Whenever the CIA, or the FBI, or any of the other intelligence agencies acquire sensitive information, they are required to keep the Congress informed. Anything like this is given first to the chairman and myself."

"So, you, along with the chairman— believe it is Senator Ryder from Virginia—know more about what is going on than anyone else?"

Fitzgerald bit his lip, and with a quick, darting glance, denied it.

"We're supposed to be told whatever the intelligence agencies have learned. We weren't always told everything they knew."

"Can you be more specific?"

"The Russian investigations. There were occasional attempts at suppression."

He let this hang in the air, a suggestion the implications of which could be expanded, or compressed, according to whatever conclusion you had already reached about what Walter Bridges had or had not done. Then he removed any possible ambiguity.

"There were attempts, every step of the way, to prevent the truth from coming out. Everything' almost everything, you heard was true. And what you did not hear was true as well, and it was lethal!"

I stopped him before he got too far ahead of the story. He knew everything that had happened, but the jury did not.

"The beginning. What happened, what did you learn that eventually led you to believe that you had to…? What about the Russian investigation?"

"It needs to be divided into several different but ultimately interconnected parts. Before the election, before the campaign had even begun, before Walter Bridges became a candidate, he and others around him—friends, members of his family, business associates—had connections, relationships with various Russian individuals and entities. These were, so far as anyone knew at the time, perfectly legal. American investors in Russian enterprises—gas and oil, construction, technology, that sort of thing. Russian investors in American enterprises—mainly real estate, high-rise buildings in New York, golf clubs, resorts, and various industries, including high tech companies who were doing business around the world. There was nothing suspect about any of this. It was seen as nothing more sinister than the workings of the new world economy everyone was always talking about. Money, capital, moving from bank to bank, country to country, at the speed of light, the instantaneous electronic transactions that have come to dominate modern commerce. But there was still that other side of things. Money moved from place to place, but so did the people who had it. Americans who were doing business in Russia spent time in Moscow; Russians who did business in America or Europe spent time in New York and Paris. Relationships were formed, friendships—apparent friendships—were made, understandings were reached."

"Understandings?"

Fitzgerald nodded, a cynical, knowing look on his face.

"There is a difference between men and women in public life, and people who live their lives in the private sector making money." He shook his head, marveling at how things had changed. "When I first got into politics, someone told me—and it was something everyone new to politics was told—never to do or say anything you didn't want to read in the newspapers the next morning. A married man or woman who holds public office who sleeps with someone not their wife or husband faces a scandal that, even today, will either drive them out of office or make their next election more of an adventure than they ever wanted. A private businessman staying in a Moscow hotel isn't thinking what may happen to his chances in the next election. With the Russians, it's all very subtle. They were subtle enough with Walter Bridges."

There was an audible gasp in the courtroom, not because anyone had ever seriously doubted Bridges could have done the kind of things in his private life that had been endlessly chronicled in the tabloids, but because Fitzgerald was apparently about to confirm that the stories were true.

"Bridges was never someone who knew, much less practiced, the virtues of restraint. On this one trip to Moscow, he spent a week in the most luxurious suite of Moscow's most expensive hotel. The cost meant nothing to him, and he certainly did not haggle over the price of the various high-priced Russian call girls who kept him company at night. He had to have known—everyone knew—that foreigners, especially rich, influential ones, were kept under close surveillance. But like a lot of wealthy men used to getting whatever they want, he, apparently, believed that what happened to other visitors would somehow never happen to him. He didn't follow anyone's rules, and he was, then and always, too reckless to follow his own, if, in fact, he had any.

"It was only at the end of that sybaritic week, the last night he was there, that what he thought his great, good Russian friend, a man he had been doing business with, told him over dinner—told him as if he was delighted—was that he understood that he had had a really good time. And before Bridges could say anything, he assured him that the secret of what he had done in a Moscow hotel would 'always be safe with us.' Not safe with me, your supposed good friend—safe with us. Even Walter Bridges could figure out what that meant.

"That was only part of the story, one of the ways the Russians acquired a means of influence over who, at that point, was simply another brash, rich American. Well, not simply that. He had already begun to speak out, to make a name for himself, at least among the tabloid journalists and cable news shows who liked nothing better than someone who would attack celebrities and well-known politicians, someone who seemed to like calling other people names. But it is safe to assume that no one in Russian intelligence, no one in the Russian government, ever imagined this same rather vulgar, boorish fool—those are the words they used among themselves, the Russian intelligence operatives, to describe him—would ever be a candidate, much less actually become president.

"They did this—Russian intelligence—as a matter of course, but there was also a very specific reason. Bridges was someone they thought they could use for reasons that had nothing to do with politics. He owned hotels, he owned casinos, he had an interest—a financial interest—in dozens of different enterprises. The Russians needed ways to move money. The Russian economy was controlled from the top, but not like what it was under Lenin and Stalin and the others who came after them when the Communist Party was in control and Russia was still part of the Soviet Union. It was not socialism in one country anymore, it was not even an attempt at socialism. The state-run industries had been sold off, given away, to a few well-placed people, all of whom became extraordinarily rich. Russia became an oligarchy, or in the eyes of those who had to live there, a kleptocracy—a government of thieves who had stolen what rightfully belonged to the Russian people. The oligarchs—people Putin trusted, and Putin himself—were worth billions. The question was where to put it, where to keep it safe, safe and untraceable. Walter Bridges, and people close to Bridges, provided one of the answers.

"It is very simple. You run a Russian bank. You have money from various Russian mobsters. You invest that money in an American construction project, or you loan it out through some third party to an American investor who uses it to pay off a loan he owes to a different bank, a legitimate bank. And now, if you are one of the Russian oligarchs, you have gotten rid of money you did not want anyone to trace, and have instead acquired through the loan you made what looks like a legitimate American investment, and with it something even more important: a chokehold on the American who now owes you a billion or so dollars that he may or may not be able to repay.

"What I have just described is not some hypothetical case. It is what the Russians actually did with Walter Bridges. They hold, through various intermediaries, the mortgage on the biggest building he owned. What they had on him from his time in that Moscow hotel became, in a way, security for his debt. He might be able to use the bankruptcy laws to avoid paying other creditors, but he would not be able to bankrupt out of this. They did not have to threaten him, both sides understood the game. No one was harmed, no one lost money; it was business as usual. The Russians were laundering money. Walter Bridges ran his companies. When Bridges needed money, when one of his businesses was in trouble, he could go to any bank he wanted to. The problem was that he was in trouble so often that there weren't many banks interested in giving him, for the second or third or fourth time, the help he needed. But there was always one source he could use. I say one source, not one bank. The Russians were too smart, too careful, to use one bank alone. There were dozens of them, banks in different parts of the world they either controlled or had sufficient capital in, banks that would, following direction, make whatever loan Bridges required."

For the next two hours, I handed Fitzgerald one document after another: bank statements, financial transactions, loan applications, the long, tedious, Byzantine record of the ways in which Walter Bridges had done business with the Russians. He examined each document, identified its origin and explained in clear, concise language what it meant. Then I handed him a folder full of photographs. Before he had opened it, St. John was on his feet, renewing the objection he had made earlier, in chambers, when he and I met privately with Judge Silverman.

"Your Honor, the prosecution objects to the introduction of these photographs into evidence. They serve no legitimate purpose. They are salacious in the extreme, and prove nothing relevant to what the jury is here to decide."

The jury, and everyone else, was immediately interested. The word "salacious," used in court, had that effect. Silverman waited to see if I wished to reply.

"The jury is asked to decide not if the defendant killed someone, but whether there was a lawful excuse. Whether there was such an excuse depends, in this case, on what kind of person the victim was, whether Walter Bridges was a man who could control his impulses, a man who held himself to the normal, civilized standard of behavior, or someone, as the defense contends, willing to do anything he wanted and damn the consequences. These photographs tend to prove the latter."

Silverman did not hesitate. He seldom did.

"For that purpose alone, they are admitted."

Fitzgerald opened the folder and thumbed through them.

"They're all photographs of Walter Bridges."

"Is he alone?"

"No, he is with several different women."

"Can you tell from the photographs where they were taken?"

He held one up and examined it closely.

"There is a menu, a room service menu, I think, open on the lamp table next to the bed. It's written in Russian. And, here, at the top of the photograph, it is marked Moscow with the time and date."

At my instruction, the clerk took them from Fitzgerald and handed them to the juror sitting in the first row, in the corner closest to her. I stared into the middle distance, careful not to watch the jurors' faces as one by one they looked through the photographs of a naked Walter Bridges in all his pale ugliness cavorting on a garish golden four-poster bed with painted harlots nearly as hideous as he. When the photographs had been passed all the way around, when the last juror had given them back to the clerk, I hazarded a glance. If anyone was stunned or surprised, they did not show it. They seemed almost indifferent, as if they had grown used to Walter Bridges's notorious lack, not just of morality, but of even minimal good taste. Those, and there were several, old enough to remember the rumored indiscretions of John F. Kennedy might have been forgiven if they thought it still proved something that the women Kennedy had known had all been volunteers. Fitzgerald did not say that, but then he did not have to. He may have been accused of murder, but he conducted himself with decorum. He looked at the jury as if he wanted to apologize for what they had just been forced to see.

"These photographs, are they consistent with what you learned as the ranking member of the Senate Intelligence Committee?"

"Yes, they are."

"Is there any doubt, based on what you learned, that the Russians had this information, and that the Russians had substantial financial ties with Walter Bridges?"

"No doubt whatsoever."

"But this was all background, wasn't it? Until he became a candidate. What happened then, once Walter Bridges emerged as the likely nominee of his party?"

"Some of it," he began, looking directly at the jury, "you already know. I don't mean what you read in the papers, what you saw on television. I mean what you learned here, in court, when Michael Donahue testified for the prosecution. He can deny it all he wants, but the fact is he met with the Russians, and he had others do the same thing. We don't know—we may never know—who made the first contact, whether it was someone in the Bridges campaign or someone from Russian intelligence. We know, and there is no doubt about this, that they met, not once or twice, but dozens of times. We know what they discussed. We know how, over time, those discussions changed."

With my arms crossed, I followed the movement of my feet as I slowly walked a few steps in one direction and then back again, concentrating on every word; listening intently not just to the words, but the sound they made, the rich, clear, bell-like sound that made you listen even closer. There was seduction in that voice of his. The more he talked, the more you wanted to hear. And he knew it. You could see it in his eyes, the absolute, unshakable certainty that he could convince everyone of the truth of anything he believed. It was the gift of the politician who had never lost an election, the gift of the lawyer who had never lost a trial, a gift that belonged only to those who could first convince themselves that they were never wrong. It was the gift of arrogance, the gift that almost always led to your own destruction.

He had said the discussion, what went on between Bridges and his people with the Russians, had changed. Before he explained how, I had a question.

"You referred a moment ago to the testimony of Michael Donahue. In addition to what he testified—that he had dinner with a Russian at a Paris restaurant but did not know he was a Russian general, much less the one in charge of their cyber warfare program—did he, to your knowledge, have any other meetings with high-ranking Russian officials?"

"At least three others. Twice with the Russian ambassador in Washington, one with a Russian banker. That meeting took place in Zurich."

"There were no other meetings?"

"General Rostov, the man he had dinner with in Paris. That was the second time they met."

I wondered if Reynaud had known about this.

"There were five meetings, then? Was that second meeting with Rostov also in Paris?"

"No. They met two months before. I said there were four meetings because the second time Donahue met with the Russian ambassador is when he was introduced to Sergei Rostov."

"The general was here, in Washington, in the United States?"

"He and Donahue spent the better part of the day together."

"At the Russian embassy?" I asked, just to be sure.

"They never left."

CHAPTER

SEVENTEEN

"Tell me everything!" insisted Tangerine when she picked me up from the third floor of the hospital parking garage.

She looked astonishing, sitting behind the wheel of her car, her chin tilted up and a smile on her lips, her eyes vibrant as a summer rainbow. I forgot all about the trial. All I wanted to do was watch. She drove up the steep, narrow exit that spiraled to the street outside.

"Tell me everything that happened, Antonelli!" She laughed, turning the wheel hand over hand through the passing white concrete maze. "Don't leave out anything. I couldn't watch on television and you wouldn't let me come to the trial, you—"

"Had to try to concentrate on what I was doing. You're not much help with that."

Wrinkling her nose, her chin shot higher and in that thrilling voice called me a liar, and with her glowing, eager eyes told me she was glad I thought I was telling the truth.

"Later, at dinner. I promise I'll tell you everything, though there really isn't that much to tell."

We were out of the garage and on the street, weaving through traffic, daring each light to wait, and not always stopping when it did not. She seemed to take it as a challenge whether she could make it to the bridge without having to stop even once.

"I think that's called cheating," I remarked when she coasted through the last light in the park just as it turned red.

"It wasn't even close," she argued. "Live dangerously, don't live stupidly. What chances did you take today? Ask any questions you didn't know the answers to? Make any promises you know you'll never keep? Tell the jury your client is innocent when you know he is, in that wonderfully dull phrase, guilty as hell!"

I leaned against the door, watching out the window, Alcatraz in the middle of the bay shining black and gray in the evening sun.

"I've never done that...or maybe I have. You're not supposed to say whether you think the defendant is guilty or not. I think I must have, at one time or another. I've broken all the other rules, I don't know why I wouldn't have broken that one."

"Have you really? Broken all the rules?"

"In court, and in life. But I promise, lying bastard that I am, I'll always be faithful to you."

I sometimes marveled at my own weak-minded stupidity. She was the most beautiful woman I had ever seen. She took my breath away every time I looked at her. And I was promising I'd be faithful to her, as if it could ever have occurred to her that I would not. I started laughing.

"Why? What did I…?"

We had almost reached the other side of the Golden Gate.

"That story Albert told me, that story I told you—that woman in ancient Greece, or ancient Rome, the one—"

"Who would sleep with any man who promised to kill himself in the morning." She said this in a way that left no doubt she not only understood but approved of the conditions.

"That's the one. Do you think any of the men she was with also promised they would be faithful until—"

"Until the day they died. Wouldn't that have been implicit? But do you know what I think? I think that story isn't a true story and it wasn't meant to be one. I think it has a hidden meaning, that it is a kind of riddle." Her eyes got brighter, her smile got bigger. "She's asking if the men who want her are willing to die. Whether they are willing, but able as well. Remember, they are asked to commit suicide, not to let someone else kill them, to experience death. Remember what some people used to call it when a man finished, that is to say, completed the act—a 'little death.' So, maybe what it means is that what she really wants is a man who just looking at her knows that when they make love, she can give him the complete satisfaction he may never have known before."

I could not help myself.

"Thank God. Now I can kill myself more than once."

Her eyes were full of excitement.

"Only more than once?"

"I've been in trial all day."

"Are you going to tell me everything that happened? That is the other thing you promised."

"At dinner. Where do you want to go?"

"Some place quiet; some place we can be alone."

She pulled off the highway at the last exit to Sausalito, the one farthest from her house, the other side of the village. There was a restaurant at the north end of the yacht harbor.

"Here, I brought you a few things," she informed me after parking the car in the lot in front. She handed me a tan canvas hat, the kind beachcombers wore, and my dark glasses. "Put them on before we go in," she said as she fastened a silk scarf around her hair and, watching herself in the rearview mirror, adjusted her own dark glasses delicately on her nose.

I looked at her, dumbfounded.

"We're maybe forty feet away, why would—"

She became quite serious.

"There probably isn't a place in America with a higher percentage of liberals, probably nowhere where more people think you should win, that Kevin should not be prosecuted for it—whether or not they agree with what he did. But that doesn't mean there aren't people who think the death penalty would be too good for him, and—more importantly, as far as I'm concerned—that his lawyer should get the same kind of treatment. Think me crazy if you like, but crazy people aren't always wrong."

There was no way I could say no. I pulled the hat on and put on the glasses, and with my arm around her shoulder we crossed the parking lot and up the steps to the entrance. There was a long three-sided bar in the middle of a very large room, with tables scattered all around. Floor-to-ceiling glass doors and windows let in the outside light and a view across the floating wooden walkways and boats of every size and description moored next to them. Tangerine had been here before and led me to a table on the far end of the deck outside.

It was the last table left, and as luck would have it, the two couples at the table next to ours were talking about the trial. Smiling to herself, Tangerine raised an eyebrow in knowing triumph. She had taken the chair facing the restaurant and, coincidentally, all the other tables outside on the deck. I was sitting facing the water, my back to everything. The conversation had stopped, the way it always seemed to stop whenever Tangerine suddenly made an appearance. There was the same breathless pause there had been the night she had come to meet me at the top of the Mark Hopkins when she walked across the room to the bar. She removed the silk scarf and let her hair fall free, and then, taking off her sunglasses, she smiled briefly at the four faces that had turned to her. Looking up at the waiter who had come running the moment he saw her, she ordered two drinks. I looked at Tangerine with a smile of my own. The silence at the table behind me was broken by four voices now talking all at once.

"It's terrible, what happened to that judge," one of them, a woman of middle years, was saying. "Just awful. But they should have known something like this would happen. These people who thought Bridges was so great...why? Because he was always talking about violence himself."

"Listen, I know I'm the only one around her who voted for Bridges," replied the husband of the other woman at the table. "But none of this would have happened, that judge would not have been killed, if Fitzgerald had not started it. He killed Bridges. Bridges never killed anyone, and you seem to think Fitzgerald is some kind of hero. I don't understand people like you. I don't understand what is going on."

The waiter brought our drinks, and for a while, occasionally lifting a glass, we just looked at each other as we listened to what the rest of the world was thinking.

"There's a poll just out," reported the other man, a little older than the first one, and, from the brief glimpse I had of him when we first arrived, more distinguished looking. I guessed he might be a physician, or, because he dressed with understated elegance, someone in finance. "If Spencer runs for president, he wins. He isn't as far ahead as Bridges was behind. Fitzgerald would have beaten him by twenty points or more, but he has more than fifty percent."

"That's just because, through no fault of his own, he's just become president," insisted the second woman at the table. "After Bridges was killed, everyone wants the new president to succeed. The only surprising thing is that his level of support isn't higher."

"That wasn't what the poll said. It gets interesting. They asked how they would feel about Fitzgerald if he gets acquitted, if he proves he had to do what he did, if—"

"The murdering son of a bitch! He murdered the president. Who gives a damn what—"

"If you'll just let me finish, Charlie, I'll explain. The question was if it turns out that Bridges was about to do something that was a clear and present danger to the country, and Fitzgerald acted to stop him, do you think Fitzgerald should run for president and would you support him if he does? Almost sixty percent said yes."

"Wait a minute, you just said that Spencer gets more than fifty percent."

"Separate questions. They did not ask what would happen between Spencer and Fitzgerald, just what did they think of each of them."

The first woman thought everyone was making a mistake.

"The way the question was asked. *If* Bridges was about to destroy the country. *If* Fitzgerald stopped him from doing it. *If* Fitzgerald saved the country. A lot of ifs."

"We'll know soon enough. Fitzgerald started testifying today."

"In the trial no one can watch."

"You know what I don't get," said the only one of them to have voted for Bridges. "A guy like Antonelli. How the hell do you justify doing what he does, defending someone like Fitzgerald who already confessed to what he did? Far as I'm concerned, the guy who shot the judge shot the wrong person."

Staring down into my glass, I raised my eyes just high enough to see Tangerine start to say something. I reached across the table and held her wrist.

"Tell me about your day," I said quietly, shaking my head to let her know that I had heard it all before and that nothing was going to change his mind. She nodded what I assumed was her agreement, and then signaled the waiter. He was there almost immediately.

"Would you..." she whispered in his ear. Then, while he stood there waiting, she reached into her purse for a pen and a sheet of note paper. Her eyes sparkled with a truant's excitement as she scribbled a brief note and then gave it to the waiter, who practically fluttered with delight at carrying out her order. A few minutes later he returned with a bottle of the restaurant's most expensive wine. Nodding in our direction, he presented it to the table behind me, along with the note that, she explained to me, read simply, 'With the compliments of Mr. and Mrs. Joseph Antonelli.'"

"You wrote that? Mr. and Mrs..."

"Sure, why not? They don't know you haven't married me yet."

There was one thing I now had to do. Turning around, I moved my chair close to the other table and looked at the Bridges voter who thought I should probably be killed. He was red-faced with embarrassment, but he believed what he believed, and that was not going to change. I told him he was in good company.

"You know your Shakespeare. One of his most memorable lines, in the mouth of someone at the beginning of a rebellion, 'The first thing we'll do, let's kill all the lawyers.' But before that happens, if you ever find yourself in trouble, if you are ever accused of a crime you didn't commit, I hope you'll call me. I'll do what I can for you."

He could not help himself. He smiled, and the grin on his face growing larger, he said that if he ever killed anyone, I would be the first call he would make.

"In that case, I hope I never hear from you."

I liked him. That was the simple truth of it. But I was proud of Tangerine for the classy thing she had done, and she was proud of me, and we sat there so pleased with ourselves you would have thought us two teenagers who had just discovered what it meant to be invincible. Nothing could touch us, not now, not ever.

"Keep your promise," she reminded me after we had ordered dinner, and our friends at the other table had grown content with us and with each other.

"Promise?"

"To tell me everything that happened today in the trial."

But before I could start, she began telling me.

"I watched what they were saying on television. They can't have cameras in the courtroom anymore, so they have reporters who watch for a while and then come out and tell what they saw. So, you see, I know a little. I know that Kevin was your first witness, and that you spent most of the day asking about what he knows about what the Russians had done with Bridges, and some of his people, in the days before he first became involved in politics. That doesn't tell me anything about what really happened, though, does it? What was it like, what did it feel like, how did the jury react? Could you tell?

She started poking at the crab louie she had ordered. I took another drink, trying to remember what had happened and the best way to describe it.

"The first thing that—"

"No, first tell me about the judge, the new one, Leonard Silverman. How different is he? Or is he different from Evelyn Patterson?"

"He's older, quicker—quicker than maybe any other judge on the bench—and gentler than any man I know."

"Gentle? In what way?" she asked, her musical eyes glittering with anticipation. "He doesn't raise his voice, doesn't get angry, never says a harsh word, even when someone has spoken that way to him. Gentler, because he's wise; because he knows people better than they know themselves; because, knowing their failings, he is always able to forgive their sins. Gentle, like that?"

I listened, I heard every word, and then I listened again to what she had said, and knew that if I tried for a hundred years, I would never be able to describe Leonard Silverman any better. And she had never met him.

"Something like that," I replied, tilting my head to the side in baffled surrender to the strange, enigmatic power she had to see into the heart of things of which she had not known the surface.

"There aren't many like that, are there? I don't mean just judges, butr people altogether. If you meet two or three in your whole lifetime, you've done better than most, haven't you?"

She picked again at her food, but she was too interested in what I could tell her to think about eating.

"What is the jury thinking, how did they react when Kevin was testifying? You get a feeling about things. Tell me what it was."

"There were two sets of motion at once: Fitzgerald moving toward the witness stand as if he could not wait to get there, and twelve jurors moving forward in their chairs to get as close to him as they could, close enough to hear every word, close enough to see even the smallest change of expression. And they didn't stop, they didn't get tired of it, they didn't lose interest. Some of his testimony was riveting, compelling—he has that gift, that way of speaking that makes you want to listen, that makes you want to hear more. But he could have been dull and listless, the worst speaker you have ever heard, and you still would have been mesmerized by some of the things he talked about: the way the Russians handled Bridges, the way they took their time, building relationships, friendships, establishing a sense of trust. They were only businessmen, bankers, men with connections who knew how to get things done, investors with more money than they knew what to do with who only wanted the kind of safe investments they knew he could offer. The Russians were brilliant; Bridges could only see what was right in front of him: the next deal, the next opportunity, the next way to make money.

"Everything Fitzgerald said today was believable because he didn't say anything that has not been talked about, and rumored, before. The last two years, it's about all anyone has talked about. The jury believed him, but we had to have more than what everyone had been told. We had to have proof. There were dozens of documents, most of them the kind that will cause your eyes to glaze over in less time than it takes to read the title on the top of the page. This jury treated it all like twelve rabid accountants, getting more excited with every number they heard cited. It was extraordinary, the way they seemed to hang on every word. Part of it was Fitzgerald. He has this trick he uses. I've seen him do it before. He's tried it with me. He'll stumble over a word, correct a figure he has just quoted or read, and flash that bashful smile that makes everyone want to believe him, and apologize for the mistake. He wants you to believe that he thinks you must know more about this—understand better what these dull reports he is reading mean— than he ever could. And it works. They think they do, or that they should, or at least ought to try."

A smile started onto her mouth, the cynical nostalgia about what she had once considered the innocent fraud of a rising star.

"When he was mayor, he would go to some dinner, say, in Chinatown. He would have a few words of greeting in Chinese and would always make sure to pronounce them with an awkward self-consciousness that seemed to show how important he thought it to try. And you're right, it worked. They loved him more than they would have if he had spoken Chinese perfectly. It proved the effort, and the effort proved his goodwill. But," she continued, tossing her head in a way that expressed a doubt, "is that enough to work with a jury? He isn't running for office, he's on trial."

"I'm not sure," I admitted, "that he thinks there is a difference."

The people at the next table left, but not before thanking us for the bottle of wine. My new friend, the Bridges voter, shook my hand and wished me well. I thought he might almost have meant it.

"It's what happens when you're famous," said Tangerine with a laugh after they were gone. "He can think Joseph Antonelli should be shot dead, until he meets Joseph Antonelli, and then he can't imagine there is any nicer man in the world—just like other people. I'll bet you anything that is what he'll tell his friends tomorrow."

"That isn't what he'll tell his friends tomorrow. He'll tell them with wide-eyed wonder that that son of a bitch Antonelli is married to the greatest-looking broad he's ever seen!"

"You think he'll say 'broad?'"

"Only if he's on his best behavior."

"So he won't hate Joseph Antonelli anymore, he'll envy him—is that what you are saying?"

"That is exactly what I'm saying—as if you needed to hear it. Now, what do you want to know about the trial?"

"The photographs. Everyone is talking about them."

"That's another good reason not to televise a trial."

"That bad?"

"Worse." I realized now the reason they were so utterly appalling. In a way, it was almost funny, especially when I was sitting across from her. "Do you ever...? No, of course you wouldn't, wonder how stupid we look. most of us, I mean, when we're naked? Especially men, and especially when we're aroused. There we are, slumped shoulders, arms and legs too skinny or too fat, stomachs, some of them, like beachballs that haven't been sufficiently inflated, or inflated to the point of bursting, with hairy chests, or chests with no hair at all, with any number of scars and other disfigurements on our faces which, even without that, are usually grotesque enough, with sagging mouths and sagging eyes, crooked noses and missing teeth. And then, if we weren't ugly enough, an erection that makes us look like a broken down door with a misshaped handle dangling upside down from somewhere near the middle. There is a reason we invented clothes. And now, to our great discomfort, we discover that our president looked even more grotesque, naked and aroused, than almost anyone we could imagine outside a circus freak show. When those pictures were passed around the jury box, they could not wait to get them out of their hands."

"Then why...?"

"The same reason that the prosecution introduces photographs of the victim in a murder trial, the same reason St. John introduced the pictures of Bridges lying dead on the floor of Air Force One—to prove that something really happened, and, though no one will ever admit it, to make the jury as angry, as repulsed, as you can. Although, in this case, I did it less for that reason than to prove that Bridges had something to fear from the Russians."

It was getting dark. A few lights flickered on the hillside across, what at this end of the bay was perhaps less than half a mile away. A short man with a short beard and a round face got into a rowboat and headed for his sailboat anchored a hundred yards offshore. Three seagulls alighted on the railing of the deck a few feet from where we sat, waiting with imperious impatience for what someone at a table might be willing to share. Tangerine tossed them a broken piece of French breach. They ate it, and seemed offended when they were not offered more.

"The deserving rich," she observed. "What will happen tomorrow? How long does Kevin testify?"

I threw my arm over the back of the chair and crossed one leg over the other. The seagulls thought it meant something for them and hopped closer. Tangerine laughed, and handed them the bread she had left.

"Go away, you greedy birds. Find someone else to show your ingratitude!"

They ignored her.

"I didn't want you there today," I began to explain.

"I know, you weren't sure it would be safe. But it's safe, isn't it? What if I come tomorrow?"

"Then I wouldn't have anything to tell you tomorrow night."

"You can tell me the meaning of everything I see. It will be easy," she added quickly, to forestall my objection. "We'll do the same thing we've started to do. I'll bring you in, in the morning, drop you at the hospital, like today. Then I'll park near the courthouse, watch the trial, then drive back and wait for you. You'll be able to avoid all the reporters, and I'll get to watch you work."

I thought about it. I had liked it when she was in court, I liked knowing she was there, that close. But there was something I had not told her.

"It's better if you don't. When I got there this morning, there was a mob scene outside. It wasn't like before. No one was shouting obscenities, no one was picking fights. The murder of Judge Patterson has had at least that much effect, but the tension is still there. You can feel it. Something is going to happen. Someone is going to start something, do something, and people will start shoving, pushing, and when that happens, punches will start being thrown. There are cops all over the place, but there is a point at which that becomes a provocation, an invitation to show your rage and defiance. Don't come. If you did, I wouldn't be able to concentrate on what I'm doing."

She did not say anything for a few moments. Though she had eaten next to nothing, we were finished with dinner. She sipped on coffee.

"It's nice you worry about me, Antonelli," she said presently. "I'm not sure anyone ever has before."

I did not have to ask what she meant. She could have anyone she wanted, she always could; why would anyone ever think her vulnerable and alone?

"What else about today, Antonelli? What else happened in the trial you haven't told me about?"

Scratching my chin, I tried to think of something that others might not notice.

"The jurors. Five men, seven women. Two Asian, one Hispanic, one black. What you might expect. One of the women is five months pregnant. She was asked if she wanted to be excused, whether she thought because of her pregnancy she would rather not serve. The woman, Alice Milham, said she thought she owed it to her child—this was to be her first—to meet her obligations as a citizen. No one was really surprised. Alice Milham is an Army veteran, served two tours in Iraq. That's why this jury is a little unusual. There are five veterans, two of them the two oldest men, both in their sixties. The other three, including Alice Milham, are all women, young women in their twenties or thirties, who joined up. One of them will be foreman, I'm sure of it. When they enter the jury box every morning, all the others defer to them. St. John thinks that because Bridges was commander-in-chief, and they are former military, they're more likely to think there is no excuse for what Fitzgerald did. He's wrong. They're the best chance Fitzgerald has. They're one of the reasons I wanted those photographs put into evidence. The chain of command is one thing, but their sense of honor, of sacrifice, of doing whatever you have to do for your country, is everything."

CHAPTER

EIGHTEEN

I started where Fitzgerald had ended his first day of testimony.

"Michael Donahue met twice with General Rostov, once at a restaurant in Paris, but the other time, the first time, in Washington, at the Russian embassy. Is that what you told us yesterday?"

Tricia Fitzgerald brought her husband a different change of clothes every day. This morning, he was wearing a dark blue pin stripe suit, white shirt and light gray tie. He looked more like what he was, a young and ambitious United States senator, than the defendant in a murder trial. He did not lean to one side or the other in the witness chair, but bent slightly forward, just enough to emphasize his intense interest in the questions and his eagerness to respond.

"That's correct. Two meetings. The one at the Russian embassy lasted nearly all day."

"This meeting took place before Walter Bridges had the nomination?"

"It was in early June. Bridges did not have the nomination yet, but it was pretty certain he was going to get it."

"Do you know what was discussed in that meeting? Was it just General Rostov, or was the ambassador also involved?"

"They were both involved—Rostov and the ambassador. There were three main lines of discussion," he said as his eyes moved from me to the jury. "The Bridges campaign and how they might help; how relations between Russia and the United States could be improved; and, finally, how the world had changed, how the old attitudes needed to be replaced with a different, more informed understanding of a nation's self-interest. This came late in the day," he added, "and Donahue was doing most of the talking. The Russians listened, but did not really comment. They were clearly more interested in the first two things: the election and what might happen if Bridges somehow managed to get elected."

"Start from the beginning. What did they discuss about the Bridges campaign and, as I think you put it, how they could help?

Fitzgerald nodded twice in quick succession. He could barely wait to begin.

"Rostov told Donahue that there were things about the other party's candidate, Madelaine Shaw, that would be extremely damaging if they were ever made public, that there were things about some of the people in her campaign, people who had been close to her for years, who would cause the kind of scandal that could disrupt, and possibly even destroy, her candidacy. A lot of it was financial—money paid for things that were never done, contributions that had never been reported and that instead of going into the campaign had gone into various off-shore accounts—tens of millions that could not be explained.

"You have to understand," said Fitzgerald with a grim, determined expression, "the Russians did not believe for a moment that Bridges could win. That was not what this was about. They wanted to help him only as a way of hurting Shaw, to weaken her as much as possible. They were very good at this. I'll get back to this in a minute. Madelaine Shaw was going to be the next president of the United States. That seemed a given. The Russians hated her. They had had dealings with her before, when she was in government. They thought her overrated, a lightweight, someone who would never take a chance on anything, someone—and from their point of view this was decisive—who would always stand in their way, because it allowed her to seem more tough minded than she really was. The goal was to make the election as close as possible, and in that way deprive her of any chance to claim a mandate of what she, and her party, wanted to do. That was the reason they were so eager to use people like Michael Donahue, to get him, and some others, involved. They needed people on the inside, people who could tell them the best time to release what they had, how to do this over time, so each new disclosure would add to the overall, cumulative effect that whatever you thought of what Madelaine Shaw wanted to do for the country, whatever policies she wanted to pursue, whatever changes she wanted to make, you could never trust her."

Fitzgerald sat back, a rueful smile at the corners of his mouth, the grudging admiration for a scheme of Machiavellian proportions.

"Rostov, the ambassador, they're sitting there with Donahue over lunch, safe to say what they really think about a woman all of them despise. The ambassador, who had been in Washington for nearly a decade, who knows everyone; Donahue, who had only ever visited, a tourist from out of town, new to politics but certain, because he's read a few books, that he knows why everyone in Washington is wrong; the two of them, with Rostov nodding his agreement, talking about what an extraordinary thing it is that a woman with so little to show for a life's work in politics and government could actually find herself this close to winning the presidency.

"'Everyone knows she's as crooked as they come.' That was a line the ambassador kept repeating, and every time followed it with the almost casual remark that the material he had seen that proved it was 'overwhelming.' All Donahue knows are the rumors that, like everyone else, he has heard. But the Russians have proof. Or so they tell him. That is one idea they plant in his mind. There is another one to which Donahue is particularly susceptible. Everything in Washington is fixed. Nothing is done, legislation is never passed, decisions are never made, unless money changes hands, unless the lobbyists for special interests agree. And nothing happens at all, money is never spent or offered, unless it does not threaten the permanent interests of the real government, the one that had never been elected and holds all the power—the Deep State you heard him testify about in court. Everything is rigged for its advantage. The ambassador asks—and there is no one more subtle, more insidious at this sort of thing—'What makes you think those same people can't make sure the election turns out the way they want it to? Isn't the whole system rigged? Do you really think they're going to let someone like Walter Bridges get elected so he can tear down everything they have built?'"

I was leaning against the front edge of the counsel table, one foot crossed over the other, listening, like the jury, to a soliloquy on the study of political intrigue and influence. Fitzgerald had a way of telling a story that made you feel you were there, inside the room, listening in person to the beginning of a conspiracy that would change the way everyone thought about their country and the people leading it.

"There was a kind of genius in the way they handled Donahue. They would tell him something, stunning in its implications, and then dismiss the importance of what they had just told him with the suggestion that there was more, much more than that. And every time they mentioned something, it was accompanied by some remark that while they did not have this information themselves, they were reasonably certain they could get it. They wanted Donahue to take the initiative; they wanted him to express an interest. They wanted to have a way to protect themselves when questions started to be asked—as they surely would be after this material started to be released—a way to make everyone believe that some independent source was doing this on their own. Donahue believed everything they told him. They had the same interest; they wanted to do anything they could to make Madelaine Shaw seem illegitimate, a woman who cheated her way to the nomination and would, given half a chance, steal the election. And if any proof was needed that she was not qualified to hold the office, there was the question of what she would do if she actually won. The question, in particular, of what she would do about this country's relations with Russia."

"The second thing discussed that day at the Russian embassy?" I asked.

"Yes, that's right," replied Fitzgerald as he rubbed his forehead. He stared at some point in the middle distance, concentrating, as it seemed, on how to explain the precise nature of what had taken place. "This is where it gets complicated, where things begin to converge. When I testified yesterday, when I described what the Russians had learned about Bridges, the various relationships that had been formed with him, the material they had compiled, I talked about how they had made certain that Bridges knew what they had. You had to, unfortunately, see some of the photographs that had been taken of Bridges in a Moscow hotel. But now, suddenly, all of this, all the material they had gathered, everything Bridges knew they had, became relevant in ways they had not imagined. Think what a surprise it must have been. They could not believe their good luck. Walter Bridges, a rich, mindless American in the judgement of their intelligence services, someone who because he did not care where the money came from, they had been able to use as a conduit for money they had reason to hide, is now a candidate for the presidency. He isn't going to win, but that is not important. What is important is that he now commands the national stage. What is important is that, in addition to all the speeches he is going to make, all the interviews he is going to give, he will debate, not once, but several times, Madelaine Shaw on national television. He can attack her at any point where she is vulnerable. He can, with a little helpful advice, attack her for her failure to understand how Russia, instead of an enemy, can become an effective and valuable partner in the fight against terrorism. That is what they really want, and, whatever Donahue may know about what the Russians have on Bridges, they know Bridges knows. And why would he object to doing what they want? The only thing he knows how to do is attack, and there's no one he likes to attack more than someone who stands in his way." Fitzgerald gave the jury a long, significant look. "The Russians knew what they were doing."

We went back and forth, question and answer, rounding out his testimony about the Russian involvement in the election, until a few minutes past noon. We finished that line of inquiry and were ready to move on to the still more vital discussion of what happened after the election, after Walter Bridges, to everyone's astonishment, became president. Judge Silverman recessed the proceedings for lunch.

I did not eat, and neither did Fitzgerald. We sat together in a small conference room, going over one last time the explosive revelations that would either save his life or send him to death row. At one thirty we were back in court and in front of a jury that had lost nothing of its sense of anticipation and a courtroom packed with reporters ready to take down every word. I started with the question the whole country had been waiting to hear.

"Senator Fitzgerald, why did you kill Walter Bridges?"

Fitzgerald did not hesitate. I did not doubt that he had been thinking about the question from the moment he killed him; I did not doubt, really, that he had been thinking about it long before that. He must have thought about it from the time he first decided that it was something he had to do. It was part of the equation, the justification, for what, as he knew better than anyone, no one had ever done before. That had become clear to me. He was not some crazed assassin, willing to kill and be killed in return. He had never intended to die in the attempt. He was always going to go to trial. The death of the president had, in his mind, become necessary, but so was his own vindication.

"It's very simple. Walter Bridges was going to make sure we did not have another election. He was right in the middle of doing it. That was the reason he had come to California."

You could have heard a pin drop, the silence in the courtroom was that profound. Everyone was holding their breath, afraid they might miss what he was going to say next, the explanation of this extraordinary allegation.

"You say he was going to make sure there was never another election. How was he going to do that?"

"It started with what the Russians did. They knew how to get into computer systems, how to find out what people communicated electronically.

It's all well-known now, but what hardly anyone paid attention to was how they created stories, put them out on the internet, sent them directly to people they wanted to influence, thousands, maybe millions at a time, false stories, pure invention, but with enough connection to what was really going on to create uncertainty about what was real and what was not. That gave some of the people around Bridges the idea. If the Russians could do this, why can't we? Not to try to influence a Russian election, but here, at home, use the same technique to make the American electorate think what they wanted. They knew," insisted Fitzgerald, a warning in his eyes, "that they had been lucky, that the Russians could not have done what they did if Bridges had been running against a candidate with nothing to hide and who could at least give a halfway decent speech."

Fitzgerald bent closer to the jury, as if to take them into his confidence. He talked to them as if they knew as well as he did the lengths to which Bridges had been willing to go.

"You heard one of them testify that Bridges would have lost by more than twenty points against me," he said, shaking his head to dismiss the suggestion that this had very much to do with him. "He would have lost by that much to anyone who ran against him. He knew it, they all knew it. They had not expected to win the presidency, but now that they had it, they were going to keep it. They had only one appeal—fear. You make people afraid of terrorism by always talking about the danger, by insisting that you're the only one who knows how to fight it, by promising that you know how to end it. Safety, not freedom, is what you preach. And it works. No one tries to argue when you spend billions on wars in the Middle East. But what fear do you appeal to if you want to make sure you won't, or rather, can't, be defeated in the next election?"

He looked at the jurors one by one, telling them with that look that they could trust him to tell them everything he knew. It made a silent pact that he trusted them to grasp in all its dreadful implications the secret, the state secret, he was about to reveal.

"The Senate Intelligence Committee, the House Intelligence Committee, the FBI, the CIA, every intelligence agency we have, and almost every reporter in Washington, were investigating the same thing: what the Russians had done in the last election, and whether anyone in the Bridges campaign, including Bridges himself, had been involved, whether there had been, to use the word everyone was then using, 'collusion' between Bridges and the Russians. I'm on the Intelligence Committee. There was not any doubt what had happened, no doubt that Bridges himself had been involved. The only thing missing was the kind of proof that would satisfy everyone, Democrats and Republicans alike, those who had voted for Walter Bridges and those who had not.

"The truth was we didn't have enough. There would have been enough, but there was not time. Bridges, the people around him, and especially Michael Donahue, knew they had to do something, because if they did nothing, if they just sat by, even if they tried to stop the investigation, eventually, there would be enough evidence, and with the evidence the kind of public demand nothing could resist, for impeachment proceedings to begin. This was not Nixon, who understood he could not survive impeachment; this was not Clinton, who understood he could survive a scandal. This was a case where articles of impeachment would include a charge of treason. No one, least of all Walter Bridges, could survive that. They had one chance: convince everyone, or at least a majority in the House and Senate, that the Russians had done a good deal more than anyone knew."

Becoming more intense with each word, the sense of urgency palpable and real, Fitzgerald slammed his hand on the arm of the witness chair and with a penetrating stare held the jury mesmerized as he went on.

"The Russians had managed to gain access—hack their way into—the computer systems that keep the records of registered voters. It was much more extensive than anyone knew, and the meaning of what the Russians were doing obvious to anyone who cared about the integrity of our elections. The Russians were planning to take over the computers that tabulate the results and change the outcome. The Russians, not the American electorate, were going to decide who governed us.

"That was the fear they thought they could exploit. They were careful. They knew they could not just come out and say they were going to cancel the next election and then keep postponing it until they could guarantee that each vote would be counted the way it had been cast. No one, not even members of their own party, would stand for that. They appointed a presidential commission to look into the fictitious allegation that there had been massive voter fraud. The commission concluded, without a shred of evidence to support it, that there had been, or rather, because they were careful here as well, that there could be. Could be. That was crucial because it seemed to dovetail neatly with what all the people who voted against Bridges had been saying: that the Russians had interfered with our election and that kind of interference could never happen again. The system was rigged, the system did not work, the system could be manipulated by foreign powers. It did not matter the nature of your complaint, whatever it was, it led to the same conclusion: something had to be done, the system had to be protected, it had to be made safe from any possible abuse or interference."

Pausing, Fitzgerald looked at me. He knew what the next question would be.

"Was that the reason the president came to California to meet with those Silicon Valley executives we heard about earlier? To discuss ways in which the system could be protected?"

"No. He met with them because they were part of a covert cyber warfare organization Michael Donahue had set up. Their task was not to protect the system; their task was to penetrate and disrupt it."

"But why would the president want to do that? What good would that do him?"

"Because they were going to do it in a way that would be traced back to the Russians. That was the genius of it. You have heard of kings and tyrants, men like Hitler and Stalin, you've heard of tin pot dictators who keep their hold on power by starting wars so that support for them becomes a test of your patriotism. No one can turn their back on their country and its leadership when the country is faced with the possibility of invasion and defeat. Now, today, though Bridges played the terrorism card for all it was worth, it doesn't take a war. All that is necessary is the failure of a system, the electronic lifeline that holds the democracy together. If Bridges had lived, they would have done it: revealed a Russian threat so invasive and expansive that the only way to defeat it would be to start all over. It might take years—and remember, while the system is being rebuilt there would doubtless be new and different threats. There might never be an end to it. We would all have to trust the government to do the right thing."

I could not wait for Raymond St. John to ask the obvious next question on cross; I could not let him have that advantage.

"But if you knew this, knew that was what they were planning, why didn't you tell someone, why didn't you report all this to the FBI? Why did you have to kill the president?"

"Because I couldn't prove any of it. Or rather, I could not prove every part of it. The evidence was all there. But each thing, taken by itself, did not prove a crime. Bridges set up a commission, the commission reports that voter fraud could happen, and might already have happened. Donahue calls together a group of cyber warfare experts. It would have been malfeasance not to get the best trained people to assess the nature of the threat. They know why they are doing this, but there wasn't anyone who was going to tell us on the record, in testimony before the Intelligence Committee, even in closed session with a promise of anonymity. Too many things leaked out. No one was willing to take the chance."

"But you knew?'

"Yes, absolutely. There was someone, a private source, from one of the intelligence agencies. That person, whose identity I have sworn to protect, had Donahue under surveillance. He had been under surveillance since the meeting he had in June before the election with Rostov and the Russian ambassador. That was the other reason I knew there wasn't any time, that I had to stop Bridges when I did."

"The other reason?"

"My source, the one who told me. Someone had him under surveillance, and probably me as well. The night after he told me, he was killed, found dead in his apartment. The police said he died of an overdose. He had never even smoked marijuana."

Raymond St. John was perplexed, or so he pretended, when he got up from his chair to begin his cross-examination.

"You think you may have been under surveillance, is that what you just testified?"

"It's quite possible," replied Fitzgerald, formal, polite, ready to answer any question the prosecution cared to ask.

"Because your source, this person who told you what the president was really up to, an attempt to subvert the government—"

"Subvert the government, that's exactly right. I couldn't have said it better myself," interjected Fitzgerald.

Trying to hide his irritation, St. John smiled to himself, and moved closer.

"You, and your source as well, were probably under surveillance, with the result, again, according to your testimony, that he was killed?"

"That's what I think. Yes, that's correct."

"To stop him, I assume, from telling anyone else?"

"Yes."

"Because that would be the last thing the president, and the other people involved, would want anyone to find out, is that what we should assume?" he asked, raising his eyebrows as if in anticipation of what he expected to hear.

"That is certainly what I assumed."

"But your source wasn't the only one who had this damaging information, was he?"

Fitzgerald was not quite sure what he meant.

"He wasn't the only—"

"You knew. He told you. It was only after that that he was killed—if he was killed. Which raises the question: if they had you under surveillance, if they knew what you had been told, why did they invite you on Air Force One for a private meeting with the president instead of having you killed as well?"

Fitzgerald dismissed it out of hand.

"Probably because it would have been a little difficult to make my death look like an accident. Probably because," he continued, throwing back his head in sheer, undisguised defiance, "as you may remember from the testimony of one of your own witnesses, I had on three separate occasions requested a meeting with Bridges in the White House. Each time I accompanied that request with a message that I wanted to discuss what he intended to do about the integrity of our elections, that I had learned something so troubling that I had written a contemporaneous memorandum of everything I had been told."

To St. John's astonishment, Fitzgerald reached into his inside suit coat pocket and pulled out a typed three-page document.

"Here, would you like to read it? Everything my source told me the night before he was killed, everything Bridges would have done if I had not stopped him!"

St. John ignored him. The only interest he had in what Fitzgerald had given him to read was to remind him that if he thought it evidence, his lawyer could always decide to introduce it. Then he moved on.

"You say you uncovered this plot, that no one else knew of its existence. You're the ranking member of the Intelligence Committee. Did you provide this information to the chairman the committee?"

"No, I did not. There wasn't anything I could tell him."

"Because, Senator Fitzgerald, you didn't have any evidence to back up this conspiracy theory of yours, isn't that the reason?"

"If I had evidence—the kind of evidence you mean—I wouldn't have had to do what I did, would I? I could have stopped it cold. If my source had not been killed, if—"

"If...yes, we understand, Senator Fitzgerald. You had no evidence. There wasn't any, which means you couldn't—"

"I didn't say there wasn't any; I said I didn't have it. I knew what was going on, but I couldn't prove it." He turned quickly to the jury. "If someone tells you that he has just seen the man who murdered your wife or husband, and after he tells you who it is, that same person kills him as well, are you really going to let someone tell you that you don't know what happened?"

"Your Honor!" protested St. John. "The witness isn't answering my question, he's giving a speech."

"Maybe you should ask better questions," I observed before Silverman had time to react.

Silverman looked at Fitzgerald, then he looked at St. John, and then, finally, he looked at me.

"If we're done now, perhaps, Mr. St. John, you might want to ask your next question."

"You had no evidence, but you had to stop him?" he said with cynical disbelief. "Isn't the truth, Senator Fitzgerald, that you killed him because you could not stand the fact that this political neophyte, this man you thought a charlatan and a fraud, had what you wanted more than life itself—the presidency? It drove you crazy, didn't it, that someone like that, an ill-educated, blustering fool, the most ill-prepared man ever to occupy the office, a man who should not have been elected county sheriff, had done what you had spent your life wanting to do? Isn't it—"

"Isn't it time you asked a question? Isn't it time you let the witness answer one?" I suggested with the polite contempt for an honest, if misguided, mistake. It put St. John's teeth on edge.

"Perhaps you would like to ask them for me, cross-examine your own witness. Who knows, with you to tell him what to say, he might even just once tell the truth."

I took the challenge in good stead, and played it for everything it was worth.

"Yes, of course; I'll be glad to help. Senator Fitzgerald, isn't it true that you acted solely for the purpose of saving the country from an attempt to destroy our system of free elections, and for no other reason whatsoever?" I asked with as much severity as if I were the one prosecuting him for murder.

For one of the few times in his sober life, Raymond St. John went red with rage.

"Your Honor, this is—"

"The result of your invitation. Next question, Mr. St. John."

He took two quick steps forward, then two slightly slower steps back. Four steps to bring him back into control. He looked at Fitzgerald and continued his cross-examination as if everything had gone just as he had planned and expected. He bore in again on Fitzgerald's well-known ambition, only now he added what until the last minute I was not sure he would. It got close to what I had sometimes thought myself about why Fitzgerald had done what he did.

"Walter Bridges had what you wanted, and you became convinced he was not going to give it up. Isn't that the crux of your testimony here today, that he was going to make sure there would not be another election? Isn't that what you said?" he asked, or rather, demanded, as he moved within an arm's length from where Fitzgerald sat.

"He was going to stop us from having another election. That is what he was going to try to do. Yes, that's right!" Fitzgerald fired back. "That's exactly right!"

"And if you stopped him, stopped Walter Bridges from doing that, you would have saved the country, isn't that what you testified?"

"I had to do it. I had to save the country. I had no choice. You would have done the same thing!"

"You saved the country. You're not a murderer! You're a hero, the greatest one the country has ever had. You knew what would happen then, didn't you? You wouldn't be convicted of a crime—we don't do that to people who save the country! We elect them to high office, we ask them to lead us, we make them president if we can. That's why you killed Walter Bridges, that's why you had no choice—it was the only way you could get what you wanted, the only way you could take his place, the only way you, instead of Walter Bridges, could become president! Isn't that right, Senator Fitzgerald? You wanted it so bad you committed murder!"

I tried to salvage what I could, repeating on re-direct some of the questions I had asked before about what he had learned about what Bridges was planning to do, and why, once again, he had decided there was no other way to stop him, but St. John's cross-examination had been devastating, among the best I had ever seen. I left the courthouse thoroughly depressed, wondering whether there was anything I could do to avoid what now seemed almost inevitable.

CHAPTER
NINETEEN

"I was there today, sitting in the back. The prosecutor, St. John, is rather good, isn't he?"

Jean-Francois Reynaud looked at me with sad, wistful eyes, and a slight, dubious smile of encouragement. It was a French way of telling me that things might be bad, but they could always get worse.

"No, Raymond St. John isn't bad at all, better than most. What he did, at the end..."

"Yes, but that may not have been so effective as you think. When someone gives a speech, or a teacher gives a lecture, what do we remember? The first and the last things said. I believe that is a rule without exception. What you start with, what you end with, always has the largest impact—at the time when everything is still fresh in your mind. It is what you will remember later as well, until someone tells you what you heard, then the same rule applies again: what they tell you at the beginning, and what they tell you at the end, is what you think important. So, at the end of the trial, when you give your closing argument—and perhaps even before, in whatever you manage to bring out through the testimony of your other witnesses—what St. John ended with today will not be first or last anymore, will it?"

It was a little after nine o'clock. I had come back to the city from Sausalito because Reynaud had left a message with Albert Craven that he had to see me and that it could not wait, but there did not seem to be anything urgent in his voice, nor did he seem to be in any great hurry to tell me what was so important. I was actually relieved, or at least I did not mind, if he wanted to take his time. Perhaps it was the way he could detach himself from what was going on all around him, the sense that even the business of his own government had nothing to do with him personally, that he was only an observer, always interested, but never quite involved. He made me feel that he was a spectator, and that, in his presence, I was one as well.

"I used to watch trials fairly often when I was young. My father was a lawyer. Quite a good one, too; one of the very best there was in Paris, years ago, after the war. He never really liked it, I'm afraid. He would have preferred, like his father, to go into politics, but he was, if I can put it like this, the prisoner of his name."

"The prisoner of his name?"

"Reynaud. His father, my grandfather, was Paul Reynaud, premier of France, the last one before the German occupation."

"Reynaud. Paul Reynaud." I repeated the name with the innocent surprise of a new discovery.

"You know about him?" asked Jean-Francois, surprised that I did.

"Not much, I'm afraid. But a little. Didn't he head the government, or what there was of one, when the Germans were about to take Paris and the government fled to Bordeaux?" I remembered something else. "Didn't he have a mistress who insisted that surrender was the only thing left to do?"

Reynaud's head bobbed side to side, keeping time to the rhythm of his family's remembered past.

"Yes, she was, in her day, quite beautiful, and quite the worst thing that ever happened to my grandfather. She was not a stupid woman. The Germans had destroyed the French army; there was not an army left to fight. There were two choices: move the government to North Africa, where you would have the French navy at your command, or surrender on the best terms you could still negotiate. She knew the war was lost, but for her, and a great many others, there was more to it than that. The war was lost because France deserved to lose. We were weak, decadent, too divided even to form a government that could last more than a month or so. The Germans, with their discipline and courage, were the wave of the future. Our future, the French future, would belong to those with the foresight and the courage to see this and to act on it. My grandfather, Paul Reynaud, would not do this, but she made his life so miserable with her constant interruptions, her constant unsolicited advice, that he was too distracted to come to any definite decisions, too preoccupied to understand that events were moving too quickly, that there were other forces, other interests, at work. Before he knew what was happening, he was out of power and the government dissolved. Marshall Petain and Pierre Laval took control. General deGaul left for England, the German armistice was signed, and the German army, with Hitler in attendance, marched down the Champ Elysees.

"After the war, deGaul returned in triumph, and while no one thought of Paul Reynaud as a traitor, the way they did, for example, Pierre Laval, no one wanted to be reminded of what had happened in the last days before the fall of France. My father practiced law and lived an essentially private life. It is also, if I can make my own confession, the reason why I joined our foreign service instead of trying my luck at a career in politics. I did not want to be a lawyer, and I had an interest in, shall we say, politics at a higher level, the politics among nations."

I wondered whether that was also the reason—whether he had also been a prisoner of his name—that he had never risen about the rank of French consul in a foreign country.

"I didn't mean to burden you with the ancient history of my family, but sitting in court today, watching Senator Fitzgerald, listening to what he said, I was put in mind of what happened years ago with the fall of France. Marshall Petain became the figurehead of a government that depended on the Germans. He had been a hero of the First World War, the French general given credit, though not all of it was deserved, for the German defeat. We lost millions of men in that glorious victory, an entire generation. Petain was in his eighties, shrewd, vindictive, mean-spirited, and in the early stages of senility, but everyone still thought of him as the savior of France. When he went on the radio and blamed the French defeat on the cowardice of politicians, everyone believed him; when he insisted that the honor of France required that we submit to the German victors, there did not seem any alternative.

"Petain gave the new, collaborationist government legitimacy. The real power, however, was Pierre Laval. It is a name that, even today, is still reviled. He believed, like my grandfather's mistress, that France had become rotten to the core, that the French could not govern themselves. Unlike Petain, who had spent his life in the army, Laval had spent his in politics, a member of parliament who had seen governments come and go with the seasons, a man with deep-seated resentments against all those—and there were a great many—who had conspired to keep him from holding any important office. Laval was now in charge, but of course only to the extent his German masters allowed. This is where it gets interesting, and why I started to remember this while I was watching your trial."

We were in Reynaud's favorite, and, from what I could tell, his only restaurant. As usual at this hour, it was nearly deserted. An elderly couple was lingering over a passable dinner in the far corner. Two old men, probably regulars, were sitting at the bar. We were in the booth farthest from the entrance. The bartender, who at this hour doubled as the waiter, caught the signal from Reynaud and brought a bottle of California champagne. With a bittersweet glow in his eyes, Jean-Francois sipped approvingly from his glass.

"Everyone hates Pierre Laval. He helped the Germans round up the Jews. This is true. It is also true, however, that he did it as part of a deal he made to help the Germans find Jews who were not French. The Germans, in return, would not try to find or take prisoner any Jews who were. You made the point in this trial of yours that Fitzgerald was acting under the law of necessity, the law that says it is sometimes necessary to sacrifice one life to save others. Laval's situation was similar, though, for a number of reasons, including the numbers involved, not identical. Here you talk about sacrificing one; there you were talking about thousands. But still, he had only one way to save anyone. There is another difference. Laval could not know how long the Germans would keep their word; whether when they had all the other Jews they would start taking the French Jews as well. And there is also this: Laval was trying to save lives; Fitzgerald was trying, according to what he claims, to save, to protect the basic institutions of the country. That is the difference that really caught my attention."

Jean-Francois drank some more. His pale blue eyes had a marvelous clarity, the perfect mirror to the marvelous clarity of his mind. He put the glass down on the table. A lost memory, the hint of some long-buried thought, seemed to occupy his attention. He searched my eyes, as if he half expected me to know the answer to a question he had not asked and was not quite sure he knew how to.

"Because, you see," he continued, "that is what Laval thought he was doing as well: saving his country, saving France, from what he was certain would be worse treatment if instead of collaborating, of trying every chance he could to get better terms, better conditions, he and the government he led tried to resist, to oppose, the Germans and what they wanted. The Germans had won; they were never going to be defeated. That is what he thought; that is what nearly everyone thought. You do what you have to do to survive; you do what you have to do so that the country can survive. The law of necessity all over again.

"But—and this is really my point—what may seem necessary at the time, may not have been necessary at all. You know," remarked Jean-Francois with a burst of enthusiasm, "Laval, my grandfather's mistress, Petain, some of the other generals and Admiral Darlan, they all thought they were doing what was necessary. And so did Charles deGaulle. Notice the change. For deGaulle, resistance was necessary to the honor of France, to what it meant to be French, to French history, to French culture and tradition, above all to French independence. Laval, by the way, also understood this. In one of the most poignant things I have read, Laval made the remark that if he could have been anyone, it would have been Charles deGaulle.

"So what does this have to do with Walter Bridges and Kevin Fitzgerald?

Only this. There was a necessity for the death of Walter Bridges, but it was not the one that Fitzgerald talks about. What the prosecutor, Raymond St. John, said today about why Fitzgerald did what he did was absolutely correct, but still only half right."

I looked at him in dumb amazement. I knew him well enough to know that he knew what he was talking about, but I did not know what any of it meant. He reached into his briefcase, sitting next to him, and pulled out a large, sealed envelope.

"This came in late last night. This time you can keep it. My government decided—rightly, I think—that it was too important to keep secret, whatever the cost."

When I started to open it, he placed his hand over it.

"Take it with you. Even though it's Friday night and you have all weekend, once you see what it is, you'll be up all night, deciding what you should now do with the witnesses you will want to call."

There was not any way I was going to wait, not after what he had just said. He only shrugged his shoulders when I went ahead and opened what he had given me. There were perhaps two dozen typewritten pages inside. I did not finish reading the first one. Reynaud was right. I was not going to be able to sleep.

"This is all…?"

"Oh, yes, there isn't any doubt. And, as you will discover, it gets more interesting with every page. Fitzgerald is an even more fascinating character than I thought before. I'm not sure I've ever come across anyone quite like him. He is what a hundred years ago we would have called a truly historic personality. Tell me, if you can—I know there are limitations on what a lawyer can say about his client—but does he know anything? About history,

I mean. Does he ever talk about Bridges's death in those kinds of terms? I heard what he said in court, I heard what St. John said about him—his motivation, what he may have thought would happen—but has he himself put it in the broader context of history?"

I looked down at the open envelope and thought about what it meant, and what it was going to mean, and I suddenly remembered several things at once: the three revolutions that had, at different times, been used as parallels to what Fitzgerald had confessed to doing.

"He became interested in the Russian Revolution. He did not study it in college, but after he was in the Senate and he began learning things about the Russians in the Senate Intelligence Committee. We had a few discussions, starting the first time I met him, before I had decided to represent him, about the Russian show trials of the 1930s when Stalin was getting rid of as many of the original leadership of the Bolsheviks as he could, the ones who had come to power with Lenin and were still committed to what they thought were the revolution's original principles. Fitzgerald was fascinated by Bukharin in particular, the way someone could be convinced—could convince himself—that the truest thing he could ever do, the only way he had to save what he believed in, what gave meaning to his life, was to lie, to insist he had betrayed the Soviet Union when he never had."

A curious half smile quivered for a brief moment on the lips of Jean-Francois Reynaud.

"Bukharin knew when he did that that his death was unavoidable," he remarked. "He believed in history, history with a capital H, and believed that his death would contribute to history reaching its desired, and inevitable, end. Fitzgerald wants to make history of his own."

"Which you can only do if you seize the moment, if you act when history—if you want to call it that—has created the circumstances the makes it possible," I replied. "If there had not been a French Revolution, if there had not been the Terror, if there had not been the kind of chaos that made everyone desperate for a new order, Napoleon could never have become emperor of France. If there had not been a revolution in Rome, if Caesar had not become dictator in everything but name, he would not have been assassinated and the civil wars would not have happened and Augustus could not have destroyed the Roman republic once and for all."

"Yes, precisely. In all these cases, the same result. Someone emerges—Augustus, Napoleon, Lenin—who seizes the moment and is swept into power by what in effect is popular acclamation. Fitzgerald, whether he knows any history or not, understood what the death, the murder, of Walter Bridges could bring about, the chance that might not occur for another hundred years, the chance to become in the eyes of his country the only one they could trust to restore what they thought they were in danger of losing. St. John was right in what he said about Fitzgerald, but he had no idea the real dimension of Fitzgerald's incredible ambition."

Reynaud finished off his glass, poured himself another and watched with eyes that became nostalgic the endless lines of soft rising bubbles.

"When this is over, I'm going back to France. My wife is there now, getting everything ready." He put the glass back on the table and, leaning over it, glanced at the envelope. "You might want to come over for a long vacation. You and your bride to be. Things may get difficult here. This really is what everyone said it was going to be: the trial of the century, the trial that will change history—just not in the way everyone thought it would."

"You're going back to your castle, somewhere in the south of France?"

Reynaud emitted a modest, self-effacing laugh.

"A castle? Well, yes, with respect to its historical classification. But that is a little like calling something a house in the country without making any distinction between a twelve-hundred-square-foot house in Carmel, or a twenty-thousand-square-foot monstrosity in the hills above Palo Alto. Yes, we own a castle, a very nice six-bedroom home, built five hundred years ago in a place called Pont-du-Casse a few miles outside Agen, which is four hours southwest of Paris on the high-speed train. Albert stayed there, as I told you, years ago, with one of his wives. But come, you and the beautiful Tangerine, and while you look at the French countryside, I'll look at her. And we can sit around at dinner—my wife is one of the best cooks in France—and talk about everything that happened at the trial and everything that happened after. Whatever it is, it will certainly be worth talking about."

I said I was grateful for the offer, and that I knew it was something Tangerine would want to do. He stopped me with a sudden look of the utmost seriousness.

"You don't understand. You don't know it yet, but when the trial is over, the one thing you will want more than anything else is to get out of the country. You won't be able to avoid the questions. Everyone will want to know everything. You won't have a minute to yourself. There won't be any privacy. Don't regard this as an invitation; regard it as a means of escape."

The whole time we were talking, I kept thinking about what he had done for me: the intelligence reports—the secret intelligence reports—he had allowed me to see, and to use.

"All right, we'll come. And thank you," I added quite seriously. "But there is a condition. Tell me why you have done this, given me this help, and tell me how you got them. They can't all have been from French intelligence. Those photographs of Walter Bridges in that Moscow hotel—they had to come from the Russians."

It seemed to amuse him. He drank more champagne. His face lit up at the memory of what he had been able to do. It was not so much that he wanted to share as to explain the secret of his accomplishment.

"No one speaks any more, especially in this country, of old money and new money. Now it's only money, the only difference how much of it you happen to have. But, at least in France, there are still old families. There used to be two hundred of them that, whatever form the government took, decided everything of importance. That isn't true anymore. But as I was saying, there are still old families. My family is one of them. We all know each other, we help one another when we're asked, and when we can. When this first happened, when Bridges was murdered, when Fitzgerald confessed, when, despite that confession, I learned there was going to be a trial, it was not difficult to anticipate what was going to happen, that the country would be divided, and that the only thing that could keep that division from becoming a permanent condition, an endless source of bitterness and hatred and suspicion, was if everyone learned the full truth of what had happened. Whatever that truth turned out to be. That was the reason I was there that night at Albert's place. I wanted to meet you, to make my own judgment, to decide how far we—not just my government, but people I know—should go in giving whatever assistance we could. But again, always for that one purpose—the truth, whatever it was. Fitzgerald had confessed. The truth had to be found in the reasons. With you as his attorney, I felt confident that these reasons, and all the evidence connected with them, would be brought out into the light.

"I did not have to depend on my sources in French intelligence. Or rather, to be quite clear about it, they did not have to depend on French intelligence. We were responsible for the surveillance of Donahue, and some others, when they were meeting with someone in a Paris restaurant or a Paris hotel. But we get things from German intelligence, British intelligence, most intelligence services in Europe. No one trusted the Americans anymore. We did not—we could not—share anything with them. We could never be certain what might be passed to the Russians, or what the Russians could find out on their own. The photographs of Bridges in the Moscow hotel. They came through German intelligence who got them from a Russian double agent they employed."

I tapped my hand on his latest, and last, offering.

"And these?"

Jean-Francois clasped his hands behind his head and stared up the ceiling.

"Someone in American intelligence who works for us. But that is a secret I never told you," he added as his gaze descended to my own, waiting, eyes.

He picked up his glass and took a long, slow drink, then checked his watch, decided it was time to go and signaled the bartender to bring the bill.

"How does it feel?" he asked as we shook hands outside the restaurant.

"How does it—"

"To know that there is now no chance, no chance whatsoever, that you are going to lose this case?"

I did not doubt Reynaud was right. Although I had seen only the first page, there was no question what the verdict would be. How I felt about it, however, was a question I was not sure how to answer. Perhaps it would answer itself as the trial, with the evidence I now had, told the story no one would have thought possible.

It was nearly midnight when I got back to Tangerine's place on the hillside in Sausalito. I could see her through the window as I started down the steps to her chocolate shingle-sided home, running barefoot to the door to greet me as if I had been away for months. And in that moment, when she threw her arms around my neck and told me that she loved me and missed me, I felt almost as if I had.

"We've been invited to France," I told her as I tossed my jacket on the chair and settled into the corner of the sofa. "That's not really true. You've been invited to France, the guest of Jean-Francois and his wife, Chantal, at their castle somewhere south of Bordeaux. He said I could come along, but only if you didn't object."

She did not hesitate; she did not stop to think. Things worth considering she decided immediately.

"I can be packed and ready to go in an hour." Her legs stretched straight out in front of her, she slid lower in the chair facing me, and mocked me with her laughing eyes. "The only question is can you be ready that soon?"

"As soon as the trial is over. One more week should do it."

I got up and went toward the kitchen. She grabbed my hand as I passed and held me there.

"One more week? Do you mean it, we'll go to France, to anywhere, when it's over?" She let go of my hand and stood up. "Do you want something to drink?"

"No. Yes. I have to make coffee."

"I'll make it. Why do you need it? You're going to be up all night. The reason Jean-Francois had to see you. It's that important?"

"I'm afraid so."

"It's bad? It hurts your case?"

"I don't know if it's bad or not. All I know is that it means I'm going to win."

She did not ask me to explain, she did not ask why I was so equivocal about this sudden certainty that the verdict was all but assured. She brushed past me and made the coffee.

"Is there a lot to do before Monday?" she asked when she brought me a cup of coffee at the dining room table where I had put down a long yellow legal pad and my fountain pen. The documents Reynaud had given me, still in the envelope, lay just to the side.

"What was he like, I mean really like?"

"You mean Kevin, don't you?"

"I know you never knew anyone by that name, I know you never knew anyone, before you met me, but, yes, what was he like? What did he care about when he was mayor?"

"Is it important? Is it about the trial?"

"It could be. There are things I don't understand, things about him that might make a difference. If you were asked to describe him, what is the first thing you think of, the one overriding fact that leaps out?"

"Ambition. I know, a lot of people have that, especially if they're in politics. But that wasn't the kind he had. I tried to tell you before. Remember? When I said he wanted to be president, and maybe something more than that. Don't ask me what more than that means. Maybe it's what he has been saying all along: that he wanted to save the country. There was always this sense of dissatisfaction with him. It was not just that nothing was ever enough—that whatever office he had was just a step farther along the path he wanted to go. You had the feeling that nothing would ever be enough. If he had been a writer, a really great one, he would have thought the Nobel Prize for literature somehow, not exactly below him, but not the measure of what he really could do."

She looked at me with cool, limpid eyes, gently berating herself for her failure to find a better way to explain someone who remained, for her, essentially an enigma.

"I don't think he ever knew what he wanted, except the next rung on a ladder you could never stop climbing."

It seemed to me to explain a lot more than she thought.

"But always within the rules, the accepted way in which things are done?"

"Yes; until now, of course. I never would have thought him capable—I think I told you that. However necessary he might have thought it was. I suppose it only proves you can never know what someone is capable of. But you're going to win, Antonelli," she said with a smile that insisted she had never doubted that I would. "And you're not sure that you should? I think I knew that about you that first time we met, at Albert's home, when, harlot that I am, I waited for you outside, hoping to seduce you. Imagine my astonishment when I discovered that it was more interesting when I failed. I learned that you see both sides of everything—even what you want and why you shouldn't have it. But at least that is one dilemma you'll never have to face again."

I was as lost as I was dazzled.

"Dilemma?" I said, managing to stumble over just one word alone.

"When you want me. There are no more reasons why you shouldn't have me." She let that thought linger for a moment, and then, getting to her feet, placed her soft, warm hand on the side of my face. "Except, of course, for one. You have work to do."

She had taken two steps when she stopped and looked back.

"Would you mind, would it bother you, if I slept for a while on the sofa? That way I won't feel that far away."

"Yes, it will bother me; no, I don't want you to go anywhere else."

I started reading through what Reynaud had given me, each page more damning, more decisive than the last. I read slowly, stopping every few minutes to jot down a note on how best to use what I had just learned, which witnesses would now have to be called and the order in which I wanted them to testify. The pieces fell into place, the story began to tell itself. The question looming over all of it was the defendant himself, whether I should, or should not, put Kevin Fitzgerald back on the stand.

I kept working until the black night had begun to turn gray. There would be time tomorrow, and the day after that, time to go over everything until I had it all down by heart and could go into court and know everything a witness would say before the witness knew himself.

But I could not get Fitzgerald out of my mind. It did not matter that I was now all but certain he would be acquitted. He was, if anything, more of a mystery than he had been before. It seemed strange, looking across at Tangerine, the woman I was going to marry, sleeping soundly on a sofa just a few feet away, that she had once been involved with him. Though perhaps not as strange as that she was now involved with me. We like to think we know what is going to happen to us, but none of us do. We turn a corner, decide to stop somewhere for a cup of coffee, we go to a dinner, the way I did, not because I wanted to, but out of a sense of obligation, an indebtedness I felt toward Albert Craven, and the last thing we ever expected to happen becomes the central fact of our existence. I looked at her, laying asleep on the sofa, and I could not imagine what my life would have been like if I had not met her. It seemed the easiest, most natural thing in the world to do what I did next: picked her up in my arms and carried her to bed and slept with her until, late the next morning, I woke up.

CHAPTER TWENTY

"The defense calls Jonathan Reece."

The announcement that I was recalling to the stand the prosecution's own witness, the one St. John had called first in the trial, set the court buzzing. What was the defense up to, what was I planning? St. John did not know, but he did not give any indication that he was at all surprised.

Reece took the stand, wondering why he had been called to testify again.

"Your Honor," I said after a single glance at the witness, a glance meant to be a warning. "Mr. Reece is the first of several witnesses called by the prosecution I intend to call back. I would ask the court's permission to treat Mr. Reece, and the others, as hostile."

By giving his permission, Judge Silverman allowed me, in effect, to cross-examine them all over again. I got right to it.

"Mr. Reece, you testified that Senator Fitzgerald was always making false accusations about the president. Isn't that what you said?"

Like everyone else, Jonathan Reece had been following the trial. He knew what other, subsequent witnesses had said. He knew what Fitzgerald had said, and he knew about the evidence that had been produced proving that Michael Donahue had met with the Russians. It was not difficult to guess that his main concern was to distance himself, if he could, from anything that might suggest he had been involved.

"Is that still your testimony, Mr. Reece?"

"Yes, that's what I thought—at the time."

Standing at the far end of the jury box, as far from the witness stand as I could, I forced him to speak loudly.

"At the time? Does that mean you no longer believe that what Senator Fitzgerald had been saying about President Bridges was untrue?"

Loyalty, even misplaced loyalty, does not simply vanish overnight. Bukharin had found the meaning of his existence in his belief in the infallibility of the Communist Party. With nothing like the same intellectual background, Jonathan Reece had found his in Walter Bridges and his vision of America. There were still limits on how much he would concede.

"There may have been more to the Russian connection, the nature of their interference, than I had been led to believe."

"More than you were led to believe," I mused. Folding my arms across my chest, I gazed down at the floor and took a few slow steps forward. Raising my eyes just high enough to look at him, I asked, "You also testified that Senator Fitzgerald had on several occasions requested a meeting with the president, did you not?"

"Yes, that's right. He did."

"Tell us again, what was the reason Senator Fitzgerald gave? Why did he want to see President Bridges?"

Reece tried to shrug off the question, as if the reason, even had he been able to remember it, was irrelevant.

"Let me remind you what you said, what you told the jury, the first time you were asked. You said that Fitzgerald wanted to tell the president what he had found. Now that you have been reminded, do you remember why, according to your sworn testimony, the president refused to see him? Never mind. Let's not waste any time. I'll tell you what you said: 'The president knew it was a bluff—that the FBI didn't have anything.' Remember now, Mr. Reece? Now, after everything that you, along with the rest of us, have learned, do you still believe that was the reason? Do you still believe that Senator Fitzgerald was bluffing?"

Shifting his weight around in the chair, Reece bit hard on his lip and rapidly blinked his eyes.

"I'm not really sure. Maybe not. Maybe he knew something about the Russian business."

"The Russian business? Are you aware of what Senator Fitzgerald said in his testimony last week? That there was a plan to destroy our system of free elections?"

With both hands, Reece shoved himself up from the witness chair.

"I don't believe that. I don't know anything about that. I wouldn't have been involved in anything—"

"I'm sure you wouldn't have, Mr. Reece. No one is accusing you of anything. You worked for Walter Bridges, but not directly, did you? You worked for Richard Ellison, the president's chief of staff, correct?"

"Yes, that's right. And he never would have—"

"You used a phrase in your testimony when you were asked about the reason why the president refused to see Senator Fitzgerald, even though the senator had requested such a meeting on three different occasions. By the way, when did Senator Fitzgerald do that, when did he request those meetings?"

"The first time was ten days or so before the trip out here."

"Which means all three requests were within that same ten-day period. Didn't that suggest that the senator, at least, thought that whatever he wanted to talk to the president about was urgent, that this was not some routine request to discuss pending legislation?

"No one thought it was urgent."

"Because no one in the White House trusted Senator Fitzgerald, because—and this is what you said when you testified before—he wanted a meeting with the president so he could tell everyone that he had discussed with him 'things he could not yet reveal.' Isn't that what you testified."

"Yes, but—"

"Was that what you thought, or was that what someone else thought? What I am asking, Mr. Reece, is did you come to this conclusion on your own, or did someone else—the president himself or someone on his staff— decide this was the senator's motivation?"

"I'm not sure who first decided that. It's what everyone believed."

"Is it what you believe now, Mr. Reece? Or do you believe that the senator wanted to meet with the president to confront him with what he had discovered in the hopes that the president would change his mind and call off the attempt to subvert our democratic way of government?"

"I don't know," admitted Reece. "I wish I did, but I don't. All I know is that the reason I gave you, that Fitzgerald wanted to use a meeting to publicize himself, is the reason the president said he would not see him."

"Until he arrived in San Francisco, and Senator Fitzgerald was invited on board to meet with him on Air Force One?"

"Yes, that's right."

"The president told you to bring Senator Fitzgerald on board. Were you alone with the president when he asked you to do this?"

"No. Ellison was there, and so was Donahue. They were both just leaving. Everyone was getting ready to leave the plane."

"How long had you been with the others in the president's cabin?"

"Not long. Ellison asked me to come in. The president asked me to get Fitzgerald."

"The two of them—Ellison, who was the president's chief of staff, and Donahue, who is now chief of staff to the new president—they did not like each other very much, did they?"

The question surprised him. He looked at me in a way that suggested he was not sure what I wanted to know. I gave him the same look back.

"They didn't like each other? The question isn't that difficult."

"They worked together."

"Rivals, and not always friendly ones, is that not a fair description? Let me be more specific. They despised one another. They hated each other. Donahue thought Ellison, the man you worked for, an intellectual lightweight, a political hack Bridges hired because he supposedly knew his way around Washington, but, as it turned out, did not know how to get anything done. Ellison, for his part, thought Donahue a pretentious egomaniac who thought he could use Bridges to change the course of history. They hated each other. It was all out war, a war Donahue has won, hasn't he? Ellison, your boss, is on his way out, and Donahue now runs everything. How long do you think you have, Mr. Reece, before you find yourself out of a job?"

"Objection!" announced St. John, doing his best to appear confused. "I don't know where this is going, but it doesn't seem to have any obvious connection to any of the issues in the case."

"I have no more questions of the witness, your Honor," I said when Silverman looked to me for my response.

There were two people with Walter Bridges when Jonathan Reece was sent to get Fitzgerald. The jury now knew what I knew: that they despised each other and that, it was safe to assume, a power struggle had been going on behind the scenes. The jury had heard Donahue deny under oath everything with which I had confronted him about his meeting with General Rostov in that Paris restaurant. They had heard Fitzgerald testify that there had been other meetings as well. Everything Fitzgerald said had not just been sworn to, but documented. Now they were going to hear from a witness whose credibility had just been established by the sworn testimony of someone who knew that Richard Ellison and Michael Donahue were sworn enemies. I called Ellison to the stand with the warm greeting of a long-lost friend.

"Mr. Ellison, we're glad to have you back. There are just a few questions, a few matters we need to clear up."

It was difficult to keep a straight expression. Richard Ellison's photograph could have been used in an illustrated dictionary next to the word "puzzlement." That baffled expression of his was such a permanent part of who he was that it was hard not to think that every morning when he looked in the mirror to shave, his first reaction was to try to remember the name of the stranger staring back at him. He placed his elbows on the arms of the witness chair and began to rub his nervous hands together.

"When you were here before, a witness for the prosecution, you testified that you spoke to Senator Fitzgerald when he came on Air Force One."

Richard Ellison's wavy hair, a black shiny hue in the courtroom lights, made his pale face seem paler still. The dark suit he wore, though different than the one in which he had testified before, was still a size too large. He nodded slowly, and carefully, in response to my question, before, finally, he answered that he had.

"You said you were standing just outside the president's cabin, and that the two of you exchanged a few words. You said—and this is what struck me at the time—that he was nicer than you expected, a 'much nicer person'— those were your exact words—than you had thought before. You said he suggested you ought to come to San Francisco sometime for a few days, and that if you did, you might never leave. Do I remember what you said accurately?"

"Yes, that's what I said. And that's what he said—about San Francisco, I mean."

"Well, Mr. Ellison, we all hope you have that chance," I said in as friendly a manner as I could. "But now, we need to get a better understanding of some things than we had before. I want to go back a little, before the election. You weren't directly involved in the Bridges campaign, were you?"

"No, I was with the national party."

"When Bridges was elected, you became his chief of staff?"

"Yes, he asked me, and I was glad to do it."

"Part of your job was to hire the rest of the White House staff?" I asked, as if the question answered itself, though I knew it did not.

"Yes, and no. There were people the president had already asked to serve in various positions, people—"

"Like Michael Donahue?"

"He was one; there were others."

"Others like Jenny Ann Carruthers." It was not a question. "In fact, the White House was divided from the very beginning between those like Donahue and Carruthers who had been involved in the campaign, many of them close to Bridges before he ever became a candidate for public office, and those, like yourself and Jonathan Reece, who had not been involved with the campaign but had spent years in politics and government. And is it not true, Mr. Ellison, that this division was characterized by a strong antipathy: that you wanted a government that got things done in the normal, traditional way, while, on the other side, the side that Michael Donahue was part of, wanted to break up everything, destroy the old political alliances, start all over, build everything from the bottom up?"

"There were differences, differences of approach, that's true, but I'm not sure I would go that far, that I would—"

I turned on him with a vengeance.

"You know what has happened in this courtroom!" I shouted. "You know that there is now evidence of massive collusion with the Russians! You know that the president of the United States was involved in a plot to stop the next election from even taking place! The question, Mr. Ellison, the only question, is how far you were involved? The question, Mr. Ellison, the only question, is were you, or were you not, a co-conspirator? Did you, or did you not, participate with Walter Bridges and Michael Donahue in a plot to destroy the basic institutions of this country?"

"No, I did not!" he bellowed, rising straight up from the witness chair. "The first I heard about this, the first I ever heard that anything like this was even possible, was when I heard what Senator Fitzgerald said in his testimony last Friday!"

"And when you heard it, you believed it, didn't you?" I asked, so quickly, and with the same friendly smile I had shown just a moment before, that he just looked at me and for a moment did not know what to say.

"His testimony, the evidence…it seems impossible. I wouldn't have believed it, but—"

"But if anyone could have been involved in something like this, Michael Donahue would be the first one you would think of, wouldn't he?"

Ellison did not want to believe it about anyone, but he could believe it about Donahue. He would not believe it about Bridges without more proof.

"But Donahue had a lot of influence with him, didn't he?"

Reluctantly, he agreed.

"It was Donahue who did not want him to meet with Senator Fitzgerald in Washington, wasn't it?"

"He didn't want Fitzgerald to get anything we didn't have to give him. Fitzgerald was the enemy. But there was another reason. I think he was afraid what the president might do, what he might say. And that if he said anything he shouldn't, Fitzgerald would use it."

"About the Russians?"

"I don't know. Maybe. I didn't know, until now, anything about it. I believed what we were told, that it was all a fabrication, things taken out of context, twisted, misinterpreted." With a plaintive look, he added, "What else could we believe? We were working for the president of the United States. He was being attacked by his political opponents. And those people would do or say anything!"

"The day you came out here, had there been any discussions about having Senator Fitzgerald meet with the president when you arrived?"

"No, no discussions I was involved in."

"It's a six-hour flight. What did you discuss with the president?"

"Not that much, really. We went over the speech he was going to give; we spent some time talking about the legislation we were trying to get Congress to start working on. We talked about a couple of appointments he wanted to make, whether there would be a problem getting them confirmed."

"When did you have this conversation?" I asked, pacing slowly in front of the jury box.

"Right after we took off. Thirty, forty minutes, then he had other things he wanted to do, other people he wanted to talk to. Half an hour, forty-five minutes, that was about all you could ever get. He did not like to spend too much time on any one thing."

"The early part of the flight...but you saw him again, when you landed?"

"A little before that. I thought he wanted to go over the speech again, talk about the arrangements that had been made—who was going to introduce him, the kind of off-the-cuff remarks he should make—but all he wanted to talk about was Fitzgerald and what he should do."

"Because he didn't want to see him. Isn't that what he wanted to tell you, that Fitzgerald might be waiting at the airport, but that didn't mean he was going to do anything beyond shaking his hand and saying hello? Walter Bridges did not want Fitzgerald on the plane, did he?"

Ellison was even more puzzled than usual. He could not understand how I had come to know this. Nothing had been said about it at the trial, he was sure of it.

"When you were asked to come to the president's cabin the second time, he wasn't alone, was he? Michael Donahue was there with him, wasn't he?"

Ellison's head snapped back. A crooked grin broke sideways across his mouth.

"How did you...? Yes, Donahue was there."

"The president wasn't in a very good mood, was he?"

I was guessing, but after what Carson Youngblood had told me, it seemed unlikely that someone as famous as Walter Bridges for never forgetting, or forgiving, a fight, would suddenly become even tempered and affable.

"Not particularly, no."

"Not particularly, no?" I repeated with mocking laughter. "He and Donahue had been arguing, a shouting match that got ugly, a knockdown, drag out fight, and all because Bridges did not want to see Fitzgerald and Donahue insisted that he had to. Isn't that what happened?"

"I don't know anything about a fight. I wasn't there. I was in another part of the plane, meeting with my staff, for most of the flight. As I told you, after that first meeting with the president, I didn't see him again until I was called to come back, ten, fifteen minutes before we landed."

"And when you got to the president's cabin, he was there with Donahue and he wasn't happy. He did not want to see Fitzgerald. Is that correct?"

"He said he didn't think it was a good idea, but that Donahue thought it was."

"What did Donahue say? Why had he changed his mind about a meeting with Fitzgerald?"

"He said that Fitzgerald had let everyone know that the president was refusing to see him, despite the fact that he had made three separate requests for a few minutes of the president's time. Fitzgerald was going to be there, waiting with the others, and knowing Fitzgerald, he was probably going to stage something that would dominate all the television coverage. If we let him have a private meeting on the plane, we could solve both problems at once: Fitzgerald would have his meeting and the only television coverage of it would be whatever we decided to tell the press."

"He didn't say anything about using the meeting to keep Fitzgerald from finding out what was really going on, what they were really planning to do?"

"No, nothing like that."

"But Donahue wanted the president to do it, and the president agreed, but he didn't like it?'

"That's pretty much it. The president did not like Fitzgerald, and when he didn't like someone, the last thing he wanted was to be in the same room with them."

"Remind us, if you will, Mr. Ellison," I said quietly as I turned to the jury. "You said when you testified before that the president agreed to meet with Senator Fitzgerald, but for only ten minutes. Do I remember that right?"

"Ten minutes. He must have told me three different times. Ten minutes. Then I was to come in and break it up. Not one minute more."

"And that is what you did—waited ten minutes from the time you let Senator Fitzgerald into the president's cabin; waited ten minutes exactly and then opened the door, ready to tell the president that he did not have any more time, that the meeting had to end, and then, to your astonishment, you found the president laying on the floor and Kevin Fitzgerald, the knife still in his hand, standing next to the body. What did you do then?"

"What did I do…? I started shouting as loud as I could."

"You didn't think to go toward Fitzgerald, try to wrestle the knife away, because, after all, you could not really be sure, could you, that the president might not still be alive?"

It had all happened so fast, the president on the floor covered with blood, Fitzgerald and the knife, he had not had time to think, and then, before he could do anything, the Secret Service burst inside. It was over before he knew it. Which was another way of saying he was frozen with fear.

But I was not there to call him a coward. I had another, deeper purpose.

"You were looking straight at him, and Fitzgerald was looking straight at you. You had just come through the door, whatever he was doing, he must have turned."

"That's right. He looked right at me. I'll never forget it."

"What is it, precisely, that you'll never forget?"

It seemed an odd, even a perverse, question. What did someone who had just murdered the president of the United States look like? Ellison could not even guess what I might mean.

"Was his face contorted, full of anger, full of rage? Did he look like a homicidal manic, a man who, in the very next moment, might come after you?"

Ellison had not thought about it, and now that he had to, he seemed surprised, and uncertain.

"No, he didn't look like that at all. There wasn't any anger, any rage. And no, I didn't think he was about to come after me. I'm not sure how I should describe it. He didn't seem afraid, like he wanted to get away. He looked like he was trying to figure out what he should do, now that he had just killed the president."

"I want to be sure of this. You walked in, found him with the knife still in his hands, the president dead on the floor, and you did not feel that you yourself were in any danger?"

He shook his head, and seemed to think back on what he had seen.

"No. Maybe I should have, but no, I didn't."

It was an answer that at least let him think himself not a coward after all.

"Thank you, Mr. Ellison, that's all I—no, I'm afraid there is something else I need to ask you. You were chief of staff under President Bridges. Under

President Spencer, Michael Donahue occupies that position. He's moved up into the position you held, and you..." I smiled at the jury before I added, as kindly as I could, "Perhaps you'll have a chance to spend some time with us, here in San Francisco, after all."

No one, including Raymond St. John, had any idea what I was doing. The strong suspicion was that I did not know myself. But if I wanted to grasp at straws, asking questions that I might better have asked on cross-examination when the prosecution first called the witnesses I was calling now, there did not seem any reason to interfere. When Judge Silverman asked if St. John wished to cross-examine Richard Ellison, St. John barely rose from his chair to barely whisper that no, he did not. Silverman then had an announcement of his own.

"Because of other matters which require the attention of the court, the next witness will be the last one called today."

He looked at each of us, St. John and me, a reminder of what he had told us that morning in chambers.

"Mr. Antonelli?"

"Yes, your Honor. The defense calls Milo Todorovich."

The head of the president's Secret Service detail, Todorovich, reported to the director, but Youngblood would not have told him anything about our conversation late one evening on the other side of the Golden Gate. Or so I assumed. Because as soon as I asked the first question, I was almost certain I was wrong, and that Youngblood had told him everything.

"There was a violent argument on Air Force One, on the flight out here, between Walter Bridges and Michael Donahue, wasn't there?"

"And then some," replied Todorovich, leaning forward, eager, as it seemed, to describe in detail everything that had happened.

"And then some?" I asked, raising my eyebrows.

"Bridges—the president—was in a rage. He was often in a rage, especially when someone was saying something about him he did not like."

"Did Donahue say something about him he didn't like?"

"No, I don't think so. No one who worked for him—so far as I know—ever did that, at least not to his face. It was something else, something about Fitzgerald. What you need to understand," he went on, looking at the jury in the same measured way he had learned to survey the faces in a crowd. "What you need to know, is that there were some people, just the mention of their name would set him off. Fitzgerald was not the only one, but I would have to say he was at the top of the list."

"Did you know the reason why Bridges disliked him so much?"

"Disliked him? There was that, all right, but that wasn't the reason, that was the effect. He was afraid of him, afraid of what he could do—what he might do. He was scared of what Fitzgerald was doing, the investigation into his dealings with the Russians; scared that if he somehow survived whatever that investigation uncovered, he would have to face Fitzgerald in the next election, and that Fitzgerald would win in a walk."

"Is that what he and Donahue were arguing about on the flight—what Fitzgerald might find out, what was going to happen in the next election?"

"I can't say for sure. I wasn't in the room. I was just outside, but the door was partway open and I had spent enough time around the president to know when he was getting ready to start throwing things."

Todorovich had been called by the prosecution, but he was my witness now, more than willing to tell everything he knew.

"They were arguing about Fitzgerald, whether Bridges should meet with him at all?"

"Yes, that's right. Bridges didn't want to do it. He refused. Said there was no way he would give 'that son of a bitch the time of day.'"

"But despite that initial refusal, he finally agreed to do it. What did Donahue say—if you know—that made him change his mind?"

"He told him that he didn't have any choice, that Fitzgerald already knew too much, and that they had to 'keep him in the dark'—those were Donahue's words—about what they were really planning. He told him, reminded him, that everything was almost ready, that after they met with the people they were going to meet with after the speech, things would be put in motion no one could stop."

I walked back to the counsel table and stood directly behind Fitzgerald. I wanted the jury to look at him when they looked at me.

"This is extremely important, Agent Todorovich. As best you can remember, those were the words, the exact words, that were used by Michael Donahue to the president: that they 'had to keep Fitzgerald in the dark,' and that, after they met later that night with certain people—cyber warfare experts, from what we have learned in other testimony—something would be 'set in motion that no one could stop'? Are you sure, absolutely sure, that is what was said?"

"I'm trained to take a bullet for the president. I'd do the same thing for the truth."

"Which means, doesn't it," I asked, stealing a glance at Raymond St. John, "that if Walter Bridges had lived, whatever he and Michael Donahue were planning to set in motion would have started?"

St John was about to object. With a sudden, quick question, I cut him off.

"One last thing, Agent Todorovich. Jenny Ann Carruthers, the White

House communications director, wasn't on that flight, was she?"

"No, she stayed in Washington."

"Am I wrong in thinking that this was the first, and only, time that Walter Bridges made a trip, an official trip, without her?"

"No, you're not wrong. She had gone on all the others."

We were finished for the day. The courtroom cleared out and I was left alone with Fitzgerald. His two guards stood on the far side of the room, past where the clerk had her desk, having a conversation of their own.

"I'm not sure I know what you're doing," said Fitzgerald, expecting an explanation. "Is there a reason you kept asking about the meeting I tried to get with Bridges, or the argument about whether Bridges should do it?"

"There is a reason, and more than just one."

He thought he understood.

"Because you could then bring out that the reason Bridges agreed to see me on the plane was part of their conspiracy, that they had to keep me 'in the dark' about what they were really planning. But I knew what they were planning to do, what they were going to do about the election."

"But you didn't know when. You didn't know it was going to be that soon, and whatever they thought you knew, they could be reasonably certain you did not know that."

"Who is left? What are you going to call?"

"Two more. Carruthers and Donahue."

"Because of what they'll have to admit now that all the other evidence is in about their involvement?"

I ignored the question, or rather let him interpret my silence as the agreement he expected. I signaled the guards that we were finished and got up to leave.

"One last thing, Kevin. You need to know something. You're going to win, you're going to be acquitted. The only question is whether you really want to be."

Perhaps for the first time in his life, Kevin Fitzgerald was too stunned to speak.

CHAPTER
TWENTY-ONE

Tangerine drove me into the city, the way she now did every morning. It had rained hard during the night and the water sprayed behind the wheels of the cars on the Golden Gate even as the heavy gray clouds began to splinter and break apart under a bright rising sun. A rainbow arched across the bay from the city to the Berkeley Hills. The air was fresh and clean, and if it had been anywhere but San Francisco, you might have thought it the start of spring instead of the beginning of fall.

"It's your voice," I said when we were halfway across the bridge. "That's what I forgot to tell you. Reynaud thinks you sound French when you're speaking English; Albert thinks it sounds like silk velvet or burnished brass, he isn't sure which."

"French, silk velvet, burnished brass? What are you talking about?" Her eyes never left the road in front of her, but she laughed at the way she knew I was looking at her. "Jean-Francois thinks I sound French?"

"He's right, you do."

"I didn't know you spoke French."

"I don't. But that's how you sound."

"Unintelligible?" She laughed again, this time quietly, and in a lower tone.

"It's the rhythm, the way everything you say seems subtle and intimate. It makes everyone feel you are sharing things you would only share with them."

She did not laugh, she only smiled.

"Silk velvet, burnished brass—that sounds like Albert's favorite combination: some brand of whiskey and some jazz recording from his collection. Yes, I remember," she added, her eyes flaring open at the memory. "George Shearing, the once famous jazz pianist. It was the name of one of his albums, if I remember right."

"I don't think that is what he meant. Silk velvet—smooth and rich and bright and full of excitement, but never loud. Burnished brass seems as good a way as any to describe how you speak."

I could have been talking to her about anything, as long as it kept my mind off the trial, but her voice was magical and I wanted to talk about that. She had an answer, of course; she always did.

"So now you can call me a brassy, bossy…?"

"Burnished, something bright and finely polished."

"And what, Mr. Antonelli, shall we say about that seductive voice of yours? How to describe the voice that if a hundred people were shouting all at once would be the only one anyone would want to hear, or would be able to remember later? I've never heard a voice like yours before." And then, with a quick sideways glance to let me know not to get too full of myself, she added, "You could have worked in a carnival, or sold things on the radio."

"After today, I may be looking for a new career."

"If there is one thing I'm certain of, it is that you'll never have to look for something else to do. Even if you wanted to, you can't. You promised we were going to France."

We reached the end of the bridge and passed through the toll plaza. She headed for the exit that would take us to the hospital from where I would take a cab. I put my hand on her wrist.

"Drop me at the courthouse, then find a place to park and come in. Lives are going to be changed today. You need to be there."

The courthouse was under siege. The trial was drawing to a close. There were, as everyone now knew, only a few more witnesses to call, and then closing arguments. Today, tomorrow, maybe the day after that, and the case would go to the jury, and then, finally, there would be an end to it. Kevin Fitzgerald would either be the assassin half the country was convinced he was, or the man who had saved the nation as the other half believed. I fought my way through the horde of reporters clamoring for a statement, a few words, anything they could use to show the world what might be going to happen. With the help of the police, I made my way into the courthouse where, because cameras were not allowed inside, I was followed by just a handful of newspaper reporters to the courtroom.

Fitzgerald, dressed impeccably as usual, had been brought in before anyone else. I took my place next to him and immediately began a last-minute review of the questions I had listed in my longhand scrawl on a yellow legal pad. I never read a question to a witness, I never used a note. There was not time, not if you wanted to hold a witness, keep them so intent on making sure they heard what you were asking, so caught up in this fast-moving conversation that they could not stop to consider what they wanted to say or how they wanted to say it.

Raymond St. John took his place at the other counsel table. The clerk sat at her small desk. The court reporter set up her machine. The doors at the back were opened and the reporters and spectators were allowed inside; counted as they came in to the limit of the courtroom's capacity. Fitzgerald bent toward me to ask a question. I had not finished with my list and with a slight movement of my head let him know it would have to wait. The bailiff announced that everyone should rise, that court was in session and that the Honorable Judge Leonard Silverman was presiding. Two steps before he reached the bench, the judge, never one to waste even a moment's time, waved his hand in the general direction of the bailiff and told him to bring in the jury. Bounding up to his chair, he waved his hand again, the signal that everyone could now sit down.

"Mr. Antonelli, are you ready with your next witness?"

"Yes, your Honor. The defense calls Jenny Ann Carruthers."

She had been sworn in before. I did not have to ask her to state her full name for the record, but she did not know that, and I wanted to remind the jury that there was something essentially false even in the way she identified herself.

"Jennifer Anastasia Carruthers," she replied when I asked.

"When you testified before, you were asked why you had not accompanied the president on his trip to California. You replied, 'There wasn't really any reason for me to come. The speech had been written, all the arrangements made.' Do you remember saying that?"

She was surprised that I thought it so important that I would quote back to her the reasons she had given; even more surprised that I had done it from memory.

"Yes, I believe that is what I said."

"Is that still your testimony? Is that still what you want this jury to believe?"

"That was the reason I didn't come."

"Those same reasons would have applied to any trip the president made. This was the only trip you did not make. What was different this time?"

She seemed suddenly nervous and uncertain. I was standing behind my empty chair. I moved to the corner of the counsel table. Fitzgerald was sitting below me on my left.

"It can't be because you hadn't been involved in what was going to happen after the president arrived. You testified—I remember it quite well—that the trip was 'partly my idea.' You testified—I remember it quite well—that you thought the president should make the trip, out here, to California, 'to take the fight to the senator's home ground. He had left us no choice.' Isn't that what you said?"

"Something like that, I think."

"Something like that. You also told us—admitted—that according to your own polling, Senator Fitzgerald would have defeated Walter Bridges in the next presidential election fifty-six to thirty-two, an astonishing margin. Isn't that what you said? Didn't you say 'something like that'?"

Anger shot to her eyes. She gripped the arms of the chair.

"I also said that if the president had lived, if he had not been murdered, he would have turned that around. He would have been re-elected."

"The trip was your idea, you wanted to take the fight to Senator Fitzgerald on his home ground, because with that kind of margin to overcome, there really wasn't any choice. Is that what you were trying to say?"

"That's exactly what I was trying to say."

"But despite that, this was the only trip you missed. Was it because, as you also testified, you had to stay in Washington 'to work out our communications strategy'?"

Added to the other reasons she had given, it seemed a reasonable excuse.

"Yes, that was important, and as I said, I—"

"Whose communication strategy? The president's, or the one you and Michael Donahue knew you would need?"

Her face went rigid, her eyes went cold.

"What are you talking about? What communications strategy would Michael Donahue and I—"

"The one you used, the whole series of press briefings, press releases, interviews, after Walter Bridges was murdered!"

The life came back in her eyes, and she seemed suddenly triumphant. I was a fool, and she could prove it.

"How could anyone have done that before it happened?"

The next question was out of my mouth almost before she had finished.

"Did you know you were under surveillance, that the meetings you had with Michael Donahue, the late-night telephone calls, were all recorded?"

I opened the thin black finder in which I had placed the intelligence reports Reynaud had given me.

"Here, for example, let me read what you said the night before that trip you decided you could miss. The call was made from your cell phone at ten seventeen eastern time. It reads as follows: 'Carruthers,'" I began. Then I changed my mind. "No, I think I'll wait. But let me ask you, Ms. Carruthers, and I would remind you not only that you are under oath, but that this will be your one and only chance to tell the truth about what happened, and why it did."

She sat there, ashen faced and almost immobile, staring at me as if I were the devil incarnate.

"Did you, or did you not, discuss with Michael Donahue the great danger the Bridges presidency was in? Did you, or did you not, agree that what Senator Fitzgerald had learned would almost certainly lead to the president's impeachment?"

Her mouth was too dry to speak. She asked for a glass of water.

"Do you want me to repeat the question?"

"No. The answer is yes, but not the way you seem to think. We knew, and not just Donahue and me, but nearly everyone in the White House, what the polls were saying. We knew—as I testified—that the Russian investigation was making things difficult, that—"

"Did you discuss with Michael Donahue that what Senator Fitzgerald had discovered would likely lead to impeachment?"

"There was that possibility," she conceded, finally.

"Senator Fitzgerald did you quite a favor, didn't he?"

"I'm not sure I understand what you mean. He killed—"

"Killed Walter Bridges, is that what you're going to say? And if he is found guilty of it, you have a new president, and you're rid of the one candidate that even he can't beat."

I looked long and hard at her, smiling with the secret she still was not sure I knew.

"I have no more questions of this witness, your Honor." And then, before she had taken two steps, I announced, "The defense calls Michael Donahue."

They passed each other, and after seeing the look on her face, he must have known he was in trouble. He could not possibly have known how much. He had just taken the witness stand when Raymond St. John said he had a matter for the court that had best be discussed in chambers.

"If the defense has evidence - transcripts of recorded conversation - the prosecution has the right to know it." He turned to me, sitting next to him in front of Silverman's spartan desk. "Unless you were just bluffing, trying to make Carruthers think you knew something that you really did not."

"I wasn't bluffing," I replied with a reluctance that caught his, and the judge's, attention. "In some ways, I wish I were."

I reached inside my briefcase for the thin black binder I had used in court, and then I reached inside again.

"These are copies, one for the court, one for the prosecution. If there is any doubt concerning their authenticity, if you want me to offer proof that they are what they appear to be—transcripts of conversations between Michael Donahue and, amongst others, Jenny Ann Carruthers—there is someone in the courtroom, a representative of the French government, willing, if necessary, to provide it. I would ask that it be done on camera. I don't have any objection if Mr. St. John is included in the court's interview, but there doesn't seem to be anything to be gained by making the source and methods of this information more public than is necessary."

For the next few minutes, Leonard Silverman and Raymond St. John read through the intelligence reports I had been given by Jean-Francois Reynaud.

"My God!" muttered Silverman in astonishment after he had finished the first few pages. "What do we do now?" he asked an equally astonished Raymond St. John.

"I think we get to watch Joseph Antonelli."

I did not know what the jury was thinking, or what the witness imagined, when the three of us came back into court, looking more serious, and more determined, than when we left. Silverman placed his right arm on the bench and with an air of great anticipation, looked down on Donahue. St. John rested his elbows on the counsel table, folded his hands together, and peered at the witness with narrow-eyed intensity. I stood at the end of the jury box, my right hand gripping the railing. I began with what seemed an utterly routine question about what he had testified before.

"You testified that when you had dinner with General Rostov, you did not know he was a Russian general and you did not know he was in charge of Russia's cyber warfare program. Is that still your testimony?"

He was nothing if not brazen. He said it was.

"You're aware that last week Senator Fitzgerald testified that not only did you know it was Rostov, you had met him before, that you had, in fact, spent the better part of the day with him at the Russian embassy in Washington?"

"I'm aware of what he said."

"Then you're also aware that in addition to his own sworn testimony, evidence was introduced, including the transcripts of what was said in that meeting you had at the Russian embassy?"

"I'm aware that documents were introduced; I'm not aware that they were authentic, that they have been verified as being true."

"You deny, then, that they're true?"

"I deny I've ever done anything that wasn't done to protect this country."

"Protect this country! Yes, I understand. That was the reason you came up with this plan to use the threat of Russian interference in the next election as a way to cancel it, to postpone as long as you had to even the possibility that Walter Bridges would have to leave office, wasn't it?"

"No, I never—"

"Yes! Along with Jenny Ann Carruthers, and who knows how many others, you had it all worked out. It was the reason for the meeting—the meeting that never took place—with people who could penetrate the computer systems used in our elections and make it look like another country—Russia—was behind it!"

"No, that isn't true! It was the other way around. We were trying to stop them from doing anything like that again."

"The reason why you were going to meet with those cyber security people isn't really important, is it?"

It stopped him. Thoroughly confused, he threw up his hands. The question did not make sense.

"The reason for the meeting did not matter, because the meeting was never going to happen. On the flight, the last flight Walter Bridges would ever make, you argued with him. You had been opposed to any meeting with Senator Fitzgerald, and yet, now, suddenly, you were all for it. You knew Fitzgerald would be there, didn't you?" I asked, shifting ground so fast he could not keep track.

"Yes, he was going to be there. It was the normal—"

"In fact, the day before the flight you called his office to make sure. You did that because you had to be sure. He had to be there. Everything depended on it."

"Everything depended…?"

I stared at him, daring him to deny it, daring him to tell me I was wrong.

"He had to be there, because without him, your plan would never work. You had already decided your first plan would not work," I said, as if I were reminding him of a well-established fact. "You couldn't use a phony cyber attack to delay, much less cancel, a presidential election. Walter Bridges might think he could get away with something like that, but you—and Carruthers, and anyone else in the White House who was halfway sane—had to know that the House, the Senate, whoever had a majority, would never go along with anything that unprecedented, that extreme, especially with Kevin Fitzgerald going after everything he could find. It wasn't going to work. There was going to be an election, and you, and everything you wanted, all the great changes you wanted to make, the new American revolution you intended to lead, the one you wanted to use Bridges to accomplish, was going to be defeated in an electoral landslide. It was over. Bridges was a disaster. Something had to be done. You studied history. What did history teach you? When something becomes necessary, necessary to save the country, you do what you have to do. Isn't that what you were doing: following, like Kevin Fitzgerald, the same law of necessity? Isn't that why you did what you did? Isn't that the reason why you, not Kevin Fitzgerald, murdered Walter Bridges?"

It felt like an earthquake, the one everyone had been expecting, the one that would level San Francisco and send a tidal wave to the shore. The courtroom shook from side to side, the floor began to roll beneath my feet. The noise was so loud no one heard the gavel with which Judge Silverman tried to stop it. I kept staring at Donahue, and he kept staring back.

"That's ridiculous! Insane! He confessed. He testified under oath!" he cried, stabbing his finger at Fitzgerald, who sat, thunderstruck, in his chair.

"The law of necessity, Mr. Donahue! Kevin Fitzgerald walked into the president's cabin to confront him with what he had discovered, what, as you know, would destroy his presidency, and found Walter Bridges lying dead on the floor. You were there, Mr. Donahue, remember? Richard Ellison had left, gone outside the cabin to wait for Senator Fitzgerald. He thought you had left as well, gone out the other entrance, the one that leads to the president's bedroom. But you didn't leave, you stayed and, alone with the president, you went up to him as if there were some last things you wanted to tell him. That's when you stabbed him in the throat, severed the artery, causing almost instant death. You thought that when Fitzgerald came in he would be caught, the only one in the room, and charged with murder. It never occurred to you that Fitzgerald would confess and try to argue that he had killed the president to save the country."

I picked up the transcript and handed it to Donahue.

"Read it out loud, the first page will be enough."

He would not do it. I ripped it out of his hands and read it out loud myself.

"'Carruthers: Did you do it? Did it work?'

'Donahue: Better than we could have hoped. Fitzgerald has been taken away. They found him with the knife in his hand.'

'Carruthers: It was the only thing we could do. He wouldn't have had a chance against Fitzgerald. Now we have Spencer. What could be better than that?'"

I tossed the transcript onto the table.

"Everyone who testified in this trial, every witness—with one exception, Milo Todorovich, who would have taken a bullet for the president, and was willing to take one for the truth—lied. Every one. And they all did it for the same reason: they thought, they believed, that what they thought necessary—for themselves, for their country—was more important than the truth. The truth for them was whatever they wanted it to be. You lied, Mr. Donahue, not just to cover up your crime; you lied for the same reason you committed that crime: this bizarre belief that history is on your side, that you somehow understand what history requires. In this respect, you and the defendant are not really that much different. You think history has a meaning, and that you know what it is. Kevin Fitzgerald thought that history provided, not very often, perhaps only once in a lifetime, or even once in a century, a chance to make history. The difference is that he confessed to a crime he did not commit so that he might have that chance, while you lied about a crime you did commit so that you might have the chance to change the country into something it never wanted to be."

There was dead silence. I did not even bother to tell the court I was finished with the witness. St. John did not get up to ask to cross-examine. Judge Silverman turned away from Donahue and stared, without seeing, at the courtroom crowd. I did not know how long it lasted, but finally, Leonard Silverman brought us back to the safety of settled procedure.

"Mr. Antonelli, does the defense have a motion it wishes to make at this time?"

The habit was so ingrained, I knew without thinking the useless motion made routinely when the last witness has testified and the case is about to go to the jury.

"Yes, your Honor. The defense moves for a judgment of acquittal on the grounds that based on the evidence in this case no reasonable jury could return any other verdict."

"Mr. St. John, does the prosecution wish to oppose the motion?"

The consummate professional, and a thoroughly decent man, Raymond St. John stated that the prosecution did not.

"The motion is therefore granted," announced Silverman. "An order of acquittal will be entered on the record. The defendant is free to go."

Free to go, but where? He was not the savior of his country as he had wanted everyone to believe. He was worse than a joke, a man who had lied about a murder, confessed to a crime he had not committed, undergone, quite willingly, torture as part of this unconscionable ruse, and all for the purpose of claiming an exaggerated importance that would make his name live through the centuries. He turned to me to offer an explanation, to excuse what he had done. He had saved the country, he insisted, imploring me to believe him. If he had not done what he did, discovered what they were planning, if he had not decided to make that confession, there would not have been a trial, and without a trial, Donahue and the others would have gotten away with it. He had saved the country, he repeated. And he was glad that he had.

"You've been acquitted," I reminded him. "It's up to you what you do next."

And with that, I turned and walked away. Sitting in the front row, right behind him, where she always sat, his wife, Tricia Fitzgerald, looked like a bride left at the altar. She did not know what to do or what to think.

The crowd outside, all the reporters, all the cameras, all the others who had come to see what finally would happen when the trial reached its conclusion, melted away. There had been no victories, only defeats; defeat for Michael Donahue and who knew how many others who wanted what Walter Bridges wanted more than they wanted Walter Bridges, defeat and either execution or life in prison without the possibility of parole. And defeat for Kevin Fitzgerald. Not a single reporter wanted anything to do with him. He had become an embarrassment, and no one in public life ever recovered from that.

I drove back with Tangerine in almost perfect silence to the house on the hill in Sausalito. She did not know what to say, and I did not want to talk about the trial, or anything else. We drove over the Golden Gate in the dying light of early evening and I looked back at the city, shining as bright and eager as all the best yesterdays you could remember, and then I looked at her and knew that tomorrow, and all the tomorrows after that, I would think each new yesterday better than the last.

"We're still going to France?" she asked as she pulled into the drive.

"Do you still want to?"

"More than ever."

We spent a month in Paris, idle tourists, wandering from place to place, stopping for a glass of wine in some cafe we found deserted in the afternoon, sitting together on a bench in the park behind Notre Dame just above the river in the cool warmth of the October sun. With a guidebook in hand, we went everywhere and saw everything, and were so entranced with each other that at the end of the day we could not remember what we had seen. History was all around us—the Bastille and the French Revolution, the Arc-de-Triumph and Napoleon's wars—and the only history we cared about was ours. We had dinner late at night, and made love until morning. We never spoke about the trial.

Jean-Francois Reynaud was waiting for us at the station when the train from Paris arrived. He seemed glad to see me; he was thrilled to see Tangerine.

"I almost didn't recognize you," I remarked as we walked outside and headed for his car. "It's the first time I've seen you without a coat and tie."

It was more than that. He had nothing more to worry about. There was no more official business to conduct, no more late night clandestine meetings with an American lawyer he had, perhaps without the entire knowledge or approval of his government, decided to help. There was a new spring in his step, and his smile, at least when he looked at Tangerine, was incandescent.

"Chantel can't wait to meet you—both of you," he said as he drove through the streets of Agen in his new Peugot.

The castle was only a few miles away. We turned off the two-lane highway and a few blocks later passed through a gated entrance to a mile-long dirt and gravel road that wound through a thick hillside forest and across a short bridge to Jean-Francois's idyllic three-story country home. His wife, Chantal, tall, thin, elegant and quite beautiful, had heard the car and was waiting on the front steps.

Chantal greeted Tangerine with the open generosity of long-time friends. Their laughter echoed behind them as they followed Jean-Francois, who was carrying our two suitcases under his arms, up the staircase to the enormous bedroom on the second floor.

I stayed outside for a while, looking out over the lawn and the garden, the fountains and the green sculpted hedges, the only sound the laughter from the open window above. I thought about Kevin Fitzgerald and the choice he had made, and I thought about how many lives had been destroyed in the trial. History could write about what had happened, and the story would be nothing like what Kevin Fitzgerald or Michael Donahue or any of the others so eager to leave their mark on time had wanted and expected. They wanted to do something great and memorable, and became not the heroes they imagined, but fools and charlatans, criminals and imposters. If there was such a thing as history, its main purpose seemed to be to treat with violence and contempt anyone who thought he knew its meaning.

I heard Tangerine's laughing voice calling from the window, and in that moment the mystery of time's meaning disappeared.

THE END

About the Author

D.W. Buffa was born in San Francisco and raised in the Bay Area. After graduation from Michigan State University, he studied under Leo Strauss at the University of Chicago and served as special assistant to U.S. Senator Philip Hart. He received his J.D. degree from Wayne State University in Detroit.

His book *The Judgment* was nominated for the Edgar Award for Best Novel.

D.W. Buffa lives in Northern California.